the twilight
of
lake woebegotten

the twilight

of
lake woebegotten

HARRISON GEILLOR

Night Shade Books
San Francisco

First Edition

Printed in Canada

ISBN: 978-1-59780-284-0

Night Shade Books
http://www.nightshadebooks.com

"If there ever had been, or could be, a Tree of Knowledge, instead of God forbidding man to eat thereof, it would be that of which he would order him to eat the most."

—The Emperor Julian

PRETTY MUCH DUSK,
MORE OR LESS

NARRATOR

This document here is mostly the diary of a young woman, not to be confused with *The Diary of a Young Girl*, better known to some as *The Diary of Anne Frank*, though to get technical it's really called *Het Achterhuis*, which translates as something closer to *The House Behind* or maybe *The Secret House* or—sorry, got caught up in a digression there, it's a symptom of my problem, that problem being omnicognizance. When you know everything, it's hard not to share that knowledge, even though I don't technically know *everything*. I can see everything that's ever happened, and look into the minds of the people who were there, which gives me a pretty wide view, I admit, but you can't necessarily trust anybody's *thoughts* to be true, and anyway, there are still some pretty unknowable unknowns: whether there's a God or a Devil or a Higgs boson is just as mysterious to me as it is to you. Plus, I'm limited to knowledge of everything that's ever been or currently is, which leaves everything that ever will be as big a void for me as it is for everybody else. Which is alternately a terror and a comfort, depending.

But yes, this is mostly the journal of a young woman, or an old girl—someone in that borderline twilight world between being an adolescent and an adult. She didn't write it like a true journal, though, as things were happening, but as an account of relevant events afterward, which makes it not really a "journal"—the word started out as French, *diurnalis*, for "daily," so if it's not daily, it's maybe not technically even a journal, oops, there I go again—but that's what Bonnie Grayduck called it, so we'll go along with her, no reason to make a fuss. But there were things Bonnie didn't know, or didn't think were important enough to record, or didn't want to think about, that have some bearing on the events in her life, which is where I come in, with my aforementioned omnicognizance, you see, to fill in the gaps. Where Bonnie had thoughts on a matter, I'll let her thoughts stand without outside interpretation or contradiction, even though to call someone like Bonnie merely an unreliable narrator is an insult to good upstanding unreliable people everywhere and also to me, since people mostly call me The Narrator, because I have a habit of narrating everything that's happening around me in real-time.

I know, it's pretty strange, not very sociable behavior, and I apologize, but I can't seem to help myself, I've always been that way. There's a theory about how humans develop their thought processes, you see. At first, children don't think like we do, in words, because they don't have words. Then they get words and they go through a period where they talk, and little kids can *talk*, and so they go on and on about everything that happens around them, saying everything that comes into their heads. Then they go to school, and the teachers tell them not to talk so darned much (or if they don't go to school, annoyed adults passing by tell them the same thing), and the kids start to subvocalize, whispering to themselves about what's happening around them, and eventually that subvocalization goes absolutely silent, and the insides of their heads start to resemble the insides of most of ours: a string of thoughts, a stream of consciousness, which is largely composed of words.

For whatever reason, I never grew out of the stage where you narrate your whole life. It used to be just what you'd call an eccentricity, but since I started knowing everything it's become a downright liability, so I've turned to the written word to pour some of these words out. Maybe if I let some of that knowledge out here, I can hold it in elsewhere, like when I go to the grocery store or the bait shack. Mostly I'll try to keep myself out of this story, since I don't really have too awful much to do with the bulk of the action, though I guess I'll address the issue of who I am and how I got to be omnicognizant and all that later, if it seems warranted.

But for now, I'll tell you a little story about a fella in my town—that's Lake Woebegotten, and I'll spare you its whole history, though it costs me some effort: enough to say it's a small town in Central Minnesota and it's got a good-sized lake and a bunch of townspeople, most fairly good-hearted, with a few exceptions. I'll tell you about one of those people, Gunther Montcrief, who does have a good heart, even though he's got a pretty lousy liver. What Gunther saw out in the woods one day is as good a place to start as any, and better than most.

And after Gunther, I'll let Bonnie have her say. But, really, her journal is nothing at all like *The Diary of Anne Frank*. I'm beginning to wish I hadn't even brought that up. For one thing, that diary ended after the girl writing it died.

The same can't be said of the diary you'll be reading soon...

Gunther Montcrief—who wasn't technically the town drunk, but only because he didn't technically live in town—stepped out of his fishing shack down by the marshy shore of Lake Woebegotten and scratched himself in places too indelicate to mention in print. He wore his bright orange long underwear, which made him look like a slightly misshapen traffic cone, because deer hunting season had just opened, and it wouldn't do to get shot by a hunter as drunk (or drunker) than Gunther was himself. Also because he couldn't remember where he'd put his pants.

He squinted at the sky, taking a minute to think whether it

was dawn or dusk, and finally settled on the latter, since the little bit of light in the sky was in the direction he recollected as west, or at least it had been the last time he checked. Gunther, who wasn't as old as he looked but was still pretty old, reached both arms above his head and listened to the cracks and creaks of his body and took a little walk around the fishing shack to his favorite pissing tree. He had a pit dug some distance away for when he had to do more involved excretory business, but his steady diet of dried fish, beef jerky, and whiskey made bowel movements a semi-weekly event at best.

While he was unloading a goodly portion of the day's liquor onto his chosen tree—the bark was all discolored, and moss didn't grow on this side anymore, terrible thing, probably had to do with global warming—he heard a deer scream.

People tended to think of deer as quiet things, and they were, if you happened to glimpse one at a distance, bowing its head to a stream in particularly picturesque fashion, or freezing with its head cocked because you snapped a twig while you were sneaking up on one, but they could be noisy, too. Mostly they snorted or grunted or made a kinda sheep-like bleating sound, but twice before in his life he'd heard deer scream, both when they were injured badly but still some distance from death. A screaming deer sounded a lot like a screaming woman, or more accurately a screaming deranged female clown with the hiccups.

He might have thought it was a woman (or even a clown, stranger things had happened) except he saw the deer come bounding out of the trees, not straight toward him but at an angle toward the lake. The sun was getting on toward all the way down, so it was hard for him to make out what exactly came racing out of the woods after the deer, but it wasn't a dog, not even one of them hairless ones, and it couldn't possibly be a man, not with all the leaping and snarling and bounding sideways off of trees it was doing. Seemed like a pale spider the size of a man, more than anything, and Gunther looked down at his hands—one still occupied in aiming his pee at the tree, though the stream had dried up—to check if they were shaking, because he always got the shakes real bad if the delirium tremens hit him. But now that he thought about it he had better than two pints of whiskey inside his belly, so he probably wasn't hallucinating, at least not due to alcohol *withdrawal*. He couldn't recall ever seeing things while drunk before, as he was more of a "black out" than a "see pink elephants" type of drinker, but he knew there was a first time for everything and nothing new under the sun so he didn't rule it out.

The spider-thing—which more and more looked like a man who *moved* like a spider—sprang into the air about six or eight feet high and came down on the deer, which screamed again, but altogether more briefly. The hunter snarled and bit and slurped at the dead deer for a while, and Gunther took a moment to tuck his personal privates back into his long underwear. Suddenly wearing bright orange didn't seem like such a good idea, so he sort of scooted back toward his shack, hoping to slip inside unnoticed, and maybe just coincidentally lay hands on his .22 target pistol, which was the only one of his many guns he hadn't sold off over the years.

Before he made it to the shack, though, the deer-eating man snapped his head up and looked straight at Gunther. The fella had a snow-pale face, apart from all the smeared-on deer blood, and dark hair, and he was dressed in a faded denim shirt and blue jeans and muddy boots, pretty normal stuff, which made it all even weirder, in a way. Gunther and the deer hunter weren't more than thirty-five yards apart, close enough that Gunther could have probably hit him with a football, not that hitting him with a football would've helped matters much, and not that he had a football anyway. Having seen the way the man moved before, flying through the trees, Gunther didn't even bother to run. He fell back on a lifetime of experience at polite conversation, because if he was going to be disemboweled by a fella who ate raw deer, he wasn't going to have his last words be something rude. "Hey there. Some weather we're having. Looks like it might turn cold soon. Good day for hunting though."

The man looked at him for a moment, then turned and raced off into the woods.

"Well now. That's different." Gunther scratched himself and went over to the deer, just a little buck, which was awful dead, and had such nasty neck wounds that it had been beheaded, more or less. Shame to let that much venison go to waste. Gunther thought about whether it was a bad idea to eat a deer that some weird fella had been gnawing on, what with diseases and such, but he figured if he cut away the chewed-on part, it might be okay, and anyway, he'd have a lot of whiskey when he ate it, and what with alcohol being a pretty good disinfectant, there shouldn't be any problems.

He considered maybe mentioning the deer hunter to the police chief, Harry, next time he saw him down at the Backtrack Bar, but decided maybe he'd better not. Deer season was open, after all, and if you could hunt with a bow or a gun, why not with your bare hands? In a way, that was even more sporting. Where was the crime?

Even half drunk he could butcher a deer—he'd been doing it since he was a boy—so Gunther got his ropes and winch out and hoisted up the deer and hung it by its back legs from a tree branch so he could skin it. Normally he would've bled the deer first, but its throat was pretty well cut already. Even so, he was surprised at how bloodless the thing was when he started cutting it up. The hunter hadn't eaten much of the deer's flesh at all—and how could he, when he'd been focusing on the neck, which was just a mess of veins and tendons?—but he'd sure drunk enough of the blood.

Gunther had tasted a bit of deer blood himself when he was a boy, the first time he went out hunting successfully. Lots of hunters had that tradition, to taste the blood of your first kill, and it hadn't been so terrible, but it also hadn't been so tasty he'd be tempted to make a meal of it. Oh well. None of his business. Be a boring old world if we were all the same. Still, it was a hell of a thing, and the story might be worth a drink or two at the Backtrack Bar. Then again, perhaps silence was best. He'd hate for folks around town to think he was crazy when they already thought he was a shiftless drunk. A man had his pride, after all.

OPEN BOOK

FROM THE JOURNAL OF BONNIE GRAYDUCK

I f anyone ever finds this, they'll assume it's fiction, which is funny, since I don't even read fiction really, let alone write it. But it's filled with enough impossible things that it will never hold up in a court of law as evidence to convict me of anything (as if there's a cop in the world who could bring me in): clearly it's all just a lot of nonsense, product of an overactive imagination. But it's *important*, and I know in a few hundred years my memory will fade and I won't remember how I got to the place I've reached at last, so I thought I'd better write it down, and that requires imagining someone besides me will read it someday, so: hello, dear reader, and this is the story of the best of my life.

The day I saw Edwin for the first time, I stared at the concrete expanse of the runways at the San Jose International Airport while my mom fretted beside me. "You don't have to do this, Bonnie," she said. "I'm sure all this unpleasantness will blow over. I mean, no one can really believe you *meant—*"

"It's better this way, Mommy," I said, patting her knee. I still have a hard time believing I share genetic material with someone as flighty and distractible as Miranda Grayduck— but having a mother who loses her train of thought anytime she hears a loud noise or sees something shiny had proven useful over the years. "Just until things blow over."

"But you haven't spent any time with Harry since you were

twelve years old," mom went on, digging through her suit-case-sized purse in search of something—who knew what. "You two have barely even talked on the phone if it wasn't your birthday or Christmas. I know he loves you, but—"

"Are those new earrings?" I interrupted, and Miranda touched her earlobes, smiled, and rattled on about the little shop in Santa Cruz where she'd found them long enough for me to say, "Goodness, I'll miss my flight. I'll call you as soon as I get there, I love you, don't worry, it's all for the best."

She spent a little more time rummaging and babbling, but I managed to peel myself away and get my bags out of the trunk, and eventually Miranda took the hint. At least with the security checkpoints she couldn't come with me to the gate. Once she drove away in her ridiculous yellow hybrid—a gift from my stepfather-to-be—I instantly felt lighter, as if part of me were soaring through the clouds already. I wasn't particularly excited about spending my senior year of high school in the tiny Minnesota town of Lake Woebegotten with my dad Harry, better known to the locals as Chief Cusack. (As a bastard in the original sense of the word, I'm saddled with my mother's last name instead of Harry's. Miranda says Grayduck is a Native American name, but really, doesn't every other white person in America think they have some Choctaw or Blackfeet or Cherokee blood back in their ancestry somewhere? Or, what were the Indians up near Lake Woebegotten called—Ojibwe?)

Anyway. A little lake town way up north, where I hadn't even visited in five years, was hardly my idea of paradise, but staying in Santa Cruz had become decidedly uncomfortable because of some recent unpleasantness. It was really just a misunderstanding, or maybe not a misunderstanding, more of a misfortune, since I'd been reasonably sure no one would ever trace the whole thing back to me. And who would have expected anyone to care so much about something so unimportant, some*one* so insignificant... Oh, well. Just because you're smarter than everyone else doesn't mean you can't make mistakes. Santa Cruz and I just needed a little mutual cooling-off period.

I made a big production out of struggling with my luggage when I got into the airport, and soon enough a scruffy twenty-something with a huge backpack hurried over, gave me his best impression of a winning smile, and offered to help carry my bags. I gave him a half-strength smile of my own, loaded him down with my bags, and directed him toward the desk for my airline. People are willing to do all sorts of things for a pretty girl (I'm not being conceited; I just know my strengths, and being pretty isn't even the strongest of them), but it's better if you act like you don't *know* you're pretty. If you position yourself as too sophisticated and cool and aloof, the losers are afraid to approach, but if you act clumsy and lost and helpless, they decide you might be just barely in their league after all: and losers are easy to manipulate. Being cold and distant and perfect has its uses, but it attracts a different sort of prey: smug, confident, arrogant men. Men like that are good if you're playing a longer game, though. They can pay great dividends, especially if you're not yet eighteen and can mention your jealous father the cop—even better because it was true, and no reason to mention he was chief of police in Lake Nowheresville, Minnesota thousands of miles away—and statutory rape and oh, didn't I mention I was underage, oh dear, I thought you knew, I thought that's what you were *into*!

But I decided that once I got to Lake Woebegotten I wouldn't play any of those games anymore. The place was too tiny, anyway, and who would I play with, Norwegian bachelor farmers? Some bald bank manager or the guy who ran the car dealership or the podunk grocery store? No thanks. This was a chance for a fresh start. To simplify and purify my life, and just be The New Girl... which meant I'd probably have my pick of country bumpkin boys. There might be some entertainment value there. I vaguely recalled they grew them big in the Upper Midwest.

I ditched the loser bag-boy at the security line, not even bothering to thank him—no incentive, when I'd never see him again—and breezed through the gates without being groped or bombarded with radioactivity. Having translucent skin as pale as milk (or "the color of lutefisk," as one of my Minnesotan relatives had memorably said once, shudder) is an advantage in a world of scary foreign terrorists, even with brown hair and eyes to go with the paleness; I don't look dangerous at all. Which just goes to show how much faith you can put in looks.

Once I got to the gate, I upgraded my flight to first class— it was on Miranda's credit card, and she'd never notice. She didn't even look at her statements when they came in the mail, just threw them in a pile for a year and then shredded them. I got on board as soon as the jetway opened, took my seat and my complimentary beverage—I didn't bother trying to get booze, because alcohol doesn't do much for me, just takes the edge off the world—and frowned when a businessman sat down beside me. First class was booked solid. Disappointing. Fortunately, the doughy man paid me no attention—gay, probably—and to my surprise he opened his briefcase and took out a *book*, of all things, not even a Kindle or an iPad, but a big fat hardcover printed on actual paper. There was no dust jacket, but I could read the title: *The Historian*. Bleah. Who'd want to read about a stupid historian? Or about anything, for that matter, apart from the occasional book of useful non-fiction? Why read about other people's imaginary lives when you could have a real life of your own?

I took out the MP3 player I'd stolen from Dwayne, my mother's boyfriend. Dwayne was dreadful, in his late thirties and at the tail end of a career as an arena football player, which was the kind of football you played when you'd never been good enough for the real game or just weren't good enough *anymore*. Despite being a cliché jock, Dwayne went to a lot of rock shows and thought he was hip, but there was nothing on his iPod from the past fifteen years, just a lot of grungy alterna-junk from the '90s. Oh well. Better than listening to the mooing and lowing of the other passengers getting on board and shuffling to their cramped coach seats, to travel in discomfort and misery and empty-headedness like the livestock they were.

I put in the earbuds, scrolled through Dwayne's playlists— they were named things like "Rockin Good" and "Brutal Jams" and "Break Shit"—until I found something that looked promising. I closed my eyes, listened to some classic rock band called Soundgarden sing about how they were feeling Minnesota, and began the journey into the rest of my life. Once we started taking off, I considered looking out the window to see the world drop away, shrinking until all the people bustling around the tarmac looked like ants, but I didn't bother. That's pretty much what people look like to me most of the time anyway: ants.

PHENOMENOMENON

NARRATOR

"It was one of them unexplainable phenomenom-enons," Gunther said, swaying a little on his customary stool at the Backtrack Bar, while Ace the bartender ignored him. Gunther had forgotten his resolution to keep quiet about what he'd seen in the woods, which didn't matter much, because no one paid any attention to him anyway, so he embellished. "Red eyes he had, and fangs as long as ice axes, and he tore that deer to pieces. Completely to pieces. Nothing left but red sludge, like cherry pudding."

"Never heard of cherry pudding," Ace said, flipping channels on the TV, though one station full of fuzzy snow looked more or less like another to Gunther's untrained eye.

"It's pudding," Gunther told Ace, or maybe his beer, since that's what he was looking at most intently. "But cherry-flavored. Maybe I should've said 'blood pudding.' Since there was so much blood?"

"What's this about blood?" The town's head (and very nearly only) cop Harry Cusack eased onto the stool next to Gunther, who grunted a greeting. Harry was all right. He'd been known to lock Gunther up for drunk and disorderly, but he always let him go after he'd dried out, and true, he made you clean up your own puke if you let loose in the cell, but he'd give you a cup of coffee afterward to clear out the taste. "Don't tell me you witnessed a crime, Gunther, because I can't think of anyone in the world who'd be a worse witness

13

than you, officially speaking."

"A blind deaf-mute, maybe," Ace said. "With a felony conviction and a history of mental illness." He paused. "Or that boy Clem who works over at the Half Good Grocery for Dolph, he's dumber than a bag of hog snouts."

"But if you did see something," Harry said, putting a companionable arm around Gunther's shoulders, "I'd be pleased to hear about it. My daughter's coming into town tonight to stay with me for a while, and if there's a criminal element hanging around, I may as well clean it up before she gets here."

"No crime," Gunther muttered. "Unless killing a deer with your bare hands is a crime."

"Maybe animal cruelty, depending. And killing animals is part of the homicidal triad, you know, indicative of a budding serial killer, right along with bedwetting and setting fires."

"You'd think with a name like 'homicidal triad' that actually committing homicide should be one of the three," Ace said, to general lack of response. Some bartenders stood there, not paying any attention, as their regulars babbled on about this and that. Ace was pretty much the opposite.

"So when and where and who was this?" Harry said, peeling the label off his bottle of Krepusky's Red Ribbon Beer.

Gunther marshaled all his mental powers and attempted recollection. He wasn't a stupid man, not at all; he was just an extremely drunk man, and it was his grave misfortune that stupid and drunk were often indistinguishable even from a very slight distance. "Yesterday, 'round about twilight, out near my place. Don't know who. Some fella, maybe seventeen, eighteen. He didn't look like anything special, but he moved fast as a greased pig with a lightning bolt up his ass."

"That's pretty fast," Harry allowed.

"He jumped on the deer, and it was like a bird of prey falling out of the sky and landing on a little bunny rabbit or something. Just bite, tear, rip. When the fella saw me looking, he ran away."

"Hmm," Harry said. "I reckon you ate the deer? Turned my evidence into steaks and jerky?"

"Uh," Gunther said, and Harry sighed.

"That's all right. Keep your eyes open, though, and if you see that fella around, let me know? Somebody who'd run down and kill a deer bare-handed... I'd say that at least warrants a friendly conversation."

"You missed the part where he said the guy was some kind of supernatural wolfman dracula monster," Ace said. "With red eyes and big teeth and who knows whatall else."

"Hmm," Harry said, and drummed his fingers on the bar. "Well, that's all right. What good's a story if you don't gussy it up a little to make it even better?" Harry laid his money on the bar, and Ace pushed it back to him, a little ritual Gunther had witnessed with jealousy a million times—he damn sure paid for *his* drinks, and sometimes Ace got a wild hair and wouldn't even *sell* him any booze, let alone go giving it away—and told Gunther to stay out of trouble.

"Another whiskey," Gunther said, after ascertaining that enough of his Army pension money remained in his wallet to justify the extravagance of whiskey you drank inside a warm bar instead of a cold fishing shack.

"Only if you promise not to tell any more stories about pudding," Ace said. "You're making me hungry."

"You really want me to go tromping around the woods, what, looking for tracks or something?" Stevie Ray said. He was Harry's assistant and the only other employee of the Lake Woebegotten Police Department, though he was only a part-timer, and in his other job as back-up bartender and sometime bouncer at the Backtrack Bar, he'd become very well acquainted with Gunther Montcrief. "On the say-so of the most notorious drunk in town?"

"I take your point, but Gunther doesn't usually tell wild stories." Harry propped his feet up on the big desk. "He usually tells *old* stories about the combat he's seen and the women of negotiable virtue he met during his years stationed in the Pacific, but this? This is new. If there's a feral fella running around the woods eating deer, don't you think we should know about it?"

Stevie Ray sighed and pulled on his earflap hat. He went outside and walked around the back of the police station—which was more a general-purpose civic building that happened to have a jail cell in it—and took a moment to breathe the autumn air. Tomorrow was the first day of September, and winter would be along a month or so after that. Stevie Ray tried to live in the moment, but it was hard not to think about what the future might bring.

After making sure he was alone, which wasn't too difficult in a town as small as Lake Woebegotten, he took out his cell phone and scrolled through the contacts to a name that just read "Dr. S." He waited a moment, then said, "Hey, doc, Stevie Ray here. I just thought you should know, somebody saw one of your boys running down a deer out by the lake."

He listened a moment, then sighed. "It matters because it was the part of the lake by the Ojibwe reservation. You don't want to upset the Woebegotten Band—" Another pause to listen. "Well our witness didn't say anything about the hunter being *hairy*, and was pretty specific about it just looking like a normal fella apart from the super-speed and whatnot, so no, I don't think it was one of the boys from the rez. If it wasn't one of yours, then who? Don't tell me there are other—no. Okay. No, I don't know which one it was, probably Edwin or Garnett, if it'd been Hermet the witness probably would have mentioned the fella was the size of a grain silo. Just have a talk with them, okay, before I hear from Mr. Noir? I don't know how I got roped into being the go-between and peacemaker between you... Ha. Yes, all right, I'm a peace officer, fair enough. So help me by keeping things peaceful."

He closed his cell phone and sighed again, this time just for his own benefit, because if you couldn't feel sorry for yourself once in a while, where was the pleasure in life? He trudged around the building toward where his truck was parked by the curb. He'd have to go wander around in the woods for a while now, just to keep up appearances for Harry.

Ordinary people like me shouldn't have to mess around with folks like the Scullens, he thought. The ones on the *other* side—the few elders on the reservation who knew the secret of the Scullens, and had secrets of their own—were bad enough, but at least they were human *most* of the time. The Scullens were never human at all anymore. Really made a guy want to pause and reflect on how his life had gotten to this point, maybe wish things had gone a different way, but oh well. If wishes were horses, beggars would eat.

IMITATIONS

FROM THE JOURNAL OF BONNIE GRAYDUCK

I got off the plane in Minneapolis and went to the baggage claim, where I made a great show of almost falling over while attempting to haul my bag off the carousel. On cue, a couple of frat boy types jumped in to help me carry them. Nobody likes to see a pretty girl overexert herself, except in certain situations of a private nature, the dream and hope and imagination of which situations certainly motivated the strapping young men who offered to serve as my luggage-bearers.

So they were probably none too pleased when a police car—rather mud-splattered but still recognizable—pulled up to the curb and a big man in a law officer's uniform climbed out of the driver's seat, gave the fellas his best hard-eyed cop glare, and took the bags from them. "Much appreciated," he said, "but I can help my *daughter* from here." The brothers frat exchanged a glance and mumbled something to me which I didn't bother to hear before they slumped off into the terminal.

"Thought I was going to have to take a cab, Daddy," I said, leaning in to kiss his slightly stubbly cheek.

"Aw, I'm sorry, hon, I'm not used to all this big city traffic, I didn't time it right."

"And a police car? Do you want me to ride in the back like a criminal?"

"I wouldn't advise *that*," Harry said, popping the trunk

and loading my bags in. What an *interesting* trunk. I noted with interest that Harry had to shove aside crime scene tape, road flares, orange traffic cones, boxes of ammunition, and some interesting-looking gray plastic cases which probably contained more lethal cop supplies. Harry went on. "I make the drunks clean up their puke when they have an accident back there, but drunks are, as a rule, pretty terrible when it comes to hungover car detailing. You can ride up front with me." He grinned. "I'll even let you run the lights and sirens. You loved doing that when you were little."

"I'm not so little anymore, Dad." I thought about pointing my chest at him and giving him *that look*, the one I use to make Miranda's boyfriend uncomfortable and to distract male teachers and other officials who were maybe starting to make dangerous mental connections that linked me and certain unsavory events, but I held back. Harry was predisposed to be on my side, a protector and ally, and there was no reason to poison a well that could be so useful. Funny how I'd never thought about the advantages of living in a town where I was the only daughter of the chief of police. You could never underestimate the benefit of having friends in high places, even in a low place like Lake Woebegotten. "But that sounds like fun."

Once we were in the car and on our way, Harry said, "How's your mom?"

"Oh, you know Mom. She's fine."

Harry grunted. "Listen, I know being driven to school in a cop car wouldn't be much fun, so… I got you a car."

"Really? But all those years when I was a little girl I asked for a *pony*," I teased.

He laughed. "I don't see you cleaning up after a pony, Bonbon."

Ha. I'd cleaned up worse things. I gave him the laugh he thought he'd earned, but I had to grit my teeth a little. "Bonbon." I'd forgotten that nickname. "Seriously, Dad, a car? That's really nice of you." Saying "dad" felt funny, but it didn't take a genius at social engineering to know that calling him "Harry" would cool the warmth he felt toward me.

"Well, don't expect anything too fancy. You remember my friend Willy Noir?"

"Hmmm... no."

"Old buddy, lives down by Pres du Lac, we used to go fishing with him when you visited in the summers, and we still go hunting together sometimes."

I'd come to stay with Harry in the summers from ages five to twelve, but the years from before I was nine or so were pretty fuzzy, all running together into one blurry boring summer. But I remembered Pres du Lac, the itty-bitty Indian reservation on the far side of Lake Woebegotten, even if I didn't remember Mr. Noir. "Ah, fishing, my favorite activity. Was there ever a year when I *didn't* fall out of the boat?"

He laughed. "Maybe one. I thought you did it on purpose, just for the attention. Anyway, Willy's getting on in years, doesn't drive much anymore, so he sold me his old truck. Like I said, nothing fancy, but it runs good, and it's survived a lot of winters—"

"How many winters are we talking about?" Being the exotic new girl in school wouldn't work as well if I had to drive some old beater. I could work around it, but it was certainly a handicap I'd need to overcome.

"Let's just say the truck remembers when Eisenhower was president."

Oh well. I made grateful noises, and after that we lapsed into a silence that might have been uncomfortable for Harry, but wasn't for me. We drove away from the city limits, such as they were, and into the endless flatness of the prairie. Less the middle of nowhere than the far outer reaches of nowhere. I was used to cliffs, ocean waves, hills, redwoods, cars with surfboards or kayaks on top... but this was just flatness, and trucks spattered with mud. I was thousands of miles from the sea. How awful. Without the ocean, where do they hide the bodies?

I kid. I'd never hide a body in the ocean, at least, not without taking a boat some ways out first. Tides are a bitch.

After an interminable period, we reached the tiny town of Lake Woebegotten. Downtown was like something from a movie: park with a bandstand, City Hall with a dumb little dome, square grassy town common, little mom-and-pop stores. One stop light. A single parking meter, which was pretty funny, since there were a million empty places to park for free. It looked like the kind of place tailor-made for fourth of July parades and speeches by local politicians and ceremonies crowning the Pig Queen or whatever they had here. The sun should have been shining and making everything look even more corny, like Pure Americana Extract, but it was pretty overcast. Funny, I remembered summers in Lake Woebegotten—hot, sticky, and humid—but I had no idea what autumns and winters were like. Guess I was going to find out soon.

Harry pulled the police car over to the sidewalk. "I know you probably just want to get home and stop traveling, but there's not a thing to eat in the house but a freezer full of walleye and maybe some maraschino cherries, so how about I pop into Cafe Lo here and get us something to eat?" A horrible thought must have occurred to him. "Uh, are you, you know... Like your mother?"

I raised an eyebrow.

"A vegetarian," he said.

"Oh, no," I assured him. "Absolutely carnivorous."

He made a show of wiping sweat off his forehead in a broad gesture of relief. "I remember you used to eat a hamburger of your own and then do your best to eat mine too, but all those years you've been out in Santa Cruz, I wasn't sure..."

"The hippies did not convert me," I said.

"Burgers it is. Julie makes the best ones I've ever had, even better than her grandpa who used to run the diner."

I was happy to sit in the car while Harry went inside. I'd been traveling all day, and I was tired and puffy and probably a bit smelly—hardly ideal for a first impression, and I had a feeling anyone I met in this town I'd be seeing again and again.

I looked out the window toward the town common... and that's when I saw him. Or, rather, *them*, but even from the first moment, it was really mostly *him*.

There were five of them, walking across the grass like kings and queens of the Earth. The wind itself seemed to hold its breath in their presence. They *looked* like teenagers, but they *moved* like they owned the town. In a way, they were an odd bunch: three boys, two girls, all different... but all physically striking. It would have been remarkable in an individual, but with all of them together, the effect was almost overwhelming. The girls were gorgeous, irritatingly so, even in jeans and button-down shirts—I might not be the prettiest girl here after all, which could complicate matters, though I could already see ways to use it to my advantage. They were even paler than me, though one was a petite red-haired thing and the other was proportioned like a runway model and ice blond. Of the boys, one was nearly seven feet tall, black-haired, dressed in red flannel and big enough across the shoulders to be one of Dwayne's linebacker friends. Another was blond, shorter—though still tall by any ordinary standards—and muscular in a wiry sort of way.

The last was slimmer, wearing a long dark coat that was halfway stylish, with a mop of brown hair almost exactly the same shade as mine. He had cheekbones so sharp you could have used them for bottle openers, and his lips... More about his lips later. He was the one who fascinated me the most instantly, and when he turned his head and looked at me, I felt an electric shock pass through me. He didn't stop walking, and if I hadn't been staring at him with all of my considerable attention I might not even have noticed, but he *hesitated*, a long pause between one footfall and the next, and he stared right into me in that instant before walking on, murmuring to the others, who didn't so much as glance at me. Who *very conspicuously* didn't so much as glance at me, I thought.

Harry reappeared with brown paper sacks and plastic cups. "Who are they?" I asked gesturing toward their departing backs. "Do they go to my new school?"

After glancing and squinting, Harry nodded. "Oh, sure, those are Doc Scullen's kids. Well, not his *kids*, he's only maybe ten years older than they are, they're adopted, or foster kids, or something, except for the Scales, who are cousins or off-relations of the doc's wife.... Let's see, the big bear of a fella is Hermet Scullen, and the little redhead is Pleasance, and the one in the long coat is their brother Edwin. The blonde girl is Rosemarie Scale and the other guy is her brother Garnett. Heck of a family. Just moved here two, three years ago, but the Doc's been a great addition to the community, and the kids seem all right, never get into any trouble."

"Maybe I'll meet them at school tomorrow," I said.

"You could fall in with a worse crowd," Harry said agreeably.

BROOD TYPE

Harry's house was a little gray farmhouse just outside town, bordered on three sides by fields, with a stand of trees in the back. Hardly a match for mom's house over by Westcliff Drive in Santa Cruz, but I could cope. And there in front of the house was a truck—my truck, I guessed. I'd been expecting a beat-up old pick-up, possibly with the vague stink of pig manure clinging to it... but this... the thing was almost as big as a tractor-trailer rig, glossy black, with bulging headlights, a grille like a giant robot's grin, and a flatbed in back big enough to carry a normal-sized pickup truck.

"It's a 1938 Ford V8 one and a half ton Marmon-Herrington," Harry said, getting out of the car and beckoning for me to follow. "All wheel drive. Marmon-Herrington made trolley cars—and *tanks*—but they also did business with the military converting ordinary trucks into, well, pretty much super-trucks. This one used to belong to the Belgian army, Willy says, which means it's more well-traveled than me, and I don't doubt it's made it through a few wars and could make it through a few more." He coughed. "I know it might be... a lot of truck... but it's gonna be the safest thing on the road by a good margin. Those little aluminum tin cans rolling around on the highways today couldn't even make a dent in her."

"Her?" I strolled over to the truck and patted the hood, which was so tall I'd need a stepladder to look inside. "I think it's definitely a him."

"Well, anyway, it runs great, Willy's grandson Joaquin is some kind of mechanical genius. Still a stick shift, though. Is that going to be a problem? Your mom said you could drive a manual, but this one..."

I'd once driven a tractor trailer to the edge of a cliff and then put a cinderblock on the gas pedal to send it over the edge, so I wasn't too worried about wrestling with an old Ford's transmission, but there was no need to go into specifics. "I'll manage. I love it, Daddy. Thank you."

And I really did. I've always found it easier to love objects and machines than people. If you maintain them properly, and know how to use them, machines will do exactly what you want them to, every time, without variation. If only people were half so reliable.

Harry led me into the house, and we feasted on our burgers and fries. The place was exactly as I remembered but—cliché, I know—it seemed smaller. I don't know if it was all his years as a bachelor or just some sort of fundamental self-sufficiency, but Harry didn't hover around me or try to make much more small talk. He took my bags upstairs to my room, which was just like it had been the last time I visited. I doubted the sheets had even been changed; Harry probably hadn't changed *his* sheets in the years since I'd been here last. The room was essentially an anonymous place for a summer visitor. Well, I was settling in now, for at least the next several months. I told Harry I was tired after my long day, and he gave me my space.

I got ready for bed, locked my door, and stretched out on the bed... which crinkled under me. I pulled up the covers and hissed through my teeth. There was an old plastic cover underneath the sheets. I'd had some... issues... with bedwetting when I was younger, and I felt a surge of humiliation and anger that Harry hadn't thought to remove the plastic since my last visit.

But no matter. Old news and ancient history. Tomorrow

was a new day at a new school in a new town—anyway, new enough. I felt myself on the cusp of possibility. I was a little anxious, but only because there were so many unknowns. What would the other kids be like? The school was much smaller than my old one, just a few hundred students, and I was sure the entire senior class had deeply entrenched loyalties and ancient feuds stretching back to elementary school. I could navigate the social minefield at my own school blindfolded and hopping on one leg, manipulating opinions and opening old wounds at will to achieve my own ends, with never a misstep—all right, *one* misstep, which was why I was living in Lake Woebegotten now—but Lake Woebegotten High was going to be a whole new world, one I'd never even glimpsed, a place without maps or guideposts.

I closed my eyes, took deep breaths, and listened to the silence. No rolling waves, no hiss of passing cars, no cries of seagulls or college kids: just quiet, and the creaking of the house. Yes, I was going into uncharted territory, but I had the power of being a novelty in a place where novelties were likely highly prized... and people were essentially the same all over. Seen one, seen them all.

Except for the Scullens, and the Scales... especially Edwin... they looked like something else. Something *interesting*.

I love things that are interesting. They're as hard to come by as a perfect crime.

The next day I woke up early, because it pays to be up and around before anyone else, but I underestimated Harry's Minnesotan work ethic: he was gone by the time I rose, with a note on the kitchen table weighed down with the keys to my beautiful monster of a truck. Blah, blah, will try to be home for dinner, blah blah, have a good first day at school.

I showered, and considered my wardrobe. Autumn in Lake Woebegotten was colder than winter in Santa Cruz, so I'd invested in new cool and cold-weather clothes. I had some incredibly cute things, but I also had some... ordinary things.

Call it protective coloration. Blending in with the rest of the herd. The temptation to dress myself in something cool and stylish and eye-catching, taking Lake Woebegotten High like a hurricane (or I guess a blizzard would be more appropriate given the locale) was strong, but it violated my fly-below-the-radar resolution. So I settled on a baggy-ish green sweater, and jeans, and black boots. Hair down, just a little make-up. I examined myself in the too-small mirror on the little girl's vanity in my room and nodded at my reflection. Completely inconspicuous, like a little harmless bird. There was no point glamming up: I'd seen Rosemarie Scale and Pleasance Scullen walking across the grass yesterday, and I knew my own strengths and weaknesses enough to know I wouldn't be able to overshadow them. So the situation called for a different approach.

I pulled on a black coat and walked out to my truck, which I was already thinking of as Marmon, and climbed inside the cab. And I mean *climbed*—a shorter girl, like that little snip Pleasance, would've needed an elevator to get behind the wheel. I cranked it up and the engine roared like a furious lion before settling down into a low grumble. The radio didn't work, but the heater did.

I shifted into gear and pulled forward, and despite being what felt like ten feet up in the air, driving Marmon was remarkably easy. Of course, back home, it would have been a nightmare—ever parallel park a school bus?—but in Lake Woebegotten, where there were more parking spaces than pigs and idiots, it should be fine. I'd never been inside the school before, but I'd been there at some cruddy little summer carnival they had in the parking lot years ago, so I knew how to find it. A few minutes later I was pulling into the muddy gravel lot marked "Student Parking." There weren't any spaces marked out, and only one or two other cars parked haphazardly around, so I just parked as close to the school as I could and hopped out.

Santa Cruz High has big columns out front in a sort of

faux-Classical style that's not uncommon for institutions of lower learning in central California, while Lake Woebegotten High was just a few low brick buildings with flat roofs clustered around a brick courtyard, and a scattering of trailers the color of old snow off to one side. I went toward the biggest of the buildings and stepped into a hallway that was like all school hallways, probably: scuffed floors, fluorescent lights, beat-up walls punctuated by beat-up doors. I found the door marked "office" and pushed my way inside to a cozy little space that could have been a dentist's waiting room. A woman with orange hair and a face like tapioca pudding in a plastic freezer bag looked up at me and smiled. "How can I help you?"

"I'm Bonnie Grayduck. I'm—"

"Oh, yes, Harry's daughter, of course." She reached into a desk drawer without looking and pulled out a little map of the school—like such a dinky place needed a map, you might as well make a map of a gas station or a public toilet—and my schedule. English, Government, Trigonometry, French—oh well, those years of Chinese I'd taken would go to waste in this wasteland—then the blessed interval of lunch before Biology and Gym. Biology. Maybe this would be one of those classes where they let you dissect cats or pig fetuses. You can learn a lot about the world from cutting up animals.

I confirmed that where I'd parked was fine and took the slips I had to get all the teachers to sign, I suppose to make sure I actually showed up for classes. As if there weren't ways around *that*. I had a little time before my first class, so I strolled around the halls a bit, glancing at the map, getting the lay of the land. Other students began to arrive, but I didn't pay them any attention—at least, not so's they'd notice.

Just before the first bell rang I crumpled up the map into a ball and tossed it into a trash can. I wouldn't need that anymore. I've always had a good spatial memory. In English class I introduced myself to my teacher, a balding rabbit-faced man who might as well have been named Mr. WhoGivesACrap, who told me I could take any open seat. I chose a desk in the very back corner of the class, where I had my back to the wall and could see the door. Other students filed in, but none of them made an impression on me. None of *them* were there— the Scullens and the Scales. The rest of these people might as well have had used wads of chewing gum for faces, as far as I cared. The styles of clothes were different, and these kids were altogether a whiter bunch than my old Santa Cruz High classmates, but they were still part of the great undifferentiated multitude, to be noticed only if I had need of them.

There were lots of glances and murmurs my way, but I mumbled responses to questions and stared at my feet. Let them think I was shy awkward new girl.

The morning went on that way, with no particular moments of note. I made a couple of brief points of contact with some of the more vivacious girls, the kinds who might see a shy new girl as a project, someone to take under their wings. Always let people think they have the power; it's much easier to control them that way. At least this way I'd avoid the awkward dance of trying to figure out where to eat at lunch.

And lunch is where I saw them again.

HAIRY STORIES

NARRATOR

Stevie Ray sat with his back resting against a tree near the postage-stamp-sized Indian reservation of Pres du Lac, trying not to doze off. He yawned, closing his eyes, and when he opened them again, three elderly Native American men dressed in flannel and denim stood in a loose semi-circle around him. Stevie Ray glared. "Indians creeping up silently on a fella through the woods? You don't think that's a little stereotypical?"

Willy Noir grinned. "We weren't all that quiet. Maybe a guy who didn't hear us coming should think about having his ears checked out."

Stevie Ray stood up and offered his hand, but no one shook it. He sighed. "Dr. Scullen would like me to apologize on his behalf for his idiot son trespassing on your lands, if he did, which maybe he didn't, but he probably came close, so anyway, he's sorry."

Willy glanced at the other two tribal elders, who had faces as impassive as carved wooden—damn it, stereotyping again. As the only black man in the entire town of Lake Woebegotten, Stevie Ray was keenly aware of racial things, but heck, these guys *were* taciturn and inscrutable and other such things. Then Willy leaned over his walking stick and spat on the ground. "Never had a wendigo apologize to me before," Willy said. "Can't say as I like it much."

Stevie Ray rolled his eyes. "This wendigo stuff. We both

30

know the Scullens and Scales aren't wendigo—"

"Wendigos," Willy interrupted. "The plural is wendigos, not wendigo, they're not like deer or moose."

"I thought it was Wendigeaux," one of the elders said. "With an x. Like the French do it."

"Wendigi, maybe, like octopi and cacti?" Stevie Ray said.

"Wendigos," Willy Noir said, unperturbed.

"Well, all right," Stevie Ray said. "The point is, they're *not* wendigos. They're... you know." He put his hands to the corners of his mouth and made fangs of his index fingers.

Willy shrugged. "Our legends don't really have *those*, but we have wendigos. I don't think it's a bad description. Wendigos used to be human, and then became something else, something immortal. They eat human flesh. The details are a little different, maybe, okay, but do your—" Here he imitated Stevie Ray's fang gesture "—do they fear sunlight, or garlic, or crucifixes, or holy water, or have obsessive compulsive disorder? They don't exactly fit the stories perfectly, either, do they?"

Stevie Ray shrugged. "No, I guess not. But in the legends there are all different kinds of—"

Willy interrupted. "And maybe one kind is a wendigo. My people—especially people like *me*," he said meaningfully, "are sworn to protect the world from the wendigos. And the world needs protecting from the Scullens and the Scales, so I say they're wendigos." He wiped his mouth. "And yes, one of them was on our land, though I think he strayed over by accident in the midst of blood lust during pursuit of a deer. He ran right off our land again, and killed whatever prey he was chasing outside the limits of the rez, but trespass is trespass. I'm willing to concede it was an accident. No doubt about whether he was here or not, though. I can *smell* him."

"That's not so difficult," Stevie Ray said, "assuming he was out on a sunny day."

One of the other elders snorted, and Willy cracked a smile. "You're not so bad, Stevie Ray. Why do you play Renfield for those things?"

"Let's just say I have some philosophical interest in avoiding an all-out race war," Stevie Ray said blandly. "Between you... hairy folks... and the ones you want to call wendigos." *Also because the Scullens pay me a lot.* "Besides, I don't work for them, I work for both of you, as a liaison. Did you have a message to take back to the Scullens?"

"Just this. If it happens again, and one of the boys comes onto our land? Don't expect them to come back."

Stevie Ray sighed. "I've seen those boys play hockey, Willy. They play rough. Could be one of them against you three wouldn't be a fair fight. Could be it might be a little dangerous."

"Could we fight a wendigo as we are now? No. But you know... we're not too hairy right now. We can get hairier. And one of the things that makes it easy to get all hairy—that makes it hard to *not* get all hairy—is having unnatural flesh-eating animated dead things on our land. Besides... what makes you think there aren't any *young* people in Pres du Lac who've inherited our gift?"

"Okay, okay." Stevie Ray held up his hands. "I'll pass on the message, least I can do, I was just saying, that's all. But, you know, for flesh-eating dead things, they aren't so bad. They've found, ah, non-human sources of nourishment. And they brought a lot of money to the economy. Dr. Scullen has a way of forgetting to send the people he treats bills, too. I mean, their kind may be known for drinking blood and treating humans as playthings, but heck, some people think *my* kind are all good at playing basketball, and some people think *your* kind are in touch with the spirits of ancient wisdom or else that you're all drunks, so maybe these kind of generalities aren't such a good idea, I don't know, I couldn't say, but it just seems to me."

"I know they're behaving themselves now. That's why we made the truce with the Scullens—well, not we, but my ancestors, and I was awfully annoyed to see them come back here a couple of years ago. But we also know it's an effort for them to stick to food that doesn't think and talk and have hopes and dreams. You have to understand, Stevie Ray, things like that live forever unless you stop them from living... and when you live forever, the chance of you making a mistake or losing control isn't a question of whether or not, it's just a question of when. And when they *do* slip, when they witness a car wreck or something and start smelling blood and lose control of themselves... aren't you glad to know me and my occasionally hairy friends and family are around to protect you?"

"Great," Stevie Ray said. "Werewolves are going to protect us from vampires? That makes me feel real comfortable, as a human."

After Stevie Ray left, the quietest elder said, "Did he say werewolves? He thinks we're *werewolves*?"

"That fella," Willy Noir said, "is a fella who watches too many dumb movies, is what I think."

A LITTLE LUNCH

FROM THE JOURNAL OF BONNIE GRAYDUCK

I gazed across the cafeteria, and there they were, sitting in a little island all their own in a corner: the Scullens and the Scales, leaning together and talking among themselves, like they were a species apart. (That was a feeling I could relate to.) I became aware of a sort of twittering and realized the girls I'd "befriended"—a blonde called Jessica or Jenny or something, I'd call her "J" and she'd think it was a nickname, and Kelly, a petite brunette, though she looked like a heifer in comparison to Pleasance. "Those are the Scullens and the Scales," J said. "I know, I saw you looking at Edwin, he's a *dream*, but he doesn't date, I don't know if it's a religious thing or what, they keep to themselves." I detected a note of bitterness in her voice, and knew he'd rejected her—or, more likely, failed to notice her existence. "But at least he's single," she said, pitching her voice low. "The other ones are... *together*. The big one Hermet and the blonde one Rosemarie, and Garnett and that tiny little Pleasance. I don't care if they *aren't* related by blood, I know Dr. Scullen and his wife adopted them, but they all live in the same house, so I think it's unnatural, they might as well be brother and sister, it's just not right, and Garnett and Rosemarie really *are* brother and sister, the Scales, but I guess they're not dating each other, so—"

"Have they always lived here?" I interrupted, still gazing at Edwin. His jawline... his nose... his *lips*...

J shook her head. "They lived up in Canada or something I guess? But they're American, Dr. Scullen was just working up there. They moved here a couple of years ago, and they live a ways outside of town, mostly keep to themselves."

"He will be mine," I said. I probably shouldn't have said it out loud, but there you go.

J giggled. "It's good to aim high," she said, a little doubtfully.

"I wonder if I have any classes with him," I mused. If I didn't, I'd have to see about making some adjustments.

Kelly said, "Let me see your schedule." Classes had been going on for a week, I realized, so she might have some idea of his movement. After poring over my schedule for a moment, she said, "You have biology with me after lunch. Edwin's in that class. But are you really going to..."

"I might say hello," I said.

Just then Edwin happened to look up, and caught my eyes. He stared at me, and frowned—hardly the reaction I wanted. He looked away, said something to his pseudo-siblings, and then all of them got up from the table and left together.

I walked with Kelly to biology, a long low room with lab tables fitted with gleaming metal fixtures to attach Bunsen burners. "Good luck," Kelly murmured before taking a seat at one of the tables. Naturally, she already had a partner, which made me wonder who I'd be stuck with—I hoped not that baby-faced nerd Ike who'd chattered at me in one of my earlier classes and trailed me like a yapping dog to the cafeteria. I'd smiled at him, because having a geek in reserve could be useful, but I didn't want to make *conversation*, I just wanted to observe Edwin and plan.

I took my slip of paper to the teacher, who read it at least five times before ever so reluctantly signing it. When I turned back to the tables, every one had its requisite pair of students... save one.

Edwin sat at the table, and I walked toward him, eyes shyly downcast. If he had a reputation as someone who didn't date, a charm offensive wouldn't work. I needed to draw *him* in, be a shy and tantalizing enigma. I might contrive to accidentally touch his arm during class, or—

I noticed his face. I mean, I'd *been* noticing his face, but I really noticed his expression now, and it was furious. He must *really* enjoy sitting alone, because he didn't like the idea of a lab partner. Or did he just not like the idea of *me* as a lab partner? It hardly seemed possible that it was a personal dislike, as we'd never even spoken—how could he have anything against me? People *loved* me.

I sat next to him, and he moved to the far end of the table, his chair scraping. He stopped looking at me, at least, staring down at his hands, clasped white-knuckled before him on the table. As the teacher lectured—something about parasites—Edwin never moved a muscle. His jaw was clenched so hard I was afraid his teeth would break. I did my best to ignore him... but even though I'm normally the world's champion ignorer, it *bothered* me. There are so few things I want, after all, and I usually get them—but if he was like this, he would be hard to win.

Up close, he was even more beautiful, unfortunately, and I thought about moths drawn to flames, and flies to flytraps. I was not happy with being the moth; I was much more accustomed to being the flame.

When class ended, Edwin sprang to his feet and bolted out the door. The A/V nerd, Ike, intercepted me at the door. "Hey," he said. "You need help finding your next class?"

"It's gym class," I said absently. "I'll take a wild guess and assume the class is in the gym."

"Hey, that's my class, too!" he said, as if we'd just discovered a mutual passion for something incredibly obscure, like 16th century antique furniture or dressing up in Ewok costumes.

"Mmm," I said, and Ike took that as an invitation to walk with me.

"Man, did you kill Scullen's dog or something?" he said, and I twitched a little, though I hadn't killed anyone's dog in ages.

THE TWILIGHT OF LAKE WOEBEGOTTEN • 37

"What are you talking about?"

Ike shrugged. "He acted like you were his worst enemy, and he hardly ever even seems to notice anybody."

"Oh, was that the boy at my lab table?" I asked innocently. "I didn't talk to him."

"Yeah, Edwin Scullen. He's a weirdo anyway, so screw him."

This from someone who probably still had Spider-Man bedsheets. "Mmm," I said again, which was all the encouragement he needed to chatter on about himself and his stupid friends and their plans to go to the lake sometime before the weather got too cold.

In gym class Coach Syph gave me a uniform—eww—and I stood around and avoided playing volleyball. I'm good at volleyball—I'm good at everything—but I wasn't interested in being recruited to any sports teams or otherwise calling attention to my athleticism, something that had been a problem in the past, as I have a competitive streak it's hard to tamp down. I'm trying hard to be content with just *knowing* I'm better than everyone else, without having to demonstrate it all the time, so I flubbed a few serves and missed a few volleys and generally made myself unremarkable.

People are much more surprised when you dislocate their shoulders or choke them unconscious or chase them down in the woods if they think you're physically graceless.

WISE COUNSEL

FROM THE JOURNAL OF BONNIE GRAYDUCK

I didn't see Edwin or his siblings again that day, though I did have to dodge Ike a few times. I wanted to stalk Edwin out to the parking lot, see what kind of car he drove, all that sort of thing, but I had to turn in the papers my teachers had signed. I walked to the office, where the orange-haired secretary was deep in conversation with one of the oldest men I'd ever seen. He was scrawny, with dirty whitish hair, and I could see the shape of his skull under his face, and the veins and muscles in his neck sticking out, like all his infrastructure was showing. He had on a nice gray suit, though, made only slightly silly-looking by a little red bow tie. The man gave me a smile that was all teeth and no eyes. "Ah, the chief's daughter. Hello, dear. I'm Superintendent Levitt—well, I was, before I retired. I allowed the county to woo me back, and now I'm acting principal."

He was obviously some kind of ancient pillar of the community, but there was something funny about him, but also something kind of familiar. Those eyes... they were the eyes of someone who knew a joke nobody else did, and the joke was on *you*. "Nice to meet you," I said.

"Enjoying our school so far?"

"Everyone has been very nice," I said carefully.

"Mmm, well, why wouldn't they be?" He patted the secretary on the shoulder—was I imagining things, or did she flinch away from his hand a little? Interesting. "Just step on through there—" He pointed down a short hallway "—and chat with our guidance counselor, Mr. Inkfist, for a moment before you leave."

"Oh, I'd love to, but I should get home, my dad will be—"

"I imagine Harry's at the three-car pile-up that just happened over on the state road," Mr. Levitt said blandly. "Or so my police scanner would suggest. You have a few minutes to get some guidance." Another cold smile, and then he just stared at me, and I knew he'd keep right on staring until I went where he said... or didn't, but if I didn't, there would be consequences, and what those consequences might be, I couldn't entirely predict. Also interesting. Two interesting things in one day... though Edwin was a rather more pleasant sort of interesting than this cold-eyed old man.

More to get away from him than anything else, I went down the hall to the office he'd indicated, a tiny closet of a thing. A middle-aged man with gray hair at his temples was sorting through a pile of folders in a distracted way, so I knocked on the door. He looked up. "Yes? Ah, yes, Miss, ah, Harry's daughter, um—"

"Bonnie Grayduck."

He nodded, a pained look on his face. "Grayduck. Not Cusack, that's right. Your mother's maiden name."

I seesawed my hand. "Well. I think it's only a 'maiden' name if she ever gets married, which she hasn't, yet. And she never wanted Harry—Dad—to adopt me, so Grayduck it is." His discomfort was delicious. "It's okay, Mr. Inkfist. Being a bastard isn't so bad."

"Ah, well, youthful indiscretions, and, ah... We've gotten off. I mean. On the wrong, er, footing. Foot. Feet."

I slung my bag onto the floor and dropped into the chair across the desk from him. "Does it bother you, me being born out of wedlock? It's only... that happened a pretty long time ago. And I didn't have much to do with it."

"Of course not!" He held up his hands. "No blame accrues to you, that is, not that there's any *blame* of any sort, officially speaking of course I don't have an opinion about it one way or another, which doesn't mean *you* should have a child out of wedlock, not that I'm suggesting you're the sort of girl, that is young woman, who—who—" He sighed and put his head in his hands.

Light dawned. "You're... *Pastor* Inkfist. I remember, Harry took me to your church when I used to visit when I was a little girl."

He looked up and smiled weakly. "Not a man of God anymore, though I hope still a *godly* man, I try to be, but, oh, well, of course I'm strictly secular, technically speaking, here on school grounds, and ah—"

"How's the wife?" I said. He wasn't wearing a wedding ring, but I could still see the pale patch of skin where it had been for who knows how many years.

He chuckled and shook his head. "Did Harry tell you? That's... Well. Hard for me to counsel my flock about their own marriages and other travails when my own wife... when I wasn't able to keep my own marital house in order. My wife is fine. Last I heard. Though we don't speak often. So, things being as they were, or as they are, I put aside my calling, and chose to serve in another way, here, as a guidance counselor, instead of standing in the pulpit."

Standing in the pulpit with everyone staring at you, I thought, *thinking how your hussy of a wife did... whatever it is she did. Or how you did whatever it was you did, though to look at you, I bet it's all on her.*

"So." He laced his fingers together and rested his hands on top of the desk. "I just wanted to see how you were settling in, on your first day." His smile was a tiny bit strained, but far more genuine than that old lizard Principal Levitt's.

"Not bad," I said nonchalantly. "I've met some nice people. Especially the Scullens and the Scales." I watched him carefully, and was rewarded with a tiny frown.

"I don't know them well," he admitted. "They've only been in town a few years, but they seem like a good family, or families, or… no, family."

"They don't go to your church—your *old* church—then? I was hoping to see them there."

He shook his head. "No, they, ah, no."

"So they're Catholics." In Lake Woebegotten, you were Lutheran, or you were Catholic, unless you were that crazy guy Gothic Jim who lived in the woods and worshipped the moon or Satan or whatever. Harry was Lutheran, and so, by extension, was I.

"No, they don't attend Father Edsel's church either," Mr. Inkfist said. "They… I suppose they're not terribly spiritual. Good people though, very good, especially Dr. Scullen, he does a lot of wonderful things for the community. Still, it's good you're making friends already, I'm delighted, I know it must be hard moving to a new town, a new school, leaving everything you knew behind."

"I look at it as a fresh start," I said. "The beginning of the rest of my life. A good, sharp separation from the life you used to know can be good for you—shake you out of your old habits, force you to think about the decisions you've made and how you got where you are in life, and where you want to go."

"That's a very healthy attitude," he said doubtfully. "Well, ah, did you get your teachers to sign… Oh, good. Everything looks to be in order. If you have any problems, or need any help, about school or anything else, don't hesitate to ask."

"Sure thing, Reverend," I said, and rose, walking out of the office, and putting in a little extra sashay as I went. Might as well give the ex-pastor something nice to sin about later in his lonely bedroom.

PSYCHOSOCIO

NARRATOR

After the Grayduck girl left, Principal Levitt appeared in David's office in that way he had, materializing like smoke rising from a hole in the ground where something noble or useful used to be. "Counselor," he said. "How was your meeting?"

David hemmed and hummed and even hawed a bit, wondering if Levitt had been listening at the door; it wasn't beyond him. But he owed Principal Levitt his livelihood—he'd given David this job, saying a man needed useful work to keep him occupied, especially if his wife and his faith deserted him, in that order. Principal Levitt had actually been School Superintendent Levitt until his retirement a few years back. He'd agreed to come out of retirement and effectively accept a demotion to run Woebegotten High after the old principal, Mr. Jorgenson, ran off with the old guidance counselor, also coincidentally named Mr. Jorgenson (no relation), along with the entire contents of the football team's booster club fundraising account. So here they were: David not entirely sure what he was supposed to be doing, and Mr. Levitt so profoundly overqualified that he could probably float through the days with his eyes closed. One day, David thought, it would be nice to feel confident and not full of doubt, but now that he'd lost his path to God, that day was probably even more distant than it had been a year ago, when—

"Inkfist!" Levitt shouted, and David snapped out of his reverie.

"Erm, sorry, I was thinking about, ah, what was the question?"

"The Grayduck girl," Levitt said patiently, sitting in a chair across from David. "What do you think of her?"

"Oh, she seems nice, ah, gregarious? She's already making friends, I think she'll do fine—"

Levitt sighed. "You didn't read her file, did you?"

David winced. "I *skimmed* it, I didn't have much time, I'm afraid—"

"You skimmed it, but overlooked the letter from her old principal, right on top? Maybe you should read it." Levitt moved papers around until he found the folder on David's messy desk, removed a single sheet—a photocopy of something written on a sheet torn from a legal pad—and handed it over.

David read it. Then he read it again. He considered reading it a third time, but that would only get him more upset. "That girl... she did *this*?"

Levitt shrugged. "Nothing proven, of course, no charges brought, nothing official, which is why that note isn't written on school letterhead, I'd guess. But the principal clearly put enough stock in the rumors to send us a note warning us to keep an eye on young Bonnie, just in case."

David frowned. "Do you think her father knows? I mean, how could he *not* know?"

Levitt shrugged. "The girl lived with her mother. The mother knows, no doubt. But a girl like that... I bet she has her mother wrapped around her finger and firmly on her side, so they may have decided to keep it from Harry."

David blinked. "Should we tell him?"

Levitt laughed. "You're so prompt to violate student-counselor confidentiality?"

"Ah. I didn't—I didn't realize there was such a thing."

Levitt showed his teeth. "You might have read your

orientation packet, David. You have to maintain confidentiality with your students, with three exceptions: if you think the child is being abused, in which case you're legally obligated to tell the law, though in this case the law is Bonnie's *dad*, so let's hope Harry isn't the child-beating type, it could get awkward; if you think the student is going to kill herself or someone else, you tell me, and I'll refer it to a psychologist who has an arrangement with the school; and in the case of a student disclosing something that could cause serious and foreseeable harm, like plans to run away from home or set a house on fire. Do any of those apply?"

"Ah. No, though the bit about serious and foreseeable harm could be arguable, I think, if this letter is accurate, though there's nothing to say she'd do something like that again… But, technically, Bonnie didn't tell me anything, so it wouldn't be a breach of confidentiality to tell Harry—"

"So you are paying attention," Levitt said, in his dry voice, like the rasp of lizard scales on sand. "Good. That's true. So call up Harry and tell him you think his daughter is… what? A monster?"

"Ah, I guess I'd say… troubled? Confused?"

Levitt's eyebrows went up. "Troubled? You wouldn't go so far as to say *psychopathic*?"

David made one of the array of noncommittal noises he'd mastered over the years.

Levitt clucked his tongue. "Or, in your considered professional opinion, is she more properly termed a sociopath?"

David nodded sagely for a moment, cocking his head thoughtfully, then gave in to the inevitable. "What's the difference?"

The old man sighed. "Trick question. *Technically*, no one is a psychopath or a sociopath anymore—they're sufferers of Antisocial Personality Disorder now, and even back in the '50s the distinction was disappearing, with the terms used interchangeably. But some people say there are two varieties of APD. For instance, maybe psychopaths have poor impulse control, and they're more fearless, risk-seeking, and incapable of internalizing social norms. Psychopaths are louder and easier to notice. Sociopaths, though, have better impulse control, they can hold their tempers better, and don't often take unnecessary risks—they can control themselves, and they're better at passing as... for want of a better word... *normal* people. Psychopaths are incapable of love, while sociopaths *can* love, and intensely, though being the object of their love can be extremely dangerous—they might just kill a pretty waitress who flirts with you, for instance, or burn your house down to encourage you to move in with them. A sociopath is a selfish lover—they don't respect rules or boundaries, and deep down they don't much care about *your* needs, they begin to see you as an extension of themselves. Probably sounds romantic, to someone who's an idiot. Passion and madness are so thinly divided, wouldn't you say?"

"I've... never thought about it," David said.

Levitt continued. "Then again, some people flip the words, and say sociopaths are the ones who are obviously crazy and can't fit into society, while psychopaths are the manipulative con men who cruise through human society like sharks. You shouldn't use either term, really, though people still do, even doctors, even though neither one really means a damn thing exactly. But psychopath or sociopath, organized or disorganized, both lack empathy, both have a propensity for violence—or at least a willingness to engage in violence more easily than other people do—and deep down, they don't believe other people are real, not entirely, not like *they* are."

"Ah," David said. "I... I'm not sure Chief Cusack would like hearing his daughter was a sociopath. Or a psychopath. Or anything like that."

Levitt grinned. "You think? I think so too. Probably it's all a misunderstanding, anyway, the principal's note is careful to say it's just rumors and rumblings, nobody's sure." Levitt shrugged. He looked at the ceiling for a while, long enough that David looked up there too, wondering if there was a water stain in the shape of Jesus or something similarly arresting, but it was just acoustical tile. "Who are we to say lack of empathy is a bad thing?" Levitt mused, still looking up. "There's a movement among people with APD, self-diagnosed and medically diagnosed, to be considered just... non-neurotypical. Not crazy. Just... different. They call the rest of you—ah, us—'empaths,' some of them. They're just not like the rest of the human race. Perhaps even superior, their minds unclouded by sentiment, capable of a sort of ruthless rationality. What do you think of that idea?"

"I think it's something I'd have to think about a lot more before I had any thoughts about it, if you see what I mean," David said.

"That's what I like about you, Counselor. You fully commit to failing to commit. Well, let's keep this letter to ourselves—" Levitt plucked the note from Bonnie Grayduck's old principal from the desk. "—and keep an eye on Bonnie. If any of her friends... meet a bad end... we'll make some discreet inquiries. No reason to bother Harry when this could be nothing, hmm?"

"Of course," David said, delighted to have the decision taken out of his hands. Having Mr. Levitt make decisions for him was almost as good as having the church or God telling him what to do, though his moral compass, David had to admit, was likely a bit more uncertain in its orientation.

BIOLOGICAL IMPERATIVES

FROM THE JOURNAL OF BONNIE GRAYDUCK

E dwin was in the office, talking to the orange-haired receptionist, when I got out of my meeting with the guidance counselor. He was leaning over the counter, speaking to her in a low voice, and I was suddenly viciously jealous of their proximity: why the hell did that old woman get to be this close to his perfect face? I overhead him say, "But you have to let me transfer, I'll take any other biology class, any period, it's very important—" Then his head snapped around, and he stared at me, nostrils flaring, eyes narrowed. It's taken me a lot of practice, but I'm good at reading expressions, and his said: I'm angry, surprised, and also maybe a little afraid. An odd reaction, especially since he didn't know me at all—and he'd have nothing to fear from me anyway. "Never mind," he muttered, turning and not quite running from the office. One advantage of him running away from me: I enjoyed the opportunity to watch a certain portion of his anatomy on the way out.

I walked thoughtfully out to the parking lot. The logical conclusion was that he'd been trying to get out of our biology class so he wouldn't have to sit next to me anymore. That sort of behavior might hurt a girl's feelings, if she had any. I couldn't figure out *why* he'd do that, though—we hadn't interacted at all. I'd never had someone take such an immediate, instinctive dislike to me, and I must admit... I found it an intriguing challenge. Most people are as easily manipulated as a set of children's building blocks, and I can put them together or pull them apart in whatever combinations amuse me. But Edwin was something I *wanted*, and he didn't want *me*. Maybe this is what they mean by "playing hard to get"?

But I was being silly. Edwin was a teenage boy. He wouldn't be hard to get—none of them are, at least, not once I managed to get them hard. Then *I'd* be the one playing come-here/go-away, playing with *his* mind—

My jaw started aching, and I realized I was grinding my teeth, an old habit from my childhood that I'd left behind, like playing with matches. I climbed into Marmon—the parking lot was nearly empty, so there was no danger of me smashing up the cars parked around me as I maneuvered the Great Wheeled Beast—and drove toward Harry's house, planning my plans, and plotting my plots, and beginning to think I might have some fun in Lake Woebegotten after all. Getting someone to fall in love with me might be almost as much fun as destroying someone's life.

And if love didn't work out, I could always fall back on the destruction.

Harry brought home more burgers and fries from that diner, and I made a little face. "Eating like this once in a while is fine, Dad," I said. "But I'd rather avoid the pimples, greasy skin, and thunder thighs, thanks. Don't you ever cook at home?" Then again, home cooking in Lake Woebegotten probably meant casseroles where cream of mushroom soup and mayonnaise were the main ingredients, with a crust of crumbled corn chips on top.

He looked a little shamefaced. "Well, I'm pretty busy, so I do eat a lot of takeout, I guess that's not so good for you. When you used to visit, you loved eating pizza and burgers every night of the week. I guess I didn't think... I could go by the grocery store and pick up a few things." He sounded doubtful.

I rolled my eyes. "Leave me some grocery money every

week, I'll do the shopping." It was a role I'd taken on back in Santa Cruz, too, since left to her own devices my mom wouldn't have anything in the fridge but a bottle of mustard and sour milk and some rotting organic produce she'd forgotten to eat.

Harry grinned. "It's a deal. I can't promise I'll be home for dinner every night, what with the job and all, but I'll do my best—"

I waved my hand. "It's okay, I'm good with the lone wolf thing, I'll make stuff that generates lots of leftovers."

Not long after that, Dad got a call on his radio—somebody got drunk and fell down a flight of stairs, and Harry had to go make sure there wasn't any foul play—so I had the big old house to myself. I considered trying to find out where the Scullens lived, maybe doing a little judicious stalking, but despite Marmon's many fine qualities, he wasn't an ideal reconnaissance vehicle.

I settled for locking my door—it didn't have a lock originally, but I'd brought a few hook-and-eyes and sliding bolts with me in my luggage, along with a battery-powered screwdriver, so that was okay—and plugging in my vibrator (the battery-powered ones are way too weak, don't believe the hype) and thinking about Edwin, wondering if he was that pale and smooth and perfect all over.

Tomorrow, the games would begin. Tomorrow, I'd start winning.

Except tomorrow came, and Edwin *wasn't there*. I spent the whole morning living halfway into the future, half-flirting with baby-faced Ike by rote, playing some little Queen Bee games with J and Kelly—backhanded compliments, subtle undermining, setting them at odds, really basic stuff, but essential for shifting around the social pecking order to favor me—but mostly just thinking *Edwin Edwin Edwin*. Then lunchtime came, and he wasn't at his table. His semi-siblings were all there, but no Edwin, boy of my waking dreams.

In the middle of some stupid babbling Ike was doing about taking a trip to the lake I stood up, strolled over to the Scullen/Scale table, and gave them my biggest wide-open smile. "Hello," I said. "I'm Bonnie."

They all stared at me. Their faces might as well have been carved in marble. They were all so *pretty*. Was Dr. Scullen secretly a cosmetic surgeon, practicing at home on his foster brood, making them into images of perfection? I let my smile drop. "Anyway," I said. "I need to talk to Edwin. Is he here today?"

Rosemarie and Pleasance rose to their feet, picked up their trays, and walked away like I wasn't even there.

Blood rose into my cheeks. Cut dead by those pretty bitches, in public, in front of *everyone*? Oh, no. Oh, no, no, no. Not okay. There would be consequences.

Hermet the giant got up, glanced at me, grinned like a moron, and lumbered out. That just left Garnett, who sighed. "Sorry about that," he said. "They're just... Edwin had to go up to Canada for a little while."

"How long?"

Garnett shrugged.

"Very helpful." I went back to my table, where the convocation of lesser beings stared at me. I sat down, and went back to eating, and J finally said, "What was *that* all about?"

"I just wanted to borrow Edwin's notes from biology class for the week before I moved here," I said. "But he's not around."

That answer didn't seem to satisfy any of them, but they didn't push, and fell back into their mewing and bleating routine soon enough.

So Edwin had taken a sudden trip to Canada. Interesting. It was insane to think he'd left town because of *me*... but in my experience, most things in the world *do* seem to revolve around me. And if they don't start out that way, they get there eventually.

Biology class with no partner was a bit of a bore. Indeed,

the whole week was pretty useless. No Edwin meant nothing of *interest*. I used the time well, of course. I discovered that the grocery store—Dolph's Half Good Grocery, "It Isn't Half Bad!"—was immensely easy to shoplift from, as the cash register was either run by a profoundly stupid and inattentive teenager, or by the owner, Dolph, who spent most of his time flirting desperately with various housewives. I learned the faces, and very nearly the names, of every other kid in the school, and put together a mental map of the school's social network, with all the fault lines and exploitable components marked red in my mind's eye. A fairly simple and typical structure: jocks and cheerleaders, rich kids—around here I gather that meant their fathers owned lots of pigs—nerds, "slednecks," the general slush of unremarkable losers, a lone goth, a pair of hippies, some band geeks, etc. All easily comprehended and exploited.

But the Scullens and the Scales didn't fit in. They were a little island off to the side, sharing connections only with one another, not hooked into the greater organism that was the school culture, and that meant they were essentially untouchable by all my preferred methods. Character assassination was pointless when they obviously didn't care what anyone thought of them. Humiliation was out of the question; Rosemarie and Pleasance couldn't be humiliated any more than the sun could be frozen: they *embodied* dignity and grace, which should have made them easier to topple or tarnish, but, frustratingly, somehow didn't. I couldn't turn them against each other because I didn't have any leverage, or any way to *get* leverage. There were more direct approaches to comeuppance—I'd used them in the past—but increasingly, direct acts of violence seemed to be best used as a last resort, and probably indicative of a failed imagination. Far better to lead your enemies to destroy themselves.

But I didn't give up. I like a challenge. And I can be very patient.

I just wished Edwin would come back. Plotting to destroy Rosemarie and Pleasance was fine, but when you have your heart set on seduction, assassination is a poor substitute.

RETURNITY

FROM THE JOURNAL OF BONNIE GRAYDUCK

My first weekend in Lake Woebegotten was also un-eventful. A girl can get sick of uneventfulness. I mostly concentrated on making myself at home in Harry's house, re-organizing the cupboards in the kitchen to better suit my preferences, and taking over the upstairs bathroom completely, quietly exiling all Harry's crap to the smaller downstairs bathroom. He didn't object. He struck me as a remarkably easygoing guy, which made me wonder how he'd ended up with my train wreck of a mother in the first place—though it did explain how he'd managed to put up with her for seven years before they broke up. Harry wasn't around much. I tried to plot more against Rosemarie and Pleasance, but I couldn't see any way to get to them that didn't involve going through Edwin. What if he never came back?

On Monday, people greeted me by name at school, Ike nipping at my heels, J becoming increasingly cold toward me—she liked Ike, for some reason, perhaps a fat-cheeks fetish, and his obvious fascination with me bothered her. She kept spending time with me, though, in the best frenemies tradition, and for my part, I stopped flirting with Ike, and the other boys, too. Not to make J happy, though—mostly because I didn't want Edwin to get any mixed messages... even if he wasn't here to receive them. Word could get back to him through his luminous siblings, after all.

But that day, when I went into the lunch room, the Scullen and Scale table was full again: Edwin was back, chatting and laughing with his family as always. I didn't stare—I *didn't*—but he happened to look over at me just as I looked over at him, and our eyes met, and this time, there was no mask of hostility on his face, and he even gave me a little half-smile. I ignored him, pretending to pay attention to the prattlings of my tablemates, until Kelly whispered, "Edwin Scullen is staring at you."

"Doesn't cost anything to look," I said breezily, and bit into my chicken sandwich.

"No, he's really staring. Wow."

I shrugged, but I was secretly gratified. If he were fascinated with me, for whatever reason, that was something I could use. I very deliberately didn't look over at him again. No reason for him to know *I* was fascinated, after all. Ike went on about the trip to the lake again. I gathered cases of cheap beer and bags of undoubtedly skank weed would be involved. Typical teenage stuff, but not unpleasant, in a provincial way, and I found myself agreeing to join them. I just wished I'd brought some good stuff with me from Santa Cruz—my mom had an old back injury that got her a medical marijuana card, so she always had plenty in the house, and was sufficiently scatterbrained that I could take more or less as much as I wanted. Not a luxury I had with a cop as my dad. Though maybe if I could get access to the evidence locker...

After lunch I sailed out of the cafeteria, the gears in my mind locking and meshing and spinning beautifully. A lot would depend on how Edwin reacted to me in biology class. If he put up his wall-of-silence again, it would be tough; the Scullens were a tricky bunch, but if I could find a crack, I could exploit it.

Our lab table was empty when I arrived in class, even though I'd dawdled so I could make a nice entrance, and I had a flash of worry—was Edwin ditching? I sat down, looking without much interest at the microscope set up in the middle of the table. Just when I was ready to give up on him, Edwin burst in, looking like an underwear model late for a shoot, his hair beautifully tousled, his cheekbones so prominent they could have been handholds on a beginner's climbing wall.

I looked away from him, down at my notepad, and ignored him thoroughly, though of course I noticed when he sat in the chair next to mine—and didn't drag it as far away from me as possible this time. I continued ignoring him, doodling, though I realized I was doodling skulls, so I quickly started transforming them into flowers and other innocuous things with lots of dense little pen-strokes.

"Hello," he said, and while it wasn't the first time I'd heard his voice, it was the first time he'd spoken to *me*, and a shiver started in the soles of my feet and the top of my head all at once, one shiver traveling up, the other traveling down, with both shivers meeting in the middle—well. Slightly *lower* than the middle, to be totally honest.

I glanced at him. His eyes were focused intensely on me, and they were dark blue, like young stars. "Oh. Hi." Back to my doodle. My interesting, interesting flowers.

"My name is Edwin Scullen."

"Mm. I'm Bonnie. Grayduck."

He chuckled warmly. "Oh, I know who *you* are."

Promising. "Oh? Why would you pay any attention to someone like me?"

"I think you're certainly worth paying attention to," he said earnestly. "And it's a small school, a small town. You're the police chief's daughter. Why, you're a celebrity."

This from one of the untouchable Scullens, but I didn't get any sense of condescension or mockery from his tone, and those were tones I was highly sensitive to—since I often used them myself.

Just then Mr. Whatever explained what we were doing with the microscopes (some bullcrap with looking at slides and identifying some other bullcrap), and I gave Edwin a hapless little smile. "Could you start? I always break the slides, I'm so clumsy."

Edwin heroically fitted slides in the microscope and peered through the eyepiece, and I looked in a few times too, and we drew pictures of the structure of whatever it was we were supposed to be looking at, and it was all strictly business. At one point his hand brushed mine, and it was ice-cold—that was a bummer. I was hoping to get Edwin into bed sometime, and cold hands also meant cold *feet*, which were no fun under the covers. Ah, well. Somebody that beautiful had to have *something* wrong with him, and lousy circulation wasn't so bad, really. I was no closer to understanding why he'd been a total asshole before, only to be a gentleman this time. Maybe he'd been gone for a week of rehab or something—he did have a certain heroin-chic quality about him, all pale and everything, with the fine blue tracery of veins just barely visible beneath the skin of his wrists. But a week wasn't long enough to kick any sort of habit. Mysterious. I don't like mysteries, unless they're mysteries I benefit from.

Once we finished the lab—well in advance of the bleating sheep elsewhere in the classroom—he turned the searchlight of his attention away from tiny glass slides and back to me, where it belonged. "How do you like Lake Woebegotten so far? I know it's hard to start over in a new town."

He was a transplant, too, I remembered. "Oh, I used to come here when I was a kid, to visit Harry—my dad. So it's sort of familiar. It's been, oh, maybe five years, but absolutely nothing's changed, as far as I can tell."

"Lake Woebegotten does have a certain timeless quality, I've heard," Edwin said. "My adopted father Argyle's family lived here, oh, in the early 1900s. The house where we live, on the north side of the lake, way back in the woods? It's been in the family for generations." He cocked his head. An adorable gesture. He basically exuded adorable. How could he go from looking like a dangerous rock star one moment to cuddly boyfriend material the next? He was as changeable as floating clouds viewed under the influence of psychedelic mushrooms. "This must be very different from—where is it you're from? Somewhere in California?"

"Santa Cruz," I said. "On the central coast."

"The name sounds vaguely familiar," he said.

"Ever see that old movie *The Lost Boys*?"

His eyes widened. "Ah? The one about..."

"Vampires, yeah, it has Pee-Wee Herman and Kiefer Sutherland before he got all old? The amusement park in the movie is the Santa Cruz Beach Boardwalk. Not that they called the town Santa Cruz in the movie, but it was shot there, maybe you heard about it that way. There were some serial killers there back in the '70s too, I guess." And more recently, though no one had realized that's what I was. "Nowadays it's mostly famous for, I don't know. Hippies, surfing, the usual. It's okay. Way different from Lake Woebegotten though, yeah."

"Not a lot of surfing happens in the lake," Edwin said gravely.

"Not a lot of ice fishing in Santa Cruz," I said.

Then Mr. Whatever came over and looked at our drawing and said we did a good job (though he was so bored and per-functory, who knew if it were true; then again, who cared?). He moved on to the next table, and Edwin stared at me again. His lips looked delicious. "Why did you come here, if you don't mind me asking?"

Ah. Well, I was hardly going to tell the *truth*—a stupid girl died, and some people thought I might be indirectly responsible, and we thought it might be better if I finished up my senior year someplace else, where there wouldn't be so much whispering and staring in the hallways. So instead I said, "My mom wanted to travel around with her boyfriend Dwayne—he plays arena football—but she felt bad about me being alone so much. And I hadn't seen Harry in ages, so I figured, I'd come spend a little time with him before I go off to college or whatever."

"Don't you miss the friends you left behind?"

Time for a little creative storytelling. I looked away, pretending embarrassment. "My, ah, boyfriend... I had a bad breakup. Actually, he cheated on me with my best friend. So, no, I didn't really want to see those people much anymore."

"Bonnie, I'm so sorry." The sympathy in his voice was warm as melting butter. "A betrayal like that... how terrible. You deserve better."

Hmm. Sounded like he'd be faithful, but also suggested he'd be jealous. Both of which could be used to achieve various effects, of course. I looked at him, frankly. "So," I said, "if I deserve better, why were you such a jerk to me last time we had a class together?"

His eyebrows went up, but just then Mr. Whatever called our attention to the front and started pointing at some crap on an overhead projector. A few moments later the bell rang, and Edwin was—*whoosh*—gone.

I'd spooked him. Oh well. I should've probably played up the wounded-bunny routine some more instead, but there was something about Edwin... I didn't want to show him the *real* me, of course, but I didn't want to hide myself utterly in a fake persona.

Ike joined me as I left the room. "Saw you talking to Scullen," he said, rather sullenly. "He seemed nicer today."

I nodded. "I still don't know what his problem was, but he seems to be over it." We went to gym class, where I pretended physical incompetence, as per usual, until I could finally get back to the only kind of competition that actually matters: real life.

In the parking lot, I started up Marmon and drove slowly out of the lot. There was Edwin, standing by a Subaru station wagon with some of his faux-siblings. He looked up at me, and his eyes were the color of pale blue skies this time, almost ice-blue. Weird. I'd heard of eyes that changed color depending on a person's mood, but that's just dumb—any changes like that are just the effect of light reflecting differently off the iris, and the fact that the iris changes shape as the pupil dilates or contracts. But Edwin's eyes were dramatically lighter now, so maybe....

If so which mood did that particular shade of blue I'd seen in biology class indicate?

I'd find out. It was a problem vulnerable to an experimental solution.

GODS AND MEN
AND SO FORTH

NARRATOR

S tevie Ray took his hat off when he entered the priest's
office, because it seemed like a show of respect was in
order, even if Stevie Ray himself didn't have any particular religion. He was, he supposed, technically an atheist,
though it seemed to him just about everybody was an atheist:
even Father Edsel, because even though he had faith in his
Holy Trinity, there were thousands of other gods he didn't
believe in: Zeus, Ra, Ahuru Mazda, Yum Kaax, Tepeyollotl,
Sakhmet, Napir, Bes, Gal Bapsi, and on and on. Stevie Ray'd
found a book in the remainder bin at a going-out-of-business
Borders in the Twin Cities called *The Encyclopedia of Gods,*
and that thing was more than 300 pages long, nothing but
the names of over 2,500 gods various people had worshipped
at one time or another, or still did—gods they'd probably
believed in enough to kill or die for (or at least change their
diet or get up early on Sunday mornings for). And he'd heard
that in Hinduism there were a hundred million gods, enough
gods that every family could have one of their own if they
wanted. Stevie Ray, who'd always fretted a bit about being
spiritually bereft, had felt better when he realized that. Edsel
and Pastor Inkfist—well, he wasn't a pastor anymore, but
still religious, no doubt—were almost as atheist as Stevie Ray
was: he just believed in one fewer god than they did, and the
difference between disbelieving in a hundred million gods

and a hundred million and one gods just didn't seem all that significant, really.

It was a shame, in a way, though, because if Stevie Ray had believed in a god—or at least the right god—he might have worried less about the family of vampires living in town. As it was, in the absence of a god to pray to, he'd decided he had to go and talk to Edsel.

Father Edsel wasn't a tall man, but he was a big man, with a big personality, a big bushy beard, and wild eyes, like a biker gang boss who'd decided to take holy orders. He'd been a priest down in Texas or someplace, but he'd done something bad and got sent up here to Lake Woebegotten. Not the kind of something bad where he'd molested little boys or anything, though the church wasn't above sending priests to tiny little middle-of-nowhere parishes for *those* offenses, either, or so Stevie Ray had gathered. More the kind of bad where he'd performed an exorcism on a little kid who turned out to have a neurological disorder, and gotten a lot of bad publicity for the church. Edsel was loud, formidable, pigheaded, bombastic, and other such adjectives, but he had a quality that Stevie Ray needed, mainly: he believed in evil, and in demons, and in abominations before the Lord, and such things as that, which had made it easy for Stevie Ray to convince him the Scullens and the Scales were actually vampires. It had been harder to convince him *not* to sharpen up a bunch of wooden stakes and round up some of the dumber parishioners and arm them with pitchforks and torches, though. But Edsel wasn't *stupid*, and he'd seen reason eventually, and agreed to just keep a watchful eye. But now, Stevie Ray was worried, so he sat down with the priest in his office and sipped a cup of bad coffee and talked for some time while Edsel scowled at him from under those hirsute caterpillar eyebrows.

"So you think a war is brewing, then," Edsel said finally, leaning forward across his great oak slab of a desk.

Stevie Ray sighed and shifted on his uncomfortable chair. The furniture in here was really terrible, the seating equivalent of hair shirts. "I'm not sure it counts as a 'war' when it's five or six fellas on one side and six on the other, maybe it's better to call it a feud or something, but yeah, I think the tribal elders and the Scullens—and the Scales—could come to blows over this thing. I don't think the boy, Edwin, meant to stray onto the reservation, he was probably just tracking a deer and didn't realize he'd hit their territory—it's not like there are signposts out there in the woods. But technically it's a breach of their treaty, so..." Stevie Ray shrugged. "I'm just concerned, is all. I'm trying to make things peaceful, you know, but—"

"I'm not opposed to the devil-worshipping heathens from Pres du Lac killing the bloodsucking undead fiends, and vice versa," Edsel said thoughtfully. "In fact, if we could manipulate this into a full-on war of evil vs. evil..."

Stevie Ray pressed the heels of his hands to his eyeballs. Talking to Edsel gave him a headache. "Father, please, the elders aren't devil worshippers. They hate vampires—or wendigos, as they say—worse than anybody. All right, all right, worse than anybody except *you*. But what I worry about is collateral damage. The Scullens haven't bothered anybody in the years they've been here, and in a year or two they'll have to move on anyway, because people will start to notice they aren't aging and wonder why the 'kids' haven't gone off to college. I was really hoping to keep things nice and quiet until they left, knowing they won't be back for at least a few generations, long after it'll cease to be my problem. But if they start trying to kill each other over a breached treaty, the town could get caught up in the mess."

"I am a man of action, Stevie Ray. What action would you like me to take?"

"Just be ready. Get your... people ready. So if something *does* happen, we can step in, at least to protect the townsfolk. Vampires are tough, I know that, but the tribal elders tell me guns will slow them down and blades will cut off their heads and fire will burn them."

"And fragmentation grenades will fragment them, I'm

sure," Edsel said. "So the Interfaith Vampire Slayers may finally see action, then? How wonderful."

Stevie Ray nodded. Edsel had access to truly startling quantities of weaponry, mostly because of his crazy friend Cyrus Bell, who was widely believed to be the single most insane person in town, outranking even Gothic Jim the Satanist and that odd fella on the outskirts who talked to himself all the time, called The Narrator by those locals who called him anything at all. Cyrus ran Cy's Rustic Comfort Cabins and Bait Shop, which had been pretty popular before the internet came along and allowed past guests to provide warnings for potential future guests, who mostly chose to give the place a pass after hearing about Cy's warm and outgoing personality and the way he liked to stand in your doorway for three or four hours telling you about how the moon was a hollow spaceship full of alien biologists studying Earthlings like ants under a microscope and how he'd stopped wearing underwear entirely because underpants were an Illuminati conspiracy designed to lower the sperm counts of working-class men. Because of Cy's assumption that some kind of attack—from space, or the government, or the depths of the earth on account of all the lava men down there—was imminent, he'd spent a lot of years going to gun shows, writing to fellas who put ads in the back of survivalist magazines, and acquiring various sorts of ordnance, which he kept in an old bomb shelter underneath one of the cabins which was eternally closed for renovation. Stevie Ray didn't like knowing about that little treasure trove—his boss Harry would have been troubled, to say the least, at the quantities of explosives and such just inside the town limits—but it was sort of a comfort, what with the vampires and werewolves. Sure, silver bullets and wooden stakes were traditional, but a Saiga 12-gauge semi-automatic shotgun with a ten-round magazine would take your head clean off whether you were man, beast, or some kind of beast-man. And then there were the rocket-propelled grenade launchers Cyrus had bought off a white supremacist militia who'd gone out of business recently. They'd get the job done, too, assuming the job was "utter obliteration."

"We could strike pre-emptively," Edsel said. "Burst in on the Scullens en masse."

"Right," Stevie Ray said. "And when Harry investigates, and traces it back to you and Cy and your buddies, you'd be okay spending the rest of your life in prison? Nobody *believes* in vampires, Edsel. And these ones haven't even committed any crimes."

"Their existence is a crime against God and humanity."

"I thought you believed in redemption?" Stevie Ray said. "Isn't that the difference between Catholics and Lutherans? Lutherans believe in predestination, and you don't?"

"That's one of the differences," Edsel said. "But there can be no redemption for the undead. You have to confess and repent and be absolved before you die—and they're already dead. The fact that they're still walking around... it's a walking desecration. Besides, even if Argyle Scullen is telling the truth about subsisting on animals alone, he wasn't *always* so scrupulous."

"He says he hasn't killed a human being since the 1500s, Edsel," Stevie Ray said. "And I know for sure he's saved a whole lot of lives in the time since then. You've seen it yourself."

"There is no statute of limitations on murder," Edsel said sternly. "In the eyes of man's law, *or* God's."

I wish I could have more reasonable people as allies, Stevie Ray thought, but he was limited to the sort of people who'd believe in vampire doctors and high schoolers and werewolf Ojibwe, which didn't leave him with a whole lot of choices. "I'll be in touch, okay?" Stevie Ray said. "Don't do anything until you hear from me?"

"I will wait," Edsel said, in his implacable prophet-on-a-mountaintop voice. "God's judgment is long, and God's will is undeterred by the passage of time."

After Stevie Ray left, Edsel got on the phone. "Cy? Listen:

The Omega Scenario is almost upon us. Be ready." He listened for a while, made a face, and said, "Yes, that's right. The aliens will be here soon. They've been experimenting on people, as we've discussed, making wolf-human hybrids and bat-human hybrids and—of course, we shouldn't talk on the phone. Yes, that's right, there's no telling who's listening. Yes, Cy. I know. I agree. Cy. Take yes for an answer."

Edsel hung up and sighed. It would be nice to find allies who weren't insane, he thought. But Cy had the guns, and he was righteous, even if he was misguided. Still—aliens! Ridiculous.

Everyone sensible knew demons were the problem. And Edsel's crack team of Interfaith Demon Hunters were the solution.

Once he actually recruited them, anyway.

ACCIDENT PRONE

FROM THE JOURNAL OF BONNIE GRAYDUCK

So the next day I nearly killed Ike with my truck.

I was driving Marmon to school, pulling into the parking lot. There's a bit of hill right at the entrance of the parking lot, and the driveway slopes down to where the parking spots are—it's really just an unlined field of oil-stained gravel. The slope isn't huge (not even enough to sled down in winter, really), but it's there, and the incline was enough to almost doom Ike.

Marmon wasn't complaining any more than usual, and I never felt remotely unsafe in him, since he could crumple any other car on the road like a beer can crushed against a frat boy's forehead. Which turned out to be the problem.

I pulled into the entrance to the parking lot, and there were just a few other cars there, including Edwin's Subaru, parked about fifty yards away, right near the school buildings. Edwin was leaning on the hood, talking to his sorta-sister Pleasance.

Ike was parked a lot closer to me, and he was just getting out of his little Volvo. He waved at me, grinning like an idiot, and gestured to the empty space next to his. Anything for a moment's proximity to me. It would have been sweet if I could have thought of a way for him to be remotely useful to me. He stepped into my path and started making big exaggerated air traffic controller gestures, as if guiding Marmon in for a landing. For the school's "funny kid," Ike wasn't all that funny, but it was park where he wanted or run him over, so I hit the brakes to slow down.

But the brakes didn't respond. I pushed harder, and the pedal sank mushily into the floor. *Oh, fuck*, I thought. Vehicular manslaughter, here we come.

Adrenaline does things to your subjective time sense, and kicks your attentiveness up a few notches. I didn't panic: I pumped the brakes, but that didn't achieve anything, so I stomped down on the emergency brake. Not much help there, either. Marmon was rolling downhill, and locking the back wheels with the emergency brake didn't really stop my momentum—it just made my back end start to drift a little to the left. I tried downshifting, but Marmon's got touchy gears, and I mostly just made horrible grinding noises. "Move!" I shouted, but Ike just looked at me, his stupid grin gradually melting into a quizzical expression. It occurred to me that I could swerve Marmon into one of the other cars and stop *that* way, but apart from the fact that such action would be terminally embarrassing, it probably wouldn't save Ike's life: If my front end struck something, it would probably just slew my back end around, and I'd end up killing Ike via sideswipe rather than head-on collision. There just wasn't *time* to do much of anything except mow the stupid kid down, and that would lead to all sorts of unpleasantness. I'm not overly concerned with the sanctity of human life, but something so public, against someone who'd never wronged me, was hardly my idea of a good time.

Ike realized I was going to hit him, and started to dive out of the way, but Marmon's a big truck, and if he was lucky, he'd end up with just his legs crushed instead of his whole body—it wasn't going to get much better than that.

Suddenly, I saw Edwin's face at my window, even though moments ago he'd been at the far end of the parking lot. He streaked in from the side and body-checked Marmon like a football player making a tackle. The truck swung hard to the right, much more sharply than I could have turned it. I bounced in my seat hard enough that the top of my head hit

Marmon's ceiling. Son of a *bitch*. Marmon, pushed hard off course, crunched into the rear of Ike's Volvo. Ike, meanwhile, was standing up unharmed and dusting himself off, gaping.

Edwin eased open my door and clutched my hand: those icy fingers again. "Bonnie, are you all right? Did you hit your head?"

"Um, a little." I rubbed the top of my head and stared at him. "Edwin, how did you *do* that?"

He frowned. "Do what?"

"Push Marmon—my *truck*. He weighs three thousand pounds, and you moved him like a tackling dummy."

Edwin frowned. "You must have hit your head pretty hard—I just ran over a second ago to check on you, I didn't push your truck."

Okay. Play it that way, then. Edwin was even more extraordinary than I'd realized. Was it just some temporary Hulk-out moment, like those women who lift burning cars to save their kittens or kids or whatever? But, no, it couldn't be that, he'd been at the end of the parking lot, and he'd flown over here in a *second*, faster than anything living could move. Was he... what? A kid superhero? I'm what you'd call a realist, and a skeptic, but I also absolutely trust my own senses and my mind, and they were telling me: Edwin moved as fast as lightning and shoved a ton-and-a-half truck aside like I'd push a chair out of my way. "Better check on Ike," I said, easing myself out of the truck, and he looked momentarily annoyed.

"Ike, are you all right?" he said brusquely.

"I, uh, yeah."

"I'm sorry," I said, making a great show of clutching my not-really-all-that-wounded head. "I don't know what happened, the brakes just didn't work."

"Good driving, though," Ike said, rubbing his elbow, which I guess he'd scraped diving for the gravel. "I mean, it's gotta be hard to control a truck that big, and I'd rather you dent my fender than crush my head."

I glanced at Edwin, who was looking conspicuously at

nothing, and realized Ike hadn't seen his intervention—too busy leaping for his life, I guess. I looked over at the Scullens and Scales, who were clustered around Edwin's car, and they were mostly glaring at me, except Pleasance, who looked almost concerned. Pretty soon people were pouring out of the school, and more students were arriving, and before I knew it, there was an ambulance and EMTs, and Edwin told them I'd hit my head and probably had a *concussion*. Not very nice at all. I insisted I was fine, but who listens to a girl with a head injury? No one. They loaded me onto a stretcher, which struck me as funny, because *I* wasn't the one who'd been nearly run down, and all Ike got was a band-aid for his scraped elbow and an EMT shining a light in his eyes.

Then Harry showed up, and seeing me on the stretcher freaked him out, and I had to shush him and say I was fine, Marmon's brakes had failed but I was okay—

His eyes went wide. "Oh, Bonnie, I'm so sorry, honey, I checked that car out myself, I don't know what happened, I even replaced the brake pads and all the fluids were good, maybe it's got a leak somewhere I didn't know about. I'd better call Willy Noir over to check it out, he knows that truck backwards and forwards, or that son of his Joachim, he knows everything there is to know about anything that runs or rolls, why, I hear he played with carburetors the way some little kids play with Lincoln Logs—"

Several of the onlookers and one of the EMTs joined him in discussing the various ways brakes can fail, and that led to a general discussion of horrendous car accidents narrowly avoided, and while it was nice not to be the center of unwanted attention, it was also annoying. I looked at Marmon, and there was a new dent in the driver's side door, just the right size and shape for Edwin's shoulder. He'd *bent the metal* when he shouldered the truck aside—and it was good solid *steel*, not the crappy stuff cars are made out of nowadays—and hadn't even gotten bruised in the process.

Eventually they got me in the ambulance and drove out to

the county hospital, some miles away, with Harry leading the way in his police car, lights and siren blaring. They wheeled me into the emergency room, and promptly took me upstairs for an X-ray, which at least got me away from Harry's terrified doting. I told them I was fine, that I'd barely bumped my head, and they couldn't find anything wrong at all when they scanned me. Eventually they returned me to my personal curtained alcove in the ER, explaining that I couldn't leave until a doctor signed off, which might be a little while. I was surprised to find Edwin lounging by my bed, which I refused to lay down in anyway, taking the visitor chair for myself.

"So what's the damage?" he said.

"No damage at all. No concussion. I doubt I'll even have a bump on my head." I looked at him, hard. "I'm sound of body and mind."

"I'm very glad to hear that," he said, ignoring my implication.

"Why do you get to hang around back here?" I said.

He shrugged. "Position has its privileges. When your dad's a doctor..."

Just then, a hand swept back the curtain, revealing a young, tall, blond, pale, thin man in a white coat who looked nothing at all like Edwin, but shared that same impossible-to-explain magnetic quality. It was like they were luminous beings in a dark land. Substance when the rest of us were shadows. Dolce & Gabbana in a Wal-Mart world.

"Dr. Scullen, I presume."

He glanced at me, then at the clipboard in his hands. "Ms. Grayduck. My son has told me so much about you."

Edwin winced, and I suppressed a smile.

"How's your head? My son says you bashed it pretty thoroughly."

"I'm not sure how he'd know that," I said, "when he was all the way across the parking lot when it happened."

"Mostly because you were babbling a bunch of nonsense when I opened your door," Edwin said dryly. "Sounded like head injury talk to me. Call it inductive reasoning."

"Mmm," Argyle Scullen said. "Well, it all looks fine to me. I can keep you here under observation if you prefer—"

I shook my head. "No, I'd rather get back to school."

"I daresay a day off is warranted," Dr. Scullen said.

I sighed. Harry would probably insist on keeping me home anyway. "All right, fine." The doctor told me to take some painkillers if I needed them, and to call if I had any blurred vision or vomiting. Once he wandered off, Edwin gave me a smirk and started to stroll away too. I grabbed his arm. "Hey," I said, in a low voice, and pulled the curtain around us shut. "I want to talk to you."

His nostrils flared and his eyes narrowed, and even that was hot. God, I was in trouble with this one. "What about?"

"Well, I think I owe you," I said. "Since you kept me from running Ike down in the parking lot."

"I told you, I didn't touch your truck, I just—"

"I saw the dent, Edwin." I took a step closer to him, and he couldn't retreat without crashing through the curtain, and I had a feeling he wouldn't want to look as ridiculous as *that* would make him look. "In my truck's door."

"That truck has more dents than it doesn't," he said.

"And I know them all. That one's new. And it's just the right size for your shoulder."

"What do you think happened, Bonnie? I moved a truck that weighs more than some *houses* with my own body? How would that work?"

"I'm not entirely sure." I searched his face, and his eyes were darker again, a blue so deep it was very nearly black. "But I'd like to find out."

"If I *did* save you from something," he said stiffly, "seems like you might owe me the kindness of not pressing me on this."

Ah ha. "Good. Moving past simple denials. That's a step in the right direction."

"No one will believe your story," he said.

I nodded. "I know." I know a *lot* about which kinds of

stories are plausible, and which kind aren't. "And I don't intend to go telling tales anyway. But... I'd like to know, for my own peace of mind... how did you do it? What are you, Edwin? Is Edwin your secret identity? Alien? Government experiment? Souped-up clone? I'm an open-minded girl."

He laughed. "You watch too much bad TV, Bonnie. I'm just a seventeen-year-old who was worried about you when your brakes failed. You really *must* have hit—"

"Stop," I said, and something in my tone—the utter lack of artifice, maybe, the fact that it was a word originating from the mouth of the *real* me, and not one of the thousand masks I wear for the rest of the world's benefit—made him stop. "We don't need to do this. We're past this. I know something, and I'll find out more. It will be easier for both of us if you just talk to me."

"You're crazy," he said, but he looked away.

I relaxed. If these were the parameters of the situation, that was fine. I could work with these. "Edwin," I said softly. "Really. You can *talk* to me."

He turned, swept the curtain aside, and practically ran out of the room.

After that, he didn't say a word to me for weeks.

DANCING AROUND

FROM THE JOURNAL OF BONNIE GRAYDUCK

Forget the cold shoulder; Edwin gave me the cold everything, except a cold look, because that would require actually looking at me. He couldn't avoid me in biology class, what with being my lab partner, though he did the best he could: there might as well have been a force field between us, a transparent barrier that allowed us to see but not touch, or talk, or even acknowledge one another. The first day back after Ike's near-death experience, I tried to pick up where we'd left off before I'd seen him perform acts of superhuman impossibility, saying, "Hi, Edwin," in class. That was the last time he looked at me: a stare of infinite distance, and his eyes were, again, so dark they might as well have been black.

"Ah," I said softly. "So it's like *that*."

He turned away, and didn't lay eyes on me again, and on the rare instances when his gaze necessarily swept through a portion of space occupied by me, he seemed to stare right through me.

A lesser woman might have thought: do I have cooties? Body odor? Do I need to reconsider my skin-care regime? Perhaps a change of make-up, or a lower-cut shirt, or a squirt of new perfume is in order? But I'm too aware of my faults (such as they are) and my finer qualities (innumerable), and it's hard to suffer from low self-esteem or high self-doubt when almost everyone around you is, self-evidently, little better than a bunch of grubby insects. Edwin was a higher being, obviously, but he wasn't any higher than *me*: whatever superhuman physical qualities he had were impressive, but they just made him an even more suitable mate for me than I'd thought he was before. For whatever reason, he was resisting. Afraid his secret—whatever it was—would come out, probably. But I could be discreet. Very discreet. He'd figure that out, in time. Meanwhile, I could be patient, and I could play it just as cold as he did.

"You saved my life," Ike said, for the fifth time, and for the fifth time, I shook my head.

"I *endangered* your life."

"No, you couldn't help it that your brakes failed. Most people in a truck that big, the brakes go out, they would've panicked, and I would've been a pancake, but you thought fast, and I just got a dented bumper instead of a crushed head."

I made a noncommittal noise and took a bite of my meatloaf. At lunchtime now I sat with my back to the Scullen table, which meant I had a view of nothing more interesting than my "friends" Kelly, J, Ike, and assorted hangers-on. Once Ike got a whiff of the distance between Edwin and myself, he did his best to insert himself into the gap (and that wasn't the only thing he hoped to insert somewhere, obviously). His enthusiasm barely registered as amusing, but at least it made J furious, which was something: while Ike fawned over me, J stared at me with murderous slit-eyes. For whatever inexplicable reason, she was still enamored with the pudgy little nothing, and his obvious infatuation made her seethe. The fact that I was utterly uninterested in Ike did nothing to diminish her ire, but she was firmly of the "keep your enemies closer" camp, and did her best to be my best friend/principle foe. In a way, it was cute, seeing her attempt to compete with me on a cutthroat queen bee level—like seeing a monkey dressed in a tuxedo or a chicken attempting to play the piano. She was so far out of her league that she was incapable of even recognizing that she was out of her league. I could mess with her, and at least amuse myself, while I tried to decide what to do with Edwin. Maybe start returning Ike's affection, and see if that sparked some jealousy in Edwin? Could be playing with fire, though. (I have nothing against playing with fire: when I was a little girl, I loved setting fires. But as I learned when I accidentally burned down the garden shed at age seven, fire needs to be respected and treated with care, unless you don't mind wholesale out-of-control destruction.)

Or I could play matchmaker. *That* was a thought. I'm not what you'd call a romantic, but it might be amusing to bring people together instead of driving them apart. Certainly a new challenge. And messing with people is messing with people.

"So Ike," I said. "What's the plan for this trip to the lake?"

His eyes lit up, and J's eyes darkened, so I knew I'd hit on something there. "We're going this weekend!" he said. "A whole bunch of us are going over to the north side of the lake, where there's a little beach and some nice woods. It's technically on the Pres du Lac reservation, where the Woebegotten Band of the Ojibwe live, but they don't mind outsiders visiting as long as we take our beer bottles and crap back out with us when we leave."

"Sounds fun," I said. "What I've seen of the lake looks more like a swamp."

"It's marshy on this side," Ike said. "But it's real pretty over there. Did you, ah… want to come?"

I looked at J. "Will you be there?"

She seemed taken aback at my direct address, but then, she was more passive-aggressive, rather than aggressive-aggressive. "Yeah, of course, all my friends will be there."

I turned back to Ike and gave him one of my better smiles. "I wouldn't miss it."

"Great," Ike said, all sparkles and happiness and effervescent enthusiasm. He was so uncool. "I'll bring some beers— my uncle Dolph, he owns the grocery store, and he's lousy at keeping track of inventory, I'll just lift a couple cases of cheap stuff from the storeroom next time I'm working there. And Kelly..." He lowered his voice. "She'll bring the weed."

I looked sidelong at Kelly. "Why, I've fallen in with a bunch of reprobates and delinquents. How wonderful."

Kelly shrugged. "I'm sure it's not as good as the stuff you get in California, but my cousin is in college in St. Paul, and he brings me little treats when he visits."

"Sounds like quite the party," I said. I wasn't much of a drinker or a smoker, really—I like feeling the *edge*, the *rush*, of transgression, occasionally the buzz of a little coke or meth, but only rarely the spacey euphoria of weed. (Booze is dangerous, and I partake only in small quantities. I really shouldn't lose what few inhibitions I actually possess; they keep me out of trouble.) But I could do enough that no one would think of me as the weird abstainer-kid—drinking and puffing as protective coloration.

And if I worked things right, Ike and J would be screwing in the back of someone's pickup truck by the end of the night, and ideally become so besotted with one another that they'd stop annoying me.

"Hi Dad," I said. "How's Marmon?"

Harry wiped his forehead, but unfortunately the rag in his hand was grease-smeared, so it didn't make him any cleaner—quite the opposite. "Me and Willy been working on it and we're almost there. You lost almost all your brake fluid, and damned if we can figure out why, since we've been looking high and low for a leak without much luck. It's like some kind of, I don't know, brake fluid vampire came along and sucked old Marmon dry. I swear, I checked everything before I let you get behind the wheel, and it was fine before, it's really a mystery, and I don't like those, occupational hazard in my line of work."

Ah, I thought. So maybe Marmon's failing brakes were an attempt to murder me. Interesting. More subtle than cutting my brake lines, too, which would have been obvious, but an old truck being low on fluids? Who'd think twice about that? But who had a grudge against me here in Lake Woebegotten, nasty enough to try and off me subtly?

Maybe I was being paranoid. But I'd leave my mind open to the possibility. After all, sabotaging someone's car and letting nature take its course—it was exactly like something I might do, in the right circumstances. Harry wasn't thinking of a criminal angle at all, though, despite being a cop—because I was his wonderful perfect inoffensive Bonnie, probably, and thus immune to murderous plotting.

"Will I be able to drive it this weekend? I was going to go over to the lake with a bunch of kids from school."

Harry frowned. "Which kids?"

Ah, wonderful. Pop quiz time. I dredged up their names from somewhere: Ike, and J, and Kelly, and "a bunch of other kids."

"Oh, they're a good bunch," he said, and I wondered what kids he would've *dis*approved of—if there was a bad element in Lake Woebegotten, I hadn't encountered it yet, unless you counted the Scullens and the Scales, and they were awfully well-behaved, just weird and reclusive.

"Glad to hear it. Can I take the truck?"

"Should be able to," he allowed. "But if you're going with the boy you almost hit, you might want to, you know, drive extra careful around him, so he doesn't get nervous."

"Don't worry," I said. "I don't think brake failure strikes the same kid twice."

PRES DU LAC

FROM THE JOURNAL OF BONNIE GRAYDUCK

Saturday, mid-afternoon, I met up with the other kids in the school parking lot. J and Kelly were there with a cluster of other girls I thought of by somewhat seven-dwarfish names: Chunky, Asthmatic, Pimples, Dyejob, Bangs, Eyeshadow, like that. There were a couple of Ike's friends, Derek and Skyler and enough others to achieve rough gender-parity. There were far more people than vehicles—a mini-van and a couple of SUVs would carry the excess, I guessed.

After milling around in the gravel and making small talk for a while, Ike did a head count and said, "We're all here! Everybody got a seat?"

Dyejob, who piloted one of the mini-vans, said she was full up, as were Derek and Skyler in their SUVs. "Uh oh," Ike said, "looks like I don't have a chair."

Oh, Ike, you mastermind of social engineering, I thought, but I didn't speak up. "Do you mind if I ride shotgun with you?" Ike said.

"You sure you want to be that close to my truck? After it nearly flattened you?" I didn't look at J. I didn't need to: I could envision her venomous glare perfectly. I would have been amused by it, but I wanted her to *neutralize* Ike's infatuation with me.

"I think I'd feel safer inside the truck than outside," Ike said, grinning. His attempt to manipulate his way into a car ride with me was adorable, in a way, like watching a newborn fawn try to stand up.

"I was really hoping to ride with J," I said apologetically, looking over at her in time to see her glare turn to surprise. "I feel like we haven't had a chance to talk in forever." In truth we'd never really talked, but who was counting? "Do you think you could switch places with Ike, J?"

J looked over at Kelly, and some complex best-friends-forever telepathy passed between them in a flurry of eye-widening and eyebrow-raising and micro-shrugging and nostril-flaring and lip-tightening, and then J gave me a giant smile as fake as Dyejob's blonde hair and said, "Sure, I'd love to."

Ike sulked off to sit by Kelly in the SUV, and J climbed up into Marmon's passenger seat. I waited for the rest of the procession to pull out, and fell in at the end of the line. I wasn't sure how long the ride would take—twenty minutes or half an hour, I guessed—and I needed to make the most of the time I had. I'm normally all about implication and suggestion and backhanded compliments and indirect nudging, but J had certain queen-bee pretensions, and she spoke the language of passive-aggression and subtle snideness fluently, if not as well as I did, so I decided to surprise her with the direct approach:

"So how long have you been in love with Ike?"

She went rigid in her seat and stared out the windshield, at the back of the SUV carrying the baby-faced object of her jealous affections. After a moment, she said, "Since kindergarten, I guess. How long have *you* been in love with him?"

Ah. Projection. Since she thought his chubby cheeks were squeezably sexy, she assumed I did too. No surprise there. "I only have eyes for one boy at this school," I said. The truth would make me vulnerable, to an extent, but it could also show J I was willing to open up to her. Which I wasn't, really, but the illusion of such openness could be useful. "Ike's great," I said, because if I told her I thought he was podgy and dull she'd get offended, "but... I like Edwin."

She looked at me, now. "Really? Scullen? You don't like Ike?"

"I *like* him, what's not to like, but… not that way."

"I don't understand you," J said, voice heavy with mistrust. "Ike is so sweet and good and kind, and Edwin… he's so cold and condescending and superior."

I gave a great sigh. "I know. I've always been attracted to boys like that. I don't know why. Maybe I think I can fix them."

"So… Ike… I think he likes you, though."

"Only because I'm the new girl. Once he realizes I'm nothing special, he'll get over it. Besides, when I talk to him, you know who he talks about? *You.*"

"Get out. He does not."

True, but the lie would serve me better. "He does, really. I don't even think he realizes he does it, but yeah, he thinks you're great. It's just, he's known you so long, you're so much a part of his life, you've been such good friends—I'm not sure he can see the forest for the trees. I don't know how you feel about him, but I think if he… got a new perspective on you… he'd realize what he's been looking for all along is right in front of him." Matchmaker, matchmaker, fetch me a bucket to vomit in.

"But how do I get him to think about me that way? The way I think about him?"

I've always found that offering a guy a blowjob concentrates his mind, I thought, but the moment wasn't right for *that* level of frankness, so I said, "I'm not sure, but I think if you get alone with him, maybe have a couple of beers, you might be able to think of something."

Another long silence, which was good, since talking to J was like watching mud dry. I looked out the windows at the scenery, such as it was: field, bunch of evergreen trees, field, barn, field, more trees, field, farmhouse. Off to the side, glimpses of the lake twinkled in the afternoon sun, just bright flashes of water, pretty just like anything that sparkles is pretty, no matter how shallow or deep it really is.

"Thanks for talking to me about this," J said finally. "I really thought you must like Ike."

"Yeah, that's why I tried to run him over with my truck," I said.

She laughed. "Edwin Scullen, huh? Well, he's pretty, no doubt about that. You aim high. I wish I had some advice for you, but even though his family's been in town for a couple of years, I don't know them well at all. At first we all thought they must be Amish or something, or part of a weird cult, but I guess they're just… weird." She lowered her voice. "I mean, they're from *Canada*, so maybe that explains it."

"That could be it," I said. If all Canadians had the power to shoulder moving trucks out of the way. "Maybe I should take up curling or socialized medicine to make him feel more at home."

The vehicles in front turned right, down a gravel path through the trees, past a sign that said, "Welcome to the Pres du Lac Reservation," and under that in smaller letters, "Home of the Woebegotten Band."

"Oh, we're going onto tribal land?" I vaguely remembered Ike blathering about that.

"Hmm? Oh, yeah, technically we're not in the United States anymore, weird, huh? There are only a few hundred Indians, sorry, Native Americans or Ojibwe or whatever, on this reservation. Maybe twenty teenagers, you've probably seen them around town, but they've got their own school here."

I nodded. Coppery skin, black hair: they were what passed for ethnic diversity in the Land of the Lily-White. I'd only seen one black guy, my dad's deputy Stevie Ray. Must be tough to be even a little bit different in a town like this. Good thing I was so adept at blending in. "My dad is friends with a guy from here, Willy Noir, I think his name is? He's the one who sold us this truck."

"Sure," J said, "I think his son, Joachim or something, is around our age, maybe a little younger. I've seen him around.

Pretty cute, actually, and he doesn't look 15, he's taller than Ike."

Big deal; I was taller than Ike, though I figured he just loomed unusually large in J's mind.

The caravan wound through the trees, taking more turns down increasingly poorly maintained roads which I figured would be impassable with anything short of skis come winter. Eventually we reached… not a parking lot, but a wide patch of dirt that had obviously been used as a parking lot a bunch of times over the years. And there, before us, was the lake: a vast expanse of deep blue water, surrounded in all directions by towering trees, a slice of nature primeval, apart from the crushed cigarette packs in the parking lot and the beer cans I could see in some of the bushes. Everyone tumbled out of the cars hauling coolers and dragged their things down toward the beach, which was an actual beach, though the sand was rather too brown and rocky and flecked with pine needles for my taste—but then, I'd been spoiled by the beaches of Santa Cruz. I'm sure this was a tropical paradise by local standards.

There were a couple of ancient picnic tables, and a ring of stones full of blackened bits of wood from past fires, and plenty of fallen logs and big flattish rocks to sit on. Someone had brought an acoustic guitar—shudder—and as promised, Kelly had a little bag of weed and Ike displayed his surprisingly non-terrible rolling-paper prowess. I joined the circle of people seated near the firepit and took a hit off the joint to be polite, not pulling the smoke into my lungs, just taking a mouthful, holding it long enough to look halfway convincing, and blowing it back out.

I sat next to J, and when Ike sat next to me, I gave him a smile, then stood up, gave J a significant look, and said I wanted to go stick my feet in the lake. I took off my shoes as I walked, falling over once or twice in the process to make myself look like a clumsy dork and, I hoped, give J an extra boost of contempt-based confidence. Once I had my shoes and socks in my hands I walked down toward the edge of the water, some distance from everyone else. It was maybe 65 degrees, pretty pleasant, though hardly warm enough to go wading. I dipped a toe into the water, and it was pretty icy, though not a patch on the Pacific ocean surf.

"I know some people who jump in the water in winter," a voice said from behind me.

I glanced over, annoyed, because I hadn't sensed anyone's presence, and I tend to be really finely attuned to that sort of thing: Mom always said I have eyes in the back of my head, and I was the absolute champion of hide-and-seek as a child. Makes sense: I'm a predator, and predators are hard to sneak up on. But this guy had managed it. He was clearly one of the reservation boys, not one of our bused-in party, with black hair in a long ponytail, dark eyes, and an angular but attractive face. His smile was endearingly toothy.

"Why would anyone do that?" I asked.

He shrugged. "Guess it makes them feel more alive? And bragging rights, of course. But mostly because there's not a whole lot else to do out here in the winter. I'm Joachim."

"Oh! Willy's son?"

"Yeah, how do you—oh, wait. Are you Bonnie? Bonnie Cusack?"

"Grayduck," I corrected. "I've got my mom's last name, but yes, I'm Harry's daughter."

He grinned even wider. "Me and you used to play together when we were kids, I guess. That's what your dad says, anyway, I don't really remember."

"I don't remember you either," but now that he mentioned it, I sort of *did*—running around the woods with a miniature version of this boy, playing... "Wait, did we used to play... wolf pack?"

He squinted, as if peering at something distant—maybe the past—then brightened. "Wait, that was *you*? I remembered this little blonde girl, we used to run in the woods, one of us would pretend to be a deer and the other would be a wolf, or sometimes we'd both be wolves and we'd chase down some other kid... But that was you?"

I touched my hair. "I was blonde until I was six or so," I said. "Then it got darker. Wow. Well, nice to meet you again, Joachim. You still play wolf?"

"Nah, mostly I work on old cars and stuff."

"And jump in frozen lakes."

"Not me! I don't need to feel *that* alive—being that cold would feel more like being dead anyway. My dad said you're living with Harry now?"

"Yeah. Just needed a change of scene I guess."

"I thought you lived in Los Angeles or San Francisco or something? Why would you want to move *here*?"

I marveled at his poor grasp of geography. That would be like saying, "I thought you lived in Boston or Washington, DC or something," as if they were remotely close together—though maybe he'd say that, too. If he'd never strayed from Lake Woebegotten, the rest of the world might just look like a vague undifferentiated vastness. "Santa Cruz, actually. Closer to San Francisco than L.A. And sure, Santa Cruz was nice, but... I had my reasons. And it's good to spend some time with my dad."

"Harry's a good guy." Joachim picked up a flat stone and skipped it expertly across the surface of the lake. "He goes fishing with my dad a lot, sometimes they spend a few days out here together in the winter, ice fishing."

We were rapidly moving into boring territory. I glanced over to the ring of my classmates, and saw J leading a dumb-struck Ike toward the trees. Perhaps J had arrived at my blow-job-as-icebreaker theory on her own, developing it from first principles. Good for her. "So you live on the reservation?" I said. Joachim might not be thrilling me conversationally, but at least he was differently boring; I knew exactly how the other kids would bore me if I returned to them, and the one with the guitar was butchering some country song, which gave me even more incentive to stay mostly out of earshot.

"Yeah, there aren't too many of us left, a lot of my relatives have moved up to Leech Lake, we've got some family there, but my dad says it's important for our people to keep occupying this land." He rolled his eyes. "Otherwise, who'll keep the wendigo away?"

I perked up. "The who?"

He looked embarrassed. "Oh, it's just some stories the old timers tell, though some of them take it really seriously, it's kind embarrassing, like having relatives who believe in little green men or bigfoot or vampires or something."

"Now you have to tell me. What's a wendigo? Sounds like some kind of recreational vehicle old people would drive around the country in."

He laughed, and sat down on a fallen log. I joined him. "Basically, they're cannibals. Or man-eaters, anyway, I guess since they aren't technically human, you can't call them cannibals. Unless they ate another wendigo..."

"Anthropophagous," I said to derail his tangent, and he looked at me blankly. "It means they eat people," I said. "Fun word, huh?"

"I'll have to remember that one, though I don't think I could spell it." Another toothy grin. "Okay, so here's how the legend goes, at least the way I heard it: there's a monster that lives in the woods and comes out especially in the winter. He, or it, or they, there are probably more than one—they roam around the woods, and anyone they find, they eat. The wendigos live forever, and they're strong, and almost impossible to kill, and have other sorts of powers, like maybe they can change their shape, or something—people say different things. Sometimes they just look like people, you know, only they're always very thin because no matter how much they eat, they can't ever get full—the hunger never goes away. Their skin is pale like snow or gray like death, and their lips are shredded and bloody because they chew at their own mouths when they get hungry enough. Other times, they look like monsters, or giants, much bigger than people, because every time they eat someone, they grow larger, and that's why they're always hungry—as soon as they get a full belly, they grow in size, so they're starving again. Who knows."

"Wow," I said. "Like an abominable snowman with a taste for human flesh."

"But that's not all." Despite his protests, Joachim was warming to the subject. Well, why not? Who doesn't love a good monster movie? "See," he said, "they're not *just* monsters— some of them are people who turned into monsters. Sometimes in the old days, during hard winters, people would run out of food, and get pretty desperate. The really desperate people might even resort to cannibalism. Eating other people is taboo, and the, I don't know, say the gods, they punish you for that, by transforming you into a wendigo. It's a curse."

"Huh. So, like, does the bite of a wendigo turn you into one of them? Like a werewolf or a vampire?"

Joachim shook his head. "No, I don't think so. I think if a wendigo starts to eat you, they don't stop eating until there's nothing left. But, yeah, maybe like a vampire—I read a book about vampires once that said in some stories, you don't have to get bitten to turn into a vampire, you can just be a really evil guy, and maybe you'll come back to life as one. Werewolves, too, you don't have to get bitten—there are tribes who have stories about witches who wear wolf skins."

"Does your, ah, tribe believe that?"

He shook his head. "I don't think so. Never heard any stories like that, at least. I think it's Navajo, maybe? I don't remember."

"I guess when you have wendigos you don't need werewolves."

Joachim grinned. "Ah, but wait, there's more. Lots of the Ojibwe—really all the Algonquin peoples—tell different stories about the wendigo. There's even a Lake Windigo up on the Leech Lake reservation. But here on Pres du Lac we've got our own twist. Which is, we're supposed to be the ones who defend the world from wendigo, or at least, defend this part of the world. I'm not real sure how we're supposed to *do* that.

Something about being empowered by the great spirits and embracing the primal power of the beasts of the earth, but I've never been real clear on what that means, exactly. There's a really old dance, no one's done it for years and years, but the elders here started doing it again a couple of years ago, they go around a fire backwards and play drums, it's weird, not like any other tribal dances I've seen. It's supposed to stop the wendigos, or hold them back, or remind people it's not okay to eat other people—I'm not sure which."

I frowned. "Huh. Why'd they start doing it again? Did somebody see one?"

Because of the dark skin and the fading light, it took me a moment to realize he was blushing, but he was definitely looking away. "It's... really stupid. Beyond stupid. I shouldn't even say anything."

I leaned in to him, letting one of my breasts brush his arm. "Oh, now you *have* to tell me."

He cleared his throat. "It's, ah... do you know the Scullens? And the Scales?"

"Dr. Scullen and his children?" I said, avoiding mention of Edwin's name. Now *this* was interesting. "Sure, I've seen the kids around at school, I guess."

"They're not welcome on the reservation," Joachim said. "The elders say they—well, at least Argyle and his wife—they say they've been here, in Lake Woebegotten, before. And they made a treaty with the elders back *then*—like my great-great-grandfather."

I frowned. "What do you mean?"

He hunched over. "God, it's so embarrassing. The elders think Argyle is a wendigo, disguised as a human. That his whole family is, which doesn't even make sense, because wendigos are supposed to be pretty much solitary. That they've lived for decades, maybe hundreds of years, and that they used to live here, and went away for a long time, and then came back. Well, Argyle and his wife came back, the rest of them are newer, I guess."

I stared at him. Edwin was clearly *something*, but I didn't think he was a *cannibal*. "Whoa. I mean, I met Dr. Scullen at the hospital. He looked pretty human to me, and he didn't take a bite out of my face or anything."

He held up his hands. "Of course not. The whole thing is ridiculous. People don't live forever. Or turn into monsters. Look at that soccer team that crashed in the Andes, didn't they end up eating each other? Nobody there turned into a monster. It's dumb."

"Okay," I said slowly. "But if your people are supposed to protect the world from the wendigos, what's with making a treaty?"

"Apparently Argyle is a reformed wendigo. Instead of eating people, he just drinks animal blood. Which, since a wendigo is by definition a monster that eats people, if you stop eating people, are you even still a wendigo?"

"Drinking blood? That sounds more like—"

"I know! I told my dad that drinking blood sounded like vampires more than wendigos, and he just told me our people don't have any legends about vampires, we have legends about wendigos, so that's what they are. Which doesn't exactly clear things up." He shook his head. "Are they scared of crosses and garlic or guys dancing backwards and drumming badly? Who knows. Anyway, they aren't welcome here on the rez. Nobody here goes to the hospital where Dr. Scullen works if they can help it."

Edwin, a wendigo. Or, better yet... a vampire. Did I believe in those things? I didn't believe in ghosts—dead people are just dead—but I found within myself the capacity to believe in monsters. And Edwin was certainly *something*, although an impossibly powerful legendary predator seemed more likely (and interesting) than rural teen superhero. This would require further investigation...

"So anyway," Joachim said, "how's the truck running now?"

"Marmon? Oh, good. Wait, did you work on him?"

"I helped Dad fix the truck up before Harry bought it, yeah."

"It worked okay except for when the brakes failed and almost killed that guy—oh, wait, he's off with J. Anyway, yeah, almost killed a classmate. Not so good. But otherwise, it's great."

Joachim nodded, scowling. "Dad told me about that. Doesn't make any sense. I don't know where the fluid *went*—"

"Maybe the Scullens stopped drinking blood and started drinking brake fluid," I said with a grin, and Joachim laughed.

Shame he was only fifteen. He looked sixteen or seventeen, at least. But if his people were the sworn enemies of the Scullens—crazy as that sounded, take it as a given—then maybe I could work out some sort of interesting love triangle situation, and push Edwin into my arms *that* way...

"Hey, Bonnie," Kelly said. "Looks like it's going to start raining here in a minute, I think we're packing up. Hey, Joachim, right?"

"Yeah," he said, looking at the sky. "You're right, it's going to piss down in a minute."

I hadn't noticed, but the darkness wasn't just a natural effect of dusk—thick clouds were gathering over the water. "Nice talking to you, Joachim. Next time Harry goes to visit your dad I'll try to tag along, okay?"

"That would be awesome!" He had a face like sunshine, so unlike Edwin's eternal broodface, but appealing in a way. And I did wonder if he'd be cute naked. Seemed like a lot of the trouble I got into in life stemmed from wondering if certain boys would look cute naked. But I was good at getting out of trouble, too.

I joined Kelly as we walked back up toward the spot where the cars were parked. "Do you mind if I ride with you?" she said, nodding toward the trees, where Ike and J emerged, hand-in-hand. "I think those two probably want to sit together on the way back. It's about time they finally hooked up—it's been like a sitcom or the first half of a romantic comedy with them, since about seventh grade. I don't know what you said to J—" (Ha, I'd even gotten her best friend calling her that, hilarious) "—but it sure lit a fire under her."

"Judging by the dazed and happy look on Ike's face, she lit up something under *him*, too," I said dryly, and Kelly giggled. She chattered at me on the drive back into town, and I made the appropriate noises, but really, I was thinking: wendigo.

No. That wasn't even remotely romantic. That would be like falling in love with a ghoul or a guy who bites the heads off chickens.

But: *vampire*. Sure, both were immortal beings who fed on the flesh (or blood) of the living, but for some reason, I couldn't tell you why, vampires were just so much more *sexy*.

LUNCH DATE

FROM THE JOURNAL OF BONNIE GRAYDUCK

I spent far too much time on the internet that night. Harry actually had broadband, which surprised me, but apparently there was a little ISP that had an office not far from the police station, and Harry'd gotten a good deal. I can see why. He's got various gaming consoles and tons of games, mostly first-person shooters, and apparently his major hobby is slaughtering computer-generated enemies with his friends online. The guy really could keep surprising me. But I guess he doesn't really get many chances to mow down perps with automatic weapons at his day job.

I looked up wendigos (Wendigen? Wendigi?) first, and it was pretty much like Joachim had told me, once I filtered out the comic book characters, movies that used that name for monsters but meant something totally different than the Algonquin tradition, and some random book where "Wendigo" was the name of a magical car, of all things.

The Google image search for wendigo was mostly pretty monstrous stuff, not a bit like Edwin, so I branched out and started searching on vampires, which was pretty much just inviting a giant river of crap to flow into my house. I'm not much of a reader, but if I was, apparently I'd have a hard time reading any novel written in the last fifty years that *didn't* have a brooding sexy conflicted vampire in it—the shelves were just full of the stuff. If I were a vampire guy, I'd run as fast as I could from the dark-eye-shadow, wedding-dress-dyed-black, ankh-wearing brigade—it amazes me that Goth *just won't die*, and worse, now those girls have websites with drippy fonts and way too much of their poetry and fanfic: ick. Some of them had a corset-and-piercings thing going on, and I know some guys like that, but mostly, just a universe of sad.

Still, target audience aside, when it came to brooding sexy vampire guys: that was more like it. Edwin definitely rocked the paleness and wiriness and the impossible strength, but the fact that he walked around in the daytime seemed like a potential dealbreaker—at least until I did a little more research, getting past the bee-stung-lipped immortal-teen-heartthrob types. Turns out there were plenty of vampires in recent fiction and old legends both who had no trouble with the sun, either because they'd evolved that way (like Stephen King and Scott Snyder's *American Vampire*) or because the whole sun thing was just bullshit—did you know even freaking Bram Stoker's *Dracula* wasn't hurt by sunshine? Sure, he slept in a coffin all day, but not because the sun would kill him or anything. He was just *nocturnal*, like, I don't know, a sugar glider or a bushbaby or a ferret something. I know. Blew my mind. Then there were Arabian vampires, who hated the dark and traveled in sunlight. So the whole sun thing was obviously irrelevant: Edwin could lay out all day and get a killer tan and it wouldn't mean he wasn't a vampire.

But the whole "Do they burn in the sunlight or don't they?" thing was just the tip of the ridiculousness: there are more types of vampires in the world than there are shades of lipstick. Vampires who can only be killed by hammering a nail through their heads, vampires who turn into mice or sheep or horses, vampires who transform into werewolves when you kill them—what a bummer *that* must have been for the first fearless vampire hunter to run across one of those—vampires who can astrally project and cause eclipses, ones with stingers in their mouths instead of fangs, ones with obsessive compulsive disorder, ones who hopped around until you slapped a holy scroll onto their foreheads to neutralize them, purple-faced vampires, vampires who slept in *plants*, vampires who fell to Earth as meteors, modern vampires who weren't undead at all but just stuck with some shitty virus like the world's simultaneously worst and most awesome STD—

Basically all sorts of things, and pretty much the only quality they all had in common was preying on human beings, usually sucking out blood, but occasionally life force or fat or tears or lymph or whatever. Some were dead, and some weren't. Maybe Edwin *was* a vampire, with "vampire" defined as "really vague catchall term for things that are human-ish but also monster-ish."

Mostly I wanted to know three things:

One: Was he a vampire?

Two: Was he the kind of vampire who lives forever and has awesome superpowers?

Three: Could he make *me* into an immortal with awesome superpowers?

Because that… that would be good. Even if it required him drinking my blood or something, well, look: Blood drinking. Yucky but not a dealbreaker, I'd met plenty of guys who were into way freakier shit, after all.

Hearing about someone else's dreams is just about the most tedious thing in the world. Pay attention next time you start to tell somebody about the crazy thing that didn't actually happen to you last night: their eyes glaze over, they make polite noises, or maybe they interrupt to tell you about the sound-and-light show that erupted in their head the night before, despite the obvious fact that you don't give two craps in a bucket about such things. They only perk up a little if you say they appeared in the dream—that does seem to interest people, as they're an essentially narcissistic species.

My mom put great stock in dreams—she thought she had prophetic dreams, though she only actually seemed to remember those dreams *after* whatever event the dream supposedly foretold, but that's cause-and-effect for you, I guess. She said it was a family gift, and that I was going to inherit it, maybe, and should always treat it with respect. She wanted me to keep a dream journal, and I did (I also kept a fake dream journal, which I showed *her*, with dreams carefully researched from reading her various woo-woo new age books on the subject, chock full of symbolism, but nothing too Freudian or kinky, of course). My actual dreams, at least the ones I remember, fall into two camps: wish fulfillment and anxiety. You know the kind: in one you're flying, in the other you're being chased through a swamp by something, only you're not sure what. At least, that's what the books say. Mine are more about murder and imprisonment, respectively, but a certain amount of personal detail is bound to creep in, it can't be helped. So I don't put much stock in dreams, and I don't think anyone should have to endure listening to someone else's dream, but that night, after my research and my speculations, I did have a dream, and if it wasn't prophetic, it was certainly at least *suggestive*, even if it was just my subconscious (which is even smarter than my conscious, and that's saying something) working a few things out. Here:

I was down by the lake again, but this time, no one else was around, and the sky was filled with storm clouds the color of a bad bruise a week away from healing. I was wearing the sort of filmy white nightdress women wore on the covers of the cheesy romance novels my mom hid under her bed (where any normal person would keep their pornography, but maybe that's the purpose they served for her). My feet were bare, and I stood in ankle-deep clear water, but it wasn't cold: more like bathwater. I sensed someone watching me, and when I turned around, Edwin stepped out from the shadows among the trees. His clothes were in tatters, there was blood smeared on his chin, and even from fifty yards away, I could see his fangs, two white curved shards of bone. He stepped toward me, arms extended, eyes more black than blue.

"Bonnie, you have to run." Joachim stood at my side, tugging at my elbow, trying to get me to follow him to a boat bobbing on the surface of the lake behind us. I was confused. Dreams about boats on water were dreams of death, weren't they, traditionally? But death was on the shore: Death was Edwin. Or perhaps it was something to do with the reluctance of vampires to cross running water? Except Lake Woebegotten wasn't running water; it was just-sitting-there water. Joachim pulled on my arm more urgently, but I didn't feel any fear at all, so I shook him off. Joachim made a low sound of distress and splashed away through the shallows, and I took a step toward Edwin, my blood-smeared Romeo. His jaw unhinged like a snake's, chin dropping half a foot, and pointed teeth rose up from his lower jaw to meet the fangs pointed downward.

Then a beast shambled between us. Shaggy, black, massive—but not a wolf, which I'd expected, somehow. Perhaps a bear, if bears were the size of Volkswagens, or maybe even a hairy ox, if those were carnivorous. The creature turned its back on me and faced Edwin, and Edwin hissed, a long snakelike tongue spilling out of his mouth—I confess, my first thought wasn't disgust, but a vague speculation on sexual possibilities—as the beast roared at him.

I didn't like that, so I kicked the beast as hard as I could between its back legs. Despite being barefoot, I kicked hard, and the creature howled and bounded away, with shocking speed, into the trees.

Edwin laughed, and his jaw reshaped itself enough for him to speak. "I've never seen anyone kick a were-bear in the testicles before. I hope I'm not your next victim."

I didn't speak—I couldn't, I don't think—but I *thought*, "I'd better be *your* next victim," and then everything swirled around, the storm clouds dropping low and becoming purplish-green fog, then pulling back, and I…

I was standing next to Edwin. My mouth felt crowded with needles and shards, but not in a painful way: in a deadly way.

I wanted so very much to *bite* something, and there was a girl in front of us, standing in the water. At first, I thought she must be me, but no: I'm the only one who's me, forever and always. This girl looked a bit like Kelly, a bit like J, a bit like my mother, a bit like Rosemarie, then like Pleasance, then like the pretty-but-formidable woman who worked at the diner—any woman, really, or Everywoman, dressed in that gothic romance nightgown I'd been wearing before. And she *did* scream, and run away, and try to free herself, and splash toward the boat, and Edwin and I ran toward her, hand-in-hand like lovers racing together to leap into the water on a summer day, only when we leapt, we didn't land on water, but on flesh, and what filled our mouths was not water. Not water at all.

I woke up soaked in sweat, incredibly thirsty, and hornier than I'd been since moving to this little town.

So there's that. I offer no interpretation.

The next school day, at lunch, Ike and J were holding hands under the table (and possibly getting to third base in the process, the way he was blushing and she was giggling), and Kelly was glassy-eyed from smoking pot out behind the gym the period before, and the rest of the herd were mewling and babbling like always. I sneaked my usual secret glance at Edwin once I was seated. For some reason, he wasn't sitting at his usual spot with his usual crowd, but at an empty table way in the far corner of the cafeteria.

I looked a little longer than I should have, probably. Edwin was a shining star, except not really shining—more like a pale and luminous moon, an object as beautiful as it was distant, and I longed to escape the gravity of the shitty little decidedly non-celestial bodies at my table and enter his orbit instead—

He caught my eye. Gave me a crooked smile. And then beckoned me over.

"Whoa," Kelly said, in a spacey-wastey voice. "Edwin Scullen is totally vibing you."

J looked up. "He is. Does he want you to go over there?" She beamed at me. "You should go see what he wants!" In her own haze of happiness, she wanted me to be happy, too—and didn't notice Ike's glare. Oh, dear. Mr. chubby cheeks was happy to take advantage of J's warmth, but maybe he was still holding a torch for me, too.

"Guess I should," I said. "He probably just forgot his biology homework or something."

I picked up my bag and lunch tray and walked over, putting my food down and sitting across from him. He looked at me with those deep dark blue eyes and a crooked smile like everything in the world was a joke and he was the only one who got it. I regarded him coolly for a while, and eventually, he started to squirm, and said, "What?"

"What, what? You're the one who crooked your little finger at me, after ignoring me for weeks."

He sighed. "I'm sorry about that. Or maybe I'm sorry about *this*. I… tried to stay away from you. For your own good."

I raised an eyebrow. "Oh? I'm a big girl, Edwin."

"I'm sure that's true, but there are some things…"

"Like what? You're a serial killer? A meth dealer?"

"I could be either of those," he said seriously. "You don't know anything about me."

"Maybe if you'd talk to me occasionally, I'd learn. So you've decided to throw caution to the wind and spend time with me?"

"I decided that the flame can't be blamed for all the moths it burns. If the moth can't control itself, maybe it deserves to catch fire."

Not a bad line—a little pretentious and a lot cliché, and you could tell he'd planned it out beforehand, but still, not bad—and I laughed. "I think you overestimate your attractiveness, Edwin. I'm not saying I don't like you—the whole man of mystery thing has a certain appeal—but I'm no moth, and you're no flame."

"Who said you were supposed to be the moth?" he said

softly. He shook himself and gave me a fairly dazzling smile, considering he was a pretty broody guy. "Would you be interested in going on a trip to the Cities with me in the near future?"

Interesting. "Road trip? What for?"

"I confess that I sometimes find Lake Woebegotten to be… a trifle provincial. Going to a real city reminds me that there's more in the world than fields and pigs and bodies of water. I don't presume to know your mind, but since you come from California, it seems safe to assume you might feel similarly?"

"There are plenty of fields in California too. Agriculture out the wazoo. But, yeah, I'm more a city mouse than a country mouse."

He laughed. "You are anything but a mouse, Bonnie Grayduck. I've never met a less mousy person."

"You sure know how to flatter a girl, Edwin. 'You're not a rodent at all!' What a sweet-talker. No wonder the girls are all crazy for you."

Edwin's smile was still genuine, which meant he could take teasing, which was promising, because even when I like people, I can't resist getting a *few* little jibes in, just to keep myself entertained and my edge maintained. "I don't care about *all* the girls," he said softly. "Just one, really."

I leaned back in my chair. "Hmm. Is this all some playing-hard-to-get fake-out? Because I can respect that. Act all mysterious to lure a girl in, then get what you want before she realizes you're just another guy? Except if you're a player, you're one who hasn't played in the two years you've been living here. I asked around. Which makes me think maybe you really *are* mysterious, and I think mysteries are interesting. And besides… I saw you shove my truck out of the way. Which tells me you're something special."

He rolled his eyes. "This again. So what am I then?"

"Probably some kind of vampire," I said, and took a bite out of my grilled cheese, looking right into his face. His expression was priceless—widened eyes, lips parted, rapid blinking, then a quick return to his superior smirk.

"You don't look much like the goth girl type. You're into vampires?"

"I'm into remarkable things and extraordinary people, Edwin. Which one are you? A person, or a thing? Because I'm interested either way."

A buzzer sounded, indicating the end of lunch period. "We should get to biology," he said.

"The study of life," I said. "What could be more interesting?"

In biology class, we finally got the chance to dissect something. On every lab table there were two scalpels and a metal tray containing the fetus of a pig.

"It's a little piggly-wigglykins!" I said. "How cute!"

"Cute?" Edwin wrinkled his nose and prodded the pig with the eraser end of his pencil. The smell of formaldehyde wasn't strong, but it was there, giving a certain mortuary sort of undercurrent to the experience. Our specimen was just a bit over six inches long, with a head small enough to hold in the palm of my hand. I'd done a few dissections in my time— out in the field, you might say, with certain stray animals I'd found in the hills above Santa Cruz—but I'd never cut up a pig before. They say pigs and humans are really similar in some ways—or is that just the taste? Human flesh is called "long pig" sometimes, right, because we taste like pork chops? If Edwin were a flesh-eating wendigo in disguise, he'd know.

Up at the front of the room, Mr. Whatever was talking about how the pigs were generously donated by some local pig farmer, and how they were all harvested from dead mothers and how their deaths would further our understanding of science and blah blah blah. We had worksheets telling us all the stuff we had to do: determining the pig's sex, identifying the parts of the oral cavity, tying the pig's legs pretty much spread-eagled before cutting open the body cavity—wow, kinky. Edwin had a look of distaste on his face, but I guess when you're an inhuman monster who preys on humankind, a dead pig must seem fairly bush league.

I got an idea. I picked up my scalpel, caught Edwin's eye, and sliced into the ball of my thumb with the blade. The thing wasn't as sharp as I would've liked—shoddy stuff for the high school kids, surprise surprise—and so it stung a bit, but nothing too painful. I sucked in my breath as a bead of blood formed on the tip of my thumb. Then I looked at Edwin.

His eyes were fixed on my thumb, and they were no longer dark blue: they were black. His jaw was clenched, lips pressed tightly together, and he'd stopped breathing completely—not like he was holding his breath, but like he'd simply forgotten the need to pretend to be breathing. "Oh, no," I said. "Sir, I cut my thumb."

"Do you need to go to the nurse?" Mr. Whatever asked, rushing over with the first-aid kit.

"Oh, no, it's just a teensy scratch." I lowered my voice and said, into Mr. Whatever's ear, "But Edwin here looks faint—I think he must have trouble with the sight of blood. Maybe *he'd* better go."

Edwin was still staring at my thumb as Mr. Whatever dabbed on a squirt of antibiotic ointment and handed me a band-aid to wrap around the wound. Mr. Whatever considered him, then nodded. "Some people are like that. Funny, his dad being a doctor and all, he sees blood all the time, but I guess you never can tell. Scullen, go see the nurse, make sure you're okay, sit out the class if you need to."

"I'd really better go with him," I said. "What if he faints in the hallway?"

Edwin grunted, and exhaled and started breathing again, but let me take his hand and lead him out of the room. Once we were a few steps away from the classroom he jerked his hand away from mine and moved to the far side of the hallway, his shoulder almost touching the lockers as he walked. "What was all *that* about?"

"Testing a theory," I said, resisting the urge to move closer to him.

"What theory?"

"I already told you."

He looked around, then said, "That I'm a *vampire*?"

"That's the one."

"Bonnie, you're being ridiculous."

"By the way," I said. "Yes, I'll go with you to 'the cities,' as my dad calls them. I'll go online and look up some goth clubs, what do you say? I'll dress in black, something long and tight that shows off my neck—"

"Stop," he said. "Please."

"Do you want to taste my blood?" I said lightly. "I wouldn't mind. I think it could bring us closer together."

He made a strangled sort of noise and fled, not heading to the nurse's office, but for the main doors. Well, well. I'd struck a nerve. Good to know.

I glanced at my hall pass. It didn't specify a destination. I had my liberty. Might as well go to the library and see if they had a copy of *Interview with a Vampire* or something. I'm not much for reading, but I finally had a subject that interested me.

SUNSHINE AND PAIN

FROM THE JOURNAL OF BONNIE GRAYDUCK

Edwin didn't come to school the next day, and I might have believed I was responsible, except none of the Scullens and the Scales were in school. I didn't say anything, of course, but Kelly must have seen me looking toward their table, because she said, "They're never here on really sunny days. Apparently they go camping whenever the weather's nice. Like, the whole family. Pretty weird, right?"

"Where do they camp?" I asked.

Kelly shrugged. "I'm not sure. They drive over to the Chippewa National Forest sometimes, and sometimes to Paul Bunyan State Forest. That's what my mom says—she's a nurse over at the hospital, so she knows Dr. Scullen. And other times they camp more locally, I'm not sure. They pretty much live in the woods. Maybe they just walk out their back door with backpacks on. I don't know what they do out there—hunt, maybe?"

"Hmm," I said. Hunting. *That* was possible—the Scullens and Scales couldn't be the only hikers out in the woods, and I bet hikers were delicious, if you liked that sort of thing. Probably disappeared without a trace all the time, too.

"Hey, do you, ah, want to go out with us tomorrow? We're going to Bemidji to go shopping for dresses for the dance."

Dance? Right. I'd seen posters. Some kind of fall formal. How exciting. "Wow, exotic Bemidji," I said.

Kelly laughed. "Hey, it's the biggest city in north central

Minnesota. And the birthplace of the late great Jane Russell!"

Wow, I thought. Quite a distinction. "Ah."

Kelly went on: "And more important, they've got a mall, which is more than you can say for Lake Woebegotten. Are you going to the dance?"

"I don't think so. I don't have a date."

"The Scullens never go to dances," Kelly said.

"How interesting for them." A little frost in my voice made her look away.

"Anyway, J and Ike are going together, of course, and I'm going with Terrence, you'd be welcome to come hang out with us if you want, but even if you don't, you could come with us to help us pick out clothes, you're from California so you're like automatically more stylish than most people around here... Never mind."

I retracted my claws. "No, thanks, I'd love to go, actually. I've never even been to Bemidji." I could make some guesses about it though: they would have fields, and at least one lake, and a lot of trees, and soon they'd be covered in a crust of snow and ice. But I wasn't going to sit around waiting for Edwin. I'd live life—or whatever simulacrum of life I could find here in the land of lakes and woe. "Count me in."

"Great!" Kelly said. "Do you mind if we take my car? No offense, but Marmon, ah..."

"Not a luxury ride. I know. But excellently designed for squashing people, you'll have to agree."

"Mind if I go to Bemidji tomorrow night?" I asked, stirring my fork around in my caprese salad. The tomatoes weren't very good—too late in the year, so they were hothouse—but I had to admit the cheese was tasty, and at least it wasn't a meal served on a bun or dipped in batter and fried or both, which was pretty much what Harry seemed to subsist on.

He dropped several slices of mozzarella on a piece of white bread, squashed another slice on top, and took a big bite of what must have been the whitest sandwich in history, chewed, and said, "What for and who with?"

I rolled my eyes, as teenage girls are expected to do. "My friends Kelly and J. They're going to some mall to pick out dresses for a dance next month."

"Hmm. They're nice kids. You going to the dance?"

"I don't think so. I don't want to go stag—or what is it when a girl goes to a dance by herself? Going doe?"

"I guess it'd be 'going hind,' actually," Harry said, and grinned. "Doesn't sound too good, does it? Not sure I'd want a daughter of mine going hind."

Harry could surprise me like that. He was not a dumb guy, and was actually pretty funny. Far more perceptive than Mom, which was a drawback in general, but I was living an honest and virtuous life these days, so it hadn't caused me many problems yet.

"Well," he continued, "I can't see why not. It's a Friday night, and we haven't discussed curfews or anything, and despite the badge and the gun I'm not necessarily all that authoritarian, so let's just say, use your judgment, don't be home too late, and don't make me worry about you. I know a few of the cops over in Bemidji, nice enough guys even if they do put on airs what with working for a pretty big city." (Bonnie here: let me note that Bemidji has a population of about 14,000 people. Santa Cruz—not a particularly large city by California standards—is four times more populous than that. Nevertheless, Bemidji is to Lake Woebegotten as New York City is to Lizard Lick, North Carolina, pretty much, so I guess Dad had a point.) "So I can make a call and have an APB put out for you, which would be pretty embarrassing for you if you weren't in any trouble, so call if you're going to be too late. Fair enough?"

"Works for me, Dad," I said. Calling was no problem. Keeping up social and family appearances was one of my personal specialties.

I went to bed, and I dreamed of Edwin again. No bears this time. Not much blood, either. We were camping, out in the woods, and… let's just say we didn't do any hunting. We never even left the tent.

Another bright and sunshiny day, another total lack of the Scullens and the Scales. I didn't believe for a moment they were camping, especially after Edwin told me he found Lake Woebegotten too countrified for his taste—why would he want to lower his civilization quotient even further? (Okay, possible answer: his parents forced him. But I had a hard time imagining anyone forcing Edwin to do anything.) Wasn't it more likely that his absence on the first two consecutive cloudless days since I'd arrived in Lake Woebegotten had more to do with his vampirism?

Fine. That's not actually more *likely*, the answer to a question like that is pretty much never "yes," I understand, but it's certainly more *interesting*. Maybe his sort of vampires are only vulnerable to direct sunlight or something. Perhaps vampires are like clematis (a plant that has always sounded like a particularly banal sort of sexually transmitted disease to me): they thrive best in partial shade. It was a theory, anyway. Or maybe I'd *really* scared him away by pressing the issue, cutting my thumb and showing him the blood. That was the possibility I didn't want to dwell upon: that I might have blown my chance at true love and, not incidentally, eternal life and awesome predatory powers. I took comfort in Kelly's claim that the Scullens always disappeared on sunny days, but damn: you'd think the boy could at least *call* me. Vampires don't have cell phones? Vampires don't *text*? Maybe he was hundreds of years old or something and didn't have the hang of totally everyday modern technology. And, eww, that was kind of a gross thought. If Edwin was all kinds of ancient, wasn't his obsession with me the next worst thing to being a pedophile? (Or, at the very least, an ephebophile, like the high school teacher I slept with the year before I moved to Lake Woebegotten said *he* was: obsessed with sleeping with late adolescents, which is only illegal for the *first* few years of their age-15-to-19 uber-fuckability window, depending on where you live.) But if he was that old, *everybody* was a child by comparison, unless they were dead like him, so he had no choice but to be a dirty old man, unless he wanted to be a necrophile. The moral complexities of vampire-human love matches made my head hurt, so I did what I always did when confronted with such a moral problem: decided morals are for losers and the weak, and, thus, utterly irrelevant for me.

I hoped to hear from him eventually. We were supposed to go to the Twin Cities soon, and the weather was going to be clear all weekend. I don't like being stood up. If someone's going to be stood up on, I want to be the one doing the standing.

I got through another day in school, made unspeakably tedious without the distraction of Edwin. Biology was increasingly ridiculous, as my lab partner had been absent more often than not—at least Mr. Whatever seemed inclined to cut me some slack on that point. How did Edwin get away with ditching so often? I needed to learn his secret. Maybe having a doctor dad meant he could get doctor's notes to excuse his absences, but how far could you push something like that? The Scullens and Scales were all old enough to drop out of school if they wanted, but still, it seemed pretty unlikely Edwin would ever be able to actually graduate with so many missed days. That also pointed to him being a vampire: he obviously didn't give a crap about his future, which made sense, when you figured his future would last potentially forever. What did getting a diploma matter?

Then again, why did Edwin and his quasi-siblings go to a public high school at all? It didn't really make any sense. Sure, they looked young enough that they *should* be in school, but everybody thought their family was hardcore weirdos anyway, so it would've been easy to claim they were being home-schooled like a bunch of religious kids. Maybe Edwin and his brothers were just hungry for sweet teenage girlflesh, then— but what about those bitches Pleasance and Rosemarie? Were they eager for human contact to fill the empty hours of their lonely immortal lives? That didn't make a lot of sense, either. Wolves don't hang out with sheep for kicks. And my dad hadn't mentioned a rash of disappearances or bodies turning up drained of blood in the past couple of years. What kind of vampires didn't *feed* on the human cattle around them? If I could drain and kill these morons I would.

So… maybe I was an idiot. Maybe Edwin hadn't shoved my truck. Maybe he was just a cute guy from an oddball family, and I'd driven him away by being all vampire-talky, coming off like a crazy bat lady. I had to consider the possibility that I *was* crazy.

Look. I know I'm… not like other people. I'd say I'm "non-neurotypical." I don't empathize the way the rest of you do (which is a blessing—it means I can think clearly). I don't get the warm fuzzies very often, Edwin being an exception, but even then it's more of a hot wetness with a side of cold calculation rather than any kind of warm fuzziness. Wikipedia says I have Antisocial Personality Disorder, which is dumb, because I'm all kinds of social—I love society, society is like the ocean to my shark—and I have plenty of personality, and it's only a disorder if it messes up your life, and my life is awesome. I've never been formally diagnosed, and I never *will* be, because I'm smart enough to avoid that, but it's not like I've never seen a serial killer profiler show, and it hasn't escaped my notice that in my youth I exhibited the famous homicidal triad of setting fires, killing animals, and (fuck you) wetting the bed. (Plus, there's the fact that I've committed homicide.) So I was already what some people would call "crazy," though probably antelopes think cheetahs are crazy—antelopes must be like, "Those crazy bastards just go around *killing* us all the time, it's like they don't even respect our individuality or right to life, and do you see how they're always running so fast all the time, like eighty miles an hour? That shit isn't normal. Those cheetahs need professional help." Sucks to be an antelope. Rocks to be a cheetah.

So, fine, crazy, or "mentally ill," as defined by some. But

was believing in vampires—more specifically, believing the boy I was crushing on was secretly a vampire—was that a whole different kind of crazy? A crazy that *wasn't* actually completely and obviously advantageous for me? A crazy that I *did* need help for? And how could I get help for *that* without risking giving away my other flavor of crazy, the kind I didn't *want* any help for?

Maybe I wasn't even crazy. Maybe I was just so bored in Lake Woebegotten that I was desperately trying to make things more interesting, so I was imagining vampires and were-beasts where there were just cute boys. (Hmm, mental note: Edwin and Joachim three-way? Or, better, the two of them fighting over me, a real shirtless brawl with lots of rolling around in the mud, mmmm.) Not a nice thought, though it could've been worse: I could've imagined an alien bodysnatcher invasion or a zombie apocalypse or something cliché like that.

Okay. Deep breath. You see all that brooding up there? That mostly happened during biology class, and gym, and while J took me aside in the hallway and told me she was so glad I was going with them and she hoped I'd go to the dance and thanks again for helping Ike and her realize how they feel about each other and so on and on and on. (I found friendly J even more annoying than pissy J. Maybe getting her and Ike together was a mistake. I'd hoped they would wander off in a dizzy dippy haze of mutual sentimentality and hormone-frenzy, but they'd folded me into their love story and now I was stuck playing a role in their personal narrative that didn't fit me too well, really. Oh well. I could always break them up later if things got too boring.)

I decided I needed to see Edwin. I needed to find out what he was: if I was nuts, or if I was incredibly perceptive and living in a world that was weirder than most people supposed. After this trip to Bemidji, if I didn't hear from him on Saturday, I'd find some pretext to go out to his house—Harry would know the way, and I could get it out of him with some kind of casual questioning, I was sure. If they lived in a castle with coffins for beds, that would tell me something, and if they had a basement full of human blood-slaves, that would tell me even more. And if they were just normal people who liked to keep to themselves, well—at least then I'd know.

When school ended, Kelly drove after me in her little red Honda so I could leave Marmon at home and drop off my books and crap. I took shotgun, and we picked up J, who was on her cell chattering at Ike for the first fifteen minutes in the car. I couldn't imagine what two people like them could possibly have to talk about, and after listening to J's side of the conversation for a quarter of an hour, I wasn't enlightened at all: it was an endless series of "Oh gods" and "I knows" and "For reallys!" which she actually says, yes, for reallys. But finally some vestigial sense of social appropriateness sifted through J's brain—or else she lost reception as we drove among the woods and fields and barns and lakes—and she snapped the phone shut and leaned forward between the front seats and started fiddling with the radio and turned on some kind of girl power pop and her and Kelly started singing along, and I thought: this is what it's supposed to be like, isn't it? This should be happiness. Me, with my girlfriends, singing and acting self-consciously raucous, going on a road trip, maybe later sneaking into a bar with our fake IDs (Kelly had a fake ID and she'd gotten one for J; she was a bad girl in a good girl's life, which made her slightly more interesting than the baseline) and getting tipsy. Trying on clothes and gossiping.

I fake-smiled and hooted and hollered and inside I was thinking: please, please, please let there really be vampires. Let there be more to my world than *this*.

ENTER THE VAMPER

NARRATOR

Gunther Montcrief was taking his habitual pre-dawn piss when someone standing behind him cleared his throat.

"Just a damn minute," Gunther muttered. "I'm draining my tank here, arright?"

"Oh, do take your time," a polite voice said.

Gunther tucked his business away, zipped up his pants, and turned around, squinting in the dimness. Three figures stood by his fishing shack, one standing a little bit in front, the other two apparently looking off at nothing in particular. "You look like you're posing for an album cover," he grumbled. "Who are you and what do you want?"

"Where's that 'Minnesota nice' I've heard about?" the one in front said. He stepped forward, and something about the way he moved, all fast and spidery, was weirdly familiar.

"Hey, I know you," Gunther said. "I saw you chase down a deer and rip its throat out with your own teeth."

For some reason, one of the others laughed—turned out it was a woman, well how about that, too dark to tell if she was anything nice to look at though.

"I think you're mistaken," the leader said. "I do not eat…"

"You don't eat?" Gunther said.

The man sighed. "I wasn't finished. I was pausing for dramatic effect. I do not eat—"

"So don't eat, please yourself, though I always liked a little

110

lunch myself, maybe a frito pie. I mostly drink these days, truth be told, nobody to cook for me and I was never much good at taking care of myself that way, but a little fish doesn't go amiss, I was about to fry up some walleye for breakfast, you want some, oh, wait, you don't eat, how about your friends?"

"I do not eat *deer*," he said. He sounded like he wanted to *hiss* the words, but the lack of sibilants in the sentence made that pretty difficult.

"So what do you eat, then?" Gunther wandered toward his shack. If he was going to talk to weirdos in the woods he wanted a drink to fortify himself.

"We *drink*," one of the backup singers—a guy—said.

"Well all right then," Gunther said. "We've got something in common. I'll pour us something, but I've only got two glasses, so the bunch of you will have to share." He found a half-empty—no, why be a pessimist, a half-*full*—bottle under a blanket at the foot of the mound of blankets on a raised wooden platform he used for a bed. "Bourbon," he said. "That'll do, that'll do." While he was in the shack, just to be on the safe side, he picked up something else, and put it in his coat pocket. He stepped back out, and his visitors hadn't moved. There was a touch more light in the sky now, and he could tell they were a young and pretty bunch, though dirty, carrying beat-up bags with them. "You backpackers then? A bunch of, whaddya call it, hippos? Peace, love, all that?"

"We are travelers," the leader said. "Nomads, you might say. Hunters."

"Why do you insist on playing with your food, Jimmy?" the man behind him said.

"Silence, Queequeg," the leader said. "We're going to be sporting. We're going to give him the chance to *run*."

Gunther squinted. "Eh? What's that?"

"We are going to let you run," Jimmy said. "You will have a brief head start. Then we will pursue you. And when we catch you, we will consume you. It's very simple. Whenever you're ready."

"Oh," Gunther said. "You're crazy, then." He drew the .22 target pistol from his pocket. He'd been a champion sharpshooter in his day, and even put bullets in a few living humans during one of the wars, and since he was well-lubricated with cheap whiskey his hands weren't shaking a bit. A .22 wasn't much gun, but it was pretty good for killing folks at close range, because the little bullet didn't usually blow out the back of the head, but tended to bounce around inside a fella's skull, doing all kinds of damage. Harry'd probably give him hell if he found out, there'd be no end of fuss and maybe even some jail time, but Gunther figured he could always just bury 'em somewhere, and nobody'd ever know.

He aimed and squeezed the trigger, pop pop pop, three shots to three foreheads, and they all fell down. Gunther sighed, *then* the shakes started, and he bent at the waist and threw up the entire contents of his stomach, which still smelled fairly alcoholic. Just because he'd killed before in wartime didn't make it easy, and while he'd managed to think of them as just targets while he was doing the job, they sure looked like dead people now. He wiped his mouth and stepped forward to examine the bodies. "Well that's a mess if ever I saw one." He looked down at the leader—pretty enough to be a girl—and the neat hole in the center of his forehead. Pretty good shot, at that, and—

Something started coming out of the hole. *Worm?* Gunther thought. But how would a worm get in the body that fast, let alone come crawling *out*?

Not a worm. A bullet, deformed by its passage through the skull, pushed out of the wound, where it rolled down the forehead and fell on the ground. Jimmy groaned and opened his eyes, which were crossed and funny-looking, as the hole in his face closed up, healing seamlessly. Jimmy bared his teeth, and his canines were an inch and a half long and pointy.

"Well that's not something you see every day," Gunther said. "You're, what's the word, drink blood, hate garlic, right? Vampers. Bunch of damn vampers, pardon my

French." Jimmy started to get up, so Gunther shot him in the eye, which made him lay back down again. Now, what did you do with vampers? Sunlight, well, that wasn't true, there was some sunshine coming down now and they weren't burning to a crisp or anything at all, so that was disappointing. Wooden stakes? There was plenty of broken wood around the place, and he had a mallet somewhere, but he had no idea where, so something else might be better. The other two started to stir, so Gunther made them both cyclopses too, let's see you grow back *eyes* in a hurry, nasty little things, no better than tapeworms or leeches or liver flukes. Cutting off their heads?

Wasn't a darn thing in the world, excepting some insects, that kept going after you cut off its head, at least, not for long. Now all he needed was an axe, or maybe even a shovel would do, he was sure he had one or the other or both around the back of the shack. He found his good shovel—no sign of the axe, wasn't that always the way, but you went to work with the tools you had, not the tools you wished you had—and walked back around the shack. The one called Queequeg and the girl were still there, but one-eyed Jimmy was nowhere to be seen.

"Well, hell," Gunther said. "It was a nice long life I guess, and nobody lives forever." He hurried over to Queequeg—funny name, and you'd think it would be some kind of ethnic, but he was just a white fella with dreadlocks—and put the shovel blade on his throat. He stomped down hard with a foot, and it reminded him of being in the war, digging latrines in the mud. The shovel cut into the neck nicely but didn't sever the spinal cord, and there was no spurt of blood, but the fella's eyes popped open and he reached up and grabbed the handle right where it joined the blade and wouldn't let go, no matter how hard Gunther tugged.

"Kill you," a ragged voice said behind him. "Eat you."

"I thought I got to run?" Gunther leaned on the shovel all casual-like and looked at Jimmy, who was still one-eyed. Maybe if he shot him again… but, no, he'd used all six shots in the revolver and hadn't reloaded, probably his kids were right and his brain *was* pickled in alcohol, imagine forgetting something like that at a time like this, not that he even knew where his ammunition was, buried in all the junk in the shack probably. "Or you only like playing games if you're sure you're going to win, is that it?"

"That's it exactly," Jimmy said. "Vile old man."

Gunther spat at the vamper's feet. "Go on, then. Just do me a favor and don't turn me into one of you. I'd rather be dead than a human-shaped hookworm." He gave the shovel another stomp, and Queequeg gurgled.

Jimmy leapt for him, and Gunther's last thought was, *Drink up, vamper. I hope you like the taste of Hepatitis B. Heh heh heh heh heh.*

CHASING THE CLOUDS

FROM THE JOURNAL OF BONNIE GRAYDUCK

The trip to Bemidji took I don't know how long—not as long as the god-awful endless trip from the airport, anyway, though way longer than seemed reasonable just to get to some crappy mall, and it was Girl Power all the way. Fortunately I dropped a few little Santa Cruz tidbits here and there—beach parties, surfers attacked by sharks, thumbnail sketches of the picturesque freaks who panhandle or distress the tourists downtown—and before long they were happy to let me talk about me, mostly. Which is only right and proper, because I am fascinating, and they are dull. We'd left right after school, but it was almost dark by the time we hit Bemidji.

We got to the mall, which is called the Paul Bunyan Mall: a little clutch of low buildings and a parking lot, and I swear I counted *two* K-Marts, one at each end, but maybe that was a hallucination brought on by boredom and carsickness. Seriously, though—there are strip malls in Santa Cruz with more stores than this place has. Still, it's miles beyond anything you could find in Lake Woebegotten, with chain stores that had recognizable names, even, and lots of clothing stores. We parked close to the main doors (there weren't a lot of cars there) and I followed the giggling twosome of J and Kelly into the local temple of capitalism and what passed for local fashion.

You've never seen so many sequins or so much lace or

so much pink in your life. J and Kelly tried on various horrible things, and I made encouraging noises, wondering if I could talk them into wearing truly eye-wrenchingly dreadful gowns by pure enthusiastic willpower alone. We gave a lot of thought to hair clips and purses and shoes, of course—I was, briefly, distracted by some of the shoes myself, I admit, I'm not made of *stone*—but after about 90 minutes of grueling shopping, with the two of them showing no signs of slowing down, I told them the flickering fluorescent lights were starting to give me a migraine, and I couldn't take it anymore. It's one of my basic techniques: cultivate the impression that you're a delicate flower, easily wilted and distressed. People give you extra slack, and you can always surprise them later if you need to, by being... unexpectedly vigorous.

Being true girlfriends, they offered to cut their shopping short immediately, but I told them no, don't be silly, I'd just go take a walk around for a while, I'd meet them at the pizza place we'd passed on the way in for dinner, how would that be? It took some convincing, but they agreed to let me wander off on my own, as long as I promised not to stray too far—there were, they said, probably "lots of drunk guys from the University" wandering around. I assured them I'd be fine.

I pulled up a map on my phone once I got out the door. Not surprisingly, there was a big-ass lake in town—Lake Bemidji, of course. Just far enough away for me to walk there and walk back in time, probably, and the whole way as flat as flat could be. There were a couple of cemeteries, too, and I considered walking up to one, strolling picturesquely among the gravestones, thinking long thoughts of blood and death and solitude and longing, but moping has never really been my style, and blood and death should be reserved for *happy* moments. I'm a fairly chirpy girl, as long as I get what I want.

I decided it would be more fun to look for one of those drunk college guys and see if I could get into—and out of—some trouble. I had a rather wicked little knife in my purse, a canister of pepper spray, and my own unflappable good nature. Edwin wasn't the only one who could take off on hunting trips, after all. I'd been so good for so long—how could I be expected to keep that up?

For the longest time, I didn't think I was going to get assaulted at all. I wandered toward the lake for a while, then cut over toward the University, and I barely passed another living human being. The air was brisk but not really cold, and walking kept me warm. Don't get me wrong, I like walking okay, but what I'd really hoped for was a little stalking or an altercation and some kind of—well, some kind of ructions—that could lead me into a situation where I could plausibly claim self-defense. Is that so much to ask?

But finally, about twenty minutes after I should have turned back, I hit a promising block.

Assuming you aren't outnumbered and can avoid getting physically overpowered—always a big assumption—it's pretty much perfect for my purposes to be a girl, alone, having a strange guy approach you on the street. There's not a jury in the land that would convict a girl who committed some act of violence against said guy, as long as you don't let yourself get carried away into overkill. The only reasons I don't hang out in dangerous places and hope for some guy to come along so I can stick a key in his eye—just by way of letting off some steam—are because it's always possible the guy will have friends, which is no good, because I don't like it when the power balance shifts away from me, and because if it happens more than once or twice the police *will* start to wonder why it is a nice girl like me attracts so much trouble.

But here I was, alone on a block where there was only the sort of bar that doesn't even have a beer sign in the window, which meant I was obviously looking for trouble, or a good time, or some combination of the two. So what if I just wanted to take a walk and clear my head and get away from J and Kelly and their prosaic little minds? My intentions wouldn't count for much with the kind of men who frequented establishments like this. They were beasts, officer—absolute beasts. I'm lucky to be alive with my virtue intact. Etc. It's ironclad.

I got a little flutter of anticipation when a guy a few years older than me stumbled out the door and started fumbling with a lighter. He was quite focused on his cigarette ritual, and I thought he wouldn't notice me as I walked across on the other side of the street—but he happened to look up, hearing my footsteps I guess. Then he tucked the cigarette behind his ear—charming affectation—and grinned, strolling across the street to intercept my path. He was a little shaggy, but not unattractive compared to most mere mortals—of course, next to my beautiful Edwin, he might as well have been a grinning chimpanzee or a medieval peasant with no teeth and shit in his beard. Not that he had a beard, really; he had a little soul patch sort of thing just under his bottom lip, which had probably been the height of stylishness in some movie he'd seen from the early 2000s. More alarmingly, he had a tattoo of a spiderweb on his neck, which suggested he had either exceedingly poor impulse control, a substance abuse problem, or no concept of consequences. I kept walking, but reached into my pocket, where, on my keyring, I had my pepper spray—a gift from my dad. Harry had insisted I take it with me, and I hadn't argued—he said it was more potent than the commercially-available concoctions, practically mace, despite the adorable little canister. All I needed was an excuse.

"Hello beautiful," the guy said, stepping in front of me. He was wearing a Bemidji State University sweatshirt. "I didn't realize this neighborhood was next door to heaven, but it must be, with angels like you going by."

A cheesy pick-up line? Maybe he was planning to lull me and then lure me somewhere secluded so he could rob and murder me. "Move aside, please," I said politely, and was gratified when he took a step toward me instead.

He acted like he hadn't heard me. "Normally I bitch about

how you can't smoke in bars anymore, but having to come out in the cold sure paid off this time."

"I'm sorry," I said coolly. "You used to be able to smoke in bars? I didn't know that, but then, I wasn't born in the *Eighties*."

He gave me a funny look, then laughed, deciding I'd made a joke. "Look, I don't normally just walk up to people on the street like this, but, hey, want to come inside that bar over there? My name's Rufus. I'll buy you a drink, name your poison."

Maybe he had a bunch of friends in there. Maybe he was the least scary one—I could hardly imagine anyone *less* scary, even with the spiderweb tattoo—and had been sent to bring back a victim for them all to attack together.

Or maybe he was just a slumming college boy hoping to get lucky outside the bar when he'd struck out on the inside. God, wouldn't *that* be boring. "No poison for me thanks," I said. "Now, move aside, please." If he didn't move this time, I'd be totally justified in spraying him in the face with unpleasant stinging compressed chemicals and then laying into him with the pointy toes of my new boots a few times. Harry would probably even tell me I'd done exactly the right thing. If he actually touched me in a way that left a mark, I'd be in a position to do much nastier things—strikes to the groin, hooking a finger into his eye to scoop out those bullshit-brown eyes, palm-smash to the nose, maybe driving some bone splinters into his brain...

But he just sighed. "Angel flies too high for the likes of me. I understand."

He stepped aside, and just then the door of the bar opened, and two more guys stepped out, about his age, but less cute—one was a bit bigger and broader and scruffier, the other scrawnier and wearing glasses, neither visibly tattooed. "Hey, douche, how long does it take to smoke a fucking—Hello." The one who'd spoken—the bigger one, of course—grinned at me. "Man, you totally found something better out here, it's nothing but skanks in the bar tonight, I don't know why we come to this place."

Three of them. Hmm. That was a bit much, even if they weren't particularly intimidating. Probably if I attacked one with sufficient viciousness the others would back off, but it was always possible they'd leap to his defense out of some misguided sense of all-for-one honor; boys were weird that way. But if I had no choice—

"We come for the 25 cent bottles of Pabst," Rufus said. "But, this one, nah, she's not into it. Guess she's got places to be."

"Shit, you blew it," the other guy said. "Hey, sugar, I'm way more charming than this loser, why don't you give me a chance?"

"Ease off," the boy with glasses said. "It's not cool, a bunch of guys crowding around a woman on the sidewalk, you know? You have to have some empathy, put yourself in her position." Then, to Bonnie, "I apologize, we're harmless, really."

"I knew you shouldn't have taken that women's studies class," the other guy complained. "I thought it would be a great place to meet chicks, but it's filling your head with all kinds of shit."

The boy with glasses shyly smiled. "Ah, you know, this isn't the best neighborhood, if you're walking somewhere, it might be better not to go alone, I mean—"

"Oh, you're gonna escort her, Mr. Chivalrous Knight?" the biggest boy said. "Oldest trick in the book, sister, don't fall for it, he'll be wanting to show you his etchings next."

I was trying to decide if an opportunity for deniable violence could be salvaged from this increasingly innocuous situation—maybe I'd let four-eyes take me for a walk, then attack him, and later claim he'd gotten inappropriate—when a car came screaming around the corner, taking the turn with such velocity that the vehicle slewed around almost sideways. The car was long, low, and silver—a midlife-crisis car, a penis substitute, you know the kind, but I have to admit, it *did* look kind of sexy and powerful, clichés are clichés partly because they're effective, after all. It was a pretty potent interruption, and probably ruined my plans... but as you've probably figured out by now, I don't mind surprises, as long as they're *interesting* surprises.

The car zoomed straight for the boy with glasses, who was in the middle of the deserted street walking toward me, and he dove back to the sidewalk by the bar, where his taller friend gaped at the car. Rufus started cursing and backed up right against the chain-link fence surrounding the empty lot beside us. The car stopped beside me, the passenger door flying open, and a voice from the darkness within said—"*Get in.*"

I obeyed, giving Rufus a little wiggle-fingered wave as I pulled the door shut, and then the car screamed away, swerving toward four-eyes and the other boy on their side of the sidewalk, just enough to send them skipping back toward the bar in what I assumed was pants-wetting terror. It was all I could do not to laugh out loud.

"My hero!" I said, looking at Edwin in the driver's seat, but he didn't seem to share my mirth—his jaw was clenched so hard he might as well have had tetanus. "You came out of nowhere to save me," I purred, reaching out to caress his cheek. "Who knows what those boys might have done to me?"

"The one with glasses," he said, choking the words out. "He had... he had so much *lust* in him." He glanced at me, his eyes taking in my short skirt.

"Did he?" I said, surprised. I thought I was good at reading people, but I hadn't seen lust on his face, and Edwin had only seen him for seconds, through a car windshield at that. "Are you sure you aren't... projecting?"

He almost laughed at that. "You *are* a sight to incite such feelings, but he could have been dangerous. He wouldn't stop staring at your, ah, chest, and your, ah, legs, and, ah, you know. Your butt." He gritted his teeth again. "Listen, distract me, would you?"

"From what?"

"From what I'd like to do to those *boys*. From turning this car around and going after them and making them regret messing with you."

"Go ahead," I said lightly. "Someone should teach them a lesson."

He shook his head. "It… wouldn't stop with being a lesson. You have to be *alive* after a lesson in order to learn anything, and I… don't trust myself right now. So, please talk? About anything, really, the more trivial the better."

"I guess murder would be an overreaction," I acknowledged, thinking. "All right, well, there's my mom, who's been sending me some fairly insane e-mails lately, I mean, more insane than usual, mostly about her dreams and how she's afraid something bad's going to happen, but I'm pretty sure it's just separation anxiety or empty nest syndrome or something…" I prattled on in that vein for a while, letting myself be a touch more catty than I usually am in my public persona. It was too easy to let my guard down around Edwin.

"Where were you going, anyway?" he said after a while.

I shrugged. "Just taking a little walk. Kelly and J were shopping, I got bored. I'm supposed to meet them for dinner, oh…" I looked at the clock in the dashboard. "Really soon. When I don't show up, they'll assume I've been murdered. So don't murder me. You'd be playing right into their expectations."

"We'd better reassure them, then." He deftly spun the wheel, U-turning across empty lanes, and drove back the way we'd come, more or less.

"Are you over your bloodlust?" I said.

"As much as I ever am." He shook his head. "Did you want to have dinner with them? Your friends?"

"Not if I get a better offer."

"Would you consent to dine with me?"

He had such a funny, archaic way of speaking sometimes. "Yes. That constitutes a better offer."

Edwin glanced at me. "You don't seem… troubled, by what happened."

I shook my head. "What, getting harassed by drunk boys on the street? I'm female, and my hometown is a college town *and* a tourist town, so it's not the first time I've ever been catcalled or propositioned. I know sometimes it goes farther than that, girls can get in trouble, but it never has for me. I've got pepper spray, and I had 911 dialed into my phone, all I needed to do was hit 'send.'" And I could have stabbed four-eyes in the throat before he got so much as one handful of boob, but no need to mention that.

He nodded grimly. "The world is a dangerous place. Lake Woebegotten is small, I know, but it is also safe—peaceful."

Peaceful is boring, but there was no reason to say that.

We got back to the mall, and he parked next to Kelly's car. Her compact kind of looked like a pig parked next to, I don't know, a *god*, which was fitting enough. We got out and walked companionably to the mall, where Kelly and J were hovering around the arcade. I waved to them. "Hi guys! Look who I found!"

"Uh," J said. "Hi." Kelly waved at him shyly.

"Wait here," I said to Edwin, and pulled the girls aside. They both knew I was into Edwin. "Guys, he wants me to have dinner with him, I don't want to back out on my sisters, I know that's totally lame—"

"Do it," Kelly said. "Seriously." I could tell she'd lick Edwin if she could. Alas, Kelly was only ever going to be best-friend, other-girl material. Maybe in college she'd blossom if she got slutty enough.

J was more doubtful. "If you're sure it's okay. I mean…"

"I've got my phone," I said, patting my purse. "I'll call you after dinner and let you know I'm okay. If you don't hear from me in a couple of hours, feel free to tell Harry I'm gone and you last saw me in the company of Edwin Scullen, okay?"

Kelly laughed. "Fair enough." J nodded way too seriously. I'd have to remember to call, or they *would* have Harry after me.

I returned to Edwin, hooking my arm over his. "I have my liberty. Where are you taking me?"

"Ah, well, I don't, ah..."

"Eat in restaurants," I said. He stiffened. "In *Bemidji*," I said, and he relaxed. "Because who would eat in Bemidji?" I turned on my phone and zipped around online and found an Irish pub not far away that got good reviews and featured corned beef eggrolls, which sounded too grotesque not to try. "Let's go here. Brigid's Cross Irish Pub. You cool with that? With *crosses* and all?"

"Brigid is the name of a saint," he said, "but before that, it was the name of a pagan goddess. And I have no quarrel with crosses *or* goddesses."

He opened the car door for me—such a gentleman—and I let my body brush against his as I climbed in. Something was going to happen tonight. A boundary was going to be crossed. Things were going to be revealed.

This shit was *on*.

MY DINNER WITH DRACULA

FROM THE JOURNAL OF BONNIE GRAYDUCK

The pub was kind of cheesy from the outside—what real Irish pub would feel the need to advertise Guinness that prominently?—but inside it was nice, lots of dark wood, well-stocked bar, and best of all, some deep and discreet booths, including one that opened up just as Edwin veered toward it. Once we were comfortably ensconced, it felt like the rest of the world was somehow off in another room. We'd been together in the car, of course, but this was the first time I'd ever felt really alone with him, and centered in his attention.

"Bonnie," he said. "We really need to talk."

"Sure," I said. "The whole following-me-to-Bemidji thing is kinda stalkery. I assume you were tracking me the whole time?"

He scowled. "Well, yes, but—"

A waitress—pretty college girl, black hair, big boobs, but Edwin didn't even glance at her bosom, so that was a point in his favor—came by and took our order. Edwin just asked for water and soda bread, but I ordered a burger, making a point to say, "As bloody rare as you can make it."

When she was gone I gave Edwin a dazzling smile. "Sorry nothing on the menu appeals to you. If this were an English pub we'd be able to get some blood sausage, I bet."

Edwin sighed and leaned forward. The candle on the table cast his face in flickering shadows. "All right. Fine. I tried to avoid this, but you're a lot smarter than you let on, Bonnie Grayduck. How did you know? It's not as if I've been leaving fang holes in the necks of our classmates. My reflection shows up in mirrors, garlic doesn't bother me, I walk freely in the daytime—what exactly about my existence screamed..." He looked around, and no one was in earshot, and the loud bar atmosphere would muffle our conversation anyway. "The *V*-word."

"Ah, well, I had a little help," I admitted. "I knew there was *something* weird about you, but I didn't know what—mutant, superhero, alien? I admit, the *V*-word wasn't my first guess. But then I went with some people from school to the lake. Over in Pres du Lac."

He leaned back in the booth, half disappearing into the shadows. "Ah."

"I saw an old friend of the family—Joachim Noir. His dad Willy and my dad go way back." I frowned. "This isn't ringing any bells?"

"I don't think I know them," he said.

"Willy is apparently some big tribal deal on the reservation. Joachim and I got to talking, and he let slip some of the, ah, weirder stories the tribal elders tell. And, funnily enough, the name of your family came up. Weird, huh? And something about a treaty."

"Oh. That."

"Of course, Joachim doesn't believe any of it. Thinks it's silly superstition."

"But he told you I'm a... that the elders think I'm a... *V*-word."

"They say you're a wendigo, actually. You know—flesh-eating, inhuman monster. But Joachim says that's just because there's no precedent for vampires—oops, I said it—in Ojibwe mythology. I did some research on the internet, though, and it's all rivers of crap. So how does it work *really*?"

"There are secrets I shouldn't tell," he murmured. "But you already know the major secret... Bonnie, if you know what

I am, why are you sitting here with me? Shouldn't you be running away from me screaming?"

I raised an eyebrow. The waitress returned with our food, and I ate a french fry slowly while she tried to bat her eyes at Edwin. He never stopped staring at me. Once we were alone again, I said, "Have you not read a book or seen a movie in the past century? Vampires aren't really scary—they're *sexy*. Why would I run away?"

"Vampires should be scary," he said emphatically. "They—we—we *kill* people, Bonnie. We use them for food. Drink their blood and discard the body, like, like—"

"A kid tossing away an empty juice box?" I said. "But you're not going to do that to *me*."

He picked up his glass of water, sniffed it, and put it back down again. "I—my family—we don't do that to anyone. Argyle decided a long time ago that he couldn't prey on humans without giving up his own humanity, and he stopped hunting sentient creatures. His wife—my adopted mother—agreed with him, and so do the rest of us. In fact, I've never harmed a human. Argyle... made me what I am, now, and raised me, you might say, in his faith."

"Whoa," I said. "Vegetarian vampires. Teetotalers. Well, sure, there's lots of precedent for that in movies and TV shows too. It's how you can tell who the *good* vampires are. Or sometimes they just eat criminals and murderers." I said the last kind of hopefully, and Edwin shook his head.

"They say if a tiger tastes the flesh of a human, it becomes a man-eater," Edwin said. "I don't know if it's true or not, but Argyle says our kind are similar. It's like being an alcoholic. Nothing compares to human blood—they say pig blood is closest, but it's close the way saccharine is close to sugar. Not quite right. There's an aftertaste. To taste human blood is to crave it more, and to risk losing control, so we avoid it."

So much for my fantasies of Edwin and I as a continent-crossing team, me luring victims and helping to dispatch them for his supper. And here I'd been looking forward to doing my part to put dinner on the table.

"Okay then." I took a bite of my burger—not rare enough, nobody makes them rare enough, but juicy enough to dribble down my chin. "So what do I have to worry about?"

He sighed and rubbed his eyes. "Bonnie, you don't understand. I've become attracted to your personality, and certainly your beautiful looks, but the first thing that drew me to you was your *smell*. Humans have flavors. Vintages. Bouquets. Most of them are neither offensive nor inoffensive to me, but occasionally, one smells *especially* good."

"So I'm like fresh baked cookies and you're in overeaters anonymous, huh?"

"Indelicate, but apt. I greatly fear I might lose control around you, Bonnie."

"So drink up." I took a sip of my soda. "I don't mind. If it's consensual, where's the harm? Turn me into one of you—we can be together forever."

His eyes widened. "You... want to be with me?"

"You're the hottest guy I've ever met," I said, honestly—see, I can be honest sometimes. "And you have the whole awesome superpower thing going for you. Of course I do."

"You're young, Bonnie. Forever is a *very* long time. You don't know what you're asking."

"So how old are you, then, grandpa?"

He smiled. "Biologically? Around seventeen."

"And in calendar time?"

"Well. Argyle turned me... a long time ago."

I rolled my eyes. "Enough with the vague. When?"

Another sigh. Clearly he was not happy giving up his mysteries—or maybe he just knew he was all cute and broody when he sighed. "1906."

"Ah. And *you* were only seventeen, just like *I* am, when you got changed, so why hesitate to do for me what Argyle did for you?"

"You don't understand. It was just after the great San Francisco earthquake. Argyle was there, working in what passed for a hospital in those days. After the earthquake, and the fire, he found me, trapped under rubble, my whole family dead, my own injuries grievous. I would not have survived, and he made the decision to give me a semblance of life, rather than letting me die entirely."

I considered. "Whereas I'm all young and healthy."

"Yes."

"And not in need of such desperate measures."

"Correct."

I considered. Suicide attempt? Would cutting my wrists prompt him to turn me in order to save my life? Then he'd think I was crazy and might let me bleed out. I could maybe fake an accident... but what if he didn't come and turn me into a vampire? I'd be dead, and while being a vampire would be vastly preferable to being alive, being alive was vastly preferable to being a banquet for worms. "Fair enough," I said, though it wasn't; I was just tabling the discussion. I'd bring it up again. I'd work it in. Maybe next time I'd ask him after screwing his brains out or sucking him off (assuming vampires could, you know, *function* sexually—that was a topic for another time). I find guys are in a more responsive and accommodating frame of mind after they've just gotten off. "If you don't mind me asking, if you're more than a hundred years old or whatever, why do you go to *high school*?"

He laughed. "I suppose it might seem... untoward. But I look young, Bonnie. Where else should I spend my time?"

"Why spend time with humans at all? No offense, but, well, I like this hamburger, but that doesn't mean I want to go hang out with a bunch of cows."

"Bonnie." He reached across the table, and touched me with his cold, cold hand. He basically had no circulation. Not promising for the prospect of him getting erections. His face was so earnest I wanted to laugh. "You must *never* think I believe your kind to be cattle. I consider *myself* a human, or at least kin to humans. I *was* human. I like to still be among humans, to be in their company, to remind me of what I once was. Of course, there's a certain degree of standoffishness—it's dangerous for us to get too close to humans, because we're so strong, it's easy to hurt them accidentally. You don't know how many times the coach has begged Hermet to sign up for the football team, and my brother *loves* such sports, but he'd kill everyone else on the field, quite by accident. But being in the company of humans is essential to retain our *own* humanity." His perfect lips quirked in a half smile. "Plus, have you ever spent a century with the same six people? It gets a bit tiresome. Being out in the world helps ease *that* as well."

"Okay then. I'm going to help you get in touch with your humanity. And since you're impossibly ancient, I'm going to do this the old-fashioned way: Edwin Scullen, will you be my steady?"

He laughed, and it was a wonderful laugh. I usually hate it when other people laugh—they're a *source* of amusement for me, so they shouldn't *be* amused—but Edwin was different. "It's not traditional for the *woman* to ask that. Bonnie, do you really want to be close to me? Knowing I will never age, that I can never be entirely like a human boyfriend would be?"

"Are you telling me this doesn't feel epic to you, Edwin?" I said. "That you don't feel like someone in a storybook? Have you ever felt this way about anyone before?"

He shook his head. "No, Bonnie. Never. Not vampire, not human, no one. Since the moment I met you, there has only *been* you."

"You could have fooled me. You seemed to hate my guts at first."

"Ah. That. Well." He took my hands. "I was afraid of the intensity of my feelings. Afraid of what I might do. That's why I missed that week of school—I left town, went back to Canada. We have some friends, another clan, who are—vegetarians, as you say. I planned to stay away forever, but I couldn't stop thinking about you, and I decided I would be strong. So I returned... and was besotted with you all over again." He sighed. "Do I dare to be with you, Bonnie? Despite the risks?"

"I'm a big girl," I said. "I say, yes. Let's do it. Let's be together. Or at least *try*. I think we owe it to these feelings to try."

"You are extraordinary," he murmured. "I can't believe you aren't... *afraid* of me."

"You've never given me reason to fear you," I said. "Are you planning to?"

"Never."

I figured as much. I just hoped I could avoid giving him reason to fear *me*. Because though I saw Edwin partly as a means to an end—my ticket to superpowers and immortality and becoming an apex predator—I also had feelings for him. I don't know if it's what other people mean when they say "love" (I don't know how most people, being the stupid wastes of flesh they are, can possibly be capable of love or worthy of being loved), but I felt something profound. He was interesting like nobody else has ever been interesting, and so pretty I didn't think I'd ever get tired of looking at him.

Edwin paid the check—I assumed he was rich, because of the sports car, and because how do you not get rich when you're part of a clan of vampires?—and we went out to his car. He drove me back to Lake Woebegotten, and he drove very damn fast. "Aren't you worried about crashing and killing me?" I said. "I'm just a fragile mortal weakling, you know."

He laughed. "I always drive this fast. My reflexes are phenomenal. You have nothing to worry about."

"Um, except for the laws of physics. It doesn't matter how fast *your* reflexes are, really. They're limited by how responsive the *car* is. And given the physical limitations of, you know, brakes and steering wheels, your superhuman powers won't be a lot of good if a deer runs out in front of us. You see what I mean?"

"Hmm. You make a good point." He slowed down. "I don't

usually have people in the car with me. I mean—*people*. If I get in a car accident, well. I'll miss the car, but it wouldn't inconvenience me too much."

"Turn me into a vampire," I said, "and you can drive as fast as you want."

"I'm not sure the drawbacks of turning you into an undead, blood-drinking creature of the night are worth shaving a few minutes off the drive to Bemidji," he said.

He got me back to Harry's house, and we sat in the driveway, looking at each other. After a moment I said, "Are you going to kiss me?"

"I... want to. I haven't kissed anyone in... well. It's been some time. But I'm afraid, Bonnie, being so close to you, the *scent* of you, it's overpowering..."

"Okay," I said, leaning in quick and pecking his cheek. "We'll give you some time to get desensitized or acclimated or whatever, but there'd better be vampire-human make-out sessions in our future, all right?"

Before he could respond, I scooted out of the car and went inside. Harry was on the couch, still in his uniform, playing some kind of Xbox game where he ran around with an assault rifle slaughtering zombies. "Hey, hon," he said, glancing at the clock on the wall. "You're home early."

"Oh?" I'd assumed it was late, past midnight, but that was just because time with Edwin had a tendency to stretch—it was barely nine. "Guess it doesn't take that long to hit every store in the mall in Bemidji."

"True enough." He yawned. "You eat?"

"I did."

"You have fun?"

"I did. Dresses were acquired. Mission accomplished."

"Good, good."

"I'm going up to my room to study a bit, then I guess I'll go to bed. Good night, Dad."

He mumbled a response, and I went upstairs to my room and called J—I couldn't believe I'd forgotten to do that.

"You're alive!" she said.

"I am. Everything's fine."

"So?" Her voice was excited. "How did it go? With Edwin?"

"Good. It was... practically a date."

"Wow! Maybe we should have gotten you a dress, too—you guys should come to the dance with us!"

"I'm not sure he's the dancing type," I said. I yawned artificially. "J, can we talk more tomorrow? I'm pretty tired."

She let me go after only five more minutes of attempting to pry, and promised to let Kelly know I'd made it home safe.

I stretched out on my bed and did a mental inventory. In a world full of uncertainty, I had three absolutely solid touchstones:

First, Edwin was a vampire.

Second, he loved me—or at least thought my blood smelled delicious, which, for a vampire, was probably the next best thing.

And third, I would get him to turn me into a vampire too, no matter how much scheming, manipulation, or treachery it required.

MEADOW LARKS

FROM THE JOURNAL OF BONNIE GRAYDUCK

I won't bore you with talk of how happy we were in the next week, being publicly a couple, spending every waking moment together, holding hands at school, eating lunch together (not with my crowd or his—I got the feeling I wasn't welcome with his, and I didn't want to bore him with mine), being the subject of gossip, not even having to fake the giggling girl talk with J and Kelly and the others, and with Edwin sneaking into my room every night (and steadfastly refusing to sleep with me, much to my dismay—more about that later), Harry completely oblivious to his arrivals and departures. Being able to leap up to a second-story window has its advantages.

But Happiness in a story is boring: almost as bad as listening to someone else's dream. You want "blood and ructions," as my old granny used to say—actually that's how she characterized every entertainment in the world other than the Bible, though from the little I've read the Bible has enough blood and ructions to match a hundred action movies. Still, I should cover a few things, some snippets of that happy time before the hockey game and the evil vampires trying to kill me (a few weeks before I would have considered that a tautology: saying "evil vampire" should be like saying "big whale" or "little microbe," absolutely redundant, but that just goes to show, you never know as much as you think you do, even when you're me). So:

Edwin liked to play this game when we were in my bed together, *not* having sex, and no, it wasn't a game that involved dry humping. It was called Questions, but it wasn't the same as the Questions game from that movie *Rosencrantz and Guildenstern Are Dead*. It was pretty simple. He got to ask three questions, and I got to ask three questions, and follow-up questions or requests for clarification counted against your total—but only if they were actually phrased as questions, so you could make leading statements and try to tease out more information. My kind of game, really, as it turned ordinary conversation into something you could *win*, by getting more out of your opponent than he got out of you. Edwin asked me questions like, "What's your favorite ice cream" and "What's your favorite color" and "If you were a verb, which verb would you be?" (I didn't say "murder," I think I said, "sparkle.")

My questions were more like this: "So how does this whole vampire thing work—I mean, like, physically?"

He stirred beside me on the mattress. "I'm not sure I understand."

"Your heart doesn't beat, I can tell when I press my ear to your chest, and you only breathe when you remember to, so how does that *work*? Come on—your dad's a doctor, surely he's spent some time exploring this problem."

"Ah," he said. "I see. Hmm. Well, you must understand—Argyle is interested in the question, but it's not as if vampires stand still to be dissected."

"Vivisected," I murmured. "When you cut them open when they're still alive, it's vivisection—but, wait, if you vampires are technically dead, I guess it is dissection, never mind."

He smiled in the dark: I could see his teeth gleam in the moonbeams through the window. "Quite. Well, Argyle has theories, but precious few opportunities to test them. Our blood doesn't circulate under normal circumstances, and so it doesn't circulate oxygen, and so our brains shouldn't work, but—they do. He thinks the oxygen in the blood we drink replenishes us, somehow—and, yes, I know, drinking blood should just fill our stomachs with blood, not affect the blood in our veins or brains, which doesn't circulate anyway. My mother—well, Argyle's wife—Ellen has a rather more mystical view: we take in life force, and that force sustains us."

"Huh. So it's woo-woo shit."

"Was that a question?"

I sighed. "No. I'm just surprised at Argyle. I thought he was more of a scientific vampire."

"Understand, Argyle was born six hundred years ago. He was shaped by the worldviews of the time—he still, deep down, believes in demons, and magic, and gods, and all manner of such things. And our very existence is a powerful argument in favor of that worldview. There's also the matter of… our powers."

That perked me up, but I could tell he wanted to go on, so I didn't waste a question, just waited.

In a moment he said, "Some of us have… abilities. They develop after we turn. Not *all* of us, but some. Pleasance has the power of psychometry—she can hold an object and discover things, psychically, about its history, and about its owner. That power even works in the present, assuming the affinity between object and owner is strong enough. If she picked up my favorite sweatshirt, say, at home, and held it in her hands, and concentrated, she would receive a vision of where I am now, here, in bed with you—she calls it sympathetic magic."

"Wow," I murmured. Mental note: never let Pleasance get her hands on *anything* of mine.

"Yes. Garnett can make people forget they've seen him. It's not invisibility, exactly, but… well, you just don't notice him, and if you do, you soon forget you did, if that's what he wants. There are other powers. My own, well…"

I could sense he was trying to pull a question out of me, but I stayed quiet.

"I can see through the eyes of others."

"Ha!" I said. "So you *were* spying on me. That's how you

knew that guy who talked to me outside the bar in Bemidji was staring at my boobs the whole time—you looked through his eyes! And here I thought you were just following me around."

"It's true. Argyle thinks the powers we have are... enhancements of the powers we had in life. I was always good at seeing things from someone else's point of view—and so I can *literally* see things from their point of view, now. Only humans—or things that used to be human—alas, not animals. I can't control them either, it's completely passive, but anyone within, oh, a hundred miles, I can dip into their senses and see through their eyes, as if they were cameras. I was keeping an eye on you as best I could when you were in Bemidji, but I lost sight of you when you were alone, so I jumped from person to person for a while until a barfly caught sight of you."

My very own super-stalker. It should have been creepy, but mostly it was cute. It did have certain troubling aspects, though. If he could see me *all* the time... But apparently he couldn't, so I decided to waste a question. "Why not just look through *my* eyes?"

"Ah, there, you see. It's not just your delectable smell or your powerful personality that fascinate me, Bonnie. For some reason—I can't see through your eyes. You are largely a mystery to me, you see—what you do when you're alone is utterly unknown to me, and that is wonderful. When you can so easily satisfy your curiosity as I can, finding someone who resists such casual prying is wonderful."

"Oh, too bad," I said, but I was really thinking: *Thank the nonexistent god.* It would mean, if I ever killed anyone else again, I'd need to make sure they didn't get a look at me, just to be on the safe side. But it should be okay. Edwin's attention couldn't be everywhere at all times. He could only see through one set of eyes at a time. "I was thinking I'd spend a lot more time staring at myself in the mirror after I took a shower, maybe fondling my breasts, give you a little show, but since you can't see through me—you'll have to use your imagination."

He moaned in a very satisfying way.

"So I'm unique, then. I always suspected. That's satisfying." I wondered if the limitation had something to do with my... neurological situation. If my own lack of empathy made his apparently empathy-based power go haywire. It was a theory, and as long as we were embracing magic, it made as much sense as anything else.

"That wasn't technically a question, but I'll answer anyway, since you've given me such a nice mental image to dwell upon," Edwin said. "No, you're not entirely unique. I've met a few other people who were resistant to my power over the years—there are two of them in this town, actually. Mr. Levitt, the principal at school, and the mayor's wife, I think her name is Eileen. I don't know why. Just one of those things."

"You sure know how to make a girl feel special."

"Believe me—a middle-aged woman and a seventy-year-old man don't have quite the same appeal for me that *you* do."

"I'll be middle-aged someday too, old man," I reminded him. "Unless you take steps to make sure I live forever young with you. I don't know why you won't just go ahead and do it already. We both know you'll give in eventually."

He stiffened. "Argyle's theories, about magic, about the supernatural, about redemption and damnation... I am not as old as he is, but they make sense to me, too. I am a creature without a soul, Bonnie. A monster who takes life from the living to sustain my own existence. I love you—I don't want to make you into a monster too."

"You're no monster," I said, glad he couldn't see through my eyes, because those eyes were *rolling*. Souls. Monsters. If there were souls, the angels ran out of them before they got to me, and by most definitions, I was more a monster than he was already. Maybe better not to let him know that though. I decided not to push the issue—not yet. "You're wonderful, and strong. And I have one more question, which is: How do you get erections? Because I *know* you get them. And don't say 'magic.'"

He coughed. He was so shy about some things. Pretty adorable, though also frustrating. "Ah. Well. The blood flow situation is, of course, problematic, but it's possible for us to reach... arousal... as long as we've fed recently. Fresh blood seems to do the trick."

"Huh. Blood as magical Viagra. Interesting. So have you fed recently?"

"You're all out of questions," he reminded me.

I slipped my hand under the bedspread and reached down toward his pants. "I'll just have to rely on experimental data, then."

He swatted my hand away with his usual bullshit about how he couldn't trust himself, in his excitement he might bite me and tear my throat out, etc. I argued that made an even *more* compelling case for him to turn me into a vampire already, so we could have hot invincible vamp sex, but he was adamant, and we ended up sleeping with our backs to one another, each of us sulking through the night.

Over the course of other games of Questions through-out the week, I found out a few more things: boy vampires ejaculate just like normal guys. Which is good, as I'd worried they'd spurt blood, but also bad, because I'd sort of hoped they'd have magical spooge-less ejaculations—I mean, I don't mind giving head, totally controlling a boy with your mouth and hands can be fun, but neither spitting nor swallowing ever appealed to me a bit. Ah well. You can't have everything. (On the bright side: girl vampires don't menstruate—he was embarrassed answering that one!—I guess because their bod-ies are loathe to give up even that much blood, and thus, they can't get pregnant, which is pretty intuitive but it's nice to have confirmation.)

I also discovered Edwin was a *virgin*, which explained a *lot*, and I was glad I hadn't been forthcoming with him about my own sexual history, because I quickly assured him I was a virgin too, of course. He had this whole "My first time must be with my true love" schtick going. Edwin can be such a girl sometimes. But I was his true love, he said, so it was only a matter of time, and once I got him once, I'd have him as often as I wanted, I figured. He just didn't know what he was missing—whereas I could guess what I was missing. Sex with a creature with supernatural stamina.

One day we were out taking a walk in the woods—Edwin said the whole town would be encased in ice starting from November or so, and we'd better enjoy the air while we could—and I asked him about his hunting. "So, what, do you eat pocket gophers?"

"My own weakness is deer," he said. "Though we all have our favorites. None of the animals in the world can compare to human blood, but it's good enough."

"Carob's not as good as chocolate," I said, "but if there's no chocolate—you eat carob."

"Just so. We toyed with the idea of raiding a blood bank, getting bags of old donated human blood just before it's going to be thrown out, but Argyle refused, saying the taste might be too potent, and send us out hunting again. It's very tiring to be good all the time, Bonnie."

So why bother? I thought, but there was no reason to let him know I valued human life a lot less than he did, despite the fact that he was a *vampire*. It's not like humans are rare and precious. There are billions of them, and more being made every day. "I guess deer don't stand a chance against your body, what with the super speed and all."

"Yes. It's quite unfair. Garnett sometimes hunts blindfolded, by smell alone, just for the challenge. Hermet likes to hunt bears, and once flew to Africa to hunt predators like lions, but the taste didn't agree with him. In a way, it's a shame, though. We're exquisitely engineered—or evolved, who can say?—to hunt *humans*. Hence our... well, I hope this doesn't sound immodest... our *beauty*. Our powers, whatever they may be, almost always help us hunt—even Pleasance's psychometry is excellent for learning about a human subject, to more effectively stalk them. And there are... other factors."

I could tell he was leading me into using another question, but that was okay. "Such as?"

He glanced at the sky, which was pretty much just overlapping tree limbs at this point. "You know we avoid the sun?"

"Yeah, I was going to ask about that eventually, but I had a lot of sex and violence questions to get through first, you know, and I didn't want you to think I was trying to, like, catalogue your vulnerabilities."

"Oh, the sun isn't a vulnerability. Quite the opposite. Listen, I know a meadow nearby. Come with me. It's a sunny day—I can show you." He took my hand and led me down a series of deer paths and dry stream beds, up ridges and over hills, until we stepped out of the trees into a vast space, bigger than two football fields, utterly filled with wildflowers, though it seemed pretty late in the year for those. The meadow was warm, too, unseasonably so, and Edwin began shedding his coat—which he only wore for appearances anyway, I'd learned; when you're cold-blooded, wearing a coat doesn't *help* you, since coats work by trapping your own body heat against your skin. He stripped off his shirt, too, which was wonderfully yummy of him—he was like an underwear model carved in white marble. Lickable. Extremely lickable. I was hoping he'd go all the way naked, but that wasn't the plan, apparently. Just as well. Sex in a meadow always seems like it would be so wonderful, right? But meadows just *look* good. In reality, they're scratchy, itchy, and generally filled with bugs. Avoid.

Edwin put down his shirt and coat in the center of the meadow and stretched out with his upper body on the former, gesturing for me to join him. I lay down beside him on his coat, and took his hand. "Just a moment," he murmured. We looked up at the sky for a while. A single fat puffy cloud drifted slowly across the face of the sun, and when it moved away, and the sun's rays shone on him directly—

Well. I wasn't sure what I'd expected. Maybe that he'd burst into flames or at least start smoking, despite what he'd told me. Maybe that he'd bulk up like the Hulk, or turn to stone like a troll, or fluoresce like bodily fluids under a black light.

Instead, he didn't change at all, but there was the most wonderful *smell*. "Oh my god," I said. "Is that coffee? Who's brewing coffee out here in the woods? Oh god, it smells *amazing*." Coffee is my favorite smell in the world. Once when I did ecstasy, I spent two hours making fresh pots of coffee just so I could *smell* them with my senses heightened. (I spent the other five hours having sex, of course.)

"That's me," he said.

I leaned in, and sniffed, and yes—his skin smelled *exactly* like a cup of Kona. "You—that's—wait, what?" I kept sniffing him.

"Argyle thinks it might have something to do with phero-mones," he said. "When exposed to sunlight, there's a reac-tion with our skin, and we produce a smell that's incredibly attractive to humans. It's not always the smell of coffee—the smell is perceived differently by everyone. Baking bread, fresh cookies, lemon zest—it varies. But they always come running, trying to find the source of the smell." He shrugged. "You see what I mean? We are ridiculously overengineered to capture prey. Humans don't stand a chance. But this is why I don't go to school on sunny days. None of us do. Even if we're bundled up, the sunlight touching our faces, our hands, any inch of exposed skin, produces a smell powerful enough to be detected hundreds of yards away. Unless we wore full burqas..." He shrugged. "So we avoid the sun, and choose to live in cloudy places."

"So, if any inch of skin will do the trick, why did you go shirtless just now?"

He grinned. "Well," he said. "You *are* my girlfriend."

I licked his nipple, and he gasped. "No fair. You don't *taste* like coffee." I paused, then said. "Uh, this is cool and all, but, um, maybe we should get back in the shade."

He looked at me curiously. "Why? What's wrong?"

There are certain things a girl doesn't want to say, but we have a rule about Questions, and while there were certain lies I was willing to tell, I tried to be truthful when it wouldn't hurt anything. "Edwin, I love the smell of coffee, but coffee... the smell of coffee kinda makes me have to go to the bathroom. I don't know if it's just years of associating the smell of coffee with early morning, but it's... *deeply* ingrained, and if I have to go even a little bit, the smell of coffee makes me have to go a *lot*."

He looked confused. "Oh. I... vampires don't have, ah... well. We don't urinate. Or have bowel movements."

"Lucky you," I said through gritted teeth as I ran into the trees for some privacy. Though at least it meant I'd never be forced to share the bathroom with him.

When I got back, he was dressed again, and we went back into the forest. "So," he said, delicately avoiding the fact that I'd just pissed in the woods. "My family wants to meet you. I know you've met some of them, but they'd like to... really meet you."

"Wow. Big step!"

"Would you be willing to come see us, at home?"

"Is it very gothic? Lots of spiderwebs and coffins and red velvet drapes?"

"Not very. More Danish modern, really."

"I'd be happy to come," I said. Becoming friendly with more vampires would be good—if Edwin wouldn't turn me, it would be nice to have backup plans. Even if one of his siblings was the one who brought me over, and Edwin got mad about it, he'd see reason eventually.

Plus, I still held a grudge again Pleasance and Rosemarie, and seeing enemies at home can teach you a lot about their vulnerabilities.

FOR YOUR OWN GOOD

FROM THE JOURNAL OF BONNIE GRAYDUCK

"**D**arling," he said that night, as we snuggled in bed. I'd convinced him that I always slept in a thong and a tight little tank top—boys are so credulous, even century-old vampire boys—and he was certainly affected by my attire, but I hadn't been able to get more than a kiss out of him in any of the nights we'd spent. He didn't have noticeable fangs—they popped out when he was hunting or feeding, he told me, like a cat's claws—and his tongue was very talented, and rather cold, too, which made me wonder how that tongue would feel if he went down on me. Of course, he'd probably be terrible at cunnilingus, with the virgin-ness, but he'd also probably be patient, and I suspected he'd be a fast learner. He said it was getting easier, spending time with me, which I took to mean he fantasized less about tearing my throat out and more about tearing my panties off, but he wouldn't even go to second base.

"Yes, love?" I said back. We didn't really have pet names for each other—vampires are too cool for that, I think, and I know *I* am—but the occasional "dearest" or "darling" or "love" slipped out. Not "lover" though. He hadn't earned *that* yet.

"I can't stay with you tomorrow night."

I pushed myself up on my elbow and looked at his face, limned and made beautiful by moonlight through the window. "Why?"

He cleared his throat. "Ah… practicalities. I haven't eaten in a week. I need to hunt."

"Oooohhhh. I see." I lay back down with him. "What's on the menu?"

"Whatever we can find," he said, with a laugh. "Bears, maybe. They're all fat on berries and about to hibernate this time of year."

"You tangle with bears?"

"It's not much of a tangle, Bonnie. Don't worry. We move fast enough, they're dead before they realize what's happening. Well, usually. Hermet likes to play with his food. He takes his time. Not that I'm a particular fan of bears, really—they're fine, but not my favorite."

"Right, you like deer." I made a face of mock horror. "You eat *Bambi*."

"I'm just another hunter," he said, holding up his hands. "It's good for them. Keeps their population down, so they don't starve. Everyone's happy. And being killed by me is probably less traumatic than being shot with a rifle or a bow and arrow. My kills are clean."

"Hmm. You know, you could make the argument that humans could use a predator or two to keep *our* population down. I was reading an article online that said the world will be unrecognizable by 2050. Ten billion people on Earth. Meat will be a luxury. Everybody will be eating bugs because they're easy to breed and high in protein."

"People aren't animals, Bonnie, to be culled by hunters."

I disagreed with *that*—obviously we're animals, what the hell else would we be, plants?—but I held my tongue.

"Besides, there aren't many vampires. Maybe a few hundred of us worldwide. Even if we were *all* preying on humans, it wouldn't make much difference to the human population."

"Huh. Only a few hundred, really? Why so few?"

"We don't make many more of ourselves. And why would we? It's just competition for food, after all. We live forever, barring outside intervention, so there's no pressure to bring a new generation into being. And even when we *do* decide to turn someone… the process is very dangerous. The success rate is hard to determine, but it's surely less than a third. Argyle has done it several times, he's quite good at it, but it's easy for the, ah, victim? new prospect? to die of their wounds before the taint of immortality and bloodlust is passed on and takes hold. That's *another* reason I don't want to turn you, Bonnie my darling—what if I did it wrong? What if you died?"

Hmm. I hadn't realized the odds were so bad, but it didn't really deter me. "I'll die eventually anyway, Edwin. Do you want to wait until I'm seventy and try to turn me on my deathbed? Elderly hag vampiress with her seventeen-year-old paramour."

"Oh, well," he murmured, "We don't know if it will come to that… you're so young, Bonnie…"

"Wait. You think I'm just a dumb kid, don't you?"

"Not dumb," he said. "Never that. But… well… you're seventeen. I *look* seventeen, but I'm really much older. What if you tire of me?"

I laughed. "Edwin. I'm in this for the long haul. I'm in this *forever*. I'm pretty far from being a romantic, but you hit me between the eyes, you *captivate* me. You think I'll ever meet someone else who overshadows you? Some mortal *boy*? This is eternal. This is hearts intertwined. This is soul mate stuff— and don't give me any crap about you not having a soul. I know you have a soul. How else could you love me as purely and passionately as you do?" In truth, I don't believe in souls, but he did, and the sentiment I was expressing was actually true, even if I had to couch it in slightly bullshit terms.

He took my hand, and kissed it. "Bonnie," he whispered. "You are my everything. You are the answer to prayers I dared not make, forsaken as I must be by God. And yet, I've been blessed with you."

A little too mushy for me. "So is this a Scullen family outing, then? A big hunt?"

He shook his head. "I'm going with Pleasance. She's the only one I trust to... well... not bother me about you."

"Oh? Your family doesn't approve?" Shocker. One of them had sabotaged my truck, I figured.

"I wouldn't go that far. They just worry about me. Especially now that we're, ah, seeing each other publicly."

Light dawned. "Oh, so if I vanish, the boyfriend is the first suspect. If you slip up and eat me, Harry will be all over you, and, what? You'll all have to flee Lake Woebegotten?"

"That's about the size of it. They like it here."

"So you invite me over," I said, "to a house full of vamps who don't like me? Hmm."

"Pleasance likes you." Huh. Really? "Well, none of them even *know* you, but she's disposed to like you. And my father and mother, too, are glad I've found someone, though they, ah..."

"Wish I was a nice Jewish girl? A nice Indian girl? A nice Irish girl? Oh, right, wait—a nice bloodsucking girl? Well, tell them I'm on board if they want to help me make the transition."

He sighed. "The only one who's, I would say, actually hostile, is Rosemarie, and even *she* wants me to be happy. They all do. They're good people, Bonnie, and after you come with me to visit them, I'm sure they'll see how wonderful you are, and come around."

I hoped they'd find me so wonderful that one or all of them would insist on letting me join their undead club.

I went to sleep, while he held me. I woke up in the middle of the night, having to pee, and he was awake, watching me. I wasn't even sure he *could* sleep—he was usually gone when I woke up, to make sure Harry wouldn't spot him. I yawned. "You like what you see?"

"You're a vision of loveliness. I shouldn't say this, but, the first night after I met you... I followed you home. I came through your window and sat over there, by your desk, and I watched you sleep."

I paused, seated on the edge of the bed. "Dude. Edwin. Stalker much?"

"I know. I… was trying to decide if I should drink from you. If I could stand to take just a little bit. Our venom acts a bit like rohypnol, it affects short-term memory, and I could have sipped you, made a bite in some… discreet place, perhaps your inner thigh, or under your armpit, the back of your neck where your hair would cover the marks—and tasted just a bit. You wouldn't have remembered. Just a few strange dreams, perhaps. But I couldn't trust myself to take just a taste, so I watched you, and then decided I had to leave town. You were too much of a temptation."

"Okay, but still: if I didn't like you back, Edwin, you'd be the obsessed villain in a psychological horror movie. Even *without* the whole vampire thing."

"Then it's lucky you do like me," he said. "And what is love, after all, but a reciprocated obsession?"

Edwin drove me home from school—he'd taken to picking me up and driving me home, and while I missed Marmon, his sports car was a much sweeter ride. We lingered in the driveway, him loathe to leave, me loathe to let him go, our fingers entwined. "I really must," he murmured. "Pleasance will be waiting for me." He cocked his head. "Harry is coming." He pulled his hand out of my grasp.

I shrugged. "It's not like we're half-naked in the back seat. This car doesn't even *have* a back seat. And he knows I'm seeing you."

"I know," he murmured. "But there's someone else, another car, wait, let me look." His eyes went all faraway and glassy, then he shook his head. "Oh, dear. That's… hmm."

"What is it?"

"Probably nothing. Just… no, nothing. I'll see you tomorrow. You should go inside now."

Miffed at the tone of dismissal at his voice, I took my time climbing out of the car. I'd just shut the door when a ramshackle red truck pulled into the broad dirt side yard—driven by Joachim Noir, with an older man seated beside him. Willy Noir? Seemed likely. I glanced at Edwin, who stared at Joachim and Willy with something very much like hate in his eyes, or even (was it possible?) fear. Then he revved his engine and tore off around the truck and down the lane.

"Hey, Bonnie," Joachim said, climbing out of the truck, a smile as big as the sky on his face. His father was *huge*, over six foot five, broad-shouldered, heavyset, belly like a beer barrel. His eyes were the same as Joachim's, though: so dark they were almost black, observant, very striking. Willy stared at me, then turned his head and looked down the drive, where Edwin had vanished, then back at me. He shook his head, slowly, just once.

Crap. He was one of the tribal elders. He really believed all the wendigo/vampire shit. Crap, crap, crap.

Harry pulled up next, getting out of the cruiser. "Willy boy! What are you doing over this way?"

"Been a while since we visited," Willy rumbled. "Did you miss me?"

"Hell, we played Modern Warfare together for three hours last night," Harry said, "it's not like we haven't talked, but yeah, it's nice to be in the same place where we can have a beer together."

"About that," Willy said. "I got the red ring of death on my Xbox. It's kaput. Think you could spare a controller for an old man?"

Harry groaned. "You want me to play split screen? That's brutal. Good thing I invested in the big TV. Come in, come in." He turned to Joachim. "You want to play?"

"Does Bonnie play?" he asked.

I laughed. "Not me, I'm useless—all thumbs." Of course, it's not true—I have the reflexes of a bat—but killing shapes made of polygons isn't all that satisfying for me. Like eating some kind of vegetarian meat substitute instead of the real thing.

"Well, mind if I hang out with you?" Joachim said.

I blinked. My evening *was* free, and Joachim was nice enough, and Willy hadn't started denouncing me as a witch or consorter-with-wendigos, so maybe there was nothing to worry about. "Sure," I said. Harry and Willy were already going in, discussing squad tactics and their rankings. I took Joachim into the kitchen and said, "Want a glass of soda— sorry, they call it 'pop' up here, right?"

"I'll take whatever you're having." He slid into one of the kitchen chairs, still beaming. He was so *happy*, especially in contrast to Edwin's usual pensive brood. Normally I detested seeing happiness among lesser beings, but something about Joachim's joy was infectious. He really loved life, and on his own terms. I could appreciate that.

"So who was the guy in the fast car?" he said, taking the glass of soda.

I sat down with him and spun my glass around. "A friend, who gave me a ride from school."

"Rich friend," he said. "My dad acted like he recognized him."

I sighed. "It's Edwin Scullen."

Joachim snorted. "Ha! No wonder Dad got all cold and still and serious."

I pretended to remember something. "Oh, that's right, you said he had some, ah, issues with Edwin's family."

"Just crazy superstitions. So." He took another sip. "You two dating?" His voice was casual. Super casual. Way, way too casual.

"I don't know. I guess. Sort of. Do you think your dad would, you know, tell my dad anything? Say anything bad about Edwin?"

"I doubt it. He always says that wendigo shit is tribal business, not for outsiders."

I decided to change the subject, and we chatted a bit more, then drifted out to the living room, where we watched Willy and Harry machine gun terrorists and shoot helicopters out of the sky for a while. Very impersonal mechanical mayhem. Ho-hum. Joachim made small talk, and I chatted too, but mostly I kept an ear on Willy and my dad, to make sure Edwin's name didn't come up. It didn't.

Finally, they finished up whatever they were doing and the little party broke up. Harry slapped Willy's back and told Joachim it was good to see him again. Willy paused by the doorway, looked at me, and said, "Take care, Bonnie."

"Of course," I said. "You, too." I closed the door on them, and soon after said my goodnights to Harry, and went to bed.

The next time I had Edwin alone, and it was my turn to ask questions, I said, "So what's the deal with your people and the Ojibwe over at Pres du Lac?"

He snuggled against me. "Your basic supernatural rivalry."

"Gotcha. Like in that movie where the werewolves fight vampires."

"I think you mean 'those movies,'" Edwin said. "There are quite a few of them. Which is strange, as I've never met a werewolf."

"Huh. I thought you beasts of the night all hung out together." I was vaguely disappointed. No werewolves? There was something hot about a powerful, hairy, muscled, bad-boy type that appealed. Not that I was growing bored of my pale slender Edwin, by any means, but variety is the spice of this girl's life.

"I'm not saying werewolves don't exist. But, like leprechauns, the Loch Ness monster, and delicious lutefisk, I tend to assume they don't. The Ojibwe on Pres du Lac aren't werewolves, but they do have... certain powers, and apparently they're perfectly suited to the business of killing wendigos. Unfortunately, they think *we're* wendigos, and apparently those powers are equally well suited to dispatch vampires."

"Ancient Native American wisdom," I said. "Shamanic prowess. Like that."

"I don't know the source of their power," he admitted.

"Nor have I ever witnessed it. Argyle says things were... very heated... when he used to live here, generations ago. He assures me the Ojibwe, at least some of them, are quite formidable. We have a truce, as you know, but things have been... strained of late. We're treading very carefully, as a result."

I decided to spend another direct question, because implication can be exhausting. "Why are things strained?"

"Ah. Well. I may have... inadvertently encroached on their property. I was pursuing a deer through the forest, just a spur-of-the-moment thing, really, saw it running and thought I'd have a snack. So I gave chase, and didn't pay close attention to where I was, and in the course of my pursuit, I strayed over the border. Only a *little*, mind you, but... the elders take this very seriously."

"Sure. You violated their airspace, right, and you pretty much count as an army all by yourself, so I can see how that would be construed as an act of aggression."

He sighed. "It was an *accident*. But that's why I fled when I saw Willy Noir coming—I didn't want to remind him of my existence. Argyle was... cross with me."

"I'm surprised it didn't turn into a shooting war. Or a biting war. Whatever."

"No, it's pretty much smoothed over. They believe it was a mistake on my part, not a deliberate taunt. But let's just say it wouldn't be a good idea for people of the bloodsucking persuasion to stray into their territory again. Argyle says they'll kill us immediately, no questions asked. I find it hard to believe they *could* dispatch us so easily, but Argyle assures me they can. Apparently this particular bunch of Ojibwe—at least members of some particular bloodline—have evolved or trained or altered themselves by magic to be perfect wendigo-killing machines. They're like antibodies tuned perfectly to destroy vampiric infection. Argyle sent them gifts, gold and bearer bonds, as a peace offering, but the elders sent them all back without comment. Things are still tense."

"Must be tough to negotiate a peace when you can't drop by

for a chat. Must be a bitch to talk to a hostile foreign power, I guess, since I doubt there are vampire embassies."

"Ha. No. We aren't much for diplomacy—Argyle is pretty much the only one who ever tried negotiating a peace with a hostile force. Normally we're more fight-and-slash-and-burn in our relations. But Argyle saved a few lives at the reservation, generations ago, as the basis for the truce, and that's why we're tolerated now. Unfortunately, the ones he saved are long dead, and the elders now weren't even born back then, and they aren't too fond of us there. We don't talk to them directly, at all, but we have an, ah, intermediary, a local human who does work for us."

I sat up. "Whoa, whoa, whoa." Somebody else living in Lake Woebegotten or environs knew about the Scullens and the Scales? I would've blurted a follow-up question, but I knew he'd elaborate if I just stared at him in alarm.

"Yes, I know what you're thinking, but he's very trustworthy."

"Let me guess: he's like a mind-controlled blood-slave."

"No," Edwin said. "He's like a guy trying to make ends meet who really needs money, and we pay him handsomely to act as a liaison, when necessary."

Now this *was* worth spending a question on. "Who is it?"

"Pass."

I frowned. "You can't say 'pass.' I ask, you answer, that's the rule."

He gave me a lazy smile. "I just did. I can't answer that question. Argyle says our agent must remain anonymous. Take it up with him. I'm not *about* to cross him."

I settled down, frustrated. "Hmm. So since Willy found out about me and you—I mean, I'm sure Harry mentioned it—I guess that means *I'm* unwelcome on the reservation too."

"Not judging by the way young Joachim looks at you," he said, suddenly sullen. "I'm sure he'd love it if you'd come around more often."

I laughed. "You and your looking-through-people's-eyes. He's sixteen years old, you can't be surprised if Joachim has a boob fixation."

"Nothing so crass," Edwin admitted. "But he does watch you, constantly, whenever you're around. I can't read minds or sense emotions, but he's clearly besotted with you."

"Besotted! What a word! I love it when you show your age. Joachim's cute enough in a scruffy way," I said, "but he's no immortal love god, like some guys I could name." I snuggled in closer to him.

"By my count you have one question left," he said, "but only because I'm very generous about offering information without prompting, unlike some people I could name."

"I can't help it," I said. "When I play, I play hard."

"Well? No final question?"

"This questions thing is fine," I said, "but a girl can have too much of Truth." I slid my hand under the covers. "How about we play a little Dare for a while instead?"

Reader, that night Edwin actually made it to second base. I was hoping he'd steal third, but no dice, to mix my sports metaphors.

FANGS AND GAMES

FROM THE JOURNAL OF BONNIE GRAYDUCK

Saturday came, and Edwin slipped out of my room just long enough to get his car and come over after breakfast. For once Harry was home, though he was on the phone a lot—I guess some old local drunk hadn't been seen in a while, and Harry was worried about him, putting in calls all over the place. Small-town cop who knew everybody by sight: talk about service. He hung up the phone long enough to greet Edwin, though. I'd told him we were spending time together—I'd avoided saying "boyfriend" or even "dating," but Harry is not a dumb man, so he got the idea.

"Hello there, son. Bonnie tells me she's going over to spend the day at your folks' place. It's nice of you to have her for lunch."

I stifled a grin. Being "had for lunch" at a house full of vampires wouldn't be a very pleasant prospect, most of the time.

"Yes sir," Edwin said, unfailingly polite.

"I'd love to have you over for dinner some night," Harry went on. "You're always welcome here. I'm glad Bonnie's found a... friend... to keep her company. It's always hard starting over in a new place."

Edwin glanced at me. "I appreciate the offer. We'll have to make plans sometime. Your daughter is... very special, sir."

"True enough. Take good care of her. And don't let her come home too late."

I did the requisite eye-rolling and said, "Now that the men-folk have sorted out who's taking care of helpless old me for the day..." I shouldered my purse and took Edwin's arm, out into a day that was, fortunately, heavily overcast. We got into one of his family cars (just a Jeep this time, nothing too zoomy or fancy, maybe because he was afraid Harry wouldn't approve) and set off on the long back roads of Lake Woebegotten. One field looks much like another, but my sense of direction is pretty good, and I could tell we were aimed for a spot basically on the opposite side of the lake from Pres du Lac. "So what's the plan for today? Bela Lugosi film festival? We watch Hermet wrestle an imported grizzly bear?"

He laughed. "We'll talk. Introduce you around, formally. And, we were thinking... let you see what the Scullens and the Scales do for fun."

"Blood orgy?" I said.

"Not quite. You'll see."

He wouldn't be drawn further, and I didn't pry after my first few attempts were rebuffed. Eventually we drove down a little track into the trees, then took a series of turns down unmarked side roads, with two points where Edwin got out of the car to unhook a padlocked chain, drove through, and locked up after us. He did the locking-and-unlocking at full speed, or at least the fastest I'd ever seen him move, his body and hands just blurs of movement.

"Wow," I said after the first chain was passed. "You're *fast*."

"I could pick you up and run through the forest faster than driving," he said, "but the wind of our passage might tear up your clothes, and I always get bugs in my teeth when I run that fast. Besides, that kind of exertion makes me hungry, and it's, ah, better if I'm quite sated. Everyone at the house ate until we were stuffed last night, so none of us should be... too tempted."

"That's reassuring," I said, because it was.

The car wound along a curving road, and emerged into a pastoral clearing, dominated by a farmhouse of the rambling, ramshackle, Addams Family variety. Not *quite* a gothic castle, but the closest thing you were likely to find in the Minnesota woods, complete with turrets and strange weathervanes and tall narrow windows. "Wow," I said, emerging from the car. "You guys could make a pretty great haunted house out of this. I can't wait for Halloween!" In truth, Halloween wasn't that far off, and autumn was starting to give up its place in favor of winter. I had on a coat and a hat, though Edwin scoffed at my complaints about the cold. I pointed out that he was cold-blooded, basically, and didn't know what it was like to be freezing. He pointed out that I'd been in California for too long, and compared to the wilds of Canada, Minnesota was a mild and temperate place.

"We certainly have enough monsters on the premises," he agreed, and led me up the front steps.

The house was big and rambling on the inside, too. We went through a little foyer hung with lots of coats and scarves (all for show, of course, as the inhabitants weren't troubled by the weather) into a big living room. The walls were decorated with a riot of artworks from all over the world: tribal masks, bright paintings, woven rugs, tapestries, odd bits of sculptures, framed photographs showing vistas of impossible beauty. I guess when you're a vampire, you have time to go everywhere and see everything... and yet, somehow, they'd still ended up in Lake Woebegotten. Funny old world. The furniture was, indeed, mostly Danish modern, stark couches and armchairs and low tables. Fewer lamps than you'd have expected, but they could all see perfectly in the dark, after all.

The entire Scullen clan was there, looking like a Christmas card or a photograph from a catalog. Argyle sat in one chair, beside the woman I assumed was his wife, Ellen—she was dark-haired and looked to be in her late twenties, with mismatched eyes, one blue and one green, and her smile seemed as warm and genuine as her husband's. Icy Rosemarie stood behind the couch, her arms crossed, openly scowling at me, and towering Hermet was beside her, though he leaned forward with his elbows planted on the back of the couch, chin in his hands, looking at me mostly like I was an *amuse bouche*. Pleasance was on the couch, holding hands with Garnett, and she looked delighted to see me, too, while Garnett seemed bored, and as fidgety as vampires ever got—which wasn't very, but Edwin's preternatural stillness had attuned me to tiny shifts and twitches.

"Welcome, Bonnie," Ellen said formally, inclining her head slightly. "You are welcome here."

I said, "Hi, everyone. Thanks for having me." I looked around, trying not to dwell too long on the fact that these were a bunch of alcoholics in recovery and I was a jeroboam of champagne. "This is a lovely home."

"Hello, Bonnie," Pleasance said, bouncing off the couch and giving me a kiss on the cheek. The cold bitch who'd turned up her nose at me in the cafeteria a while back was gone—she was as warm as someone dead could be. Maybe she'd just been looking out for her adopted brother, then. That kind of protectiveness wasn't entirely an impulse I could comprehend—I've certainly never felt moved to protect anyone that way—but I understood it in theory. And Edwin loved her. Maybe I could let revenge slide in her case. Everyone's entitled to one mistake. She stepped back. "Wow, you *do* smell yummy, I never noticed before!"

Everyone was silent for a moment, the whole room uncomfortable (except maybe for Pleasance, who had a certain manic pixie dreamgirl quality to her, either natural or affected). I noticed Edwin leaning in, and Argyle whispering something in his ear. Secrets already?

I glanced around, pointing toward a weird device in one corner—sort of like a keyboard, but with lots of speakers attached, and vacuum tubes, and more wires than seemed necessary. "What's that?" I said. Thinking: exotic torture device? One of Argyle's medical machines from the old days when people thought electricity and magnets could cure anything?

"It's an ondium Martenot," Ellen said. "An early electronic

music device, something like a theremin, but more versatile—"

"Wow," I said. "Do you play?"

"I do not, but Edwin does."

"Man of many talents," I said, turning toward him. "Why didn't you tell me?"

"Oh, yes," he said dryly. "Nothing gets a pretty young girl more hot and bothered than hearing you play an obscure electric music instrument from the early 1900s."

"Oh, I don't know, I think that band Radiohead used one on an album, I forget which—it makes kind of weird spacey sounds, yeah? I've never seen one before. Play for me?"

"Oh, yes, you must," Pleasance said, clapping her hands. He scowled, sighed, then allowed himself to be prodded toward the device by Pleasance.

I got the sense he was the sort of person who said, "Oh, no, you don't want to hear *me* play," while simultaneously strapping on a guitar and grabbing a pick. I didn't mind: I had an impulse for the theatrical myself, and he was certainly a pleasure to watch in performance of any kind. He sat at an ordinary piano bench, put a weird, wide ring on his finger, and pulled out a little drawer full of controls on the left-hand side of the keyboard. He didn't actually press any keys, but ran the ring on his finger along a strip in front of the keys while doing obscure things to the control panel with his left hand. Rich, lush, weirdly vibrating tones filled the space, emerging from three speakers—one rectangular, one like a stretched hexagon, one shaped like nothing so much as a fan of peacock feathers. It was the sort of music that would make you think deeply about the nature of space-time if you listened to it while tripping on acid; music to accompany the arrival of a time machine; psychedelic spaceman marching songs. I didn't think pop music was in danger of being taken by storm, is what I'm saying, but it had a certain weird prettiness, I guess. He lifted his fingers away, and the last notes faded.

"Wow," I said. "That…" I fell back on one of my dad's stock

phrases. "That sure is something."

Edwin beamed. "It's a forgotten instrument, mostly, which is a shame—" He broke off. "I certainly know how to clear a room, hmm?"

I turned around, and the Scullens and Scales had all vanished. "I don't know," I said. "Maybe they were fleeing because they don't like me, not your music."

He patted the bench, and I sat beside him. "They like you," he said seriously. "Pleasance, very much so. And Garnett, well, he likes anyone Pleasance likes, if he knows what's good for him."

"Your mom didn't seem to hate me," I mused.

"My parents both think well of you. Ellen especially, because... Well, it's not as if she has hopes for grandchildren, we're *vampires*, but like any mother, she wants her children to be happy, and I have, I confess, been very lonely. Never loving, never loved—admired, certainly, but... Nothing like this. Pleasance and Garnett have been paired off for decades, and Rosemarie and Hermet even longer—"

"Now those two," I said. "They're not about to be charter members of the Bonnie Grayduck fan club, are they?"

"Ah," he said. "They... have reservations. Rosemarie, mostly. Hermet thinks I'm quite mad—he says one of us dating a human is, ah, like a wolf dating a hamster, which I believe is rather overstating the case, especially since you're not even remotely hamsterish—but he doesn't like or dislike you, I don't think, and he's doing his best to make Rosemarie see reason."

"So what does she have against me? I'm certainly not *prettier* than she is." I'd never felt anything but waves of hostility radiating off her, and I wasn't entirely sure why. I didn't mind being an object of hatred, but I usually had something to do with *causing* the emotion.

"She didn't want to become one of us. She was turned against her will, and abandoned by her maker. In you, she sees all the possibilities that have been taken from her—a normal life, you understand?"

I shook my head. "That's dumb. She's immortal, super-naturally hot, and, I assume, has various magical powers. Whereas me? I'm cute enough, and pretty smart, but I don't compare—"

"You can have children," he said. "You have a soul."

Never planning on squirting out a brat, I thought, *and I hope there aren't souls, because I've got no interest in being judged in the afterlife.* "Oh," I said. "I guess that makes sense." Maybe I could manipulate her jealousy? Get her to turn me into a vampire so I wouldn't get to be a lucky real human girl anymore? Risky, since she might just kill me, but I'd keep the possibility in mind.

I said, "So what did Argyle whisper in your ear? Or is it a special vampire secret?"

He blinked. "You noticed that. Of course you did. He, ah... There are outsiders in town. Outside town, technically, out in the woods."

"Ooh. Wild vampires?"

"Presumably they belong to a group less civilized than our own, yes. I might as well tell you—I'm going to be watching you all the time until they're gone. You might not always see me, but I'll never be more than a second away from you."

I raised an eyebrow. "You think I'm in danger? Me, particularly?"

"Vampires are sons-of-bitches," he said. "If they find out I'm close with a human, they might think it the height of hilarity to kill you. And we know they're... interested in us. They've snooped around the perimeter of the house—we're some of the only stationary vampires in the world, so we're a novelty. They can smell us, or perhaps they have abilities that allow them to spy on us. We think there are three of them, a small pack, fortunately. Ideally, they'll never know you exist, or even stray within the limits of Lake Woebegotten, but having finally *found* someone I love, I'm not about to risk losing you."

"It's a good thing this isn't a movie," I said, "because that sure sounds a lot like foreshadowing."

"If we were in a movie, it would be a love story, don't you think?"

"Or a horror movie. Or one of those weird mishmashes that can't decide if it's action or paranormal or heartstring-tugging, and tries to be everything, and isn't very good at being any of them." *Or a serial killer movie*, I thought. *Even if I haven't killed anyone around here.* "But you're probably still impressed by movies that are *talkies*, aren't you, old man?"

"I'll show you an old man." He wrapped his arms around me, and kissed me. I bit gently on his lower lip, and he laughed into my mouth, which was actually kind of unpleasant.

He pulled away. "Come on. The others are probably waiting for us in the back yard. I promised to show you how the Scullens and Scales amuse themselves. Come and join our vampire games?"

"I wouldn't miss it for the world," I said.

I'm not sure what I expected. Paintball, only played with live ammo instead of paint? Bow-hunting one another? Mixed martial arts battles, with takedowns faster than the eye could follow? Capture the flag? War games? Any of those seemed possible: they owned a lot of land, had a lot of woods to call their own, and could have staged all sorts of impressive amusements.

Instead…

"You're going to play hockey?" I said incredulously, standing on the edge of a frozen pond, with my scarf wrapped around and around and around my throat.

"What else?" he said. "We lived for years in Canada, and now we're in Minnesota. I can't imagine why you'd be surprised." The others were already on the ice, gliding around on skates. "This, frankly, is a bit boring," Edwin said. "When we can find a sufficiently large frozen body of water, we prefer to play *inverted* hockey."

"What, where you guys are the pucks or something?"

"Oh, no. We break a hole in the ice. We climb into the frozen water with our sticks and swim out under the ice sheet. We use a hollow puck, so it floats to the top, and 'rests' on the underside of the ice. Then… we play hockey. Underwater. Swimming, in near-freezing water, slamming the puck along the bottom of the ice."

I pondered that. "You people are insane."

He laughed. "No, what's insane are the *humans* who do it—there are perfectly mortal free divers who play the same game. If I had to breathe, or was troubled by the cold, I certainly wouldn't play inverted hockey. Go to your precious internet and search around, you can find video of people playing underwater ice hockey." He shook his head. "For us, it's a welcome challenge to enliven the occasionally humdrum nature of eternity. But for mortals to do it… The living baffle me. But inverted hockey isn't very interesting for spectators, and we don't have a big enough frozen lake anyway, so: conventional hockey it is. Enjoy the show."

Something occurred to me. "It's only about 40 degrees," I said. "So how is this water even *frozen*?"

We were in the backyard, which was more or less a featureless flat expanse of grass about the size of two football fields laid side by side, surrounded on all sides by a dense growth of trees. A pond in the center of the space was the wrong size and shape for a hockey rink, but big enough for a game, and so cold it steamed in the somewhat-warmer air.

"You know how I said some of us had special powers?" Edwin said. He nodded toward Rosemarie, who skated around elegantly with a big stick in her hands. "She has the power to manipulate the weather, temperature, pressure, precipitation, things like that. So whenever we want to ice-skate, she flash-freezes the pond. It's hard on the fish, but fun for us."

"Wow." I remembered him saying their powers seemed to be enhancements of qualities they'd had when they were alive, so this made sense—I was pretty sure Rosemarie had always been an ice-cold bitch.

"Here." He handed me a pair of binoculars. "You should probably watch from the gazebo there." He pointed to a little wooden octagon not far from the house. "Keep behind the plexiglass. We, ah… play hard."

I raised an eyebrow at him, but obligingly plodded over to the gazebo, which was indeed enclosed in plexiglass. I had a feeling the Scullens had installed the protective material strictly for my benefit, since there was also a little electric space heater there to keep me warm, and neither one would be of much use to them. I sat on the bench and looked through the binoculars, which were high-quality, and gave me a great view of the action on the ice.

It seemed to be boys against girls, with Argyle standing aside as the referee or scorekeeper or whatever. Ellen and Garnett were goalies, standing in homemade-looking goals of bent metal and cargo netting. I couldn't imagine how Pleasance and Rosemarie could possibly stand up against Hermet's unstoppable bulk and Edwin's grace, but I underestimated them. Hermet was ginormous, yes, but that made him just *slightly* slower than the others. I think the simple physics of ice and skates limited how fast they could move, but even so, they were mostly just blurs, whipping around the ice, sticks flying, puck smashing toward the goals, where the goalies more often than not blocked with their bare hands. Oh, to have that kind of strength, speed, *power*… I sure as hell wouldn't waste it on stupid games like hockey.

Suddenly there was a brutally sharp *crack*, and the plexiglass barrier in front of me developed a starburst of cracks like a spiderweb made of ice. I involuntarily jumped back and almost dropped the binoculars, then lifted them to my face again, where I could see Rosemarie and Edwin screaming at each other. I couldn't hear their words, but I could guess: *How dare you try to kill my girlfriend with a hockey puck!* vs. *It was just an accident, gawd, give it a rest!*

But I had no doubt she'd aimed the puck my way. Maybe

not to take my head off, but definitely to scare me. Creatures with that kind of power and control don't make mistakes, not with the simple physical manipulation of a curved stick and a hard disc. This was a message: go away, little girl, or it might be your face that gets shattered next.

Poor Rosemarie. She had no idea what I was. She was so aware of her own monstrous qualities, it never occurred to her that I might have some monster tricks of my own.

Suddenly, the vampires stopped yelling at each other. They all stood very still, and then turned, as if all their feet were attached to the same swiveling mechanism, to look at the woods. I stepped hesitantly out of the gazebo, squinting toward the treeline, cursing my stupid mortal eyes, or nose, or whatever they were using to sense whatever it was I couldn't perceive at all. I walked almost all the way to the edge of the pond before I saw what they did, and by then, you couldn't miss it.

Three figures stepped out of the woods. There was a blur, and Edwin was suddenly next to me. "Stay close to me," he said through clenched teeth. Hermet drifted over—what? icebergs can drift—and stood between us and the newcomers.

"Are these our out-of-towners?" I said.

"Yes. We didn't expect them to approach so soon."

"So are you guys going to have a brawl?"

He shook his head. "I don't think so. It should be perfectly polite. There's nothing we want or need from one another, but it's… good manners to introduce ourselves, reveal that we mean each other no harm, that we aren't encroaching intentionally on another's territory, etc. I know it's hard for you, but just… be mouselike and quiet, please?"

"Consider me the incredible shrinking violet." I crossed my arms, watching the vampires slowly approach one another. The newcomers looked like, well, dirty hippies, or more like if two male models and a high-class hooker decided to give up their fame and fortune and go hike the Appalachian trail in clothes they stole off some hobos. They were carrying big packs, which seemed a little strange to me. What did a traveling vampire really *need*? They wouldn't carry food, they clearly weren't too concerned about clothes, and I couldn't imagine the elements bothered them much. Were the backpacks full of opera cloaks and big gold medallions?

The man in front was blond, sharp-featured, with eyes that never stopped moving. The other man was shorter, sturdier, with great ropelike dreadlocks and tattooed arms. The woman was lusher than either Rosemarie or Pleasance—*full like a tick*, I thought—all curves and bosoms and torrents of wavy, long, dark hair, which would have been unbearably pretty, except for the leaves stuck in it.

Argyle stepped toward them. "Greetings," he said.

"We didn't meant to interrupt your game," the leader said. "I'm Jimmy. Hockey, is it? Shame we didn't bring our skates."

"Perhaps we can loan you some," Argyle said. "Another time. Do you expect to be in the area for long?"

"No, no, just traveling. Yourselves?"

"We maintain a… permanent residence nearby," he said. "This is my family."

Jimmy glanced at the other man. "You… *live* around here? Doesn't the local population, ah, notice the depletion?"

"We have… a different method," Argyle said. "We—" He squinted. "Wait," he said. "Is that… *Gretchen*?"

"I wondered when you'd notice," the woman said, grinning. "Stop trying to hide behind your enormous brother, Edwin, and say hello."

He groaned. "This is all I needed. Why did it have to be *her*?"

"You know these people?" Jimmy said, at more or less the same time I did.

"They're the *vegetarians* I told you about," Gretchen said.

Jimmy laughed. "Queequeg! Did you hear that? These are the ones who eat dogs and cats and so on!"

"I don't know how people can eat that stuff," Queequeg said, in a stoner's loopy drawl. "Sounds nasty."

Gretchen walked toward Edwin—and me, though she didn't pay me any attention. She grabbed Edwin in a hug. "You little bastard," she said. "I didn't realize you'd rejoined your brood and settled down here."

"We've only been here a couple of years," he muttered, looking away.

Now Gretchen looked me up and down, frankly. "We've got a live one over here, boys!" she shouted. She reached out, as if to caress my cheek, but Edwin grabbed her wrist and held it still. They stood like that, two figures in perfect, still tension, and then she relaxed. "Oh, Edwin, you never change. Still kinky for the live girls." She looked at me. "You're not the first, sweetie, and you won't be the last."

All the blood drained from my face—another problem I wouldn't have once I became a vampire. "What is she talking about, Edwin?"

He opened his mouth, then just closed it and shook his head.

"I don't know you," Gretchen said, "but I don't have to. Because I used to *be* you. Edwin used to date me, you see—back when I was alive."

EVERYONE HAS A CRAZY EX

FROM THE JOURNAL OF BONNIE GRAYDUCK

Gretchen kept smiling. "He promised me eternity, Edwin did. But he only likes his women with heartbeats. As soon as I got myself turned, so I could be with him forever and ever and always, well, he lost interest. I guess I didn't smell so nice anymore."

"Don't listen to her, Bonnie," Edwin said. "It's not like she says. Gretchen, I think you and your... entourage... should leave."

"Oh, we'll leave," she said. "It's not as if I hold a *grudge* after all this time."

Argyle cleared his throat. "Ah. I suppose you three have some things to talk about. Jimmy, and, Queequeg, is it? If you'd like to come over to the house, perhaps take a shower, change your clothes?"

"You mind, love?" Jimmy said. "I've still got bits of that old man we ate stuck in my hair, be nice to have a shampoo."

"Not at all," Gretchen said. "I've been looking forward to having a chat with Edwin for ages, as you well know, and the opportunity to provide a cautionary tale for his latest living lover is a special treat."

"I can't believe this," I said as the others moved off. I walked over to the gazebo, thinking furiously, and sat down on the bench. Edwin came after me, and Gretchen sauntered along after that, smirking like only an immortal killing machine with boobs that were simultaneously big and perky could

168

smirk. "Edwin... you told me you were a *virgin!*" I couldn't believe he'd lied. Edwin's various depths of pathos and bathos and other *-thoses* were evident, but I'd never gotten the sense he was a liar, and I'm usually good at spotting those. If he was playing with me, just using me to gratify some kind of live-girl fetish he had, like some kind of reverse necrophiliac... then I'd bury a stake in his heart myself.

"Well, that may be true." Gretchen plopped down on a bench across from me, her back to the plexiglass barrier. "I mean, I gave him a couple of hand jobs, but we'd been seeing each other for like six months before he dared to risk orgasm." She rolled her eyes. "And he never returned the favor for fear of getting overly excited and tearing me apart with his ferocious teeth, yadda yadda."

"You said I was the first girl you'd ever loved," I seethed, not looking at her, staring at Edwin.

"You *are!*" he said. Then glanced at Gretchen. "I was... infatuated with her. Confused. She had a nice smell, I confess, but when she became a vampire, I realized her personality was a terrible match for mine—abrasive, contrary, crass, coarse—"

"Stop, you're making me blush," Gretchen said.

"Did you turn her?" I asked. I didn't actually care if he *had* fucked her. It would've been nice for him to have a little experience before we slept together—screwing a virgin is like eating a green banana. But... "Did you make her a vampire?"

"He never would," she said. "I had to get another vampire to do it, and he made me an indentured servant for ten years as payment. I just got out of that contract recently. But if you're hoping Edwin will punch your mortal-card, I wouldn't get your hopes up. Would a guy who's got a thing for pre-op transsexuals pay for his lover to get bottom surgery? Of course not. Face it, sweetie, you're just something for him to wank over. If he had a shoe fetish, you'd be a red high-heeled pump. You—"

"Shut *up*, Gretchen," Edwin said, narrowing his eyes at her.

"The love I feel for Bonnie is *deep* and *pure* and *true*, and my family likes her, unlike *you*. They always hated you. Said I was just dazzled by your breasts."

She pulled the neck of her flannel shirt away and looked down at her chest. "They are pretty dazzling."

"But Edwin," I said, "you told me yourself, what attracted you was my *smell*. If I did become a vampire, and I didn't have that smell anymore… why would you still want me?" I hadn't considered this possibility. I'd assumed we'd be together forever once I managed to get myself turned (by Edwin or someone else), but now Gretchen had raised doubts.

"No," he said, firmly, taking my hand and gazing into my eyes. "It's not that. Yes, I was initially attracted by your delectable odor, but I didn't *eat* you, did I? It's like, if a mortal man sees a woman across the room, the thing that first attracts him might be her hair, her beautiful eyes, her—"

"Tits and ass," Gretchen said, in a helpful tone.

"—other physical attributes," Edwin said. "But that's not enough to create *love*. That comes later. And even if the looks fade, when the woman, ah—"

"Gets in a disfiguring car wreck?" Gretchen said.

"—passes beyond the blush of youth," Edwin continued, "then that love doesn't fade, as it has transcended the merely physical. Once I got to know you, started spending time with you, found out how funny and sharp and smart and witty and brave you are, *that's* when I fell in love. And that's where I still am. In love, with you, Bonnie Grayduck, until the stars grow cold and the universe breathes its last."

"Huh," Gretchen said. "You know, Bonnie, I kind of believe him."

That startled me. "*Really?*"

"Yep. I don't have lie-detection powers—my abilities are if anything kind of the *opposite* of that—but I mooned around after him for the best part of a year, and I know him pretty well. He's radiating sincerity, and he's not staring at your boobs, which was all he ever did to me—back then I was dumb enough to find that flattering. So, yeah, I think he really loves you. Which kind of spoils my plan, which was to turn you into a vampire, and show you what an asshole he is. But now I'm afraid, if I do that, you two really *will* ride off into the sunset—or the heat death of the universe, same difference—together."

God. Damn. It. If Edwin had sounded just a *bit* less sincere, I could have gotten myself turned into a vampire! Yes, it would have been disappointing if Edwin lost interest in me, but I'd take consolation in the fact that I was *immortal and full of supernatural power.* The joy of being a vampire would do a lot more for a broken heart than a pint of Häagen-Dazs and a Sarah McLachlan playlist ever could.

"So I guess I need a new plan." Gretchen gave a big sunny grin and stood up. "Be seeing you around, Bonnie. Take care of yourself, Edwin. I'm going to go get a shower, and then, if your little vegetarian cult hasn't successfully brainwashed my boys into eating tofu soaked in hamster blood, we'll all be on our way."

Edwin frowned. "Gretchen. Are you... angry with me?"

"Ten years," she said, pausing in the entryway to the gazebo. "That's how long I had to be indentured to the vamp who turned me, because *you* wouldn't. I didn't think it would be so bad—what's ten years when you measure it against an eternity with the person you love? I was so happy when I told you—my master let me have two weeks to spend with you before my service began, do you remember? I thought *you'd* be so happy. But you just told me you were disappointed in me, that I'd made a terrible mistake, and after three days you told me maybe we'd better go our separate ways. So I went back to my master and began to repay him... I had no idea how terrible those ten years would be, Edwin. The things I'd be made to do. To witness. To allow to be done to *me*. It wasn't worth it. Even if you *had* loved me, embraced me, made me part of your ridiculous granola family, it wouldn't have been worth it. And since I didn't even get the consolation of having the boy I loved love me *back*…" She shook her head. "I'm not angry. Angry's not the right word. Calling me angry is like calling the sun a little warm, a glacier a little chilly, the moon a good little ways away. I'll be seeing you, Edwin. But you might not see me." Another grin, this one a quick flicker, like a striking snake or one of those fish who shoot bugs out of the air with their spit. Then she sauntered off.

"Fuck," I said.

"Fuck," Edwin agreed.

"She's going to kill me, isn't she?" I said.

"That would be my guess," Edwin said. Then he scooped me up in his arms and began running towards the woods at, I'd conservatively guess, about sixty miles per hour.

The trip wasn't exactly pleasant. Even with my face buried in Edwin's chest, the force of the wind pressing against me as he ran was tremendous, and I thought my hair would be ripped out by sheer velocity alone. He stopped running so abruptly that I jerked whiplash-hard against his immovable grasp, and as he turned his head and spat out bugs and leaves and other crap that had blown into his mouth while running, I confess, I found him somewhat less attractive than usual. He put me down gently, and I wobbled on my feet, feeling truly clumsy for once. We were in the woods—shocker—alongside another rutted dirt road. A mud-colored old SUV came bumping and thumping along, and I tensed up, but Edwin raised his hand, waving.

The SUV pulled alongside us, and Pleasance was there behind the wheel, looking tiny and harmless, though I knew she had the same core of steel and venom Edwin did. Hermet was in the back, looking rather less harmless. "Hi, guys," Pleasance said. "Climb in."

"I'll drive," Edwin said, and Pleasance rolled her eyes but climbed into the back seat with her brother. I got into the passenger seat and pulled the seatbelt on. My brain was whirring, in overdrive, overclocked.

"Uh, so..." I said. "What's the plan, exactly?"

"Drive," Edwin said. "Stop driving in a thousand miles or so. Then reassess the situation." He started down the road at high speed, hitting bumps hard enough to make me fly up against my harness. Before long we turned onto a paved road, and began picking up speed. I was surprised a vehicle that looked this old and innocuous could hit speeds like this, but I shouldn't have been—these were people who were used to having to move fast, I guess.

"Turn left up here, Edwin," Pleasance said.

"Um, okay," I said. "So, this is kidnapping, then?"

"Don't be absurd," Edwin snapped. "This is *rescue*. If we don't get you well away, and quickly, Gretchen will come for you."

"You really should've disclosed your crazy ex before we started going out," I said. "But that's another issue. *I* don't think I'm being kidnapped—but some other people might take it that way. Like my dad, for instance. He knows I went to your house, and he's expecting me to come home. Now, being police chief of Lake Woebegotten doesn't exactly come with attack helicopters and hot and cold running SWAT teams, but Harry's a friendly guy, well-liked, and I know he plays Left 4 Dead 2 online with a guy high up in the state police. If his only daughter disappears, he'll start making calls. Are you okay with having that kind of heat on you? Your family will have to pull up stakes, leave Lake Woebegotten, everything."

Edwin drove on, grimly. "We've been fugitives before. We're adept at burning up our pasts and forging new identities for ourselves."

"Okay. That's cool. So you're planning to make me a vampire, then?"

His eyes flicked over toward me. "What?" That tiny movement of his eyes was enough to tell me I had his whole attention.

"Well, you're effectively ending my old life," I said reasonably. "I won't finish high school, right? Going to college is going to be tricky. Getting a job. All that stuff."

"I can support you."

I snorted. "As the one living girl in a house full of vampires? I don't want to be a house pet, Edwin. I've got *ambitions*, you know that. I'd be perfectly happy to join your family, but only as a full member. Otherwise, if I have to be mortal, I need the freedom to do *mortal* stuff."

"This—that—I can't—"

"Pull over, Edwin," Pleasance said from the back seat. "We need to think this through."

"What? No! This is *Gretchen*, Pleasance, she was always cruel, and she's a better natural hunter than *any* of us. Plus, she's *motivated*. She won't lose interest, or get bored, or change her mind. She wants to hurt me, and Bonnie is my most vulnerable place."

"Pull the fuck over, bro," Pleasance said, rather pleasantly. "We're going to talk this out."

I found myself liking that girl more and more.

Edwin made a noise of frustration and slowed down, cutting over to the shoulder. "I can't believe this is happening," he said. "My past coming back to haunt me."

Vampires. So prone to brooding and melodrama.

"Not to point out the obvious," Hermet said, "but maybe it needs doing. There are *six* of us—vamps, I mean, Bonnie, no offense—versus three of them. And to be honest, I'm worth any two of them in a fight. Plus, I'm not sure Jimmy and Queequeg want any part of this. I say we stay and fight. I was a bushwhacker in the War of Northern Aggression, Bonnie, and I *like* to fight. You know what else I like? I like it here, and I don't want to pull up stakes just yet. I think we can take them. We should've dealt with this Gretchen thing a long time ago."

"But the *risk*," Edwin said. "What do you want to do, use Bonnie as—as *bait*? The problem with bait is, *the fish eats it!*"

"Hermet is good at laying ambushes," Pleasance said. "I think we could keep Bonnie safe."

"I have a suggestion," I said. "Or is the worm on the hook not allowed to have an opinion?"

Edwin sighed and rubbed his eyes. "Of course, Bonnie. What do you think?"

"I think you should take me home—under guard—and let Harry know you haven't stolen me away. That way, he won't call the *bigger* cops, and your family won't have to take off, and be forever remembered in these parts as weirdos who stole the police chief's daughter. And then… you lay a false trail."

"How do you mean?" Hermet said.

"I mean, I don't *have* to be bait. Gretchen thinks Edwin is in love with me—knows he is—which is why she wants to kill me, right? So she'll assume he wouldn't leave my side."

"Because I *won't*."

"But you *should*, Edwin." I gently touched his face—so sweet, so cold. "That's the point. She'll think I'm with you. She'll *expect* you to run with me. So she'll pursue you. Take Hermet, too—she got a look at him, she knows he's the biggest physical threat."

"Aw," he rumbled. "You noticed."

"The two of you take off for wherever—Canada, the deep south where I'm guessing Hermet comes from, wherever. Gretchen will chase you. Kill her when you get a chance."

"But I can't leave you here unprotected!" Edwin protested.

Pleasance cleared her throat. "Rosemarie and Garnett and I can keep watch over her."

"I'm not so sure I'd trust Rosemarie to protect her," Edwin said darkly. "After her little tizzy out on the hockey rink."

Pleasance shrugged. "Fair point. She can stay home. I'll just have her whip up some fog or something to conceal Bonnie's house… and us watching it. I believe we can keep Bonnie safe."

I could see him wavering. "But… to *leave* you…"

"It's to protect me," I said. "Besides, you really should end things with Gretchen yourself, in person. It's only polite."

He barked a laugh. "Pleasance, *promise me*, you'll take care of her."

"Or you could turn me into a vampire so I can protect myself."

Edwin looked at me thoughtfully. "Let's table that for now, all right? Perhaps if you survive this, we can talk about whether I want to risk a two-in-three chance of killing you by trying to make you immortal."

That was the closest he'd come yet to a "maybe," so I kissed his cheek. "All right. So it's a plan?"

"Call Rosemarie," Edwin said. "Get her to whip up a concealing fog so no one can see you sneak Bonnie back home. And you, Bonnie, you don't leave your house, tell Harry you're sick."

"Yes, sir," I said brightly.

"You take the car," Pleasance said. "You and Hermet. Get started on laying a false trail. I'll pick up Bonnie and run her home on foot."

"Oh, goodie," I said.

SKANK CALL

FROM THE JOURNAL OF BONNIE GRAYDUCK

Pleasance got me home—but being carried at incredibly high speeds by a woman who weighs less than you do is a weird experience. She assured me she'd keep an eye on the house, with Garnett soon to join her, then faded back into the growing shadows of dusk. Harry wasn't home yet, so I went upstairs and sat in a dark room (as ordered) and looked out the windows at the fog. Rosemarie was a bitch, but she was also a hell of a weather witch: I was used to fog in Santa Cruz, but this was a cloud so dense it looked chewy, and when I opened my window, swirling tendrils of white came in.

I heard the door downstairs slam, and tensed, then forced myself to relax. If Gretchen was coming for me, she'd probably do so silently. Unless she wanted to taunt me. That was an unpleasant thought.

"Bonnie?" Harry boomed. "You home?"

I came downstairs. "Hey, Dad." I did my best to sound casual. "I'm here."

He took off his hat and his gun belt and hung them on the coatrack, then ran a hand through his thinning hair. "Oh, good. I was afraid you'd be stuck at the Scullens. That fog out there is unreal. I'm going to have some car accidents to deal with, I bet, and I'll be lucky if I don't get into an accident myself on the way. How was your visit with Edward's family?"

"Ed*win*," I corrected, knowing he was just needling me—

maybe *that's* where I inherited my tendency to pick at people for my own amusement. Though I doubted Harry took it to the extremes I did. "It was fine. They're all very nice. But I left early, because I'm not feeling well. I think I'm coming down with something."

"You want me to call Doctor Holliday?"

"No, no, Edwin's dad looked me over at their house, he says it's probably just a bug that's going around, it'll pass on its own. I don't know if I'll make it to school tomorrow though."

He nodded, then kissed me on the forehead. So damn *fatherly*. "All right, sweetie, you just let me know if you need anything. I'll be around tonight, unless I get called for some mess out on the roads. I'll be out tomorrow—you might've heard, a fella who lives out by the lake's disappeared, so me and my guy Stevie Ray need to look into that when it's daylight. We'll be way the heck out of cell phone range, but you can call the station and leave a message on the machine, I'll call in and check from time to time."

"Sure, Dad." I went back upstairs, pulled my curtains closed, and stretched on my bed in the dark listening to music through one headphone, and listening to the empty sounds of the night with the other. It was rare to spend a night without Edwin beside me, and it was surprisingly hard to fall asleep. I didn't like that—don't like being dependent on anyone. *When I become a vampire*, I thought, *I'll never sleep again.*

But that night I was still human, so I did sleep, eventually.

Pleasance called me in the morning, as I sat eating a bowl of steel-cut oatmeal at the kitchen table. "Hey, Bon-bon," she said brightly. That hideous nickname, one she'd arrived at independently, but somehow, I didn't mind it from her. She was such a nice monster. "Edwin doesn't want to call you directly, but he asked me to let you know, it's working. Gretchen and Queequeg are tracking them—apparently the other guy, Jimmy, didn't want any part of this, and he took off, but I guess Queequeg and Gretchen are a couple, so he's along for the ride. Anyway, Edwin and Hermet are halfway to the west coast by now. They're working on setting up an ambush. With luck, this will all be over in a day or two."

"You still keeping watch?"

"Oh, yes, just in case. I'm across the road with a clear view of your front door, and Garnett's watching the back. Well, except for the *fog*, which Rosemarie says will dissipate on its own, eventually, but it hasn't, yet. I can't see a thing, but it's okay. Vampires can sense each other, so I'll know if Gretchen or Jimmy or any of them come within a mile."

"Nice trick," I said.

"Keeps us from stumbling over each other in the wild. Saves a lot of bloodshed. Not that we have blood, really, unless we've recently fed. Second-hand bloodshed. Anyway. Just sit tight."

"You're so nice to me," I said. "And I'm just a human. I don't get it." I really didn't. I wouldn't bother with humans if I were a member of a superior species.

"Don't get me wrong, you're likable enough," Pleasance said. "But I'm looking out for you because of Edwin. You make him happy. For the first time in about a century he isn't *moping* all the time. The only other girl he's gotten halfway close to in all the time I've known him is Gretchen, and that was all about lust, he never even seemed to *like* her much."

"I can't imagine why," I said. "She's so charming."

Pleasance laughed. "Just lay low."

So lay low I did. Doing *nothing* doesn't appeal to me, and I didn't dare go on Facebook or Twitter or anything, because Gretchen hadn't been dead *that* long, it seemed, and was probably pretty tech-savvy for a vampire. I'd hate for a bored status update to give away the fact that I was sitting snug in Lake Woebegotten when I was supposed to be in a speeding car out west, running for my life with a couple of dead men.

So I watched TV, and ate a bowl of ice cream—another good reason to become a vampire, I could drink all the tasty blood I wanted and not worry about putting on weight—and mostly just waited. Harry wasn't home by nightfall—he called to tell me he had to take some samples to a lab in another town, related to the disappearance case he was working on, and wouldn't be back until late. I asked when he'd be home, but his cell phone broke up before I heard the answer. There's a lot of wilderness out there, inimical to the trappings of civilization. More than I'd ever realized.

The fog had dissipated a little, but was still thick enough to limit visibility sharply, so even the view from my window was dull. I kept waiting for a call from Pleasance, to tell me things had worked, Gretchen and Queequeg were dead, I could go back to my life, so when the phone rang, I jumped on it, even though it was Harry's landline and not my cell.

"Bonnie." It was Harry's voice, but as I'd never heard it before—breathless, worried, tense. "Bonnie, there's a woman here, she says her name is Gretchen, and she, ah—Bonnie. Don't do what she says, call the state—"

His voice abruptly cut off, replaced by Gretchen's raspy chuckle. "Hi there, Bonnie. I've got your papa here with me. He's a feisty one, isn't he? So, listen. Your boyfriend Edwin *almost* fooled me. I chased him quite a while before Queequeg got a look inside the car and realized you weren't there. It didn't seem likely they'd wrap you up in a blanket and stuff you under the back seat, so I realized I'd been faked out."

Shit, I thought.

"Queequeg's still after them, don't worry, making them think I'm in hot pursuit. But I doubled back. I assume your house is under surveillance, which is why I didn't just go knock on your door—believe me, I'm not normally this roundabout. But, now, I've got your father. And I know girls like you, Bonnie. You're a daddy's girl, aren't you? You wouldn't want anything bad to happen to old Harry, would you? So I'm going to need you to come to *me*. Do that, and I'll set him free. Fair enough?"

I considered. I might be able to bait her into a trap of my

own, with Garnett and Pleasance laying in wait... but vampires can *sense* each other. If Gretchen realized I was setting her up, I had no doubt she'd kill Harry. Why wouldn't she? I'd squish a bug to get what I want, and humans are just bugs compared to things like Gretchen.

It would be inconvenient if Harry died. I wasn't eighteen yet, so I'd have to go back home with Mom... and away from Edwin. Plus, Mom would be unbearably over-protective if Harry got *murdered*, or even just vanished. She'd never let me out of her sight, because Mom is a great one for shutting barn doors after the horses are already long escaped and halfway to Mexico. Then again, I'd trade Harry's life in a moment to save my own. (Sure, he was my dad, and he'd given me life, but gratitude only goes you so far.) But if Gretchen did get wind of some other vamps laying an ambush for her, she'd probably kill Harry *and* run away, leaving me with no dad and a homicidal supernatural ex-girlfriend still on the loose. Family was important to Edwin, too, so if I let Harry get killed, he'd probably think badly of me, and I didn't want that.

My options seemed pretty limited, honestly. But maybe I could stall for time and hope inspiration would strike.

"Okay," I said.

"Great. Meet me behind the high school—"

I snorted. "Are you stupid, bitch? The Scullens have the whole town under surveillance, keeping an eye out for you and yours. Edwin can *see through people's eyes*. You think he's not checking in with the good people of Lake Woebegotten every once in a while? We can't meet here."

"Then what do you suggest?" she said coolly.

Then I got it. The idea. The perfect place. So I told her.

"Hmm," she said. "Why should I let you choose the place?"

"Hello. You have my dad. Isn't the whole point of a hostage to compel my good behavior?"

"Fine," she snapped. She really wasn't too smart—or else she thought I was dumb. "You come, then, and I'll set your father free. Maybe I won't even kill you. Perhaps I'll just take your eyes, or your legs, or mess up your pretty face, and make you less desirable to Edwin."

Yeah, right. As if. "Uh huh. I bet. You know, Gretch, it's not very impressive for you to get so hung up over some boy. Kind of pathetic, actually."

"His betrayal led me into a life of misery!" she shouted. "You have no *idea* what he put me through! I can't strike at him directly, he's too strong, but I can hurt him through *you!*" A pause. "I'm sorry. I really am. It's not your fault. It's nothing personal, really. But you're the only weapon I have to use against him. Come willingly, and I'll spare your father, and make it quick. I don't really want you to suffer. But if you try anything..."

"Yes, fine, consider all the threats read. Shit. All right. I sort of figured my days were numbered—you don't date a vampire if you want a healthy life expectancy—but I was hoping I'd at least get killed while Edwin was screwing my brains out, so I could enjoy myself. This isn't my ideal way to go."

"Life's a bitch," she said.

"And so are you."

"You're making me *want* to make you suffer now," she growled. "How soon can you be there?"

"Well, I have to elude vampire surveillance. Any suggestions for that?"

"Burn your own house down and escape in the confusion. Good distraction, there."

I sighed. "I'll think of something and then travel a hell of a distance, so give me a couple of hours."

"Fine." She hung up the phone.

I thought for a while. Then I made another call.

BEACHES

FROM THE JOURNAL OF BONNIE GRAYDUCK

Sneaking out wasn't that tough, really. I turned off all the lights and put some pillows in the bed so it would look like there was a human shape under the covers (which looks a lot more convincing in the movies, I'll tell you). Then I got all bundled up—the nights were getting cold, and I'd want a hood and scarf to conceal my face—and went down into the basement, then up the stairs to the exterior cellar entrance, which is conveniently located on the side of the house, where I didn't think Garnett or Pleasance were watching. I crept out quietly, leaving the door open rather than risking the noise of closing it again. Getting raccoons or whatever in the basement was the least of my worries. The fog would help conceal me, but I was still trying to sneak away from a couple of apex predators who were making a point of watching me, so I went slow and careful, trying to avoid where I thought maybe Garnett might possibly be.

Walking in the woods, in the fog, in the dark, is tough for ordinary mortals, but I slogged along. At least I have an awesome sense of direction. I made it out to Fincher Road as planned, and waited in a ditch until I heard the rumble of a car engine. It was an old truck, about half the size of my beloved Marmon, and the driver was looking around into the dark. I stepped out and waved, and the truck stopped. I hurried to the passenger side and slipped in, but kept my hood up.

183

"Are you okay, Bonnie?" Joachim Noir said.

"Yes," I said. "Don't look at me, okay?" I didn't want to risk Edwin looking through Joachim's eyes and seeing where I was.

"Dad told me," he said, grumpy. "Though he didn't say *why*. What the heck's going on?"

"You wouldn't believe me if I told you," I said.

"Try me."

I sighed. "Okay. Your elders are telling the truth about wendigos—well, about *vampires*, anyway. They exist. And one of them is after me."

"Uh. Seriously?" He kept glancing at me, sidelong, but I was sufficiently hidden in my hood, I thought it was okay.

"Entirely seriously."

"But, wait, does that mean *Edwin…*"

"Is a vampire," I confirmed.

"That bastard! If he tries to hurt you—"

"No, no, he's not the vampire who's after me. It's… actually his ex-girlfriend. She's got some issues."

"Whoa," Joachim said. "This is pretty crazy, Bonnie. Are you sure… I mean, are you sure they're not just screwing with you? Trying to trick you?"

"What does your dad think?"

"He took it pretty seriously," Joachim said. "When you called, I was so happy to hear from you, and then you wanted to talk to my *dad*, I couldn't believe it, I thought something happened to Harry."

"Well. Something did. The vampire has him. She said if I don't meet her—to let her kill *me*—she'll kill him."

"Holy what the crap!" he shouted. "My dad never tells me *anything*! So, what, you're going to hide out at the rez, and then… what?"

I wasn't sure how much Willy Noir had told him, and there was a lot I didn't know myself, so I just shook my head. "I don't know. I just know I need help. Edwin's family was trying to help me, but vampires can sense each other, so if they go after Gretchen, I'm afraid she'll hurt Harry. I thought your people... enemies of the wendigo and all... I thought they could help."

"Anything I can do, I will. Assuming this isn't all just some incredibly elaborate prank."

"I wouldn't mess with you like that, Joachim," I said. "You're my friend." And the thing was... he *was*. Now, I'm not saying I was *his* friend. I wouldn't hesitate to throw him at Gretchen just to slow her down if she came after the two of us, don't get me wrong, I'm not *sentimental*, but I'd never doubted for a moment that he'd help me if I called, whether because he had a crush on me or was just a genuinely nice guy or both, but it did give me a certain fondness toward him, and I wouldn't waste his life if I could avoid it.

We drove in silence for a while, back to the reservation, down the same dirt roads I'd taken on that trip to the beach where I first met Joachim, seemingly so long ago. He pulled into the dirt quasi-parking lot just up from the beach, which was empty. "So what are we doing here?" Joachim said. "Dad just told me to get you and drive you over here as soon as I could. What now?"

"Now," I said, "I go walk down by the beach, and hope this works the way I planned."

"That sure clears things up. I'm going with you," Joachim said.

I shook my head. "I'm not sure your dad would like that. This woman—she's not a woman, she's a monster—is danger-ous." I'd dealt with my share of pissed-off ex-girlfriends be-fore, but never one who could literally drain the blood from my body using nothing but her teeth. It occurred to me that my plan was very likely suicidal—I was betting on a lot of assumptions. I'm cautious, meticulous, a planner—but I just didn't have *time*, so I had to take a calculated risk.

"Too bad. I'm not letting you go alone." Joachim was cute when he got stubborn—little furrows popped up in his fore-head.

"Okay," I said.

We got out of the truck, and he rummaged around under a tarp in the back and came out holding...

"Are those nun-chucks?" I said. Though I wasn't surprised. Joachim really *was* a teenage boy, while Edwin just looked like one.

"Don't laugh," he warned, and did a complicated swoopy move with his nun-chucks, which looked like a couple of dowels with eye-bolts screwed into the ends, linked by a piece of chain. "I'm badass with these."

The image of Joachim beating up Gretchen with a pair of nun-chucks was pretty funny, but also improbable. "My protector," I said, surprised I was able to tease at a time like this... but maybe you feel more alive when you're pretty close to getting killed.

I walked down to the beach, looking around, though I knew if Gretchen wanted to, she could easily stay hidden from the likes of me. The moon was big and full, and there was no magical fog here, so the water was ashimmer with reflective diamonds... and I realized it looked a lot like my dream, the one I'd had of Edwin and a great beast. *God*, I thought, *don't let my mom's bullcrap about dreaming the future be true.* Though it'd have to be only metaphorically true, since as far as I knew Edwin was way the hell across the country. But that's the whole dream schtick, isn't it?

"Bonnie!" I recognized Harry's voice instantly, though it seemed to be coming from out on the lake, which seemed impossible, unless there was a *boat*, like in my dream—

There was indeed a boat, a little rowboat, and it came into view, but Harry wasn't in it. Just Gretchen, with her long hair streaming in the breeze, pulling at the oars and making the boat skip across the water like one of the stones Joachim had thrown last time I was here.

"Bonnie!" Harry's voice called, and my heart sank, because it was Gretchen's mouth opening: my dad's voice, emerging from her throat. Which meant this was all a trick, Harry wasn't captured, and I could've had Pleasance and Jasper jump this bitch and beat her down. Oh well. I felt dumb, but I'd have felt a lot worse if I'd really intended to sacrifice myself to save my dad—like *that* would ever happen.

Gretchen rowed the boat right up onto the sandy/rocky shore and climbed out. "What, didn't Edwin tell you?" she said. "It's a little gift I had—mimicry. I used to make fun of people all the time, you know, doing little sarcastic impressions, it used to crack Edwin *up*. You should see my Rosemarie impression. Though it's less about the voice than looking down my nose, even at people who are taller than me. Anyway, when I crossed over to vamp-hood, I carried that ability with me, only so much better! I can sound like anybody. I just called up the police station, listened to your papa's voice on the recording there—and by the way, what kind of cop shop just has an *answering* machine, really?—and boom, I had his voice down. The power's great, really awesome for luring in prey... sort of like I lured *you*. And I see you brought a little friend. Pretty dumb, Bonnie. Ha. Dumb Bonnie. Like 'dumb bunny,' huh? Good nickname for you, except, oh wait, dead people don't need nicknames."

Joachim yelled and ran toward her, nun-chucks spinning, and she just swatted him aside without even looking. He landed in the sand near the water and groaned, but didn't sit up. Oh well. Sweet of him to try. Good thing I hadn't been counting on him to save me.

Gretchen took a step toward me. "And that shit I said about not making you suffer, Bonnie? Not exactly true. Edwin's *mine*. He belongs with me. He just doesn't realize it yet. Getting rid of you might help clarify his mind."

I was afraid, I admit it—the way anyone would be, with a rattlesnake staring at them, ready to bite—but I kept my voice level and my back straight. "Of course, nothing makes a boy love you like killing his girlfriend."

She showed her teeth—and, yep, she had fangs, they sprouted right then, each as long as a forefinger, yuck.

"Getting rid of the competition is always a good way to win, little girl."

"Yes, but you did it all *wrong*. Here's the correct way: You make it look like an accident, and then, when I'm dead, you call Edwin up, in his grief, and you're *there* for him, you offer a consoling shoulder to cry on, you get back into his life, and you make him depend on you. You don't murder her *and let the boy you like know you did it*. Seriously, this is like Psychopath 101, Gretchen. You are so outclassed." Mostly, I was playing for time, but we were alone, and Joachim couldn't hear us, so it was also an opportunity to mock and to boast. I can never resist the former, and it's *so hard* having to constantly avoid doing the latter.

Her fangy smile faded. "What are you talking about?"

"You think you're a monster? Amateur," I said. "I was in your situation, back in Santa Cruz. I liked a boy, he didn't like me, he had a stupid girlfriend. So I did a little research and figured out how to disable her brakes—" (Yes, the irony of someone, I assume Rosemarie, tampering with Marmon's brakes was not lost on me when it happened.) "—and she went right over a cliff on the coast road. Boom, crash, byebye. Then I moved in on the boy for the supportive snuggles."

Gretchen seemed interested, despite herself. "Damn. Did it work?"

I sighed. "It *was* working. But see, the stupid girl had a stupid best friend, also hot, and she and the boy had the whole *shared* grief thing going, you know? They loved her like no one else, knew her better than the rest, yadda yadda. So pretty soon the boy stopped paying attention to me, and paid attention to her instead."

"So you gave up? Quitter."

"Never! I knew the boy pretty well by then, and it only took me three tries to guess his password—his dead girlfriend's birthday, how lame, but I tried her first and last names first. He used the same password for all his social networking stuff, e-mail, everything. So, you know. I sent a few messages, to the grieving best friend, ostensibly from him. Not very nice messages. I borrowed his phone and sent her a few choice texts, too. Then I hacked her e-mail—her password was *his* birthday, she must have been angling for him a long time, despite him dating her best friend, don't you hate treacherous bitches like that? I posted a bunch of... unflattering things in her accounts. Embarrassing things. Mostly photoshopped pictures of her in certain compromising situations, committing various betrayals. They got the job done. I'm pretty good with computers, manipulating images—really, manipulating anything. Anyway, pretty soon everyone hated her and thought she was a slut, and she was convinced the boy she liked was the one who'd hacked her account, so she blamed him, it was a big mess. I only meant to drive a wedge between them, you know, kill their friendship... but she was weak. She killed herself."

"Damn," Gretchen said again. "You... it's a good thing I didn't turn you into a vampire. You'd be..."

"I'd be a terrific vampire," I said seriously. "I've got the personality for it. You know, you could just turn me—I don't hold a grudge. We could work something out, maybe. Share Edwin or whatever. Boys love that threesome stuff, and I can pretend to enjoy making out with you, it's easy to fake."

"Killing you is actually an altruistic act," Gretchen said. "Who knew? I'll be doing the world a favor. Hero Gretchen saves the day."

I tensed up—thinking, *Get on with it already!* and beginning to wonder if the cavalry was even coming—but she paused. "Oh," I said. "You want to know what happened, right? How I ended up in the ass-end of Lake Woebegotten instead of in Santa Cruz soothing my cute boy back to mental health? I was pretty careful, never hacked from my own computer, but I used the school computer lab once or twice, and even though I used someone else's ID to log in so I could cover my tracks, there were witnesses who put me there at the times... certain unsavory things... were posted in suicide girl's account. Now, nobody could *prove* anything, it was all way beyond circumstantial, but you know the court of public opinion. The rumor got out anyway that I'd, you know..."

"Facebooked a girl to death," Gretchen said.

"You stole that line from an episode of *The Simpsons*," I said, shaking my finger at her accusingly. "No points for cleverness. Anyway, it was a tough rumor to dispel. The boy stopped liking me. The principal forced me to talk to a psychologist, and while it was entertaining faking her out, it was a little too close for comfort. Nobody had any idea I'd been involved with the *first* girl's death by vehicular misadventure, but if a really smart and cynical and suspicious cop got interested..." I shrugged. "I talked it over with my mom—how these hurtful and untrue allegations were making life difficult—and we decided I should come stay with my dad for a while, here in the middle of nowheresville. Where, to my surprise and delight, I met Edwin. Kinda makes you almost believe everything happens for a reason. I mean, it *doesn't*— the universe is a blind clashing machine that crushes anything and everything without curiosity or cognizance—but still, if I were a fate-and-destiny kind of girl, I'd think it was destiny that sent me here."

"What, to your death? Sorry, psycho-girl, but your fate was to be a late supper for me." She crouched, showed her teeth, and I braced myself, thinking, *Shit, they're going to let me die!*

But I should've had faith. Because just as she leapt, a shape streaked through the darkness and slammed her out of mid-air.

Despite what Edwin had said, I'd expected werewolves, because it just seems like vampires and werewolves go together like peanut butter and chocolate (or maybe oil and water, or *sodium* and water). But this thing wasn't a wolf. It was *way bigger* than a wolf, and much broader across the shoulders, and didn't have a tail, and had a lot less of a snout than a wolf did, and—

"You're were-*bears*?" I said, incredulous, as three more

bears came loping from the woods, converging on Gretchen.

"Fair enough," Willy Noir said, walking down onto the beach, squinting at me. "Were-wolf comes from the Old English *wer*, for 'man,' and *wulf*, for 'wolf.' The Old English for 'bear' is *bera*, so maybe 'were-bera' is better, but that doesn't really sound so good. The great bear is sacred to our people, and the great bear spirit gives us strength to fight the wendigos."

I wondered if there was such a thing as "dire bears," because if so, that's what these guys were—bigger than grizzlies (despite having the coloration of black bears), with jaws big enough to swallow a basketball whole.

Gretchen struggled to her feet and stumbled toward the water, looking around in panic—one of her arms was missing, though it wasn't bleeding, of course—and her eyes locked on mine.

"Yeah," I called out. "It's a trap. Took you long enough to figure that out." I looked back at Willy as three more bears knocked Gretchen down and began tearing her apart. "You took long enough, too."

"We were watching," he said mildly. "You were in no danger. We wanted to make sure she would act aggressively—we're not eager to break our treaty with the wendigos without cause."

"You don't have a treaty with that one, anyway. She's an outsider, not one of the Scullens or Scales."

He shrugged. "Forgive me for not taking your word for that. You consort with wendigos. I couldn't be sure this wasn't some trick of theirs to tempt us into war, using you as a pawn. They aren't above using humans that way. Besides, we could see you talking—it didn't look like you were about to be killed."

I rolled my eyes. "She's the kind of vampire who likes to play with her food, that's all. Lots of taunting and mocking. You didn't overhear any of it?"

He shook his head. That was a relief.

"But, no, not a trick. The Scullens *like* the treaty. They're living as much like humans as they can. I mean, come on." I gestured. "It's not like you guys aren't monsters."

"We are not monsters. We are the *cure* for monsters. At least, some of us are. I wondered if Joachim might—Oh, my." He pointed, and I turned to look.

Joachim was awake, struggling to his feet... but as he rose, he also *changed*. His clothes shredded as his muscles bugled and expanded, and black hair sprouted all over him. His face elongated, teeth popping into existence like pimples after a teenage pizza party, and he snarled and growled, then ran toward Gretchen, who was, amazingly, still struggling, even though the bits of her that were still struggling were separated by some distance.

I whistled. "Joachim, too? He's a were-bear?"

"The first change is brought on by anger and rage in the presence of the wendigo," he said. "He has been around wendigo before—seen them in town—but never with such hatred and anger toward them as he feels now." He sighed. "I should have prepared him better. I tried to tell him, but he never believed me. I might have shown him, but I am his father. I did not want him to look upon me as a beast. It will take some time to teach him to control his powers. It will be some time before he can see a wendigo without automatically beginning to transform."

"That would be awkward if he ran into Edwin at the grocery store," I said. I covered my mouth and yawned. "Think someone can give me a ride home? I don't want Harry to worry about me."

Willy stared at me. "You have ice water in your veins, Bonnie Grayduck. You should have been born a boy—you could have been a mighty warrior."

"Sexist much?" I said. "I can be anything I want, and don't you forget it."

"And yet you choose to be a consort of monsters."

"Listen," I said. "I'm grateful to you. I am. But Edwin... he's not what you think. He's actually *good*."

"He is an evil thing," Willy said. "By nature. But I will concede that, to you, he might sometimes seem to *do* good. Just be careful, Bonnie. Hasn't this brush with death given you pause? Shown you how dangerous your relationship with the Scullens can be?"

I nodded. It *had* shown me that. It had shown me that I needed to become a vampire so I could protect myself, without worrying about some big hairy guys coming to help me.

"I'll get one of the young men to drive you home," Willy said. "Obviously, it's best if you don't mention any of this to your father."

"You don't have to worry about *that*. Tell Joachim to call me when he's, ah, recovered, okay?" Joachim was busily batting what remained of Gretchen's head around on the sand. Vampires in movies often turn to dust, but in real life, they just turn into rotten meat, like anybody does. At Willy's dark look, I dredged up a dazzling smile despite my exhaustion. "Come on. Joachim *must* be a good influence on me, right? Keep him in my life, maybe he'll offset the bad influence of Edwin."

"I can only hope," Willy said. "At least tonight we rid the world of *one* of these horrible parasites."

"Wendigo," I said, looking at Gretchen's twitching remains. "Wendigoing. Wendigone."

SLAYERS ASSEMBLE

NARRATOR

"**H**eckfire," Stevie Ray said wearily. "Harry's daughter is friendly with the undead? And she knows what they are?"

"She does," Willy confirmed, shifting in his armchair. A terrible thumping and roaring sounded somewhere out behind the house, like a great beast was trying to escape from one of the sheds, but Willy didn't seem bothered by it, so Stevie Ray did his best to avoid worrying, too. "Harry doesn't."

"Well, let's keep it that way," Stevie Ray said. He yawned. "Sorry. Was out in the woods most of the day, looking for Gunther's remains." He sighed. "I guess this vampire girl you all, ah, dispatched was the one who killed him?"

"One of them," Willy said. "We think there were at least two other wendigos in the forest with her. The others may have moved on, or they may still be present." He shrugged. "The girl, at least, had a personal problem with Edwin Scullen—who, I might remind you, is the one who broke our treaty by straying onto our lands not so long ago. What if he has other enemies? What if *they* come? Accepting for the moment the dubious claim that the Scullens and Scales are themselves harmless, the same cannot be said of the rest of their kind. What if this Gretchen's friends decide *they* need to come get revenge?"

Stevie Ray squinted into the fire. He hated fireplaces. They were a darned inefficient way to heat a house. Central heat was best, but even a good woodstove did the job a lot better than an open fire. "Then we're screwed, I guess. Unless you're willing to foreswear your treaty and attack."

"No. The treaty holds. I'd rather avoid war, if I can. But my business, really, is Pres du Lac. The people of Lake Woebegotten might want to make... other arrangements."

Stevie Ray cleared his throat. "Um. Like what?"

"I know about your Interfaith Vampire Slayers," he said. "Father Edsel comes out occasionally to try and convert us heathens, you know, and to buy tax-free pipe tobacco, and we got to talking once. He was ranting about unclean monsters and so on, and I realized he knew more than most people do about the creatures in our midst. So we felt each other out a bit, conversationally, and, well. He told me that you told *him*—about the wendigos, and about my people. I'd be hurt at the betrayal of confidence, Stevie Ray, if I hadn't learned a long time ago to never trust the white man."

Stevie Ray looked at his hands, which were just as dark as usual, but refrained from pointing out that he wasn't, in fact, the white man, and that historically the white man hadn't done so good by *his* people, either, because Willy was right—Stevie Ray had betrayed a confidence. "I was afraid, that's all," he said. "I wanted to have some, well, totally human allies in case things got ugly between your people and theirs."

Willy waved his hand. "I understand. All I can say is: gather your troops. Be prepared. There may be more bloodshed. I'll help all I can."

Another thump, and an ear-splitting roar. "Forgive me," Stevie Ray said. "It's none of my business, but, ah..."

"My son," Willy said. "He went through the change for the first time tonight. It always takes a long time to come down, the first time." He sighed. "And I thought living through that boy's *puberty* was hard."

LOVE CONQUERS SOME

FROM THE JOURNAL OF BONNIE GRAYDUCK

"**Y**ou are a brave, wonderful, suicidally stupid, diplomatic-incident-causing, amazing woman," Edwin said, kissing my face all over. We were in my bed, two nights after Gretchen's very timely demise. He'd only been back for about ten minutes, and he'd already called me names, clutched me to his bosom, sobbed a bit, brooded a fair amount, and proclaimed his love in a fairly operatic fashion. He'd finally settled down to snuggling me in bed, which was rather less exhausting.

"I hope Pleasance will forgive me," I said. "I haven't heard from her since I got back, and the look on her face when I showed up at my own front door... she was so upset. I wanted to tell her, but I was afraid—I thought Gretchen had Harry, you know?"

"I do. I understand. And so does Pleasance—once she realized what you'd done, and why, she was very understanding. Rosemarie thinks you're a tactical genius, by the way. She doesn't *like* you, don't get me wrong, but she respects you, now."

Drat. I was hoping she'd keep thinking I was a dimwitted love-struck girl—that would have made taking her by surprise and killing her someday a lot easier. But oh well. I'd been forced to give up *some* of my nice-girl camouflage in the course of saving my own life. "Still, Argyle is... uncomfortable... with the way you brought the tribal elders into all this.

Their were-forms have been dormant for a long time, and now that they're active again, triggered by their encounter with Gretchen... He thinks the treaty will hold, but when they're in their beastly shapes, their hatred for us can be difficult for them to contain. Not unlike we vampires, when the bloodlust is upon us, I suppose."

"They helped me," I said. "Even though they know I'm close with you. I think you don't give them enough credit. But then, I know they don't give *you* enough credit. I can't help but think it could be worked out if you could sit down and talk a while."

"The fact that if they get angry in our presence they turn into giant bears makes negotiating a bit fraught," Edwin said. "I think our current state of détente is the best we can hope for." He nuzzled me.

"Are you sorry Gretchen's dead?" I asked. "I know you must have cared for her, once."

He sighed. "Gretchen was... passionate. Fiery. She had a lot of appeal to me at one point in my life, but she was, hmm, all sizzle, no steak? There was nothing *there*, underneath— just emptiness, need, hunger. Even when she was alive. That became magnified when she turned. She was intolerable, really. I regret what she did to herself, what she became, but no, I wouldn't say I miss her. The woman I cared about never actually even existed. She only *pretended* to be what you truly are, Bonnie: my truest of true true loves."

Given that my entire life is a series of carefully constructed masks, that was kind of funny, but the thing was, I loved Edwin, as well as I could, as much as I was able, more than I'd ever imagined loving anyone else—so I'd keep on the mask he saw when he looked at me forever, if I had to. Maybe eventually it would become my true face.

"So this vampire who turned Gretchen," I said, trying to sound only vaguely interested. "Is that something you guys *do*? Turn people in exchange for cash or prizes?"

"Vampires are like people. Some of us are monstrous and

avaricious. I'm not acquainted with the one who turned her. It wasn't either of the ones she traveled with, at any rate. I gather he lives back east, somewhere."

Hmm. Not exactly the name and phone number I'd been hoping for. Ten years of hellish service didn't sound fun, and going that route hadn't worked out well for Gretchen, but I'm all about contingency plans. Now that I knew I *could* become a vampire, there was no way I wasn't going to at least *try*, whatever it took. "What happened to Queequeg and—Jimmy, was it?"

"Jimmy isn't a bad sort. For a man-eater, that is. He seemed intrigued by our lifestyle, and took no part in Gretchen's revenge hunt. We sent him up to Canada, where there's another group of vampires like us, way out in Newfoundland—it's easier to be a vegetarian there, as there are scarcely any *people*. He says he'll give our lifestyle a try. And Queequeg, well. Hermet was quite cross about Gretchen eluding us, and I'm afraid he took it out on Queequeg."

"Wow. Is he dead?"

"Indubitably. I'll spare you the gory details."

I *like* the gory details, but I didn't say so. "So we're safe now?"

"Yes," Edwin said. "Safe, and together, which is all I want, ever. Oh, Bonnie: I have a surprise for you. This Saturday night, I'm taking you somewhere."

"Where? Our long-awaited trip to the mythical palatial Twin Cities?"

"It would hardly be a surprise if I told you, now would it?"

I might have tried to pry it out of him, but I got the sense he was chafing a bit at his utter lack of control—the fact that he hadn't *saved* me, that I'd been forced to (gasp! horror!) save *myself*—and wanted to assert some manly prerogative, so I smiled like a good little girlfriend and said, "I can't wait to find out!"

Going back to school after Gretchen's dismemberment and

so on was fairly surreal. I kept expecting to see bears come trundling through the parking lot, or to be scooped up and rushed through the halls at 70 miles per hour on foot. Mundane life was both disappointing and kind of a relief. I like excitement, but mostly only when I'm somehow directing that excitement. Edwin wasn't the only one who liked being in control sometimes. Aren't you impressed by my level of self-awareness?

I hung out with J and Kelly and Ike and the others more than usual—Edwin missed a day or two of school because of excessive sunniness. They were all atwitter about going to the Fall Formal. School dances are so lame, and I'd seen their dresses during our trip to Bemidji, so I knew it wasn't going to be a fashion extravaganza.

Then Saturday afternoon came, and when I got out of the shower, what should I find stretched out on my bed but… a formal gown. Not an ugly sequined mess, at least, but a very elegant, white, long dress with delicate beading and a low neckline. It was a *little* bit too close to the wedding dress end of the continuum for my taste, but pretty. "What in the heck?" I murmured, having picked up the not-quite-swearing mannerism from my dad and just about everyone else in this town.

"Do you like it?" Edwin stepped out of my closet, dressed in an elegant black tuxedo. He looked like the lead in a historical drama, the one all the ladies would desperately want to marry. "Pleasance helped me pick it out."

"It's beautiful," I said. "I just hope this isn't your way of proposing?"

"If I were biologically capable of blushing, I would do so now," he said, smiling. "But, no, Bonnie—when I propose marriage to you, it will be far more direct than laying a dress out on your bed."

When *you propose*, I thought. Well, well. Wasn't that an interesting choice of words.

"For now," he said, "I would be delighted beyond reason if

you would agree to accompany me to the social event of the season—the Lake Woebegotten High Fall Formal."

"Maybe," I said. "Depends. Did you get me a corsage?"

"I did."

"Will we be going somewhere fabulous for dinner first?"

"Insofar as the dining establishments of Lake Woebegotten will allow."

"Is there a limousine?"

"Of course there is."

"Will there be booze?"

"I brought a flask just for you, as I, myself, do not partake, and of course, the punch will almost certainly be spiked at some point."

"Sounds like the closest thing to fun I've heard about yet in this town," I said. "Then I agree."

"I'll pick you up at six," he said, and kissed my cheek, and disappeared out the window. It's not every day you see a guy in a full tuxedo leap right out of a second-story window. Life sure is hard to predict sometimes.

I feel like I've built up certain expectations here: including my being kind of a catty bitch. Well, and why not? Most people don't deserve my notice at all, so in a way, they're lucky to even get my mockery. So part of me is tempted to give you an avalanche of snark: about the cheesy high-school-gym party atmosphere; about the girls and their ugly dresses; about the ridiculous "family restaurant" where we had our oh-so-fancy dinner, because nothing goes better with ball gowns than paper napkins; about the lousy band and the hideous dancing by the chaperones, almost all teachers from the school. And if I did that, it would all be true.

But it's not the important truth. Because every day of life is full of petty stupidities and abominable crassness, and those are commonplace, and thus unworthy of notice and mention (unless they're especially funny stupidities).

But it's not every night you get to dance with your true

love, the most beautiful and enthralling being on Earth, just days after consigning his horrible ex-girlfriend to a miserable and violent death. On a night like that, the moonlight seems like a spotlight from heaven shining down on you. On a night like that, every song that plays is your song (even when it's, say, "Open Arms" by Journey or "Cold as Ice" by Foreigner.)

On a night like that, when you kiss that boy, and he holds you in his arms, it's possible to feel like the world doesn't deserve to be burned to ashes, the soil sowed with salt, and the survivors hunted down like vermin.

So, yes: the dance was a beautiful dance, and life was a beautiful life, and I don't have a bad thing to say about it, because nothing bad was bad enough to even slightly diminish the good.

At least, not until I went outside.

I'm going to tell you about my conversation with Mr. Levitt, and in some detail, because it turns out, even though I thought he was just a sadistic bastard, the things he said to me in the parking lot were also actually foreshadowing, and since this journal is just as much a work of literature as the diary of some Dutch girl in an attic, or those people Henry Miller and Anaïs Nin from that Jewel song, or some crazy reclusive millionaire from a million years ago, I might as well have some literary stuff in here too.

Edwin was the most attentive date ever, but he got to talking to his quasi-sisters—they came to the dance with Hermet and Garnett in, like, a gesture of solidarity or something—and my only options were to talk to Kelly about her drunk date or flee into the open air, so I chose the latter. I stepped out of the gym, pulling a shawl around my bare arms, because the reason they call it Fall in Minnesota is because that's what the temperature does: brrr.

"Why, if it isn't Miss Grayduck." This dry old reptile voice came rasping from the shadows by the side of the gym, and I jumped a little, because it's tough to get the drop on me; I usually know when somebody's there, it's called situational awareness and I totally rock at it. Pretty much the only people who didn't ping my "somebody's there" sensors were vampires and were-bears, and I was pretty sure *this* wasn't either of those. More like an unwrapped mummy or a ghoul or something, going on how old he looked.

"Principal Levitt," I said, smiling.

He stepped forward, holding a cigarette in his hands. Funny, I hadn't seen the glow of the cigarette in the deep shadow—had he been *hiding* it, like behind his back or something? So I wouldn't see him, or…? That seemed like… well, something I might do, if I were stalking someone, and if I smoked, which I don't, because, ew.

"Don't tell," he said, smiling through yellowing old teeth. "Smoking is my only vice." He wore a somber black suit he'd probably worn to the funerals of everybody he'd ever known (because he was so old they must all be dead already).

"It'll be our secret," I said. Coming outside to get away from Kelly's blather had seemed smart, but what if I'd walked into the midst of another blather-anche? Old guys could be boring like nobody else.

"Mmm. I bet you have a lot of secrets."

I thought about that. "I get kind of a gay vibe off you," I said finally, "so I'm going to assume you weren't, like, trying to flirt with me."

"Ha." He coughed. "Gay? Not exactly. Not anything, anymore, not at my age, but even in my youth my orientation was probably best described as… ha… 'opportunistic.'"

"Okay then. This just got pretty creepy. I'm going back inside."

"Do you think she screamed?" Levitt said thoughtfully.

I should have gone inside. But I said, "Who?"

"That girl. When her car went over the cliff." He made a long low whistling sound, like a bomb dropping in a cartoon, then said, "Splash. Boom."

"What do you want?" I said, crossing my arms.

"Just for you to know that someone knows what you are, little bird." He flicked the cigarette away. "Now, don't get me wrong. I don't care that you sent some girl to her death—I made some calls, I know some people out west, did you think they didn't even *suspect* you? They just couldn't prove anything about the car wreck. Or prove that you drove that other girl to kill herself. But I don't want you to be too complacent."

"There's nothing to prove," I said lightly. Then I paused. "What, are you hoping to blackmail me? You want me to fuck you?"

"I'd sooner stick my todger in an ice machine," he said.

I took a breath. "Okay. Here's what happened. I came out to the parking lot. You came on to me, said some really inappropriate things, and I just tried to laugh it off, because you're the principal—you're in a position of power over me. Then you *touched* me, and I pushed you away, and then you tried to grab my tit, and that's when I screamed for help. See? This is me screaming." I opened my mouth to demonstrate, but he held up one finger.

"This is what happened," he said softly. "They found you cut to pieces in the woods. Pieces here, pieces there. An anonymous tip to your grieving father, the chief of police, said a pale young man was witnessed fleeing the scene. The police searched your boyfriend Edwin's locker at school, and what do you know? The murder weapon was in there. Along with your bloody panties. His life got... unpleasant." He gave me a smile, like he'd just told me a joke, and my scream died in my throat. "Here's the thing, duckling," he said. "What you *want* to be? Always in control, always a step ahead? That's what I really *am*. And what I *have* been, for longer than your daddy's been alive. And I've *never been caught*. Never had to run away from home to live with relatives to avoid the heat, neither." He lit another cigarette. A thousand years old or not, his hands didn't shake a bit. "Now, people like us, we don't get along with each other so well. Product of our intense narcissism, I guess. And this town is only so big, you see? You can't have two tigers hunting in the same territory. Sure, our approaches are different—you kill classmates with *social media*, while I, ah, prefer a more direct approach, with transients and travelers. But still: we're both tigers. So know I'll be watching you. When you graduate next May, you *go*. Leave town. Stay with Mom for the summer, then go to college. But you don't stay here, or life gets bad for you."

"If you really know what I am," I said, "you know you shouldn't threaten me."

"What, you'll sic your boyfriend on me? His family doesn't eat my kind anymore, which is the only reason I tolerate *that* bunch of man-eaters in my hunting range—they don't count as murderers anymore. So what's your pretty boy Edwin going to do, drain all the blood out of my pet *dog*?"

I stared at him. He knew. He knew about the Scullens and the Scales. Was *this* the human Edwin had talked about, the one who did favors for them? If so, maybe I could have Edwin punish him—but no. Not without telling Edwin about *this* conversation, and risking Levitt revealing things I wanted to keep secret.

As if reading my mind, the old man smirked. "Besides, I can tell the pretty boy things you don't want him to know. He's trying hard *not* to be a monster. Think he'll want to shack up with a girl who *is* a monster forevermore?" He paused. "Not that I expect him or the rest of his kin to live forever. Winter's coming, Bonnie Grayduck. It's going to be an icy one. You'd best bundle up, or you might get caught in the cold yourself."

After he was gone, back into the gym, I stood for a while longer in the dark, trying to figure it out. Why threaten me? Why say those things, if he didn't want me to *do* anything? Why... *fuck* with me?

But then I knew.

He did it *just* to fuck with me. Exactly the way I would have. Purely for his own amusement. Hadn't Edwin said Mr. Levitt was one of the only people, other than me, whose eyes he couldn't hijack?

Because he *was* like me. "Ew," I said.

Like I'd ever let myself get to be that *old*.

SLAYERS ATREMBLE

NARRATOR

That night, after the dance, things got a little bit tense at the third ever meeting of the Interfaith Legion of Vampire Hunters, held in the Catholic reception hall and presided over by Stevie Ray in theory but by whoever felt like shouting the loudest—that was to say, Father Edsel—in practice.

Still, when one bit of news came out, Stevie Ray got pretty loud: "You *talked* to her? You told her you *knew*? Why... why would you *do* that?"

Mr. Levitt sat tilted way back in a plastic chair, a cowboy hat pulled down low, hiding his eyes. "Don't know," he said after a moment. "I thought it would be..."

"Funny?" Stevie Ray said, outraged.

"For her own good," Levitt said mildly. "Willy Noir tried to warn her off, you said, but *that* didn't work, so I thought, okay, maybe her beloved and respected high school principal might be able to convince her of the error of her ways." He shook his head sadly. "That girl is pretty well steeped in depravity, though, I must say. Necrophilia or what have you I guess. I hate to see mental illness in one so young. Or maybe it's just a lifestyle thing, like those what do you call 'em, gothics? The ones who wear black and too much eye makeup and silver jewelry, you know the ones? They have their own day at Disneyland?"

"I don't think Bonnie Grayduck is a *goth*," Stevie Ray said, massaging his temples. "I think she's just... enthralled, or whatever. Vampires can be very charming, you all know that."

"Vampires?" Cy said. "I thought they were moon people? From the moon?"

"They're probably space vampires, Cy," Father Edsel said, rather kindly, patting their insane weapons specialist gently on the shoulder.

"Ohhhh," Cy said. "I gotcha. That makes sense."

"I still think it must just be a disease," the former Pastor Inkfist said nervously, chewing his nails. "The Scullens, the Scales, that girl who, um, met her demise on the reservation, what if they're just *sick*? They could have, ah, porphyric hemophilia maybe? Or even a psychological condition, there's one called, um, 'wendigo psychosis,' actually, and its sufferers—"

"They're demons!" Edsel shouted. "Demons in the skins of men!"

Stevie Ray groaned. This was his crack team? His contingency plan in the event of all-out war between the were-whatevers at the rez and the vampires in the woods? He glanced over at Mr. Levitt, who rolled his eyes as if to say, "Can you believe these guys?"

Levitt was a weird case. Edsel had recruited Inkfist to the cause—said another man of God, even a lapsed one, would be good for them, and he'd even said some high-minded stuff about how fighting literal actual no-fooling supernatural evil might help clarify Inkfist's mind, and lead him back into the light of God, which would've been kind of heartwarming if Stevie Ray had actually believed in God. And Inkfist, who'd taken some convincing before he believed, had spilled his guts to Mr. Levitt, who'd always seemed pretty mild-mannered, but who took the news of deadly bloodsucking monsters in their midst with amazing equanimity.

"I still say we should just go out to their house and stake them all while they're sleeping," Eileen Munson said, not

looking up from her knitting. She was a middle-aged brunette, and you could still see the homecoming queen she'd
once been. She was the only woman in the group, and Stevie
Ray had been hesitant to involve her at all, but she was the
mayor's wife—and, everyone said, the one who made most
of the decisions, with her husband Brett pretty much just a
hand puppet who happened to hold elected office and own
a car dealership—so they'd decided to let her in on it. She
hadn't believed them until she saw one of the tribal elders
transform right in front of her, and even then, she'd just
squinted, nodded, and said, "Proof of were-bears doesn't
necessarily mean proof of vampires—not any more than it
means proof of unicorns, leprechauns, or Democrats with
two working brain cells to rub together—but I'll go ahead
and take that part on faith." She was a hard-ass, no doubt,
and if there was a need for anything really dramatic—evacu-
ation, maybe, based on a false claim about gas leaks or radon
poisoning or an imminent deadly meteor shower—she'd be
the one who could organize it and mobilize the town through
her husband's influence and her iron-fisted leadership of the
Lutheran Women's Circle.

"I don't think we need to go that far," Dolph said. He
was a big man, broad across the shoulders, a pillar of the
community, owner of the local grocery store, big and bluff
and always with a "Hey howya doing" for everybody, but in
Stevie Ray's professional estimation, he didn't have the guts
God gave a pocket gopher, and he had the soul of a cowardly
mouse. Eileen had brought him in, for who knows what reason. Sometimes Stevie Ray felt like he was running a pyramid
scheme—or a multi-level marketing business—where every
person he told about the vampires told two other people, and
so on down the chain. *At least Bernie Madoff got rich off his
pyramid*, Stevie Ray thought glumly, *and had some good times
before they put his wrinkled white ass away.*

"For now, we just wait," Stevie Ray said. "The Scullens
told me they're planning to move on in a couple of years

anyway—people will start to notice when they don't age—and they won't come back here until we're all long dead."

"They might be back in a generation or two, though," Eileen said, her knitting needles clacking. "You don't mind that? That they'll seduce our great-granddaughters, like they have that pretty little Bonnie Grayduck?"

"I don't know that it's *seduction* exactly," Stevie Ray said, "as far as I can tell it's more like true love—"

"Demons cannot love!" Edsel boomed.

"Hard to believe," Levitt drawled. "When us humans are all so loveable."

"We wait," Stevie Ray said again. "All right? No one do anything. No one *talk* to any of these people—or these *things*, yes, Father—until we have a reason to. The Scullens haven't done anything that warrants... direct action."

"But if some more of those traveling vampires come through," Levitt said. "*Those* we can kill, right?"

"I guess... I guess, yeah," Stevie Ray said. "If we can, we pretty much *have* to."

"Long as we get to kill something," Levitt said, and bid them all goodnight.

BIRTHDAY PARTY

FROM THE JOURNAL OF BONNIE GRAYDUCK

About a month after the Fall Formal, when the leaves had all dropped off the trees but the snow was only just starting to come down, Edwin came to pick me up for my birthday party. It was supposed to be a surprise party, but for a guy who has a bona-fide double life that must be protected from discovery at all costs, Edwin is pretty lousy at keeping secrets, and enough hints had dropped that I'd picked up on things—mostly when he said he had a "big surprise" for me on my birthday over and over again.

I was secretly hoping his present to me would be the dark kiss of vampirism, but I didn't expect that. He was pretty stubborn about being unwilling to risk my life and my soul. Our sex life wasn't progressing as much as I wanted, either. He kissed me pretty regularly and copped the occasional feel, but we hadn't even graduated to dry humping, let alone wet humping. Edwin was still too concerned about killing me not-so-softly if he got too excited, and our make-out sessions often ended rather suddenly with him literally jumping out the window. He said he was gradually becoming used to my scent, though, and had hopes that someday we'd be able to consummate—after we got married.

Yes. That's right. He dropped the A-bomb. The *abstinence* bomb. I think I just gaped at him, because he was so matter-of-fact about it—"Don't worry, we'll make love on our wedding night," some crap like that.

I said, "So... wait... you don't want to sleep together until we get married?"

"I think we're both worth waiting for, don't you?" he said, and I remembered he thought I was a blushing virgin. Edwin really was from another time, I had to remember that, and his dad was Argyle, who was so old he came from a time where they probably killed you with rocks if you had sex out of wedlock. *Craaaaapppp.*

Were Garnett and Rosemarie and Hermet and Pleasance married? Turns out, yes, they were, in ceremonies presided over by Argyle. Not a *legal* marriage—it's tough to have one of those when all your identity papers are forgeries and you have to pretend to be your own children or whatever every few decades—but one the Scullens and Scales considered totally binding.

Mrs. Bonnie Grayduck-Scullen didn't exactly trip off the tongue, but if that's what it took to get some hot vampire loving, I'd go along.

So: not getting turned into a vampire, and not getting laid. But he was still smart, strong, funny, and so beautiful I was content to spend hours just staring at his eyelashes, and I had to remember, we had *time*. Patience isn't my virtue, but Edwin was a hundred years old, so it made sense he didn't want to rush into anything.

I put on a pretty dress for the party (with leggings, even though I hate leggings, because there's no other way to wear a dress and not freeze in October in Lake Woebegotten. Though I heard October wasn't so bad, and that it wouldn't really start to get cold until November, when most days would barely get above freezing, and things would get steadily worse and stay mostly frozen until April or so, which I had trouble wrapping my head around. Too many years in Santa Cruz, and only hot muggy summers spent in Lake Woebegotten before that—I just wasn't *prepared*. And while I had a boy to keep my bed warm, he didn't actually come through on the *warm* part unless he'd drank down a whole deer recently. I'd have to sacrifice my thong-and-tank-top for long underwear and flannel pajamas soon, which would probably inhibit my nightly subtle attempts at seduction considerably.)

Edwin picked me up in the Jeep, and his jaw dropped quite gratifyingly when he saw me. "You look good enough to—ah." He chuckled.

"Good enough to eat? Don't you *dare*. Besides, I'm eighteen years old today, no longer young and tender, but old and stringy and tough."

"You still smell fairly fresh to me, my love, and happy birthday to you. You're older than me now, you know—not in calendar time, but in body-time."

I put my hand on his thigh as he drove, piloting the Jeep with his usual supreme and casual confidence. "My boy toy," I teased. "We definitely have a May-December thing going on." I tried to keep my tone light, but it was the one sore point between us, really—his reluctance to turn me.

"I've been thinking," he said. "And talking to Argyle. And—don't laugh—even praying. And, if you're really sure, that you want to become one of us... Argyle thinks there's a way to make the transition less dangerous."

My heart started beating faster. "Really?"

"He's been studying it, you see, the mortality rate, and he thinks it has to do with the period of transition from life to... unlife. The moment can be long or short, you see, and if it's long, as it often is, the brain is starved of oxygen, and the... subject... dies. He's noticed that the ones who turn successfully turn *quickly*, for whatever reason—metabolism, genetics, he isn't sure—while the ones who turn more slowly never turn at all. He believes, with the right equipment, a breathing apparatus to keep oxygen flowing to your brain, and a more clinical approach—injecting my venom into your veins instead of letting me bite you, as is more traditional—that the chances of success would be much, much higher than otherwise."

"I... that's... wow, Edwin." It wasn't quite what I'd envisioned—

him tearing my clothes off and sinking his teeth into my neck and ravishing me as I transformed—but I'd give up erotic romance for a hospital bed if it meant I got to *live forever and have superpowers.*

"Don't get too excited," he said. "He wants to study the problem more—he isn't confident enough in his research to do it soon—and we both *strongly* believe you should go to college and think about the possible transition for a few more years. We can get married before you go to college, now that you're of legal age, if you want to. But my father points out, rightly, that you and I are in the first throes of love, and while I do not expect my feelings for you to ever diminish, Argyle counsels caution. But if, in five years time, if you still love me, and you still want to become one of us… We can do that."

"If you weren't driving," I said, "I would jump into your lap and kiss you so hard your fangs would poke holes in your lips."

"I'm happy, too," he said solemnly. "If it can be done safely, and if we take time to make sure it's definitely what you want, I believe it could be good for us. To be together, always."

"I'll still be pretty hot at twenty-three," I said thoughtfully.

"And that way there will still be time for us to have a child," he said, casually, and at that, dear reader, my blood froze. Well, not literally—*that* would wait until I was a vampire and I went outside in Lake Woebegotten during January, I guessed—but very much figuratively.

"Ah," I said.

"Four years of college," he said, breezy as all hell. "Then, after you graduate, we focus on getting you pregnant. The baby will be born, and then we'll turn you. Unless you want to stay human long enough to nurse."

"Um," I said.

"Argyle says human-vampire offspring are incredibly rare, but not unheard of—it's hard for a vampire to mate with a human without eating their partner, you see—and they tend to be like living people, but incredibly long-lived, with their rate of growth dramatically slowed in late adolescence. They're generally granted some of the powers of their vampire parent without the need to feed exclusively on blood.

"You definitely want children then?"

He looked at me, surprised. "You don't?"

We'd never discussed it. Because I was *seventeen*. But I could see by the surprise on his face that he'd just assumed we were absolutely simpatico on this issue, even though it had never once come up. He couldn't know that I thought of pregnancy as a form of horrible parasitism. That having a human being *come out of me* was one of the most disgusting things I could imagine. That I wanted to be a beautiful perfect immortal vampire, not an immortal vampire with immortal stretch marks or an immortal c-section scar or an immortal stretched-out-vadge. Barf wretch shudder *puke*.

But fuck it. I could pretend to be baby-crazy for a few years, and take steps to make sure I didn't catch pregnant when the time came.

We made it to the Scullen house, where Edwin did his super-speed thing and opened the door for me and helped me down. I'd been over a few times since the day Gretchen interrupted the game (though, fortunately, they hadn't played any more hockey). I liked going over to their place, but there were drawbacks, like the fact that they never turned on the heat (being vampires and immune to the cold), and never had anything to eat or even drink except their weird-tasting well water from the tap. Rosemarie was always a total bitch, but she usually disappeared into her room within two minutes of me getting there and didn't try to murder me again (that I noticed), so that was fine.

But, in true birthday party fashion, when I walked inside, they were all waiting, even Bitchmarie, and they shouted "Surprise!" A big banner with my name on it hung over the ondium Martenot. They even had a chocolate cake with buttercream frosting (just a small one, since no one else would be eating it—as Edwin said, "Vampires *can* eat human food, but then, you *could* eat used kitty litter, but why would you want to?" To which I replied, "You're right, for me, it's unused kitty litter exclusively, because I have standards."

After they sang to me, which was *weird*, because vampires have eerie beautiful singing voices so it was like a choir of heavenly or possibly fallen angels singing "Happy birthday," Ellen presented me with a knife. Not a cake knife, because why would they have one of those? but a big old butcher knife with a blade that almost twinkled with its sharpness. Edwin had told me once how they strung up deer and pigs and drained their blood to keep on ice and drink later, and I guessed this knife had sliced its share of animal arteries, but it was clean enough now. "Go ahead and cut the cake," Ellen said.

I pressed the blade into the table, and they were all standing around me talking and laughing and teasing me about my age… and then someone bumped into me.

I didn't know until later that it was Rosemarie, but yeah, it was Rosemarie. The knife slipped and sliced into the meaty part of my other hand, the one I was using to hold the cake plate steady. It was a fairly deep cut, and a bright gush of blood welled up. I hissed at the pain, and said, "Ouch, be careful," snatching up a napkin to press against the wound.

I realized they'd all gone totally silent. I looked up, and all of them except for Argyle were staring fixedly at my rather profusely bleeding hand, and they'd *all* popped their fangs and started drooling.

"Everyone be calm!" Argyle shouted. "Resist, resist!"

But Garnett made a long low growl in his throat and launched himself at me.

Now, Edwin had gone all vampy too at the sight of my blood, but he had more self-control than his pseudo-brother, and he shouted and threw himself between us, knocking Garnett aside so hard he hit the ground and bounced. Argyle—grown immune to the call of blood through his years as a doctor, I guess—actually picked up a couch, threw it on top of Garnett, then jumped on the couch to hold it down. Meanwhile, Edwin grabbed me in his arms and carried me out of the house, running faster than I'd ever experienced before while I clutched my wounded hand.

He ran me all the way back to my house in minutes—my dress was ruined by the high-speed run—putting me down in the woods out back and then stepping ten feet away from me. He was pale, shaking, and looked terrified.

"Are you okay?" I said. The napkin was all crusted against the wound by drying blood, which stanched the flow, at least.

"Am *I* okay? Are *you*?"

"It's only a flesh wound," I said, trying to joke, but he didn't seem to find it funny. "I can't believe they reacted that way."

"The blood," he said. "The smell of it... you don't under-stand... the whiff of good scotch to a bunch of alcoholics... a pile of white cocaine to a recovering addict..." He shook his head.

"Well, okay, but I mean... I've been over to your house when I was on my *period* before and nobody tried to eat me."

He made a face. He was surprisingly squeamish about stuff like that—mortal bodily functions, I mean—but then, he didn't even *poop* anymore, so it kind of made sense. "That's not... pure blood. I mean, let's say you like wine—that doesn't mean you'd like wine liberally mixed with bits of shed uterine lining. But after you cut your hand, the blood that poured forth—that *was* pure, and the sight of it, combined with the smell, and you must remember, you smell *good*..." He sat down on a rock and held his face in his hands. "You could have died. Garnett could have killed you. Any of them could have."

"But they didn't," I said. "Everything was fine." I sat beside him and put my hand on his arm but he jerked away and stood up.

"What about next time, Bonnie? What if you fall down the stairs and split your lip? Any wound, however trivial, if it *bleeds*, it could…" He stood up. "This was a bad idea. I knew it from the first, but I wanted you so much, I tried to *will* it into being a good idea. But you're human, Bonnie, and we are monsters, and I can't protect you, certainly not for a few years until you're absolutely sure you're ready to be a vampire—"

"But I am sure! I'm sure now! Do it now, and I'll have nothing to fear!"

"Bonnie," he said, his voice full of anguish, "You're so *young*." He took a step back, even farther away from me. "This has to end. I'd rather have you live without me than die with me, Bonnie. And I'd rather go back to my hollow sham of a life than be responsible, even indirectly, for the end of yours."

I stared. "Are you breaking *up* with me?"

"I'm sorry." He reached into his pocket, took out some small object, set it on the rock, sighed, looked at me longingly, and then—poof. He ran, departing so quickly I almost didn't see him leave.

"Edwin!" I shouted, and I know he could hear me, his hearing was amazing, but he didn't come back. I felt dizzy, and short of breath, and like the world had turned upside down and been shaken very, very hard. That morning I'd been looking forward to marriage and vampire-dom in a few years, and now… now I was vampire *dumped*.

I looked at what he'd left on the rock. A little black box, square. I opened the lid.

A golden ring, set with the biggest diamond I'd ever seen in real life, sat nestled in the velvet folds.

"Son of a *bitch*!" I shouted. He'd been planning to propose. At my birthday party. The "big surprise" he'd mentioned hadn't been the surprise party at all. Shit, shit, *shit*.

I ran to Marmon and drove to the Scullen house. The chains blocking the roads here and there were padlocked, and I didn't have the key, but Marmon can roll through chains like I'd walk through spiderwebs, and before long, I was in their driveway.

But no one else was. All the cars were gone. They'd locked the door, but the locks in Lake Woebegotten in general are a joke, and I blew through the back door, which didn't even have a deadbolt. Inside, the furniture was covered in dropcloths, and the closets were empty. They'd cleared out and *fast*. I found my birthday banner and the remains of my bloody cake inside a neatly tied-off garbage bag on the back porch.

I prowled all through the place, hoping for some hint of where they'd gone, but there was nothing... except a note, block-printed and unsigned, in Rosemarie's room. It read, "Shame about you cutting your hand like that, you clumsy little skank. Someone as accident-prone as you shouldn't be allowed around people like us. This is for your own good." I crumpled the paper in my fist. I knew it was from Rosemarie. She'd planned this, known Edwin was going to propose to me, and rather than try to simply kill me again—probably because Edwin was onto that, after the hockey puck incident—she'd bumped into me, made me cut myself, knowing it would freak Edwin out. She'd probably been planting seeds in his mind about my vulnerability for weeks.

I sat on her unmade bed. They were *gone*, in the wind, and there was no way I'd find them again. I felt a wave of black ennui and despair wash over me, and in that cloud, I trudged out of the house.

I didn't even have the energy to burn their house down in a fit of pique before I drove back home.

MOPED

FROM THE JOURNAL OF BONNIE GRAYDUCK

I was in a bad way for about three hours. Harry, who'd planned to have a special birthday dinner with me, instead found me sitting inside playing his zombie killing game, brutally mowing down hordes of the undead with a chainsaw. I wish it had been a vampire-killing game instead.

"Honey, are you okay?"

"Edwin dumped me," I said dully.

He sat on the couch beside me. "What?"

"He broke up with me today, after the party." I didn't stop playing. My chainsaw ran out of gas so I picked up a golf club and started killing zombies with that instead. Not bloody enough. Damn it.

"Bonnie, I... I can't believe that. He talked to me, a few days ago, and he told me, ah, well. Never mind."

I paused the game, and quietly swore. "He asked your permission to marry me, didn't he? Of course he did. He's so old-fashioned."

"He did," Harry said, awkwardly putting his arm around me. "That he did. I told him I thought you were too young, and had only been seeing each other for a month, and he said he had in mind a long engagement, let you get through college first, make sure what you felt for one another was true, and I said that sounded all right to me. I mean, I'm not going to say what you can't do, you're eighteen, it's your life. And anyway, he seemed like a fine boy from a fine family. Maybe he just got cold feet, Bonnie, it could be—"

"They're gone," I said. "The whole family packed up and left."

Harry frowned. "Now I can't believe *that*. They're all gone?"

I nodded my head, and went back to playing the game, and if Harry said anything else, I didn't hear it, and he went away for a while, and then came back, and said, "I called the hospital."

I paused the game again. Waited.

"They said Dr. Scullen called, said there was a family emergency in Canada, they all had to leave, suddenly."

"Right," I said. "Sure. That sounds right."

"So maybe that's why Edwin, ah, ended things, then. He had family responsibilities, didn't think it would be fair to you, to keep things going, when he had to leave?"

"I don't really care why he did it," I said, and almost threw the controller right at the TV—but I stopped myself at the last minute. Control, control, control. Don't let anyone see the violence inside you, unless it's the last thing they *ever* see. "I just care that he *did*. He dumped me on my birthday. He's an *ass*."

"Maybe you should call one of your girlfriends," Harry said, in a tone of manly helplessness. "You know, talk it out."

I gave him a cold look and stormed upstairs and locked myself in my room. I know you want to hear that I sobbed into my pillow, and listened to sad music for days on end, and stared disconsolately out the window, or maybe even spent several months in a sort of vague zombified half-life of auto-matic behavior... but I'm just not built for that. I was mostly pissed off and enraged—I don't *like* it when people make my momentous life decisions for me—and I fumed and paced in my room, trying to think of ways to lure Edwin back, or, failing that, to find another path for myself, as I am a great believer in contingency plans.

And so, after a while, I called up a boy I knew.

POLAR BEAR CLUB

FROM THE JOURNAL OF BONNIE GRAYDUCK

"**N**ice of you to come visit me." Joachim tossed a stone at the lake, and it skipped an astonishing fifteen times before sinking under the waves. "Dad told me you called a couple of times when I was, you know. Sick. Or whatever."

"You never called me back. Something like that could hurt a girl's feelings." The Pres du Lac beach in October was a pretty bleak place, though the lake wasn't frozen yet—just incredibly cold. I found myself looking around for splotches of blood or some other sign of Gretchen's violent death here, but I saw nothing but rocks and dirt and pine needles. The world could absorb a lot of deaths before showing any sign of it, I thought. I sat on a driftwood log, and Joachim stood with his back to me. He'd always been a tall kid, but he was even taller now, at least six foot six, and his shoulders were broad, body rippling with muscles underneath the long-sleeved T-shirt he wore.

"Sorry, I've been going through a lot of changes, and you, ah… You were dating a wendigo. Sworn enemy of my people."

"You're calling vampires wendigos now? Anyway, I don't recall Edwin swearing to be anyone's enemy." I shivered and pulled my coat tighter around me. "Aren't you freezing out here without a jacket?"

He shrugged.

"I guess you probably run hotter than normal, with your

were-bear metabolism," I said. "That makes you better able to stand the cold, huh?"

Joachim turned and frowned at me. I missed his big sunny smile, even if it had been a little puppy-dog-like at times. He seemed a lot more... I don't know... *bearish* now. "That doesn't make sense. If my body temperature were higher, I'd feel the cold *more*. When you run hot, it's harder to maintain homeostasis, you know? A lower body temperature would actually be better for withstanding the cold."

I frowned. Maybe I should've paid more attention in biology class instead of mooning over unreliable vampires. "Ah. So it's just badass Native American toughness then?"

He sat beside me, a little smile quirking at his lips. "Ha. No, I'm cold, I just *grew* a lot in the past few weeks, and now none of my coats fit me anymore. Being a were-bear is hell on your wardrobe, Bonnie. I've only got about three good pairs of pants, and every time I change, I'm going to ruin one of them."

I reached over and took his hand, and he didn't pull it away. "I didn't know what Edwin was when I first fell for him," I said. "And once I *did* know... well, it was too late. I was... enthralled."

"My dad says vampires—wendigo, I mean—have traps and lures to snare minds. Did your mind get snared?" There was naked hope in his voice.

"Maybe so," I said. "But it doesn't matter anyway. He dumped me and his whole family took off yesterday."

He nodded. This wasn't news to him. "They had a big celebration on the rez last night," he said. "Fireworks and everything. People around here—the people who *know*—are glad to have them gone. I'm glad too. I worried about you." He squeezed my hand.

"Yeah, well, I'm sure I'm better off," I lied. "His family hated me anyway. When they weren't looking at me like I was lunch."

Joachim shuddered. "If they'd hurt you... I wouldn't care

about the treaty. I'd have left our land to go after them at home."

I leaned into him, resting my head on his shoulder. "You're a good friend, Joachim. You're actually my oldest friend, now that I think about it, since we played when we were little kids."

"Life sure was simpler back then."

"Mmm. How are you coping with, you know. Your transformation."

He sighed. "Dad always told me when I got older I'd start to sprout hair in funny places, but I thought he meant when I hit puberty."

I snorted.

"I don't know. When the power of my ancestors is flowing through me, when I change, it's... pretty awesome, honestly. So much power, like I can do anything. Me and some of the older guys, we transform and run around the woods some, sniffing, hunting, but we haven't gotten whiffs of any new vampires. We're patrolling, though. Dad says after a few years of no vampires, it'll become harder for us to transform. He says we're sort of like an automatic reaction to a disease, you know? Us becoming bears, it's like the body producing antibodies to fight off infection, and after the infection's gone, the body stays on high alert for a while."

"Is it, um, contagious? Being a bear? Like, if you bite somebody—"

He shook his head. "We're not werewolves. If there even are werewolves. It's a heritage thing, a bloodline thing, as far as I know."

"Interesting," I said. *Crap*, I thought. I'd had some idea that maybe I'd get Joachim to turn me into a were-bear. Being a big hairy monster didn't have as much appeal as being a cold, flawless vampire, but it was *power*, supernatural strength, and I wanted that desperately. Still... even if Joachim didn't offer any avenues to power, maybe he could offer other things. He'd always been cute, but now he was *sexy*, all muscles and raw animal energy seething just under the surface. And maybe he wouldn't have Edwin's old-school no-sex-until-marriage hang-ups...

Yes, all right: I was looking for a distraction. Looking for a rebound, maybe. Looking for a way to reassure myself I *was* attractive and desirable, after getting dumped.

But I was also hoping Edwin wouldn't be able to resist the urge to spy on me occasionally, and that he might look through Joachim's eyes, and see me flirting with him, and get jealous, and *come back*. So I decided to seduce Joachim.

And the way you seduce a boy like Joachim is with machinery.

I lifted up the tarp by the side of our house and looked at the heap of machinery underneath it. "So what is this thing, Dad?" I asked.

Harry looked up from whatever dumb yard maintenance thing he was doing and walked over. "That's my old snow machine."

"It makes snow?" I said doubtfully. "Isn't that sort of un-necessary around here?" The first flurries had fallen the night before, and though they hadn't stuck, they'd provided a hint of the winter hellscape to come.

"No, no, it's a snowmobile, you know. Two-seater, four-stroke engine, 115 horsepower..." He went on in that vein for a while, but I just let the vehicle talk wash over me. "Me and your mom used to go out riding on it back when we were together, but it broke down a few years ago, and I never got it fixed—the city has one for police business, winter rescue and such, so I just use that."

"Hmm." The snow machine was a little rusty, but it didn't look obviously broken, so I figured it was some kind of en-gine issue. "Mind if I let Joachim take a look at it? He's pretty mechanical. Could be fun for me to ride around on this in the winter."

Harry nodded. "You spending time with Joachim, then? He's a great kid, good with tools, too. If he's willing, sure, but

I can't pay him much—"

"It's okay," I said. "I think he's looking for a project anyway."

"Well, you two can use the shed if you want to work on it," he said. "You never struck me as being too mechanically inclined though, sweetie."

Like you'd know, I thought, *what with your encyclopedic understanding of my life.* "Oh, I'll limit my duties to bringing sandwiches and handing him the occasional wrench," I said.

Once we got the snowmobile moved into the shed, Joachim squatted and looked into the engine compartment, clucking his tongue and making various noises of interest and despair. "Well," he said. "Carburetor's shot. Most of the other problems are just from sitting around for a few years. It'll need new hoses. I'm a little worried about..." And then *he* went on in that vein for a while, and again, I didn't pay much attention to details.

When he was done, I said, "Can you fix it?"

"I can fix anything," he said, without apparent arrogance, just matter-of-factly—and that's when he started being *hot*, and this went from being a mere ploy to get laid or make Edwin jealous and became genuine interest on my part. Big strong guy who was casually competent and confident? Turns out, that's my type, too, at least as much as pale brooding troubled immortal. What can I say? I'm a complicated girl.

So here's the part where you'd better just insert a mental snowmobile-fixing montage. Picture us laughing in the shed, me passing him tools, us sitting on the unworking snowmobile eating sandwiches and talking, and a final triumphant activation of the ignition followed by high-fives and cheers. By then it was deep November, and the snow was upon us. Marmon had chains on his tires, and he didn't mind a little snow—weighing as much as a mountain helped—but the thought of riding this fast, nimble snowmobile (possibly with my arms wrapped around Joachim) through the woods was appealing. Like being carried through the woods in the arms of a vampire, only with a big machine throbbing between my legs: not a bad deal at all, as people around here like to say when something is awesome.

On the morning of the inaugural run, with the snow a deep blanket of white covering anything and everything, we bundled up and loaded the snowmobile into the back of Marmon and drove out to the reservation together, where the woods seem to go on forever. We parked at a spot he knew, and then took down the snow machine and I put on a helmet. (Joachim didn't bother. He said since his transformation he could heal just about anything, so he wasn't worried about flying face-first into a tree.) He took the front seat, and I climbed on back and put my arms around him. Despite what he'd said about his body temperature, he *did* feel impossibly warm to me, but maybe that was just in contrast to Edwin—hugging him had been like squeezing an ice sculpture of a boy sometimes.

"Here we go!" he shouted, and then: we were off.

The ride was surprisingly smooth, like riding a jet ski on a placid body of water, and Joachim whooped as we zoomed over the landscape, whipping past trees at a pretty fast rate. I leaned into him more, enjoying his warmth, and the speed, and the sensation of motion. Joachim hadn't even tried to kiss me, though I could tell he was into me. Normally I'm not a shy and retiring type—I don't mind being the aggressor in a relationship—but despite my growing attraction to Joachim, I couldn't shake thoughts of Edwin. All those nights in bed with him had left a mark inside me, and maybe it *was* his magical vampire powers, but I wasn't over him. Besides, what if he *was* watching? If I slept with Joachim, or even kissed him, and Edwin happened to be looking through the were-bear-boy's eyes, what if it *didn't* make him jealous? What if it made him think I'd moved on? Because I hadn't moved on. I didn't wear the engagement ring on my finger, of course, but I wore it on a chain around my neck, the cold metal and cold gem pressing against my skin, reminding me of his touch.

I'd considered doing stupid, dangerous things in hopes of spurring Edwin's well-documented protective impulses, but I wasn't about to go play in traffic or fake a suicide attempt—after all, he couldn't see through *my* eyes, so I'd have to do the death wish thing in view of witnesses, and what if he didn't happen to be spying on me at the time? What if he wasn't spying on me at *all*? Or was too far away to reach me quickly? I'd just get a reputation as a crazy suicidal girl, which wasn't what I wanted.

Joachim slowed down as we approached the frozen lake. "Can we ride over the lake?" I said into his ear.

"Eh," he said. "It's only been frozen over for a few days, the ice might not be that thick yet. Probably we should wait a while." He rode along the edge of the lake a bit, and we came upon a group of boys who'd chopped a swimming-pool sized hole in the ice—which did look pretty thin—and were in the process of stripping off their clothes.

"Whoa," I said. "What's this?"

Joachim stopped the snowmobile and we got off. "Hey, guys!" he shouted, waving, and the other boys waved, too. None of them seemed that shy about stripping down to their underwear in front of a girl, and there was a decent amount of muscly Ojibwe eye candy on display. "They're going to do a polar bear plunge," Joachim said. "Crazy bastards."

"They jump in the *lake*?" I said. "In this kind of weather?" I remembered Joachim mentioning something about this, the first time we'd talked, by the lake. It seemed so long ago.

"A lot of people do it on New Year's up at Lake Como," Joachim said, "to raise money for charity. But these guys, they just do it for the rush."

"Come on, Joachim!" one of them called. "Get in, you wuss!"

Various other hoots and shouted teasing rained down, and Joachim rolled his eyes. He leaned over to me and said, "I mean, I *can*—I'm a were-bear, you know, so I'm closer to polar bear than these guys are—but why would I want to?"

I made a decision. "*I* want to," I said, and started to undress.

"Whoa, are you crazy?" Joachim said. "You want to get in *that* water?"

"Hey, man, shut up!" one of his friends called. "When a girl wants to get undressed, you don't *stop* her."

I might have hesitated to strip down to my underwear around a group of guys I didn't know, but I trusted Joachim implicitly, and he was a *were-bear*—if any of these boys tried anything, he'd punch them onto the moon. "I think it sounds awesome," I said. "How often do you get to do something like this?"

"Okay," Joachim said doubtfully. "But, look—don't stay in for long, and don't let your head go underwater. When you hit cold water, your body reacts, you suck in a breath, you can't help it, and you *don't* want your head in the water when you inhale, all right?"

"That girl's got more balls than you do, Noir!" a boy called.

"Well, now my manhood's been questioned," Joachim said. "So here I go."

Before long, we were both down to our underwear (though that entailed taking off our *long* underwear first)—me in a fortunately rather utilitarian bra and panties, Joachim in his boxers. *So cold.* But it was so cold so fast that pretty much everything felt numb. By then the other boys had plunged in and climbed out again, howling and running in circles and slapping their chests to get their circulation back. We stepped out onto the ice—okay, never mind, the bottoms of my feet weren't numb enough for *that* not to be a shock. "Ready?" Joachim said, holding my hand.

"You only live once," I muttered, and we stepped off the ice into the water.

I've been in the Pacific Ocean without a wetsuit, and that's cold. But I'd never felt cold like this before. My whole body clenched like a fist, and the shock was so sudden my heart stopped for a second, I think. But then there was this *rush* of blood, and this huge adrenaline wave, and—I couldn't remember the last time I'd felt so physical, so in my body, so *alive*. I whooped and shouted and we splashed around for maybe two or three minutes, and then the other boys were there to help us out of the water, and throw a couple of blankets over us. I toweled off a bit, then wriggled out of my bra and panties under the blanket—the boys did a good job of not obviously watching—and then pulled on the rest of my clothes. Joachim and I took seats on the snowmobile and snuggled together under a blanket and the guys joined us, squatting in the snow, passing a joint around (I even took a puff, to be sociable, and because warmth of *any* kind was incredibly welcome right about then.) We spent a pleasant half hour before my ears started to go numb even under my earmuffs and my nose started to run rather unattractively.

My bra and panties, draped over the back of the snowmobile, were frozen solid, like I was the victim of a slumber-party hazing ritual. We said our farewells, and I pressed against Joachim as he fired up the snowmobile and drove us back to Marmon. I turned up the truck's heater and we sat there, parked on the edge of the wilderness, for a while, talking, while the truck warmed up.

"That was great, Bonnie," Joachim said. "I can't remember when I've had so much fun. I mean, it's been… a pretty heavy fall for me. For you too, I know, but… I helped tear a monster apart. I've been having nightmares. And occasionally, sometimes when I want to, sometimes when I don't, I turn into a giant monster who can smell better than I can *see*. You found out your boyfriend was a vampire, and had another vampire try to kill you, and…" He shook his head. "Our lives aren't *normal*. Not even close. But hanging out with you these past weeks, they make me feel normal. Like I can have a life that's not totally bizarre and horrible and monster-filled and unrecognizable." He held my hands, and stared into my eyes, and I stared into his, and we *almost* kissed—but we didn't, quite.

Which, it turns out, was a good thing, since Edwin came back a few days later. But I'll get to that.

A SENSE OF DREAD

FROM THE JOURNAL OF BONNIE GRAYDUCK

Joachim and I spent a lot of time together over the next few days, but none of it's really worth reporting—we didn't sleep together, and he didn't teach me magical shamanic powers, so it was all just ordinary—until we went looking for the meadow.

I'd decided that since even the fact of me swimming in my underwear with a horde of boys from the tribe of his sworn enemies wasn't enough to get Edwin to come back, I should probably start resigning myself to his absence. But I was still dreaming about him, you see; still waking up in the middle of the night and reaching out for a cool unsleeping body that wasn't there; still automatically glancing at the empty spot beside me in biology class; still gazing at the part of the cafeteria where the Scullens and the Scales had once sat, now populated by what passed for the stoner clique in Lake Woebegotten. I needed to get the taste of Edwin out of my mind, and I had the bright idea of overwriting powerful past experiences with new powerful experiences. I have no idea if that approach has any grounding in cognitive science or neuroscience or even behavioral science—I've read a bit about all of those, and they never mentioned my plan—but it seemed logical to me, and worth a try. My idea was, if I had new experiences that were similar to experiences with Edwin—either because they took place in the same location, or the music was the same, or whatever—then maybe the memories would cease to be so specific and evocative and maddening. So I'd dragged J and Kelly to that Irish restaurant in Bemidji for a "girl's night out," and watched Joachim play some of the other boys from the tribe in a pick-up hockey game—only in a place like Minnesota could you have pick-up *hockey*—out on the lake ice. I wasn't sure if the technique was working, but at least when my thoughts strayed to hockey or Irish pubs I had some *other* memory to focus on instead of one starring Edwin.

One of my strongest memories was that day in the meadow, when Edwin took off his shirt (mmmm) and revealed the secret of his mighty vampire smell-powers. So when Joachim came over one weekend I said I wanted to go walking, and, as always, the boy said he was up for anything... but he seemed hesitant. It took a bit of poking and prodding and prying, but I finally got him to tell me why: "We think there's a wendigo—a vampire—somewhere in the area. Some of the guys have been turning, and they say they caught a whiff."

I stared at him, wide-eyed, thinking, *Don't ask, don't ask, be strong, Bonnie, don't ask*, but Joachim understood and took pity on me. "Not Edwin. At least, they don't think so. We know the smell of the Scullens and the Scales. This is someone else."

"So you think he could be out in the woods now?" Every nearby vampire was an opportunity to be turned into a vampire myself—there had to be *one* I could bribe or seduce or convince or trick into changing me.

"It's possible. Whoever it is, he hasn't come onto the rez, so the elders aren't inclined to launch a full-scale hunt. We don't have a treaty with every random rogue wendigo, but there's still some worry the Scullens and Scales only pretended to leave—that it's a trick or treachery—" (I rolled my eyes.) "—so they don't want to leave the rez undefended to pursue this vamp. They usually move on pretty quickly. He may have done so already—or maybe not. Are you sure you don't want to take a walk in my territory? Might be safer."

"You saying you can't protect me?" I batted my eyelashes. For a beastly hunter of the undead, Joachim was in many ways a babe in the woods—the most basic of flirtations turned him into putty.

He smiled. "Oh, I'm not worried about *that*. But you already saw one vampire die—I wasn't sure you'd want to risk the trauma of seeing *another*."

"I have a pretty strong stomach," I said, trying not to laugh. I didn't mind seeing dead vampires—or dead humans, or dogs, or whatever—any more than I minded seeing broken eggshells or rotting apples. Garbage is garbage. "Besides, what are the odds of us running into a vampire in the snowy woods?"

"You do seem to attract them," Joachim said.

"I attract all sorts of supernatural guys," I said, flipping my hair. "I just have the right look I guess. Or odor."

He smiled. "You do smell good, actually. I don't want to *eat* you—"

"Not necessarily what a modern girl wants to hear," I deadpanned, and he blushed rather a lot, which was impressive, given that his skin is dark enough that blushing barely shows. (Edwin wasn't a blusher, no matter what outrageous things I said, but that was just because of his general lack of blood—he was actually trivially easy to embarrass, and thus, to keep off balance, which had its uses.)

"I don't want to drink your blood, then, how about that? But, yeah, you smell great—just not like *dinner*."

Maybe I was evolved to be a predator, too, like vampires were, with an irresistible scent that attracted monsters. Maybe I was meant to be a monster-slayer. If so, whoever was in charge of handing out destinies had made a mistake in my case. Monsters were some of the only things I found interesting enough to care whether they lived or died. "You smell nice too," I said. "Sort of... musky."

We were sitting on my bed, and he took my hand. "Bonnie, are you and me... I mean... I know we're friends, but sometimes I think you want more, and sometimes I think *I*... what I mean is..."

"I'm still getting over the break-up with Edwin," I said. "But I like you, Joachim. You've been great about giving me space and time. I really appreciate that. But... I do need more time, at least. If not so much space."

"Take your time, I'm not going anywhere," he said, and his grin was so big he looked like he could have swallowed the moon. You know, like that wolf, from Norse mythology, Fenrir.

I guess that comparison would work better if he actually were a werewolf. Oh well. Going with the bear thing isn't as, I don't know, poetic. "His grin was so big he looked like he could swallow a whole beehive?" I don't think so.

Though I guess I'm more like a beehive than I am like the moon.

We went walking in the snow, on high alert for vampires. At least, I was—Joachim didn't seem to be paying attention to much of anything but me, and making sure I didn't step into a hole lurking under the snow, though how he could tell where the holes were was beyond me. A were-bear thing, presumably. The forest trails were moderately snowy, with a crust of ice on top like nature's crème brûlée, and the ground cover gave off a pleasing crunch under my boots with every step, like the snap of many small bones being broken all at once.

It took us a while to find the meadow, and when we did, it didn't look much like it had before. Those unseasonable wild-flowers—had they grown under Rosemarie's weather-witch influence, I wondered?—were either dead or buried under white, which amounted to the same thing. Still, there's some-thing nice about a pristine vast expanse of snow, something that makes me want to do damage or make a mark, so we ran through the meadow laughing and scooping up snowballs, which I aimed with deadly accuracy. Joachim never hit me, even once, I assume because he thinks you shouldn't smash girls in the face with snowballs, though he knew enough to make it look like he was trying and failing when in reality he wasn't really trying at all. Though come to think of it, just barely missing a girl's head with a snowball is probably a trickier throw than merely hitting her.

We messed up the snow good, gouging trails that looped around and over and back, until we'd worked our way to the far side of the meadow—and that's when Joachim froze, and his nostrils flared visibly. "Wait," he said. "Something's here."

The vampire, I thought, and looked around, though I knew from Edwin's time spying on me in my room that if a vampire didn't want to be seen, you probably wouldn't see him. Joachim sniffed again, frowned, and shook his head. "It's a vampire, but… it smells like Gretchen did, after we were finished with her. Cold, and wrong, and rotten, but *dead*."

"Wait. There's a *dead* vampire in the meadow? Like, dead dead?"

"Like dead dead," he confirmed, and walked toward the treeline, with his head held low, staring at the ground. "Look, here, the ground's been disturbed."

He was right. In under the evergreen trees, the falling snow couldn't magically carpet over all signs of human disturbance, and there were quite a few footprints and enough splotches of dirt to indicate that someone had dug a hole and then tried to cover it up with snow and pine needles. "Shame we didn't bring a shovel," I said.

"Whatever it is, it's not deep." He hunted around until he found a thick branch, and poked it into the snow, gouging out hunks of soil, then tore off a needle-thick evergreen branch and used it as a broom to sweep away the cover.

There, about a foot underground, was the dirt-encrusted headless body of some kind of dead dirty hippie.

Joachim sniffed at the hole, then jerked his head back and wretched, like someone getting a face full of sour milk. I couldn't smell anything—cold is the great preserver, and who knew if vampires even rotted like normal people did?—but I lacked Joachim's finely-tuned senses.

"Where's the head?" I said.

"If whoever killed him knew he was a vampire—and how could they not?—it's buried separately. You want to keep the pieces apart. Let me see..." More sniffing, more walking, and deeper in the woods we found another patch of dug-up earth, and inside that...

"It's Jimmy," I said. The dead vampire's hair was only marginally dirtier from his time in a shallow grave, but only because it had been plenty dirty before. "He was with Gretchen and Queequeg, but he didn't take part in the hunt for me. I wonder what he was doing back here?"

"I'm less curious about that, and more curious about what killed him," Joachim said, frowning.

"Maybe one of your boys decided to do some unauthorized hunting?" I said.

Joachim shook his head. "No, the only way we're a match for a vampire is in our beast form, and then, we tear them apart. Anyway, we'd burn the remains, not do it like this. His head was severed by a tool of some kind, axe or shovel, I'm not sure, and I don't want to get close enough to find out. There were stab wounds and bullet wounds on his body, too. Not our style." Joachim wrinkled his nose. "Somebody threw up near here, too. I smell... used tuna hotdish. I could have done without smelling that."

I hadn't noticed either gunshot wounds or vomit, but I hadn't put my face as close to the corpse as he had. "So... a *person* killed him?" I said.

Joachim nodded. "I think so. Another vampire wouldn't have bothered with guns or knives either."

"But a *human* killing a *vampire*... isn't that like a gazelle killing a lion?"

"Pretty much," Joachim said, thoughtfully. "But I wonder, if enough gazelles got together—do you think they could *kick* a lion to death?"

"Hmm." I was thinking about other humans who knew about vampires, locally, and I only had one name: Mr. Levitt. And if he really got his jollies murdering people, as he'd certainly implied, then was it possible he'd decided to level up and try to kill a vampire?

And if so, how was it my problem? I didn't care if Jimmy died, and the only vampires I did care about were long gone. If Mr. Levitt decided to start hunting were-bears, *then* we might have issues.

SLAYERS DISSEMBLE

NARRATOR

Narrator here. This part I'm about to recount actually happened a day or so earlier than the bit Bonnie wrote about above, but I decided to put it here for, what do you call it, dramatic effect. I never much cared about that sort of thing before, but what with Bonnie's interest in fore-shadowing and so forth I thought I might as well give it a try myself. So here goes:

"That was amazing." Eileen sipped from a small glass of sherry, and her eyes were fixed and glassy, her hands trembling.

"Not quite the word I would have used," Stevie Ray said. His own hands, wrapped around a beer bottle he hadn't even sipped from yet, were steady, but that was probably just because he'd gotten his adrenaline aftershocks out by puking behind a tree. "But I might go with 'necessary.'" They were in the Backtrack Bar, where Stevie Ray worked as occasional bartender and bouncer, as if it ever got rowdy enough to need a bouncer. He had keys, and the owner Ace didn't mind if he came in after hours, as long as he kept track of everything he drank and settled up the next day. The bar closed at 1 a.m., and at 1 a.m., Stevie Ray had been in the woods with the six other members of the Interfaith League of Vampire Slayers, doing what their name implied they should do. He was still amazed they'd all survived.

"Didn't look like any moon person I ever saw." Cyrus, on

his bar stool, squinted at the ceiling, as if he might see the moon through the ceiling.

"Nonsense," Father Edsel boomed from a couch in the corner. "Did you see him? Pale as moonlight! Eyes as black as the depthless depths of space!"

He'd had brown eyes, as far as Stevie Ray could tell, but it wasn't like that was the relevant part to object to, and he didn't have the energy to combat Cy's lunacy. Besides, when you were talking about killing vampires, how was that objectively any crazier than believing the moon was a hollow spaceship full of aliens spying on you?

Well, mainly because the vampires were real, he supposed.

"I wish he'd turned to dust," former-Pastor Inkfist said gloomily.

Mr. Levitt snorted. "Wouldn't that be neat and clean? Would've spared us having to try to dig up that frozen ground. That grave was so shallow we might as well have just covered him over with some leaves."

"If he'd turned to dust," Inkfist went on doggedly, staring at the glass of soda water between his hands, "then we'd know for *sure* he was a vampire, that's all I mean."

"He has a point," Dolph said, but Eileen suddenly snapped her head up, and the focus came back into her eyes, and she sniffed loudly.

"The way he jumped around, bouncing from tree to tree like he was made of rubber, that looked like something ordinary and human to you?"

"Could've been he was on drugs or something," Inkfist said. "Cocaine gives you energy, doesn't it?"

"And the way he kept coming even when Cyrus unloaded on him with those automatic weapons? He didn't even *pause* until a few bullets went into his skull." Eileen sounded justifiably proud about that bit. She'd been the bait, playing little girl lost in the woods, but she'd had a big old .45 caliber handgun in her purse, and she'd put a bullet right in the middle of the vampire's face while he was trying to figure out who was shooting him from the shadows.

"PCP," Dolph said. "Like in the movies, the angel dust, they say fellas on that, you can shoot them point-blank and they'll just keep trying to get at you. And who told us he was a vampire?"

"I told you," Stevie Ray said. "One of the elders at Pres du Lac. They know about this stuff. In their, you know. Culture."

"Heathens," Edsel said, but without much heat, and Inkfist sighed heavily.

"But see," Dolph said, "what if it was just some fella the Indians—I'm sorry Native Americans—wanted killed for some reason?"

"You people," Mr. Levitt said. "Even if it *was*, how does it make sense for the tribe to dupe a group of people from the next town over to do their killing for them? It's not exactly a clever plan. Anyway, he was a *vampire*. What about when we cut his *head* off, and he kept trying to bite us, and rolling his eyes, and even trying to talk for a good ten minutes?"

"It's like in the French Revolution," Dolph said. "Isn't it? They cut off somebody's head, with a guillotine or such, and the eyes just keep on blinking and the mouth keeps moving, doesn't it?"

"No," Mr. Levitt said flatly. "When you cut someone's head off, there might be a twitch or two, but they don't try to *eat* you. Not if they're human. And you saw the fangs, they were as long as golf pencils—why are we even talking about this? We shot him and cut off his head and he didn't *bleed*."

"I know you're right," Inkfist said. "I still wish he'd turned to dust though. Neater that way."

"No denying that." Levitt took a gulp of rotgut whiskey like it was water. "Body disposal's a right pain in the bottom. But I don't imagine anybody will come looking for that fella. We were right up against the middle of nowhere anyhow. When the weather gets warmer we can go back and dig a better grave, if anything's left of him."

Oh goodie, Stevie Ray thought. Still, it *had* been the right thing to do, hadn't it? A couple of fisherman had disappeared the week before, nothing left but their rods and creels and ice saws and a few spots of blood on the frozen surface of the lake, and Harry's investigation hadn't turned up anything, of course. With the Scullens and Scales gone, Stevie Ray hadn't immediately thought *vampires*, but when Willy Noir called to say they'd sensed a wendigo in the area, he hadn't exactly been surprised. He'd hesitated before calling Edsel and his merry band, but not for long. How was he going to take on a vampire by himself? So they'd gone out on patrol, roaming the woods in pairs, in touch with each other via walkie-talkies and armed with some of the truly distressing ordnance from Cy's bunker, and on the third night, their bait had drawn the hunter, except they were the hunters and the vampire was the prey, or whatever. They'd killed him. He'd seemed more stunned than frightened, right up until Levitt severed his head with a machete.

The vampire, Stevie Ray thought, looked like a bear who'd just been mobbed and attacked by a whole bunch of salmon. He'd clearly thought they were ridiculous right up until the moment Eileen shot him in the face and Levitt took his head off.

Stevie Ray hadn't fired a shot or swung a blade, he'd been covering an avenue the vampire hadn't tried to escape down, but he'd puked up his guts anyway. Oh, hell. Could you get DNA off puke? You couldn't from crap, but from puke, sure, why not, had to be bits of throat and stomach lining in there, right? What if somebody found that body and found the vomit and did a test and placed him at the scene? Oh, lord, he'd have to go back out there and dump some bleach all over his own throw-up, it was the only way to be safe. He groaned. Covering up crime scenes wasn't what he'd had in mind when he became a cop.

He looked at the beer in his hand. It was his fifth. He wouldn't be going back to the woods to clean up things tonight—he'd just get lost and freeze to death. He'd already confiscated the guns they'd used, and he planned to get rid of those tomorrow morning to make sure no ballistic evidence would be recovered, so he'd go back to the woods and deal with the puke after that.

Inkfist was right. A dead body turning to dust *would* have been a lot easier.

Mr. Levitt went with Stevie Ray. They took a can of kerosene and a bottle of bleach, and trudged through the snow, and when they got to the crime scene… they saw the remains had been disturbed. "Must be animals, right?" Stevie Ray said, desperately hoping.

Levitt knelt and looked at the ground. "Not animals," he said. "Look at those footprints. People. Hmm. Wait here." He loped off through the woods—the fella was spry for someone on the far side of 70; heck, he was spry for someone 30 years younger. Stevie Ray went ahead and poured bleach over his vomit, just in case it wasn't a lost cause. Say some hunters had found the corpse. They'd have to walk a while to get a signal on their cell phones, probably. And then it would take Harry a while to get out here to the woods. Not a real long while, though—he knew the woods pretty good, and took his job seriously. He'd be calling Stevie Ray to assist, probably, but of course, Stevie Ray was already at the crime scene, contaminating evidence. Maybe if they moved the body, when the hunters got back here with Harry, there'd be no body here, no physical evidence at all, and Harry'd just think they were drunk or—

Mr. Levitt returned. "Got a look at him," he said, not even breathing hard. He was holding a pair of binoculars. "They didn't notice me though. It was one of the Ojibwe boys from the reservation, which could be a lucky break, if he's one of the ones who knows about vampires, and hates them to pieces. But the other one…"

"What?" Stevie Ray said.

"Bonnie," Levitt said grimly. "Harry's daughter. You know.

The *vampire* lover."

"Oh for damn," Stevie Ray said, numbness washing over him. "The boy was probably Joachim Noir, Harry said she was spending a lot of time with him. He's all right, Willy Noir was the one who told us there was a vampire to kill. I don't think he'll mind. But Bonnie... you're right, she did love one, but what does that mean? What will she do?"

"Let's sanitize this crime scene," Mr. Levitt said. "Should've done it last night, but we didn't have the tools or the time or the energy. Make sure if she *does* decide to tell her daddy she found a body in the woods, there's no body to find when Harry gets here. Then, who cares what she does?"

"Makes sense," Stevie Ray said. "But it makes me nervous. She'll be curious, you know, and what if she starts making waves, asking questions, sniffing around..."

"I wouldn't worry," Mr. Levitt said, pulling on his gloves. "Problems like these have a way of working themselves out."

THE INEVITABILITY OF DEATH

FROM THE JOURNAL OF BONNIE GRAYDUCK

J oachim told his dad about the vampire we found, and he took the news stoically—I'm good at reading people, and Willy Noir was hard to read, and it's not because of some "inscrutable Indian" bullshit either, since his son was an open book to me, and not even a book with lots of words in small type, but a big colorful picture book, practically a pop-up book. Willy loaded us up in his truck and drove us on a long and silent trip pretty much back where we'd come from, and then a tromp through the same old woods again, which was boring.

But things got less boring, and not in a good way, when we reached the spot where we'd found Jimmy's body, because Jimmy's body wasn't there anymore.

"But—but—I swear, it was *here*," Joachim said.

Willy Noir nodded. "I believe you. I can smell there was *something* here. But I also smell... bleach?" They sniffed around—seeing two grown men wandering around the trees with their noses in the air, sucking wind through their nostrils, was pretty comical. Turns out the puddle of puke was now a puddle of bleach.

"Whoever killed Jimmy came back and covered up their crime scene," I said.

Willy Noir nodded. "Which is all I was going to do, so— wonderful. Saved me the trouble."

I frowned. "What do you mean?"

He shrugged. "Dead wendigos superficially resemble dead humans. It's enough to get the police involved and cause a lot of difficulty, and inquiries, and when a pathologist notices peculiarities in the corpse.... Wendigos are ferocious about keeping their secrets. How do you think they *stay* secret? Whenever it seems like they're going to become public knowledge, they take steps—killing lawmen, burning down hospitals so autopsies can't be performed, making it all look like an accident, some using their mind-powers to remove memories or implant false ones. I don't care who killed the wendigo you call Jimmy—in a war, if someone else wants to attack your enemy, why complain?—but I was concerned they'd left evidence to be discovered. Apparently they realized their mistake and took steps to correct it. Fine with me." Willy fixed me with a stare. "Is that all right with you, Bonnie? Or do I misunderstand you? Are you concerned for the so-called *victim*?"

Actually, I didn't know Jimmy at all, and if I'd happened upon him one day and he was on fire, I probably wouldn't have bothered to kick sand over him. But acting like all vampires were mindless killing machines deserving of death was dumb, and, dare I say it, racist. Somehow it had never occurred to me that the member of an oppressed people could be a racist, but there it was. Nevertheless, I said, "The only good wendigo is a dead wendigo. Still. I wonder who might have killed him."

Willy shrugged. "There have always been humans who learned of the existence of wendigo, who were brave enough to do something about it. From Abraham van Helsing to Anita Blake."

Who were both fictional but I didn't say that, either.

"Anyway, that's the only wendigo we've sensed in a while," Willy Noir said. "So we're all safe now." And he trudged on back to his truck, and we trudged with him. I got Willy to drop me at home.

If I'd realized that was the night I was going to die, I

probably would have had them take me someplace else. Maybe Cafe Lo. I always liked ice cream. It would have been nice to have ice cream one last time.

You can actually make a sort of sorbet out of blood, but it's just not the same.

Harry was out of town for the weekend at some kind of small-town law enforcement convention in the Twin Cities, and I was just puttering around the house, trying to keep myself occupied and keep up appearances. I'd spoken to Kelly and J on the phone a bit, doing the fake girl-talk thing. They both liked me even more once Edwin dumped me—the appearance of vulnerability is very appealing to the weak, I've found—and in the interests of building my unimpeachable public mask, I'd nurtured our relationships. When I wasn't with Joachim, I was with them. I figured even if I wasn't marrying Edwin, I'd need bridesmaids someday. (I didn't expect them to be Kelly and J, really—college friends seemed more likely—but you could never be too careful. If I'd learned anything from the vampires and were-creatures of my acquaintance, it was that monsters have to be careful about appearing to be human.)

After I hung up with them and microwaved a bag of popcorn, I thought about calling Joachim. I was thinking it might be time to give in to the tension between us and just have hairy were-beast love. It would probably be hot and messy and passionate and wild, I thought, while I'd expected sex with Edwin would have been a precise and (of course) rather cold affair. Both had their appeal, of course, and I spent some time on the couch painting my toenails and pondering the potential joys of were-vamp-human love triangles. I figured Joachim would come running if I rang him up, and why shouldn't I? Edwin wasn't watching, he was probably on to his next piece of hot mortal teenage ass by now, having lost all interest in me the moment I turned eighteen and ceased to be jailbait, Gretchen had probably been right—

The old man was good. I have to give him that. I didn't have the senses of a wendigo, but I was a long way from un-observant, and I didn't hear him pick the lock on the back door and slip in and creep up on me in the living room at all. My preference out in the world is to sit with my back to walls, with my eyes on the entrance, but—dumb, I know—I'd come to feel safe and secure in Harry's house over the months. Why not? My dad was a cop, and for a long time I'd had a vampire keeping an eye on the place, and it's not like Lake Woebegotten is a hotbed of home invasion crime. So I was on the couch, which is in the middle of the living room, and so the old man got me, fair and square.

I felt the needle slide into my neck, and managed to get halfway off the couch before slumping down against the cushions, still aware, but with my limbs numb and useless.

"I can only assume vampires use some sort of paralytic venom," Mr. Levitt said, stepping around the couch and gently placing a hypodermic needle on the coffee table. I wondered what he'd injected me with—I was paralyzed, but not numb. Clearly he had better serial killer pharmaceutical mojo than I did. "I mean, I can't be sure, having never seen one work, but it seems likely. Draining all the blood out of somebody must take a while, right? I wish I'd seen how they feed. I don't know if it's messy or neat, though I suspect the popular image of two tiny puncture holes in the neck is less accurate than tearing out the throat and feeding from the artery."

I tried to say something—*Why are you doing this*, maybe—but could only manage a sort of grunted croak.

He seemed to understand anyway. "Remember when we chatted at the Fall Formal? How I, well, you know, suggested murdering you? The more I thought about it, the better that idea sounded. Not so much because you're a threat to me—any more than a newborn lion cub is an immediate threat to the patriarch of the pride—but you're something of a loose end, aren't you? I certainly *hinted* to you about the kind of person I am, which wasn't too smart, but you know our kind, you and I, sometimes we can't resist the urge to boast. And now seems like the perfect time to get rid of you. Your father's out of town. Your vampire boyfriend isn't keeping an eye on you anymore. So when you *are* found in a terrible state, here, well, certain people in the know will assume you were killed *by* a vampire, possibly even your departed boyfriend. Why, we may even need to bring your father into the Interfaith League of Vampire Slayers—I know, a silly name, but it makes them feel better, having an *organization*. He'd be a great addition, now that I think about it, and with the death of his daughter as a motive to drive him, oh, he'd become a scourge of the undead."

I gurgled.

He nodded. "I'd be upset, too," he said. "But this is what I do, and this is where we are, and this is how it's going to be." He grabbed me by my feet and yanked me off the couch, and I thudded to the floor, banging my head painfully on the hard wood. Not hard enough to knock me out, unfortunately. I could have done without consciously experiencing what came next. Mr. Levitt unfolded a knife bag like chefs use on those cooking reality shows and drew out a shining blade. "Messy, I think, around the throat," he said, and I tried to scream, but I couldn't, not even when what he was doing started to hurt.

I don't remember much of what happened after I blacked out from the pain, but here's what I can reconstruct, based on what I heard later:

Joachim had been lurking around my house. When I asked him why later, he got very sheepish and said having found one vampire in the woods made him worried there might be others lurking with a grudge against me, so he was out sniffing around in the general vicinity of my house, sort of on guard-bear duty. Personally, I think he was trying to work up the nerve to come in and try to seduce me—doubtless in an endearingly puppy-doggish way—but who knows? He says he smelled humans in the vicinity, but didn't smell any vampires, so he didn't worry about it, having no reason to expect humans to mean me any harm. He didn't pay any particular attention to the human's scent, either, which was good for me, as it turned out. Otherwise he would have torn Mr. Levitt apart, I'm sure, which would have been a shame.

Anyway, he got a sudden whiff of blood, he says, and worried about me, so he rushed the door. Being still in human form, and thus possessed of no particularly superhuman strength, he settled for pounding wildly on the locked front door. The noise was enough to startle "the killer" as Joachim called him. I objected, at first, but he pointed out that I *had* been killed, so it was an accurate descriptor. Hard to argue with that.

Mr. Levitt took off out the back, and Joachim finally decided to try the back door, but in such a way that their paths never crossed. Joachim rushed into the living room and found me on the floor, bleeding grievously all over the hardwood, breathing but just barely, with blood bubbling up out of my mouth. He held me in his arms and cradled me and, I imagine, wept manly tears of manly sadness, though he's never told me so.

Then things got interesting, and I wish I'd been there to see it: Edwin arrived. He burst through the back door, raced into the living room like a man made of lightning, knocked Joachim aside, and then bent over me. Joachim, in the presence of a wendigo, began to transform into his bear form, but before the transformation took hold completely, he growled, "Save her!" And then fled into the woods, I guess in case his basic vampire-killing instincts got the better of him.

So my beloved Edwin gazed into my eyes, and knelt before me, and knew I was going to die, and that he was my only hope for any kind of survival, and he bowed his head to my ruined throat, and pressed his lips against my wound, and let my blood flow into him as his essence (or venom, or virus, or whatever it is) flowed back into *me*.

And that, dear reader, is how I became a vampire.

I have *some* memory of the transition—the way you remember fever dreams. Edwin took me to his family's home, and put me down in his own room, where I sweated and writhed and howled and clawed at the air for nearly twenty-four hours. Argyle was on hand—the whole family came back when they realized Edwin was gone—but he couldn't do much for me, at that point. They weren't sure if I would make it, but on Sunday morning, I opened my eyes, and licked my lips, and croaked the word "Hungry."

Edwin fed me pig's blood, by hand, from a turkey baster, until I had the strength to sit up in bed on my own on Sunday afternoon.

Meanwhile, Joachim cleaned up the blood—he did a good job; Harry came back from the conference and didn't notice anything amiss. Good thing Levitt hadn't stabbed me on the couch. Getting blood out of cushions is hell. Joachim also did a sort of half-assed investigative job to find out who'd tried to kill me, but Mr. Levitt hadn't exactly left much in the way of evidence, and Joachim didn't know what he was looking for anyway. He didn't come to visit me during my convalescence, and who can blame him? Dropping a were-bear in a nest of vampires is a dangerous idea. All the Scullens and the Scales stopped in to check on me, except for Rosemarie. Shockingly, she wasn't thrilled at my transition to her kind, thinking she'd be stuck with me forever, now.

Boy, was she wrong.

"Edwin," I croaked, once I'd finished slurping down a bellyful of blood (which tasted like savory miso soup, more than anything else—hot, salty, delicious). "How? You were gone, you left me, why...?"

"I never stopped watching you," he murmured, touching my face gently. "Through the eyes of others. I'm sorry, I didn't mean to pry, and I really meant to make a clean break, but I knew how my heart was breaking, and if you were anything like me, I was afraid you might suffer, hurt yourself, or just allow yourself to be hurt by negligence. I was... both relieved, and perhaps a little stung, when you seemed to move on so quickly."

I laughed, but it was a rasping thing. "I was just trying to distract myself, Edwin. You left a hole in me when you left, and I did my best to fill it however I could."

"When I realized you were spending so much time with Joachim, I was... conflicted. Glad you had such a formidable protector with you, but jealous, too, of course, of your growing closeness to a sworn enemy of my kind. I watched you often through his eyes. And as the two of you grew closer, my jealousy grew. The way he looked at you... and the way I saw you looking *back* through his eyes... I knew I couldn't live without you, no matter how dangerous it might be, for either of us. I returned two nights ago, staying in the empty house of my family. I was trying to decide how to approach you, what to say, what we could *do*—run away together, elope, get married in secret and live alone on a mountaintop, I couldn't figure out the right way, the right words. But then when I saw you through Joachim's eyes, bleeding, I raced from the woods, and found you on the point of death, and knew I had no choice but to turn you." Tears welled in his eyes: they were little ruby droplets of diluted blood. "I'm so sorry, Bonnie. To take your life... I would never have done so, if there had been any alternative." He buried his head in my (completely healed) neck. "Now you'll never be able to have children." He sobbed.

Lord. Having my tubes tied supernaturally didn't bother me at all, but I whispered in his ear: "That's a shame, Edwin, but it's all right, because I still have *you*, forever, and always."

"And always, and forever," he murmured back.

I took to vampirism beautifully. By Sunday night I was walking around, and it's funny—I didn't feel stronger, exactly. I felt like I always had. But everything else in the *world* seemed... thinner? Less dense? Less *real*? Like the things that had seemed so solid and immovable when I was alive were now just so many cobwebs, to be brushed away by the merest motion of my hand. I could sense the presence of the other vampires in the house, in a way that has no analogue to my other senses—I didn't smell them, I could just... tell where they were, how close, in which direction they were moving and with how much velocity.

I sat with the family until late in the night, and they told me things I needed to know about myself and my kind, changes I could expect, drawbacks and advantages... things you mortal readers don't *need* to know. Oh, how I love having secrets, and becoming a vampire opened me up to a whole new class of secrets. When I continued to say I had no idea who'd attacked me—"I was on the couch, and I realized someone was behind me, and after that, I don't remember anything"—they vowed they would find out who was responsible and see them brought to justice... and since I wasn't actually dead and had no intention of letting Harry know I'd been attacked, I got the impression it wouldn't be *mortal* justice.

I told them I'd be grateful for anything they could do. But I had plans of my own, and they didn't have anything to do with justice. Justice is cold, remote, and abstract. I was more interested in bloody, immediate, gratifying *revenge*.

Pleasance and Ellen began excitedly talking about wedding plans—no reason I shouldn't marry Edwin now, they reasoned, since I was fully one of them. I could finish out the school year, of course, and graduate, but why not a summer wedding? Rosemarie sulked her way through the whole evening, not even looking at me, and that's when I started to have my idea, and to plan my plans.

I sat by Edwin, holding his hand—which no longer felt cold, to me; it felt exactly the same temperature as my own flesh, a reminder that everything in life is entirely relative—and smiled and nodded and talked faux-excitedly about ceremonies and flowers and dresses right along with them. I didn't really care about the wedding. I had the two things I'd wanted all along: the power of a vampire, and the devotion of my beloved Edwin.

But… it's a strange thing, and I hate to admit it… Edwin was somehow less alluring, now that I was a vampire. His inhuman beauty no longer seemed quite so inhuman, and indeed, his hair was a trifle greasy, his teeth not particularly even and straight, his blue eyes rather less dazzling. I realized that, since I was no longer in the category of prey, he was no longer the perfectly attractive predator, designed to lure me into his clutches. Don't misunderstand—he was still very beautiful—but that mysterious quality that made my breath pause and my heart stutter when he looked at me was gone. And for his part, his smiles seemed a bit weaker, a bit more perfunctory, and while gazing into my eyes he sometimes seemed to be thinking about something *other* than how absolutely wonderful I was. I can only assume it's because I lost my delicious smell when I turned.

But our love was more than just mere physical reactions, of course, it was a *deeper* love, an *eternal* love, and I didn't doubt for even a moment that it would survive certain minor and inevitable moments of disenchantment.

Love was for later, though. I had murdering to do.

ME, VAMPIRE

FROM THE JOURNAL OF BONNIE GRAYDUCK

The depressing thing was the normalcy I had to fake. Now that I was an immortal vampire I just didn't care—I wanted to eat half the world and watch the other half squirm. But Edwin explained that it would be best if I pretended to be what I'd always been (by which he meant, pretended to be what I'd always already pretended to be—a normal girl) until graduation. Then we could announce our plans to get married. If I dropped out of school or just ran away, Harry and my mom would freak and/or mobilize a manhunt, but if I played the true love card after graduation, my parents would be a lot less inclined to squawk, especially when Argyle offered to pay for my college education as a wedding present. (At first I'd thought: College? As if. But then I thought: edible coeds. And it seemed like a pretty good idea.)

So I kept having dinner with Harry most nights; kept going to biology class, even though I knew things about biology that were utterly alien to mortal knowledge; kept going to the cafeteria at lunch, even though I don't eat... chicken fingers; and kept talking to my friends J and Kelly, even though all I could think about was the pulse of life in their necks.

I'd never been an unpopular girl at school, but I was suddenly boy-nip, and in the days following my transformation I had to give Ike a stern talking-to in order to send him back to J's banal bed where he belonged. Kelly even got a little flirtatious, and I had sympathy for her inevitable lesbian college roommate, who'd be the subject of Kelly's experimentation and subsequent heartbreak when she went back home and married a typical male pig farmer or shopkeeper. (Okay, so I didn't really feel sorry for hypothetical future lesbo roommate; I just thought it was funny.)

Joachim called once to see how I was doing and to tell me he had no idea who'd attacked me, but it was awkward and weird and he didn't suggest hanging out, and neither did I. I understood—I'd become one of *them*. A wendigo. I was still Bonnie, sure, but I was also something else, and he couldn't see me the same way anymore. Oh well. You can't become immortal without breaking a few hearts. (Willy Noir didn't drop by to play Xbox with Dad anymore, either, but either Dad wasn't too broken up about it or he was just being manly and not showing it.)

Ah, but I know what you're wondering: What about Principal Levitt, my would-be murderer? How did *he* take the return of my vampire family and my own obvious-to-him transformation? I like to think he sat up every night with a shotgun in his lap waiting for me to come murder him. As if I'd be so *direct*. He didn't come to school, that's for sure—health problems, everyone said, and the assistant principal took over as acting principal—but he didn't leave town. He should have. Not that leaving town would have saved him, but at least he would have had the pleasure of annoying me slightly before getting what he deserved.

I began laying the groundwork for my plan with lots of long sighs in Edwin's presence. "What's wrong, darling?" he finally asked.

"It's Rosemarie," I said. "There's still all this tension between us. She's my family now, and I just want the two of us to be friends—or, at least, not enemies."

Edwin was quiet for a while, then said, "Perhaps Hermet and I could sit down with you and Rosemarie—"

"No," I said, shaking my head. "Forcing her to play nice, to pretend? It wouldn't mean anything, and would just make her resent me more. No, I'll just have to wait, and be nice, and hope she realizes I'm not so bad, really. If we talk when other people are watching, she'll just lie to make you and her husband happy. I want to talk to her *honestly*—promise me, Edwin, that if she ever does come to talk to me, you won't watch through her eyes?"

"I respect your privacy," he said, and I believed him, even if he did have a history of being a vampiric Peeping Tom.

"Maybe someday she'll come see me," I said wistfully, "and we can talk things over, girl to girl, but it wouldn't work if we tried to *force* it..."

I knew, of course, that Edwin would try to force it. He just wants me to be happy. He's wonderful, really. Not too good for me, of course, but *almost* good enough. He could be powerfully persuasive, and Rosemarie cared for him deeply—that was, ironically, why she'd tried to kill me at least once and probably twice, because she thought I was bad for him—so I wasn't surprised when, two days later, I heard a voice from my bedroom window.

"Bonnie," Rosemarie said, climbing through the window in a swirl of fog. She wore a sort of ninja woodsman outfit, with leather pants and a tight black top that showed off her arm muscles and her boobs. Like dressing in black could do anything to hide her in shadows when she had that radiant blonde hair. Still, the girl knew how to make an entrance, I had to give her that.

I'd wondered why Edwin hadn't come over to pass the night with me in secret, and now I knew.

"I think we should talk," Rosemarie said. "Privately." She seemed bored, but then, she always did.

"Is Edwin watching us, do you think?" I said.

"I made him promise to give us our privacy," she said. "So you and I could talk... honestly."

I glanced around. "My dad is downstairs. Do you mind if we go for a walk, talk outside? No reason for, you know, a *mortal* to overhear our business."

She shrugged. I could tell she didn't even begin to give a crap. She dropped back out the window, and after a moment, I followed. I hadn't done a lot of jumping out of second-story windows, but I'd done enough to know I liked it. Remember when you were a kid at the playground, perched up high on a jungle gym or hanging at the apex of the swing's arc, and you make the decision to jump? That delicious moment of weightless freedom, right before gravity gets a hold on you and pulls you down? I feel weightless like that so much more often now. As if I'm beyond even the reach of the laws of the natural world.

I landed on my feet in a catlike crouch. Rosemarie was already leaning against a tree, looking like the world's most jaded Norwegian supermodel. I gave her my best smile—it would have made a mortal melt and offer their throat to me, I knew *that*, but she just rolled her eyes.

I thought about what Mr. Levitt had said. About how two tigers can't share the same territory. Which, okay, is dumb: how do they get together and make little tiger babies then? But it works as a metaphor for, what, serial killers? And may-be also for bitchy vampire women. Pleasance was a harmless flake (for a blood-drinking apex predator), and Emily was the closest thing to a warm and cozy earth-mother in all of vampire-dom, but Rosemarie had almost certainly sabotaged my brakes and had definitely tried to smash my head in with a hockey puck and arranged to draw my blood at the birthday party. She was, well... dangerously close to being a lot like *me*. And, thus, a threat.

"Listen," she said, walking along the lane just ahead of me, following the winding, snowy path into the woods. (Also awesome about being a vampire: fuck snow. Nothing's colder than I am.) "I never liked you, okay? You probably noticed that. I thought you were all wrong for Edwin. Just a soppy live girl, tempting him with an admittedly pleasant smell. He's prone to these fits of romanticism, putting women on a pedestal, and—"

I'd never heard so many words out of Rosemarie. Her voice was surprisingly nasally and unappealing, which was odd, because it had seemed like smooth cold glass when I heard it as a real live girl.

Anyway, I didn't listen, really. When we passed the tree I'd had in mind, I pulled one of Harry's handguns (he has, like, four, and rifles, too) from where it was hidden in the waistband of my pajama pants. For a cop, Harry was a surprisingly deep sleeper, and anyway, gunshots weren't exactly uncommon out here, so I didn't worry too much about being overheard. I was tempted to get off some pithy one-liner before firing, but Rosemarie has vampire reflexes—sure, I do, too, but she's also got a whole lot more practice *using* them. So I passed up the chance for a zinger and just shot her in the back of the head.

She fell forward like a toppled statue, face into the dirt, not even trying to catch herself. I knew I only had moments before the wound would heal and she'd leap up and start trying to kill me in a rather more direct fashion than she'd used previously, but I was prepared: I'd put Harry's second-best wood axe behind a particular tree, and I picked it up and chop, chop, chop, off went Rosemarie's head. Didn't even take forty whacks.

Even decapitation won't necessarily kill a vampire—or so I'd learned in my little "Know your limitations!" orientation course at the Scullen home after I got turned. You have to keep the parts separated, and, ideally, burn them to ashes and then burn the ashes. I put the axe down and picked up her torso. Nice thing about cutting off a vampire's head: no bloody mess. I would indeed burn her body... but I had other plans for her head, once I dug out the bullet and threw it away to foil any future ballistics.

Killing Rosemarie was, of course, a worthy goal in and of itself. But I'm a big believer in working smarter, not harder.

"No," I said thoughtfully the next day. "No, she never came

over. Are you sure she was coming here?"

Edwin paced up and down in my bedroom, chewing on a ragged thumbnail. Nervous Edwin was not cute. I preferred languid, in-control Edwin, but I was beginning to realize a lot of his coolness had been a result of me viewing him through the eyes of enthralled prey. "Yes, at least, I think so. She told me she was going to come see you and make peace. She told Hermet the same thing."

"Maybe she decided to take a long walk and think it over?"

"It's possible, but I'm worried."

"I wonder..." I said slowly. "I wonder if whoever killed Jimmy... but, no, it can't be."

Edwin's head snapped up. "Jimmy? What about him?"

I frowned. "You didn't know? I thought... I don't know what I thought. I guess vampires don't have, whatever, a newsletter. He was killed, his body was in the woods, all shot up and stabbed and... Well. Then later his body disappeared."

"Start at the beginning," he said, in that peremptory voice that I'd once found so hot.

So I told him about taking a walk with Joachim, finding the body, how the corpse disappeared, and all that. He looked increasingly troubled. "Vampire hunters," he murmured. "You should have told me earlier, Bonnie."

I shook my head. "I'm sorry, I just didn't think about it, I mean, with all that's happened, being attacked..." I widened my eyes. "You don't think whoever killed Jimmy was the one who attacked *me*, do you? That they knew I, ah, consorted with vampires?"

"I don't know," he said grimly. "But I intend to find out."

After Edwin left to powwow with his family, I puttered around the house until Dad got home. His face was as pale as mine... almost. "Are you okay?" I asked.

He just shook his head, then sat down at the table and held his head in his hands.

"Dad? What is it?"

"I shouldn't say..." He murmured. "I just... I just got back from the Scullen house, talking to Edwin's family, but Edwin wasn't there—"

"He left a few minutes ago," I said. "What did you have to go see them about?" Like I didn't know.

"It's Rosemarie Scale," he said. "Bonnie, I'm afraid she's been killed."

I made the appropriate noises of shock and horror. Harry didn't want to give me details, but I drew them out of him. Someone had left an anonymous note at police headquarters. It was a strange note: the writer claimed to be a burglar, said he'd broken into Mr. Levitt's house in order to steal whatever he could get, and he'd looked in the chest freezer out in the garage because sometimes people hide valuables in there, you know, but instead of a bundle of cash or a cache of gold, he'd found a human head. The burglar was obviously unwilling to come forward publicly, as he'd been there during the commission of a crime, but he thought somebody should know. Harry had been willing to write it off as a joke, but thought he should investigate. He didn't have cause to get a warrant, so he just asked Mr. Levitt if he could look in his freezer, and the old man said knock yourself out, and... there was a head, in a plastic bag, on top of some frozen venison steaks, next to some frozen walleye filets.

Right where I put it. Before I wrote that anonymous note. Breaking and entering is so trivial when you're a vampire, and I'd been good at picking locks when I was alive. Screw cat burglars: bat burglar all the way.

"I have to say, he looked stunned," Harry said, drinking his fifth cup of coffee. "Makes me wonder if he was even in his right mind when he did it."

"*If* he did it," I said. "What if someone just, you know, put the head there?"

"Well, a head in a freezer is pretty damning, but it's still just circumstantial evidence," Harry said. "But we got a search warrant, of course, and brought in some crime scene techs from the state police, and we noticed some disturbed earth in the basement, and got to digging, and... Heck, Bonnie, you don't need to hear all this."

"You found more bodies?" I said, putting all the appropriate horror in my voice. I hadn't *counted* on this part—I didn't need Mr. Levitt getting convicted in a court of law, that was hardly necessary, I just needed him to look guilty—but I'd wondered if he had incriminating evidence of his *actual* crimes in his house.

"Graves," he said. "Drifters, it looks like. Hikers. Runaways. Some of them old, real old. When I think that he was a school teacher, and then school superintendent, and even your *principal*, I just... How can evil like that hide in plain sight for so long, Bonnie? I just don't understand it." The distress in his voice was so profound, like he'd realized the world was a dark and rotten place.

Well, duh.

"He's in jail?" I said.

Harry nodded. "Not here. State police took over. I know on TV the local cops get mad whenever someone tries to mess around with their jurisdiction, but I'll tell you, Bonnie—they can *have* this. I'll do my part, of course, but Lake Woebegotten having its very own Ed Gein... it's out of my league and beyond my resources and I don't mind saying so."

I stood up. "Oh gosh," I said. "Edwin must have heard by now, I—"

"Go on," Harry said. "I know you care about him, and that family. Go see him, see what you can do for them, tell them I'll do everything *I* can."

NO CELL STRONG ENOUGH

FROM THE JOURNAL OF BONNIE GRAYDUCK

Most of the family was upstairs with Hermet, who was kind of a wreck, as you might imagine. I heard a lot of crashing and thumping up there, but Edwin sat with me, his eyes kind of glazed-over. "Mr. Levitt," he said, for maybe the eighth time. "The principal?"

"It must be such a betrayal," I said, "having him turn on you."

Edwin turned his head to me slowly, frowning. "What do you mean?"

"Mr. Levitt. He was your family's, you know. Liaison? Your go-between, your human agent?"

Edwin shook his head. "No, he wasn't."

Huh. "Oh. I just assumed, since he was a human who knew about you, who knew about vampires I mean..."

Edwin stood up from the couch. "No, he wasn't our agent. But I wonder if our agent *told* him about us. Sometimes humans become vampire hunters, no treachery on the part of our agents is necessary, it happens, but this is a small town, we thought our agent was discreet, but perhaps... Thank you for coming, Bonnie, but I think I need to be with my family now. I'll be in touch soon." He rushed upstairs.

I sat on the couch and drummed my fingers on the armrest. Muffled voices drifted down from the second floor, audible to my heightened sense of hearing but not comprehensible. I guess they were discussing their plans and plots and so on.

262

I was a little miffed that I hadn't been included, but I wasn't technically part of the family yet, and they probably wanted to spare me the grisly details anyway, lest they offend my so-recently-mortal and therefore delicate sensibilities.

Then I got hungry, so I went to take a walk.

A while later I got home, and Harry was nowhere to be seen (probably at Mr. Levitt's house, AKA The Lake Woebegotten Death House, not that such a lurid name would ever catch on around here), but Edwin was there, pacing in my room. "Darling," I said. "Are you all right?"

"We couldn't restrain Hermet," Edwin said, collapsing onto my bed and staring up at the ceiling. "To be fair, only about half of us even *wanted* to. So... we set him free." .

I sat on the bed and took his hand. "Is he going after that horrible man?"

Edwin nodded. "Mr. Levitt will be dead by... possibly by now. I just hope Hermet doesn't have to hurt too many innocent people in the process. Our kind can be stealthy, and we hope he managed to sneak into the Drizzle County house of detention to find Mr. Levitt's cell unobserved, but Hermet is not, ah, the most subtle of us." He squeezed my hand. "We can't risk Mr. Levitt telling other humans about us, of course. It's unlikely anyone would believe him, but we have to be safe."

"Oh," I said. "So it's not revenge, then."

"Of course it's revenge." Edwin's voice was soft and full of, what's the word, regret? "But we've tried so hard, my family, to be above such things, to be *better* than that. But Mr. Levitt killed someone we love. We think he tried to kill *you*. There was no way Hermet could allow him to live."

Delicious. Both Rosemarie and Mr. Levitt dead, and no blame accruing to me at all—I was even hailed as a fellow victim. Beautiful, beautiful, beautiful. "When will Hermet be back?"

The silence was so sharp and crystalline that I knew right

away I'd said the wrong thing.

"He *won't* be," Edwin said a moment later. "He's not going to, to make it look like an *accident*. He's going to break into a jail cell and tear a man apart—the man who killed his wife. And when he sees that man's blood, he won't be able to resist the urge to feed. None of us could, except possibly Argyle. It's dangerous, letting us have a taste of human blood, Bonnie. It changes us, makes us lose our focus, our determination, our will to overcome our baser natures. Like with alcoholics—sometimes a single sip is enough to lead inexorably to a three-week bender. Only my worry for your safety kept me from losing control when I tasted *your* blood. We understand why Hermet has to do this, but… he won't be welcome with us anymore."

I was stunned. *They're like religious fundamentalists*, I thought. *Violate one of their silly rules and that's it, you're out, no appeals process.* But I said, "I guess that makes sense."

"He won't want to see us anyway. We'll remind him too much of Rosemarie."

"I'm sorry she's gone," I said. "I'd really hoped we could become friends. Become sisters."

"I know," Edwin said, and began sobbing blood-tinged tears into my pillow.

God, vampire boys can be so damn emo.

My only regret, and it's a big one, is that I couldn't have one last conversation with Mr. Levitt. Not that he exactly rose to the level of my nemesis, and anyway, this is a love story, not the kind of story where a heroine needs to square off against her adversary with snappy banter, but still, for all that I had to kill him and he tried to kill me, he really understood me. We were a lot alike. Not that I enjoy chopping up hitchhikers and burying them in the basement (so gauche), but our differences were only differences of methodology—differences of degree, not kind, I think is the expression. I didn't admire him, but he made sense to me. We both know the world is empty of meaning, except the meaning we make: true love, adventure, hunting, whatever. You have to make your own fun. His kind of fun was just more overt and unsubtle and crass than mine.

Which was why I was surprised he made that one last move against me, from beyond the grave. It was a very Bonnie Grayduck kind of move to make, and you know, it really *did* cost me something. You only get one dad, and Mr. Levitt took mine from me. The old fucker got me. A little.

I was out in the front yard in a chaise longue, enjoying the sun when the other shoe dropped. (I don't understand that expression. What shoe? Whose shoe? Dropping from where? Anyway.) Sure, it was somewhere around zero degrees, but it's not like the cold bothered me. I almost wore a bikini, but I wasn't entirely sure vampires could tan, so I settled for jeans and a flannel shirt. The snow all around was blinding white in the sunlight. The Scullens and Scales hid from the sun, lest someone notice how they smelled really good, but I couldn't see the point, honestly. Sure, it could be annoying to get mobbed at school, but in my front yard, what was the harm?

Harry's car pulled in. He was in a bad way lately, really overworked and stressed and, ha, harried, what with all the media heat about the town's serial killer—who'd been found completely dismembered inside his *locked* jail cell, which was pretty embarrassing for the state cops, and it was a lucky thing he hadn't been in Harry's jail at the time, at least. All that mess was stressing him out, and on top of that, he'd had to investigate a few mysterious disappearances. Not just Gunther, but a few other really marginal types around town had gone missing—a crazy Satanist (or maybe just a pagan, these people couldn't tell the difference) named Gothic Jim had vanished, along with that weird old man who usually wandered around wearing a bow tie and red suspenders and talking to himself, and a couple of other nobodies. To make matters worse, Harry's only help, part-time deputy Stevie Ray, had apparently lit out for parts unknown. And Mom was calling him all the time, screaming about how he'd let his daughter go to a school run by a serial killer, wasn't he supposed to be a *cop* for god's sake, she'd sent me to Lake Woebegotten so my senior year could be quiet, and on and on.

You really had to feel bad for the guy. Well, I mean, *I* didn't, particularly, but I could see how people would.

Harry walked over to my chair, plodding the way he did lately. He had a fat manila envelope in his hand. "Bonnie," he said. "I got this in the mail today. It's, ah... from Mr. Levitt."

I frowned. "What do you mean?"

"He must have mailed it before, you know... we caught him. I should have handed it over to the lab boys in the state police, but ah, it's not a confession, or, or anything. It's... about *you*. A letter from the principal at your old school, and a note Mr. Levitt wrote, with some... speculations. I didn't believe it, but I made some calls, and... Bonnie, your mom said you'd had a bad time of things, that a couple of your friends had passed away, but she didn't say anything about... about *hacking*, about sending fake e-mails, about this car crash, apparently there are some serious questions, and..." He trailed off, sniffing the air. "Bonnie, why do you smell like doughnuts?"

I stood up and ran into the woods. Not the most elegant solution to the problem, I know, but I wasn't thinking straight. Mom was, for all her many faults, the possessor of some great virtues: she was stupid, and credulous, and easily convinced. She might have some nagging deep-down doubts about me, but I'd convinced her it was all a misunderstanding, that I'd been framed, maligned, done wrong. Harry was nowhere *near* that stupid. And while I knew he loved me, did he love me *enough*? Enough to hide the evidence, enough to not tell *anyone*? If word got back to Edwin about the things I'd done in Santa Cruz, what would he do to me? What would his family do? Would I be cast out like Hermet?

I had some thinking to do, and I did it in the woods, and I have a hard time thinking on an empty stomach.

SLAYERS DISASSEMBLED

NARRATOR

Bonnie didn't know what happened to Stevie Ray, but I do (of course) and thought you might be interested, so here goes:

Stevie Ray was shoved roughly to his knees in the dark basement. Figures stood around him, shadowed, but he could see the red glint of their eyes. He'd met all the Scullens and the Scales over the years, but this wasn't *all* of them, and that was kind of the point. Garnett was behind him—he'd been sent to fetch Stevie Ray, and he'd done so with a minimum of kindness, dragging him out of bed in the middle of the night. Argyle stepped forward, flanked by Ellen and Pleasance, with Edwin hanging back, seemingly uncomfortable with the whole thing, which gave Stevie Ray a flash of hope... but Edwin was weak and soppy, so it wasn't realistic to think he'd be any help.

Argyle spoke. "You served us, loyally, for over a year. What made you betray us?"

Stevie Ray swallowed. "I didn't—I don't—"

Garnett cuffed him upside the head, hard enough to make Stevie Ray's ears ring like a gong. Once he struggled back up to his knees, Argyle repeated himself: "What made you betray us?"

"I was afraid," Stevie Ray whispered. "I'm just a small-town cop. I didn't want to learn about were-bears and vampires. I didn't mean any harm. I just... I wasn't even worried about *you*, but those other vampires came, they killed Gunther Montcrief, the tribal elders said they couldn't promise to protect the town, they had to protect the reservation, so...."

"So you recruited vampire hunters," Ellen said. Her earth-mama mellowness was utterly absent from her voice now; she spoke like a predator. "You told humans about us. And one of those humans killed my daughter. Isn't that right?"

Stevie Ray closed his eyes. "None of us knew what Mr. Levitt *was*, the kind of man he was, we didn't know he would kill your daughter, we didn't *mean* for this to happen."

"We chose you because we thought you might understand," Argyle said. "One of the only black men for miles and miles, often an outsider, an other, but friendly, popular among the townspeople, clearly adept at moving between worlds, you seemed a perfect liaison. But you have betrayed us." Argyle took a step forward, and Stevie Ray couldn't help it: his bladder let go, and he whimpered.

"Name names," Garnett said behind him. "Tell us everyone involved in your little vampire squad."

"I won't," he whispered. "So you can kill them, like you did Mr. Levitt? Not that he didn't *deserve* to die, but the others, they don't, they never did you any wrong, they—"

"Stupid human," Argyle said. "We won't kill them. We don't kill humans, that's the whole point. Mr. Levitt was... a different situation. Wrongs had to be redressed—some wrongs you don't even know about. But we can't allow humans to know about us."

He opened his eyes. "Then what?"

"Think of your mother," Garnett said, and Stevie Ray said, "What?" but of course he *did*, because when someone tells you to think about something (or even not to think about something) you usually do, however briefly. Her face, her voice, appeared in his mind, and then Garnett reached out and touched his head and her image dissolved like smoke.

He whimpered. "What—what did you—"

"What's your mother's name?" Garnett said.

Stevie Ray opened his mouth, but he couldn't come up with the name. He knew he *had* a mother, he must, he'd been born, after all, but he couldn't come up with any memory about her at all. "I don't know. What did you do to me?"

"Garnett can remove memories," Argyle said. "Some of us have little powers, you know. That's his. He can make people forget. Well, not *people*—humans, I mean. Very useful for us."

"You should have let me erase Bonnie's memory," Garnett said, apparently to Edwin. "Then we wouldn't have had to come back here, and Rosemarie would still be alive."

Edwin's face twisted up in agony. "I didn't want her to forget me, I wanted to know she loved me as much as I loved her, that if I was alone and suffering, so was she—"

"Now is not the time," Argyle said mildly. "Stevie Ray, tell us who your co-conspirators were, and Garnett will simply cleanse their memories. No one else needs to die, unless you give us no choice."

Stevie Ray swallowed. "All right. I guess... okay. But can you give me my mother's name back? My memories of her?"

Garnett laughed. "If I could put ideas in people's heads, Renfield, I would, but that's not how my powers work. I just take them out. Now start talking before we take a lot *more*."

Stevie Ray talked. And when he was done, Garnett emptied out his head of every personal memory he had, and they dumped him on skid row in Minneapolis, and you don't really want to know what happened to him after that.

They were gentler with the rest of the Interfaith Vampire Hunters, you might be pleased to know, just scooped out all their vampire-related memories. With Stevie Ray, they felt betrayed, I guess. Well, I don't guess. I know they did. But they didn't know who'd really betrayed them.

Not their fault. Not everyone gets to know everything like I do.

THE BRIDE WORE BLACK

FROM THE JOURNAL OF BONNIE GRAYDUCK

We didn't do the wedding and the funeral on the same day or even in the same week, because that would have been super tacky. Mom was in town sobbing and weeping and wailing all over the place, and mom's half-jock boyfriend Dwayne was there too, lurking uncomfortably in the corners of his dead predecessor's house. Everyone in town, it seemed, came by to offer condolences, including the mayor and his wife, and counselor Inkfist, and some Catholic priest, and the blonde woman who runs the diner, and the dorky old guy who runs the grocery store, and all the classmates I'd ever spoken to and a bunch of people I hadn't, and of course the Scullens, who were starting to look kind of shell-shocked, and who can blame them? It's a lot to have happen.

I was the one who discovered Harry's body, so I got lots of extra sympathy. No suicide note, but he didn't really need one, because I told everyone how he'd been really upset about Mr. Levitt's murders and the disappearances, how he felt like it was all his fault, that he'd failed the town, he was depressed and ashamed and in increasingly black moods, yadda yadda. Nobody doubted me for a minute.

The funny thing is, I didn't even have to shoot Harry myself. See, I found my power—my special *vampire* power. I can manipulate people. I always could, of course... but now I can manipulate them almost like a puppeteer manipulates a marionette. Okay, I don't take control of their bodies, but I can make… suggestions… and they get followed. After an hour of me telling Harry his life wasn't really worth living, that his own daughter was a criminal, and that he'd totally failed both as a cop and as a parent, he actually believed me. I'd been in town, pretending to have a cup of coffee (which had gone from my favorite thing to disgusting swill) at Cafe Lo, when Harry killed himself. Perfect alibi. (And a good thing. I don't know if I could have avoided drinking Harry's spilled blood if I'd been there when it was fresh.) The envelope from Mr. Levitt was just ashes, buried in a hole. No dad, which was sad—Harry was an okay guy, and he gave me Marmon, which I'll always appreciate—but also no loose ends or threats, which was more important. I mean, Mom still knew about the allegations against me, but she was in such deep denial she'd never say anything to anybody. I should probably head back to Santa Cruz sometime and get rid of her and my old principal and maybe a few other people, just to be safe, but I was in no immediate danger of discovery.

Mom wanted me to come home with her after the funeral, but I introduced her to Edwin, told her we were in love, and that I was eighteen now, and that I was going to be making my own way for a while. She was pretty shell-shocked too. People have so much trouble adjusting to new realities, don't they?

I was accepting yet another hotdish—Minnesotans and their condolence casseroles!—when Joachim arrived. He looked good enough to eat (ha, I'm a vampire now, I shouldn't say that, so I'll say what I mean, which is that he looked good enough to *fuck*) in a black leather jacket. Very vital, very alive, very bad-boy-with-a-heart-of-gold. Maybe the beast in him was coming out more, or he'd decided to stop being such a puppy and be more of a wolf (or bear I guess, not to ruin the metaphor). He took me aside and murmured his condolences, told me Harry was a good man. I gave him a big smile and a hug and a whisper in the ear of my own. Not even pushing with my powers, because while I'm happy to use that ability to get things done if necessary, I do take pride in my skills, like any artist does, and Joachim was never hard for me to guide in the direction I wanted. I patted him on the ass when no one was looking. He got the message.

After the funeral—presided over by counselor Inkfist, who I guess used to be a reverend, and wanted to be one again? So weird—I got Mom and Dwayne on a plane back to the west coast and out of my hair. Harry had left the house to me, which was nice of him, I guess. Though I was marrying into a family of robber-baron-rich vampires, so I didn't worry much about keeping a roof over my head.

About a week after the last of the dirt got thrown over Harry, Edwin and I had a little wedding ceremony in the icy back yard of the Scullen house. It was the new year, just— Christmas was not much of an event that year, as you can imagine—and it seemed like a time for new beginnings. Argyle presided (I guess he used to be a priest in the 1400s or something, which explains *so much* about his silly morality), and nobody commented on the fact that I was wearing black. They probably though I was still mourning for Harry, but, really, I just thought, as a vampire bride, black was the way to go.

Most of the ceremony was in Latin or whatever, except for some bits about how this time of happiness was a welcome relief from the recent darkness and so on and so forth, and at the end Argyle said, "You may kiss the bride," and Edwin pressed his cold lips to my cold lips, and I took his hands in mine, and I knew I'd finally arrived at the place I was always going. Tonight, on our honeymoon, we would finally make love—I guess there's something to be said for abstinence, because the delayed gratification thing *does* get you pretty hot and bothered, or as hot as a pair of animated corpses can get—and the tingle I felt at the thought of Edwin's naked body against mine almost made me feel alive again. And I decided I was alive—I *am* alive—in every way that matters.

And that's it, dear reader.

This is the part where I start living happily ever after. Forever.

ALWAYS DARKEST

NARRATOR

That's the end of Bonnie's journal. Not a bad ending, really, as far as these things go. She left some things out of the story, though, or didn't spell them out, and then there were the things that happened after the wedding, so I guess I'll mention a couple of those, if only to give you a fuller picture.

That time Bonnie got bored at Edwin's house while his family was mourning Rosemarie's death, and she went for a walk... well, she ended up at my house, a little cottage on the edge of town. I don't think she picked me for any particular reason, except I'm way out on the edge of town, nobody around, and she figured she could get away with it.

I heard a knock at my door and levered myself up from the chair where I was reading a history of the prairie, with some yodeling on an NPR radio program as background music. "Now, I wasn't expecting any visitors," I said—narrating my life, you know, like I used to do before I took up writing— "but it's never a bad time to be neighborly, so long as it's not too early in the morning or too late at night or too close to a major holiday, so I was happy enough to see which of the good people of Lake Woebegotten had come over to borrow a cup of sugar or a gallon of diesel fuel or a shovelful of fertilizer." I opened the door and said, "Who should I find on my doorstep but one of the prettiest girls in the county, Harry Cusack's girl Bonnie who just moved here from the West

Coast. I asked her how she was settling in, and she said—"
I paused, because I liked to let people supply their own dia-
logue, when it seemed appropriate.

Bonnie really was pretty, though it's hard to tell how much
was just being young and how much was true bone-deep
beauty, and of course, by that time, she was also a vampire,
which has beneficial side effects for your complexion and so
forth. But I like to think I could see something in her eyes,
which weren't brown at all in that moment, but black. I'm
tempted to say the black of empty space, but the problem
with Bonnie isn't her emptiness, because she's not empty;
she's full. The problem is what she's full *of*. So not the black of
empty space at all; the black of deep space, where dwell terrible things with terrible designs. Her smile was bright and
hard and glittering. "I'm wondering if you can help me," she
said. "You see, I'm simply *starving*."

I nodded. "Now, my mother didn't raise me to be inhos-
pitable, so if someone comes by, even if they're not hungry,
I know enough to offer them a little lunch, and I was pretty
sure I had some lemon bars and cookies and most of a cake
and of course the fixins for several sandwiches and a fresh
pot of coffee and a dab of that macaroni-hamburger hotdish
I'd had for supper the night before and—"

"I was thinking of something… fresher," Bonnie said, and
opened her mouth, fangs sliding down out of her gums. Her
eyes turned red as warning lights and she shoved me into
my house, a straight-armed push that sent me flying into
the old-timey radio I'd inherited from my own father (along
with everything else I had, from the roof over my head to the
money in my bank account to the books on my shelves). The
radio collapsed, and the yodeling cut off abruptly, and all the
breath got slammed out of me in the process, and for the first
time in my waking life, I was left absolutely speechless.

"You'll have to forgive me." Bonnie kicked my door shut
behind her and stalked toward me, her body moving sinu-
ously, like a snake, or maybe more like the body of a snake

filled entirely by squirming maggots. Drool built up in her mouth and overspilled her pouty lips and ran down her chin, and her beauty was entirely gone: being on the point of death had given me some clarity, and she didn't look like anything alluring at all anymore, but just a waxy-faced corpse walking. "It's my first time," she said, leaning down to me, twisting my head to the side, tearing off my red bow tie, and exposing my throat. "I wish I could say I'd be gentle. But gentle isn't really my *thing*."

I don't remember too much of what happened next—my throat torn away, certainly, and her guzzling my blood, and then getting dragged by my feet at high speed out into the woods, where she pitched me down a hill and into the deep snow. I don't even think she knew who I was, though she'd seen me around—people in town knew me, like I said way at the beginning of this, I guess you might say I was considered a local eccentric, less crazed than Gothic Jim and less deranged than Cyrus Bell, but still noteworthy because of my habit of constant Narration. I know her eating me was nothing personal. (I *know* it, like I know everything, now.) I also know I was her first victim (though not her last), and that's probably why she messed up the way she did. Because I didn't die. Maybe the snow preserved me or something, who can say, but I lay out there in the cold for a day and a night with hardly any blood in me and lots of her venomous saliva coursing through my veins and then I rose up and my mind opened and I knew I'd become a vampire. My special power is that omnicognizance I've been telling you about. My mother always said I was a little know-it-all. Just goes to show.

Bonnie doesn't know I'm out here. She thinks she never had children and never will—but here I am, a child of a sort, wouldn't be here in this way without her. She thinks I'm dead, just one of the disappeared—one of the several she's eaten, you see—and that my body hasn't been discovered yet, is all. I've been living on what I can find out in the woods, and haven't taken any human victims myself, because it's hard to eat somebody when you know so much about them—it's the reason farmers don't give names to the animals they're planning to eat. But I'm here, living in the woods, sitting up in trees, watching everything, the whole world like a bunch of ongoing reality shows, though I admit, I keep it on the Bonnie channel, mostly. She made me what I am today. She interests me. *That* girl wouldn't have any trouble eating a pig she'd raised, even if she'd named it Wilbur or Babe.

It's been a steamy show since the wedding, too. Oh, their wedding night was nothing much to speak of, two dead people rubbing their dead parts together like a couple of auto-necrophiliacs. When you're both cold it's hard to have a spark, maybe, though Pleasance and Garnett seemed to manage, and even Argyle and Ellen have a deep love between them even if their hearts only beat a little, right after they've eaten. But Bonnie had gotten what she wanted from Edwin, and the bloom was off the rose. Not that Edwin realized it. He'd never been inside a girl before, and as far as he knew, that was as good as it got, and if there's one thing Bonnie's good at, it's faking whatever she needs to fake.

No, the real heat is between Bonnie and Joachim. They've been meeting in secret at Harry's house, and they've got some wild stuff going on. I never watched pornography or anything like that, but they do things I'd be hard pressed even to put names to. Sometimes Joachim turns into a bear and they don't even slow down. It sure is different. Joachim is full of self-loathing, what with fornicating with a wendigo, and Bonnie whispers that she loves him, though really she just loves his heat—body heat's one of those things you don't realize you'll miss until it's gone, believe you me. She knows she's in constant danger that her husband will find out—he still can't see through her eyes, but if he decides to peek out through Joachim's peepers at the right moment, he'll get an eyeful and that's for sure—but for Bonnie, the possibility of getting caught and maybe starting a titanic battle of super-natural menfolk is part of the appeal, part of what makes it hot, and Joachim, well. Even before Bonnie could manipulate people supernaturally, he never stood a chance. He's a nice trusting boy, and the fact that he can turn into a vampire-eating monster hasn't changed that.

I tell you, I'd rather Bonnie be with weak, sentimental Edwin than with Joachim, because Joachim's a good fella who's getting ruined by her influence. I'm definitely Team Necrophilia rather than Team Zoophilia, if you want to know the truth.

Joachim's dad Willy Noir's getting suspicious—heck, he's *been* suspicious, he's just getting *more* suspicious, about lots of things, including his good friend Harry's suicide— and though I can't see the future it wouldn't surprise me if things got ugly between the Scullens and the elders (and the youngers), if the treaty broke down and some kind of a war broke out. Bonnie has that effect on people. She's trouble walking, a lie on two legs, a disaster in a black lace dress. She's pretty formidable, too, even more so now that she's a vampire, and it's troubling to think what kind of more or less dreadful things she might accomplish, given forever to ac-complish it. She doesn't show any inclination to move away from this town, at least not until she graduates high school, which probably isn't good for this town, and that bothers me, because I've lived in Lake Woebegotten my whole life, and there are good people here, every single one of them better than most, and they don't deserve whatever bad trouble she's going to bring down on them. And I don't deserve to have to know about it all in intimate detail when it finally happens, either. I understand, now, with my new perspective, that I'm an odd, cranky old fella and have been for a long time, but deep down I'm not a bad guy, and I've always thought, if you can do some good, you should.

Still. Bonnie. Well, you read all this here, I figure, if you've made it this far. You know what she's like. Makes you wonder if anybody could even stop her.

Maybe if somebody knew her every move. Knew when she

was alone. Knew when she let her guard down. Knew when she was tired, or careless, or vulnerable. If somebody could watch and wait for just exactly the exact right moment to strike. Maybe a fella like that could do something to stop her before she wrecks anybody else's life. Or unlife.

And maybe it wasn't such a smart idea of hers, making an enemy out of somebody like me.

Night Shade Books is an Independent Publisher of Quality Science-Fiction, Fantasy and Horror

ISBN: 978-1-59780-196-6 ❰ $14.99 ❰ Look for it in eBook

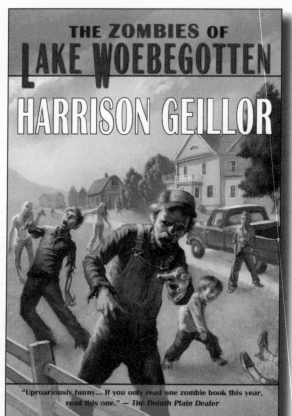

THE ZOMBIES OF LAKE WOEBEGOTTEN

HARRISON GEILLOR

"Uproariously funny... If you only read one zombie book this year, read this one." — *The Duluth Plain Dealer*

The town of Lake Woebegotten, MN is a small town, filled with ordinary (yet above average) people, leading ordinary lives. Ordinary, that is, until the dead start coming back to life, with the intent to feast upon the living. Now this small town of above average citizens must overcome their petty rivalries and hidden secrets, in order to survive the onslaught of the dead.

"I honestly thought that if there was going to be a zombie outbreak in Minnesota, it would be at the Mall of America.... Harrison Geillor has proven me wrong."
—*The Minneapolis Daily Times*

"If you only read one zombie book this year, read this one."
—*The Duluth Plain Dealer*

ISBN: 978-1-59780-224-6 ❅ $14.99 ❅ Look for it in eBook

Nyx used to be a bel dame, a government-funded assassin with a talent for cutting off heads for cash. Her country's war rages on, but her assassin days are long over. Now she's babysitting diplomats to make ends meet and longing for the days when killing people was a lot more honorable.

When Nyx's former bel dame "sisters" lead a coup against the government that threatens to plunge the country into civil war, Nyx volunteers to stop them. The hunt takes Nyx and her inglorious team of mercenaries to one of the richest, most peaceful, and most contaminated countries on the planet—a country wholly unprepared to host a battle waged by the world's deadliest assassins.

In a rotten country of sweet-tongued politicians, giant bugs, and renegade shape shifters, Nyx will forge unlikely allies and rekindle old acquaintances. And the bodies she leaves scattered across the continent this time... may include her own.

Night Shade Books is an Independent Publisher of Quality Science-Fiction, Fantasy and Horror

ISBN: 978-1-59780-290-1 ❆ $14.99 ❆ Look for it in eBook

"Terrifying, darkly hilarious, tougher and meaner and faster than a .45 hole-in-the-head—Roche delivers a fast-paced, gripping thriller where the showdowns make other zombie novelists look like they're playing with dollies."

—Violet Blue, author of *The Smart Girl's Guide to Porn* and many others

THE PANAMA LAUGH
THOMAS S. ROCHE

Ex-mercenary, pirate, and gun-runner Dante Bogart knows he's screwed the pooch after he hands one of his shady employers a biological weapon that made the dead rise from their graves, laugh like hyenas, and feast upon the living. Dante tried to blow the whistle via a tell-all video that went viral—but that was before the black ops boys deep-sixed him at a secret interrogation site on the Panama-Colombia border.

When Dante wakes up in the jungle with the five intervening years missing from his memory, he knows he's got to do something about the laughing sickness that has caused a world-wide slaughter. The resulting journey leads him across the nightmare that was the Panama Canal, around Cape Horn in a hijacked nuclear warship, to San Francisco's mission district, where a crew of survivalist hackers have holed up in the pseudo-Moorish-castle turned porn-studio known as The Armory.

This mixed band of anti-social rejects has taken Dante's whistle blowing video as an underground gospel, leading the fight against the laughing corpses and the corporate stooges who've tried to profit from the slaughter. Can Dante find redemption and save civilization?

NECROPOLIS
MICHAEL DEMPSEY

Michael Dempsey's *Necropolis* reads the way stepping over a wasted body in the rain feels. It's a noir science fiction gut punch from a strong new voice.
— Richard Kadrey, author of *Sandman Slim*

ISBN: 978-1-59780-315-1 ❦ $14.99 ❦ Look for it in eBook

Paul Donner is a NYPD detective struggling with a drinking problem and a marriage on the rocks. Then he and his wife get dead—shot to death in a "random" crime. Fifty years later, Donner is back—revived courtesy of the Shift, a process whereby inanimate DNA is re-activated.

This new "reborn" underclass is not only alive again, they're growing younger, destined for a second childhood. The freakish side-effect of a retroviral attack on New York, the Shift has turned the world upside down. Beneath the protective geodesic Blister, clocks run backwards, technology is hidden behind a noir facade, and you can see Bogart and DiCaprio in *The Maltese Falcon III*. In this unfamiliar retro-futurist world of flying Studebakers and plasma tommy guns, Donner must search for those responsible for the destruction of his life. His quest for retribution, aided by Maggie, his holographic Girl Friday, leads him to the heart of the mystery surrounding the Shift's origin and up against those who would use it to control a terrified nation.

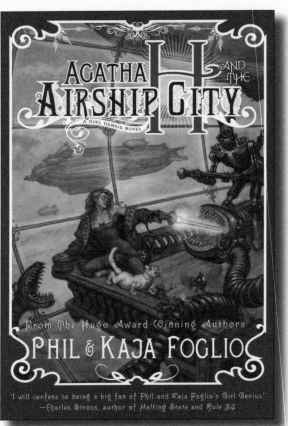

Night Shade Books is an Independent Publisher of Quality Science-Fiction, Fantasy and Horror

ISBN: 978-1-59780-283-3 ❧ $14.99 ❧ Look for it in eBook

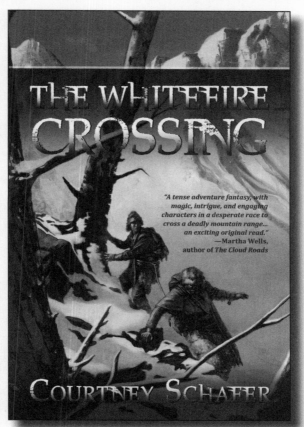

THE WHITEFIRE CROSSING

"A tense adventure fantasy, with magic, intrigue, and engaging characters in a desperate race to cross a deadly mountain range... an exciting original read."
—Martha Wells, author of *The Cloud Roads*

COURTNEY SCHAFER

Dev is a smuggler with the perfect cover. He's in high demand as a guide for the caravans that carry legitimate goods from the city of Ninavel into the country of Alathia. The route through the Whitefire Mountains is treacherous, and Dev is one of the few climbers who knows how to cross them safely. With his skill and connections, it's easy enough to slip contraband charms from Ninavel—where any magic is fair game, no matter how dark—into Alathia, where most magic is outlawed.

But smuggling a few charms is one thing; smuggling a person through the warded Alathian border is near suicidal. Having made a promise to a dying friend, Dev is forced to take on a singularly dangerous cargo: Kiran. A young apprentice on the run from one of the most powerful mages in Ninavel, Kiran is desperate enough to pay a fortune to sneak into a country where discovery means certain execution—and he'll do whatever it takes to prevent Dev from finding out the terrible truth behind his getaway.

Yet the young mage is not the only one harboring a deadly secret. Caught up in a web of subterfuge and dark magic, Dev and Kiran must find a way to trust each other—or face not only their own destruction, but that of the entire city of Ninavel.

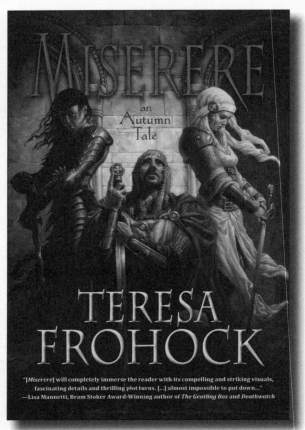

ISBN: 978-1-59780-289-5 ❦ $14.99 ❦ Look for it in eBook

Exiled exorcist Lucian Negru deserted his lover in Hell in exchange for saving his sister Catarina's soul, but Catarina doesn't want salvation. She wants Lucian to help her fulfill her dark covenant with the Fallen Angels by using his power to open the Hell Gates. Catarina intends to lead the Fallen's hordes out of Hell and into the parallel dimension of Woerld, Heaven's frontline of defense between Earth and Hell.

When Lucian refuses to help his sister, she imprisons and cripples him, but Lucian learns that Rachael, the lover he betrayed and abandoned in Hell, is dying from a demonic possession. Determined to rescue Rachael from the demon he unleashed on her soul, Lucian flees his sister, but Catarina's wrath isn't so easy to escape.

In the end, she will force him once more to choose between losing Rachael or opening the Hell Gates so the Fallen's hordes may overrun Earth, their last obstacle before reaching Heaven's Gates.

Night Shade Books is an Independent Publisher of Quality Science-Fiction, Fantasy and Horror

Look for it in eBook ❦ $15.99 ❦ ISBN: 978-1-59780-232-1

edited by
ROSS E. LOCKHART

the BOOK of
CTHULHU

Tales inspired by H. P. Lovecraft from:

KAGE BAKER   LAIRD BARRON   ELIZABETH BEAR
RAMSEY CAMPBELL   DAVID DRAKE   CAITLÍN R. KIERNAN
THOMAS LIGOTTI   TIM PRATT   CHERIE PRIEST
W. H. PUGMIRE   CHARLES STROSS   GENE WOLFE
and many others...

Ia! Ia! Cthulhu Fhtagn!

First described by visionary author H. P. Lovecraft, the Cthulhu mythos encompass a pantheon of truly existential cosmic horror: Eldritch, uncaring, alien god-things, beyond mankind's deepest imaginings, drawing ever nearer, insatiably hungry, until one day, when the stars are right....

As that dread day, hinted at within the moldering pages of the fabled Necronomicon, draws nigh, tales of the Great Old Ones: Cthulhu, Yog-Sothoth, Hastur, Azathoth, Nyarlathotep, and the weird cults that worship them have cross-pollinated, drawing authors and other dreamers to imagine the strange dark aeons ahead, when the dead-but-dreaming gods return.

Now, intrepid anthologist Ross E. Lockhart has delved deep into the Cthulhu canon, selecting from myriad mind-wracking tomes the best sanity-shattering stories of cosmic terror. Featuring fiction by many of today's masters of the menacing, macabre, and monstrous, The Book of Cthulhu goes where no collection of Cthulhu mythos tales has before: to the very edge of madness... and beyond!

ABOUT THE AUTHOR

Harrison Geillor was born in a small three-room farm house in central MN, sometime in the middle of the twentieth century. He attended one of Minnesota's prestigious institutions of higher learning, where he obtained a degree in English. Like English majors everywhere, he went on to work in a variety of jobs that had nothing to do with books or literature. At some point in his life he decided that the best way to appreciate Minnesota was to appreciate it from afar. He splits his time between Santa Cruz and San Francisco, only returning to Minnesota for smelt fishing, and the occasional family reunion.